3/2010

BROADWAY LI

secrets of M
HOLLYWOOD LI

BROADWAY LIGHTS
SECRETS OF MY
HOLLYWOOD LIFE

a novel by

Jen Calonita

poppy

LITTLE, BROWN AND COMPANY
New York   Boston

Poppy

Hachette Book Group
237 Park Avenue, New York, NY 10017
For more of your favorite series, visit our website at www.pickapoppy.com

Poppy is an imprint of Little, Brown and Company.
The Poppy name and logo are trademarks of Hachette Book Group, Inc.

First Edition: March 2010

ISBN: 978-0-316-03065-6

10 9 8 7 6 5 4 3 2 1

RRD-C

Printed in the United States of America

Book design by Tracy Shaw

Secrets of My Hollywood Life novels by Jen Calonita:

SECRETS OF MY HOLLYWOOD LIFE

ON LOCATION

FAMILY AFFAIRS

PAPARAZZI PRINCESS

Other novels by Jen Calonita:

Sleepaway Girls

For Dylan, who was well worth the wait.

one: *You've Got to Love a Premiere*

"I'm Chatty Cathy from *Inside Hollywood*—your source for all things Hollywood—and tonight I'm at the premiere of *Pretty Young Assassins*. This heart-stopping, action-packed ride stars the stunning young lady standing next to me, *Family Affair* star Kaitlin Burke. Hi, Kaitlin!"

"Hi, Cathy!" I flash her my most dazzling smile. "It's nice to see you again."

Cathy is an Amazonian tabloid reporter known for her dyed neon yellow hair and right now she's standing next to me on the red carpet at Westwood's Mann Village Theatre in Los Angeles, where my movie, *Pretty Young Assassins*, is premiering on this warm May night. Behind me there are dozens of die-hard fans screaming so loudly I can barely hear and holding handmade signs as they press against a crowd control rope on the normally quiet palm tree–lined street. In a few minutes, I'll be sitting in the cool, darkened theater with my costars and my family surrounding me, but right now I'm doing what my publicist Laney Peters calls "a necessary evil" — talking to the tabloid press. Sometimes they love me, sometimes they drag me through the mud. It depends on whether it's a slow news week.

Cathy sticks her glittery microphone in my face. Cathy's electric green paisley print mini dress is so bright it almost blinds me. "It's nice to see *you*." Cathy stares at me with her piercing green eyes, which are so similar to my own. "You look drop-dead gorgeous. Who are you wearing?"

"This is Marchesa." I give a sort of half-spin to show off my pale pink Grecian-style gown. My stylist had it short-ened from floor-length to mid-thigh, and my hoofs (aka big feet) are blinged out in strappy, sparkly Jimmy Choos. I wore my long, honey-blond hair half up and had Paul, my favor-ite hair guru, set it so that curls cascade down my bronzed back. For makeup, Shelly swept my green eyes with a very in vogue pearl blue shadow and left my tanned face bare except for peach blush and gloss. Austin said I look like a goddess. God, I adore him.

"Kaitlin, let's talk business." Cathy puts an arm around my bare shoulder and stares directly into the video camera instead of looking at me. "You've had quite a year, and it's not even half over. Your TV show goes off the air in a few weeks, you're making your Broadway debut at the end of June, and you've survived a heap of media coverage surrounding your train-wreck friendship with party girls Lauren Cobb and Ava Hayden." Her smoky voice is so raspy, I almost have to read her lips to follow along. "Not to mention all that gossip about your supposed near breakdown at a *Sure* magazine photo shoot. What's the real deal, Kaitlin?"

I do my best to keep smiling and turn on the charm that years of media training have taught me well. "Cathy, if my life were really that dramatic, it would be a movie!" I laugh even though for this particular crisis, the press kind of got it right. Not that I can actually admit that. Laney would kill me! I stare up at the famous glowing Fox tower sign perched above the theater.

"Lauren and Ava are great girls, but we haven't hung out together in a long time." I talk slowly, making sure every word I say is just right. "They like to go out, and I'm a couch potato. My nights usually involve a trip to Blockbuster, studying my script for *Meeting of the Minds*, my upcoming Broadway show, or getting takeout with my boyfriend." Cathy doesn't look convinced, but I keep going. "I'm happy, which I know is hard for some people to believe when they hear all those meltdown rumors, but they're not true. I had a panic attack. I had a hard time coping with the news that *Family Affair* was going off the air. I mean, I was losing a show that I'd been part of since I was a preschooler."

Cathy nods, but I'm not sure she's really paying attention. Her eyes have locked on my date. "It must help to have such a dashing boyfriend to lean on," she coos.

I turn to Austin Meyers, my boyfriend of over a year, and notice his face is redder than the carpet we're standing on. Cathy's right about one thing — my boyfriend is hot.

He's taller than me (which isn't hard, since I'm under 5'4"), with broad, muscular shoulders and arms. And he has the best hair on any guy I know. Austin wears it sort of long, so his bangs are hanging constantly in his amazing blue eyes, which gives me plenty of excuses to touch his face and push his hair out of the way. Tonight Austin is wearing a dark blue suit with a skinny gray tie. Very Robert Pattinson. He smiles at me nervously.

I smile back at him. "I am lucky," I tell Cathy, and squeeze Austin's hand, which has been linked with mine for the entire interview.

"Me too," Austin echoes, surprising me by saying anything at all. He's not used to getting the media third degree like I am. Austin spends his days doing algebra and playing lacrosse (he has a normal high school existence), while I spend mine in front of a camera, doing interviews, or hiding from the paparazzi.

Laney taps me on the shoulder, or should I say, jabs me hard with one of her highly laquered nails. "We have to be inside in ten." She gives Cathy the evil eye. "Last question, Cathy."

I try not to laugh as Cathy's perky expression changes to a look of pure terror. My publicist may look young and cute with her round face, long, layered blond locks, picture-perfect petite figure, and wrinkle-free face (is it Botox or youth? I may never know. Laney won't let me see her driver's license), but Hollywood insiders and the media know better. Underneath that white Calvin Klein pantsuit and carefully tanned exterior, Laney is a Category 5 hurricane. She will do anything and everything to protect her clients. Why do you think she has one of the biggest A-list rosters in Hollywood?

"Sorry to hold you hostage, Kaitlin." Cathy sounds flustered for the first time tonight. "Last question: Your Broadway run is only eight weeks. What are you going to do after that ends?"

Um…I don't have a clue.

That's the terrifying truth. I've been trying not to think about it, but it's hard not to — especially when everyone keeps bringing it up. My agent, Seth, says I've had offers but nothing worthwhile, and that's what gives me nightmares. "I'm exploring my options but can't say anything just yet," I tell Cathy. "I will say I can't wait to sink my teeth into a new challenge." There. That sounded okay. There is no way I'm telling Cathy I have no job lined up.

"Like what?" Cathy moves the microphone closer.

Uh-oh.

"Interview over. We're going to miss the start of the movie," Laney snaps, and pulls us away before I have to answer.

The flashbulbs pop as we hurry down the rest of the red carpet and past my film's oversized movie poster. It's so cool. Drew Thomas and I are hiding behind a crumbling wall, and we're all sweaty and battle-scarred. Before we head inside, Austin and I pause for a final photo in the brightly lit butter-yellow exterior lobby directly below the Mann

Village Theatre marquee. Then Laney pulls Austin and me through the theater doors and rushes us through the cavernous lobby. I glimpse mosaics, murals, paintings, and photographs of the California Gold Rush on the walls, but Laney doesn't give us time to sightsee. I guess I should just be happy I'm here for a premiere. This place has hosted some of the coolest ones in Hollywood (think *Twilight* and *Spider-Man*). It was built in 1931, and people still rave about its huge auditorium (it has over 1,300 seats), incredible architecture, and dome-like arches trimmed in gold. There are sculptures throughout the lobby and scrollwork everywhere, but my favorite thing is the six-pointed painted star on the auditorium ceiling. I won't get to stare at it tonight, though. We're running really late. Someone from the studio hands Austin and me popcorn and soda, takes a picture of us holding them, and ushers us to our seats. The lights are dimming, so I can't see where my castmates are sitting, but I know Mom, Dad, my brother Matty, and my personal assistant, Nadine, are seated behind us.

"You almost missed the credits," Mom scolds before my butt has even touched the seat.

I want to tell Mom that's impossible, but the movie is about to start, so I'll have to tell her the first of many new HOLLYWOOD SECRETS later.

HOLLYWOOD SECRET NUMBER ONE: Premieres don't start till the stars are seated — whether that's ten minutes late because you're talking to *Access Hollywood* or two hours late because your names are Brad and Angelina and you have to get your ever-expanding brood to bed first. Movie premiere start times are figurative. If the stars are scheduled to appear, no one from the studio will start the film till they arrive. The bigger the star, the later the arrival and the less likely you'll see them in the theater. Another thing to know: the lights will dim right before the biggest star shows up so that no one in the audience knows where they're sitting (if they actually stay at all. Some stars do the red carpet and then slip out the back door to avoid sitting through their new film more than once).

"The movie is starting," Dad reminds Mom, and that's enough to make her hold her tongue — for now.

I take a few kernels of popcorn, then sit back and enjoy.

* * *

Two hours and seven minutes later the end credits are rolling, and Austin follows up his praise with a kiss on the cheek, which is good, because my mom and dad are right behind us. "That. Was. Awesome," Austin congratulates me.

"I know, right?" I practically squeal. The lights are coming up, and the chatter in the theater is loud and boisterous. People are smiling and laughing, and I think they liked the movie.

Austin laughs. "Why do you sound so surprised?"

"Well, you know," I tell him without actually telling him anything. Sure, I've seen a rough cut, but my meticulous director, Hutch Adams, is known for making a lot of last-minute changes. Whatever tweaks he's made work, because I like the movie even more than I did when I saw it the first time.

"Kate-Kate, that was wonderful." Mom reaches over the seat to hug me and I almost choke on her perfume. ("It's Victoria Beckham's! She gave it to me personally and if she walked by, she'd want to smell it on me," Mom insisted when Matty and I staged an intervention to tell her that maybe she'd been using a tad too much.) Like her perfume spritzing, everything about Mom is carefully packaged. She's a tall, toned Hollywood machine who does not leave the house without Crème de la Mer on her tanned face, her blond hair blown out, and designer labels on every inch of her body. (Tonight she's wearing a Michael Kors silk tunic and black fitted Gucci pants. The underwear are probably Dolce Gabbana.) "I think your work in this puts you on a whole new playing field," Mom tells me. She has one hand on me and one on her BlackBerry, which she starts typing on furiously with her thumb. "I'm telling Seth he should start fielding offers for more blockbuster-type films or action TV shows. Maybe we can get you a role on something like *Lost*!"

Mom has been hounding Seth about my next project ever since it was announced that *FA* was ending. Mom's still not convinced that a Broadway show is going to advance my career, but Seth thinks *Meeting of the Minds* is going to move mountains (his words, not mine). The play is a teen-centric drama, which isn't an entirely new concept, but it's more

PG-friendly and comical than other teen-driven shows like *Spring Awakening*. At the same time, the show's issues — race, coming of age, peer pressure — are a step up from my character development on *Family Affair*. "This could be the highbrow *High School Musical* of Broadway," Seth declared. "Without the singing. Or dancing. It doesn't need it! This show has bite. It could be huge!"

"Sweetie, can we just enjoy the movie premiere first?" Dad tries to pry the BlackBerry from Mom's dark red fingernails. He's much bigger than she is. Matty and I call our parents Barbie and Ken, because that's seriously what they look like, even though Dad is nowhere near as put together as Mom is. Most days he doesn't even iron his standard Ralph Lauren golf shirt before putting it on. Tonight Mom must have dressed him because he's in a smart-looking beige suit. Still, I notice the white shirt underneath looks a tad wrinkled. "You can tell Seth when we meet with him before we leave town next week."

The words hit me like a bad review.

I'm leaving Los Angeles.

My home.

Next week.

And Austin is not coming with me.

In seven days, I am moving to New York for a few months while Austin will be here in Los Angeles and then in Texas for a summer lacrosse camp he's been dying to attend. I know Seth's right about the play being a huge opportunity for my career, but what about my blissful love life? Austin and I have never been apart for more than two weeks! How are we going to deal with being three thousand miles away from each other?

I guess I shouldn't complain. All this was supposed to happen sooner. Originally I was supposed to be in New York in April and start the play in May, but then the show's original London lead, Meg Valentine, got off crutches before everyone thought she would, so I got bumped back to a June start date for rehearsals and a July and August run, which is... PRINCESS LEIA WATCH!

I pull out my new iPhone — I've upgraded from my trusty Sidekick — and jot down another item I have to remember to pack for my move (I'm lost without my Leia watch). My iPhone has a dozen "note to self" lists on it already and it's only a week old.

Where was I? Oh, yeah, my new play start date. I was happy about it — more time with Austin! Yay! — but some of us weren't so thrilled.

"Mom." I hear a familiar whine. "I told you a zillion times already, I'm sure I can pull some strings and get Kates a cameo on my show."

That would be my younger brother, Matty, talking. His ego is much bigger than his actual age, fifteen. (We just celebrated his birthday.) He's signed more autographs and shaken more hands tonight than he has in his life. And this is probably only the beginning. After years of bit parts and commercials, Matty has hit the big time with his new TV show, a remake of *Scooby-Doo*, directed by my *FA* director, Tom Pullman. Matty has to be on set in late July to start shooting the season (which will premiere in October), so he and Dad have to leave New York earlier than the rest of us. I think Matty was hoping to go all *Gossip Girl* and take the New York social scene by storm, but now he's whining that he won't have as much time to do it. But what is he complaining about? He has a paying gig to come home to, one that everyone in town is gaga over. *Entertainment Weekly* is calling *Scooby* "the must-see show of the new season." And *Celebrity Insider* says it's this generation's *Buffy the Vampire Slayer*. I can't say I'm not a wee bit jealous as I stare at my brother, who looks a lot like a young Brad Pitt with his new short blond hair, green eyes, and gray Armani suit.

"Let's move, people," Laney barks, making even my long-time personal security, Rodney, jump. "The car is out front to take you to the after-party, and I want to get you guys in it before fans start asking for autographs."

"Can you imagine the horror?" Nadine quips so that only I can hear. I bite my lip to keep from laughing.

Rodney whips into work mode, puts his trademark black sunglasses back on, and uses his large frame to clear a path for my family to make our way out a side door of the theater and into the waiting Escalade idling near the curb. I follow his dark, shiny bald dome through the crowd. We slip in without commotion and are at the next red carpet outside the Crown Bar on Santa Monica Boulevard before I know it.

The white building looks as if it could be someone's house instead of a hip lounge. It has lush greenery in the front and a candlelit outdoor patio. Inside, the mood is very old-school Hollywood romantic, making me think Austin and I would like hanging out here if it wasn't so scene-y. There are chandeliers everywhere, lots of dark wood, distressed mirrors, padded walls with textured wallpaper, and intimate banquettes. In the middle of the place is an octagon-shaped bar. I hear the food here is pretty good. It's classic American bistro with burgers and flatbread sandwiches, with fish and chips thrown in. Tonight everything is being served appetizer-style. We head to the back of the place, where we have a reserved banquette; everyone drops their gift bags and rushes off to network. Everyone except me and Austin.

"So," I say softly, my voice barely audible over the DJ and the noise of the packed party. But I know Austin heard me.

Austin stares back at me. "So." He weaves his fingers through mine. "Seven days left."

I nod, looking away from his blue eyes and trying to blink back tears. I focus on his silver cuff links. I bought them for him a few months ago. They're tiny lacrosse sticks. "Seven days."

"I've been thinking of our last hurrah before you go." Austin gives me a quizzical look. "How do you feel about—"

"Katie-Kat!" Mom's voice is louder than even the DJ's, and he has a microphone. I look up. Mom is a few tables away.

She's waving her hands wildly and standing next to a short, plump man in a wrinkled dress shirt. "I need you!"

"I'll be right back," I promise Austin, squeezing his rough, calloused hand.

I scoot out of my seat and talk to Mom's new "friend," who turns out to be a TV producer working on a mid-season series about cocktail waitresses in Vegas (blech). Before I get back to my table, I see my *PYA* director, Hutch Adams, and zip over for a quick hello (with a drink in hand, he's always much friendlier). Then I run into my obnoxious *PYA* costar Drew, and though he and I aren't on good terms, I do my job and pose with gritted teeth for a few pictures. I try not to think about the fact that Drew's garish pinstriped black suit, striped shirt, and tie completely clash with my soft pink dress. (Who wears so many stripes together anyway? Does Drew think he's Ed Westwick channeling his alter ego Chuck Bass? Drew may be dark and handsome, but he'll never be as legendary as Mr. Bass.)

Next I shake hands with a few executives from other studios whom I've never met. (Seth would be happy), stand patiently and listen while an actress I barely know laments the lack of good jobs available for twenty-some-things ("Everyone wants teens!"), and do a quick interview with *Entertainment Weekly*, the sole print outlet allowed at the party. As I talk to the reporter, I sneak wistful glances at my table. Austin is talking to my best friend, Liz Mendes, who must have slipped in while I was gone. She missed the premiere because she had a kickboxing tournament. When my interview is done, I start walking quickly, eyes straight ahead to avoid being stopped again, but someone blocks my path.

"There you are, K!" Sky Mackenzie, my former *FA* costar and current *PYA* one, sounds like she's in a huff. She rolls her eyes at me. "Where have you been?"

"Sky!" I say, and without thinking I give her a hug. She instantly stiffens, but I don't care. Even with our notoriously volatile history — Sky and I never got along during our decade-plus run on *FA*, even though we played fraternal twins — I've surprised myself by actually missing her. I even miss our bickering. "How have you been?"

"Outrageously busy and in demand," Sky says with a toss of her long raven hair. She looks extra tanned (but thankfully not orange. That's happened to her before), and she's wearing a fitted, strapless silver ruched dress that she's paired with calf-length blue leggings and black Coach heels. "I went to Les Deux last week, and Winston's Bar on Thursday, and had meetings at Wagman's on Friday — they can't wait to work with me again — and I've been tanning and reading *my* script for *my* new show and..."

I stare at Sky as she talks about her packed schedule. Normally I would think she's being smug, but despite her boasting, she seems nervous, and her dark eyes have shadows underneath them. I know this girl. We practically grew up together on set. "Sky," I interrupt quietly.

She stops short and her cocky grin fades. She waves a

hand in the air, her dozen bangle bracelets sliding up to her elbow. "I'm bored."

"I know," I chime in, and put an arm on her shoulder without crushing her lacquered hair. It's an acquired Hollywood skill. "Me too."

"I thought I would love a little R&R," Sky dishes. "Time for Palm Springs, a shoot-down to Cabo, you know? But it gets old. I miss work. I *need* work. I can't wait to get on set in July. I just wish it was in town rather than in Vancouver." She makes a face, pursing her plump (fake. Shh!) lips.

"At least you have a show to go to." The words slip out and hang there. Wow. Did I really just say that? Do I miss having a show? Why am I admitting that to my supposed rival?

"Please, K, not the pity act," Sky clucks. "You're doing the Great White Way! You're going to get total cred and get some plum role working with Clooney after this. My show could be canceled after three episodes." Her eyes open wide, as if she can't believe she just admitted that to her nemesis.

I can't help but giggle. "We're pathetic."

Sky actually cracks a smile. "We are, aren't we? We've only been out of work for two months, if that!"

"Excuse me, Sky? Kaitlin?" A guy in a tux holding a video camera approaches us. "Sorry to bother you. I don't know if you know me, but I'm Ryan Joseph, Media Relations for *Family Affair*."

"Ryan!" I say, excited. I barely knew the guy, but anyone from *FA* is a friend in my book. "How are you?"

He looks relieved. "Good. Tough getting in here tonight, but Tom said if I didn't catch you two here, I might never see you together again. We thought this could be fun to post this week, before the final episode airs next week, and…"

"What are you talking about, Raymond?" Sky asks impatiently.

"It's Ryan," he says, looking nervous.

I shoot Sky a look and gently tuck a lock of my blond hair behind my chandelier earrings. "*Ryan*, what do you need?"

Ryan's shoulders relax a little. "Tom Pullman sent me. He was hoping you guys would do a YouTube shout-out for the last episode of *FA* that we could put up ASAP. Let me just call Tom and he can explain more." He punches the number I know so well into his phone, and within seconds Tom is on the line and Sky and I are listening in to his request. Something short, sweet, funny, maybe in character even. Pretty please?

Sky and I look at each other, and I see the small sparkle in her eye. We'd do anything for *FA*. "We'll do it," I answer for both of us. Sky doesn't try to stop me.

After Sky does a quick makeup touch-up and I do a pat of powder on my shiny nose and a swipe of nude shimmer gloss, I stop quickly at our table to say hi to Liz and to apologize to Austin for the delay. Next thing I know, Sky and I are huddled on the glowing candlelit outdoor patio, where it's much quieter, shooting a two-minute impromptu promo for our (almost) dearly departed TV show.

"We're back!" Sky yells, throwing an arm around me and

making me giggle as the camera records. "Miss us much?" She blows a gum bubble through her hipster wine-colored lips, and it pops loudly.

"Sky," I scold. "No chewing gum." I figure Ryan will rewind and redo, but he's still taping. Okay then. "The *Family Affair* finale is fast approaching, and you don't want to miss a second of it," I tell the viewers.

"K means business," Sky interrupts. "Don't upset her. We don't need her winding up in Cedars Sinai again." I shoot her a dirty look.

"Or Sky drowning her sorrows at a karaoke bar," I retort, and receive an elbow to my ribs. "You guys *don't* want to hear her sing."

"Or K cry. Again," Sky deadpans.

"Or Sky over-tan herself to combat boredom," I quip, and give her the evil eye.

The two of us look at each other and start to laugh. "Some things never change," I tell the camera. "Like us. You know you love the drama."

"*Family Affair*," Sky adds. "The series finale, next Sunday at nine. Be there or be…?" She looks at me.

"Square?" I question.

Sky shakes her head. "You really are a dork."

I start to laugh some more. Soon we're both uncontrollable. Ryan stops recording.

"That was clever," he says in amazement. "You guys seem like you really like each other."

We both stop laughing at once.

"Are we done here?" Sky asks. Ryan nods.

The two of us head inside, and Sky turns to me. I see the smallest of small smiles on her dark lips. "I'll see you around."

"Sure," I tell her, knowing it's probably not the case, and for some reason that makes me sadder than I would have thought. "Good luck with the —"

BOOM!

Someone pushes me and I bang into Sky, sending her backward into a waitress carrying a tray of drinks. The three of us crash with a thud so loud that DJ Bizzy actually stops spinning.

"What the hell?" Sky jumps up and shakes liquid off her. My dress and even the tips of my hair are drenched, and the poor waitress is covered in spilled drinks. Rodney is at my side in seconds and helps me up. I turn to see who I banged into, and my jaw drops. "Ava? Lauren?" I say awkwardly. "I didn't know you were invited." Eek. That sounded rude.

Ava Hayden and Lauren Cobb, two girls I spent more hours with this spring than my best friend, stand in front of me with their arms crossed. They're scowling, but they look amazing. Ava's long blond hair is pulled back, and she's rocking a cream chiffon Monique Lhuillier dress with a purple sash that I've always loved. Lauren's wearing what I think is a Roberto Cavalli sheath in black, but she's made the look her own by adding lots of chunky boho jewelery — maybe too much. Her brown curly hair is down and super shiny. For a split second I wonder whether their outfits were lifted. The two have a nasty habit of deciding to stuff new dresses into their purses at Saks, which is just one of many reasons we stopped hanging out.

"Have a nice fall?" Ava stares at me darkly, her long, thin ivory face twisted into a deep frown. Lauren laughs so hard the unrecognizable drink in her hand splatters all over, missing her dress by inches. "Sorry," Ava adds coolly. "Guess we didn't see you. Kind of like the rest of this town."

"You pushed me?" I'm flabbergasted. Yes, we're no longer friends, but we didn't end on such bad terms. We just sort of sailed away from each other — me with motor full-throttle, but still. I never said a bad word about either of them to the press and I definitely could have after the havoc they caused at my *Sure* photo shoot.

"Aw, your dress," Lauren mock sobs, and puts a hand to her heart. She cocks her head to one side, her brown eyes so wide they seem to squish her high cheek bones. "To be honest, it's sort of an improvement."

"Marchesa is so last month," Ava adds.

"K, are you going to let these D-listers talk to you like that?" Sky comes to my defense.

I remove Rodney's hand from my arm and walk over to the two of them. "Don't do this," I say quietly so that only they can hear. "We're not friends, but we don't need to be enemies. Don't we all have enough of those?"

Ava smiles thinly. "I never have enough enemies. Congratulations! You, my friend, just moved to our number-one spot."

"Why?" I'm dumbfounded. "Can't we just leave each other alone?"

"It's more fun this way," Lauren coos. "Ava and I like drama, didn't you know?"

"You mean you like any chance you can get to get some free publicity," Sky interjects sharply. The girls ignore her.

"I can handle this, Sky." I'm shaking and on the verge of tears. Everyone in the room is agape at the scene. My whisper-thin soft dress is clinging to my legs gracelessly, soaked in red wine, and I know a picture of me looking this pathetic will show up in some rag or another tomorrow, thanks to camera phones. I'm humiliated. I don't want the trouble, but if they're going to give it, then I have no choice. "I think you two should leave."

"And what if we don't?" Ava taunts. "We never miss a party at Crown Bar. Even if it's for a premiere as lame as yours." Lauren snorts.

"That's it!" Sky yells, scaring even me. "This is our movie and I won't let you talentless posers bash it — especially when it rocks and you two are just jealous that the best offer you'll ever get is for *Celebrity Rehab*." She jabs a long, bony finger at them every other word, then makes a crazy hand motion to a nearby bodyguard and to Rodney, her plum polish flashing black in the low lighting. "Toss them out."

Whoa. I need to sound more assertive like Sky sometimes.

"You can't do that, Sky, and I don't think you want to either," Ava says smugly. "We were invited. Now, go throw your temper tantrums somewhere else. You really don't want to get on our bad sides again, do you?"

"You've been uninvited," I say before Sky can answer the question. "Invite or no invite, this is our movie, not yours, and neither of you is welcome here. Not after this." I nod to a studio executive who has been watching the whole exchange. She motions to the private security.

"Ladies, you're going to have to leave," one of the guys says in a gruff voice.

"I knew you were weak, Kaitlin, but I had no idea you were this much of a baby," Ava murmurs.

"Bye!" Sky says gleefully. "I'm sure there's some C-list party happening at some totally over 'hot spot' that would be happy to have you guys."

I try not to snort, but it escapes my lips, and Lauren's eyes narrow like slits.

"You're both going to be sorry for this," she snaps.

"I doubt it," I tell her, my confidence coming back. That felt good. What's she going to do to me? I won't even be in town next week.

The security reaches for Lauren's and Ava's elbows, but they snatch their arms away, click-clacking out of the room in their matching five-inch Charles David platforms. I can't help but giggle — they look like gangly, agitated giraffes. DJ Bizzy goes back to spinning, and someone from Wagman's hands Sky and me towels. They even ask if we want someone to get us new dresses, but I decline. Sky looks like she might say yes, but she sees my face and decides against it. "We'll dry. It's hot in here," I tell the poor assistant.

"We'll just smell like the hobos down on Hollywood Boulevard," Sky quips, and then she's gone before I even turn around.

"Are you okay?" Liz rushes over. "What was that about?" Liz's dark curly hair is pulled back for a change, and little curls fall around her caramel-skinned neck, which is adorned with a big turquoise necklace that matches her spaghetti-strap mini dress. Her arms look better than the First Lady's, thanks to daily kickboxing. Despite what's just happened, I smile. One of the best parts about New York is that Liz is coming with me. She's bunking with my family while she does a summer writing and directing workshop for high school students at New York University.

"Who invited them?" Austin asks.

"I don't know," I admit. "I thought we were on okay terms, but after this episode, I guess I was wrong."

Liz sighs. "Guess your truce is over."

"Guess so." I'm crestfallen. "At least I won't be here to deal with it."

Austin looks at Liz. "Speaking of leaving town, Burke, I've figured out where we're going to go before you leave."

"Without me?" I protest.

"You were sort of preoccupied," he teases.

"It's good, Kates," Liz insists. "You're going to love it."

"So now it's a surprise." Austin smiles mischievously. "Don't try to get it out of Nadine or Liz either."

"Fine." I take a mini burger from a waiter and stuff the whole thing in my mouth. Fighting really makes a person hungry. While I chomp, I wring out the front of my dress again. Someone snaps a picture of me. And another. Guess I'll be back in the headlines again this week, after a few months off. It's weird to think I'll have to read about it at a crowded New York City sidewalk newsstand rather than on a beach lounge chair in Malibu.

"I'm going to miss Los Angeles," I say to no one in particular.

"Even all this?" Liz is incredulous as she glares at a cameraman invading her personal space.

I look around and shrug. "Even all this."

Austin puts his arm around me. "I've got to say one thing about you, Burke. You really know how to go out with a bang."

That I do.

Wednesday, May 27th

NOTE TO SELF:
Interview w/ *People* re: *PYA:* Fri. @ 1.
Ask Nadine 2 get more boxes 4 move.
UPS Pickup 4 boxes: Mon. @ 4.
Get guidebook 4 NYC.
Date w/ A: Mon. Time: TBA.
Flight 2 NYC: Tues. @ 11:15 AM.

TWO: *The Happiest Place on Earth*

"Ready to go?" Austin asks when he greets me at my door. It's only nine AM on Monday morning, which is kinda early for a date, but I'm not complaining. I have a little over twenty-four hours before I have to be at LAX to take a plane to New York, and I plan on spending every minute I can with Austin before I go. "You're wearing sneakers, right?"

I look down at my feet. Green Pumas. Check. My KUT from the Kloth boyfriend jeans are rolled at my calf, my caramel hair is pulled back in a ponytail, and I'm wearing a green Juicy tank top to combat the eighty-degree weather. I also have an ivory Diesel sweatshirt with me in case we're in A/C today. Austin's only clue about today's mystery date was to dress comfy and casual. My guess would be the beach, but he didn't ask me to pack a swimsuit so I must be wrong, especially since Austin's not wearing a swimsuit either. He's got on long khaki shorts, a cool blue American Eagle tee, white Converse high-tops, and aviator Ray-Bans on top of his head that are pushing back his bangs.

Hmm…Maybe we're paragliding? Nah. Mom would kill him, especially after how she wigged when I tried it in Turks and Caicos. Ooh! Maybe we're going on a hot-air balloon ride! I always thought it would be fun to go on one of those. But come to think of it, I've never actually seen a balloon floating over Los Angeles.

"You're all set, Austin." Nadine appears in the hallway, her thin arms loaded with boxes. "Rodney is going to meet you guys there." Nadine shipped all of our nonessential stuff last week, but Mom keeps finding more things I might need (Books that might be worth optioning for a movie! White Chloé sundress for the Hamptons! I tried reminding her that I probably won't be able to get out there that much, but she ignored me). Nadine has to head back to UPS today to ship the rest. Thankfully my suitcases are packed, so I don't have anything else to do. I purposefully planned it that way so Austin and I could have the whole day together. Plus, anything I've forgotten I can text Nadine about on my iPhone. Nadine is the most amazing personal assistant ever.

I'm so glad she is growing her hair out. Nadine's strawberry red locks are finally shoulder length, and now she can pin them back any way she likes. Today she's got her hair halfback in a clip. She never could have pulled that off last year with her pixie cut. Matty and I keep telling Nadine if she ever finds time for a boyfriend, this Ken Paves cut I treated her to will go a long way in winning him over. And why shouldn't it? The rest of Nadine is adorable too. She's tall and thin, and her look is very laid back. Nadine prefers Onitsuka Tiger sneakers over Yves Saint Laurent heels any day.

"I really owe you for this one," Austin tells Nadine.

"Nah." Nadine shrugs. "Just promise you won't miss Kaitlin's opening night performance. I don't think I could handle the drama if you didn't." Nadine winks at me.

I feel my face redden. "We should be going." I grab the front door with one hand and gently shove Austin backward with the other. "Tell Mom I'll touch base later."

After Austin powwows with Rodney to go over directions, and he and I finally get in his mom's car and hit the road, I can't take the suspense anymore. "Are you going to tell me where we're going or what?" I say, a tad impatiently.

Austin smirks. "Be patient, Burke. You're going to love this."

I eye him skeptically. Of course. I'm going to love it. I love doing anything with Austin. Which is why I'm mopey about not getting to do everyday things with him for the next few months. No dates, no drives to the farmer's market on a quiet Sunday morning, no runs to Pinkberry for much-needed frozen yogurt. No lacrosse matches to watch. My good friend Gina, who is on a CW show and is wise beyond her years, says that if I were older, the distance wouldn't be a big deal. I'd fly back and forth on my days off or meet up with him in Miami for a weekend.

But I'm not older. I'm only seventeen. And even though some actresses I know have pads in nearby Toluca Lake (which I love and so wish we would move to), my mom would *freak* if I even suggested jetting off to see Austin.

The term *PR nightmare* flashes in my head. I'll leave those to Lindsay Lohan. Instead, I'm trying to be mature about the situation and remind myself that location changes are part of my life. I go on location all the time for work. Except… I haven't gone away for this long a stretch since we started dating.

"You're going to be back in three weeks, you know." Austin reads my thoughts as he leans forward to look into the lane of the interstate we're merging onto. I still haven't gotten my license so I love to watch him drive. He looks so responsible. Plus, the wind looks good in his blond locks (not that we have the windows rolled down on the interstate, but when we're just driving to The Grove we do) and I can stare at him all I want while his eyes are on the road. I glance at the interstate sign for clues. We're heading south, but we've already passed the city limits so I can rule out a picnic at Venice Beach. We're not heading toward the water so Malibu is out too. "We'll have all weekend together and you get to wear Diane von Furner," Austin adds.

"Furstenberg," I correct. I'm amazed he got it even half right.

"Exactly." He stares at the road while I ogle his arms. "The point is, a weekend doesn't get much better than that, Burke."

"You're right," I agree. Since I'll still be in rehearsals for *Meeting of the Minds*, I'll be off the Friday night that Austin and Liz have the junior prom, so I am flying back out for it. That's another great thing about being in New York. With the time difference, I can fly back to Los Angeles and *gain* time with Austin. Going back to New York is when I'll hit major jet lag. Liz will be with me at least. She's flying back to New York with me that Sunday to start her summer program at NYU. "And then you come to New York two weeks later for my opening night."

"Wouldn't miss it," Austin says. "My mom and Hayley are really excited. Hayley's got a list of shops she wants to hit when she's in town that weekend. Mom wants to drag her sightseeing."

Austin's mom hasn't been to New York in years and his younger sister Hayley's never been so they jumped at the chance to see me on stage. "I told her she'll be doing a lot of the touristy stuff on her own," Austin adds. "I want to see you perform both nights."

I smile to myself. Austin is so supportive, just like Tom Cruise (I mean that in the most non-creepy, non-controlling way, of course). Supposedly Tom saw Katie Holmes's run on Broadway tons of times. I'm sure Austin would be the same way if he were in town.

I glance out the window again. The exit we've just passed was for Long Beach. We live in southern California near a gazillion gorgeous beaches. How could we not be going to one of them for a romantic last date before I go? I don't get it. If sand in my toes isn't in my future, where could we be going?

"You *still* don't know?" Austin chuckles. "I thought for sure you'd figure it out when we got on the I-5 south. I'll give you a hint: It's someplace you've always wanted us to go to together."

Think, Kaitlin. *Think.* Where are we going? Someplace fun, someplace casual, someplace we need Rodney to meet us, someplace this far south…There's only one place I can think of that —

"IT'S DISNEYLAND!" I shriek, causing Austin to hit the brakes for a second. "Sorry," I say in a much calmer tone. "Am I right? Am I? Is that where we're going?"

"Promise not to scream again?" he asks. "Yes."

I can feel my heart beat rev up, but I keep my lips clamped shut. Disneyland! Mickey! Minnie! The Pirates of the Caribbean ride! The Star Tours ride! Sleeping Beauty Castle!

YIPPEE!

Disneyland is one of my favorite places. Whenever Disney has some sort of event or movie premiere at the park, I'm the first to RSVP yes. And I've never been as jealous as I was of Miley Cyrus when she had her sweet sixteen there (if I could sing, and had a Disney-brand TM after my name, maybe the Mouse would throw a party in my honor too).

"Nadine set us up with a Disney cast member," Austin says, referring to what all the Disney employees are called. "We're meeting at the Californian Hotel and Spa, and they're going to take us over to the park for a personal VIP tour. They made a reservation for us at one of the character meals for breakfast, and dinner at Blue Bayou, which I know is your favorite, and we have prime viewing of the fireworks on Main Street. I think Nadine promised you'd do a quick photo op with Mickey by the castle, but they said it won't take more than twenty minutes."

"Not a problem." This is Disneyland! Anything for a ride on Splash Mountain!

HOLLYWOOD SECRET NUMBER TWO: Ever wonder why there are so many pictures in the tabloids of celebrities on roller coasters or posing with Mickey? As if celebrities don't get enough perks, going to amusement parks and places like Disney means more of them. We can usually get free park passes — especially if we stop for a photo op — but some stars can get more than just tickets. A VIP personal tour guide (think $125 an hour and up) plays host, concierge, and guide for your day in the park. The guides can't put you at the front of the line, but they can make sure you get good seating at restaurants, and tell you where the best place to view the parade is and what attractions you should hit when. Now, if your name is Brad, Angie, or even my friend Miley, then visiting the parks is probably a totally different experience. It's not like they can actually wait in line with the rest of the public and not be mauled. For stars of this magnitude, line jumping has to be a must, don't you think? Not that anyone from the Mouse House has ever confirmed that to me.

"I figured you wouldn't want the guide all day, though," Austin says, "so I told Nadine just to hook us up for a few hours and then you, me, and Rod-o are on our own. Sound good?"

"Sounds perfect," I say, and I find myself bouncing up and

down in my seat as I see a sign for Anaheim. Disneyland is the next exit. This is going to be the most perfect date ever. My right butt cheek starts to vibrate and I jump. It's my iPhone. I pull it out and stare at the text message in horror.

SKY'S CELL: 911!!!! 911!!! K!!!!! WHERE R U???

"What's the matter?" Austin replies, frowning thoughtfully. He's turned off the highway and I see the sign for Disneyland parking. "You look like you've seen a ghost."

"I sort of have." Sky's never texted me before, let alone called me unless there was a major problem. We're not working together anymore, so I can't have more lines than her. I've been avoiding the red carpet, so I don't have more coverage in *Hollywood Nation* than she does. What could she possibly be peeved about?

SKY'S CELL: Helloooooooooo...? U there???

I'd better get this over with. If I don't respond, she'll keep texting me.

KAITLIN'S CELL: It's me. I'm here. What's up?
SKY'S CELL: FINALLY! Did U read Page 6? Hollywood
    Nation? See Access?
KAITLIN'S CELL: Trying 2 avoid it. Bad 4 my self-esteem. Y?
SKY'S CELL: Boo hoo. Don't be a baby!! Must read PRONTO.
    UR not going 2 believe what

My phone vibrates again, and I skip reading the rest of Sky's text to see what Laney wants. Laney texting me at the same time as Sky can't be good. I have a sinking feeling.

Lauren and Ava.

No one printed a story about what went down at the premiere last week, so I thought I was in the clear. The rags couldn't possibly be covering the story a week later, when they have so many other juicy things to cover, like Katie and Suri's latest playdate photos or Britney's newest hair color...could they?

> LANEY'S CELL: Kaitlin, have you seen Page 6, Celeb Insider, Hollywood Nation? All have stories about your drama with Lauren & Ava. Your mom is flipping.
>
> KAITLIN'S CELL to LANIE'S CELL: That's so last week! There was nothing better to write about?
>
> SKY'S CELL: K, R U listening 2 me????
>
> LANEY'S CELL: Apparently not, but that's not the big story. This one is much worse.
>
> KAITLIN'S CELL to LANIE'S CELL: But nothing else happened!
>
> LANEY'S CELL: Maybe not, but those two heathens still managed to find a way to get press.
>
> SKY'S CELL: K!!

"I don't believe this," I mutter, feeling a dark cloud begin to settle over my head. I thought I was done with Lauren and Ava. It may have taken me a while to realize it, but those girls are a bottomless pit of bad publicity—and they love every minute of it! I've washed every reminder of them out of my life, including the clothes we bought together and that leopard print bag they convinced me to get, and yet they're still haunting me. I've steered clear of any event where they might be and then they show up at *my* movie premiere and I'm made to look like the bad guy? I won't stand for it. I hit reply all on my iPhone and write both Laney and Sky.

> KAITLIN'S CELL: I'm over it. I don't care what they said or what they did. Let's drop it.
> SKY'S CELL: Get a spine, K! I'm not letting those 2 mock ME & get away w/it! Did U C how they dressed??? And the way they made my voice sound! THIS. IS. WAR!

Dressed? Sky's voice? What the…

> KAITLIN'S CELL: What R U talking about?
> LANEY'S CELL: Kaitlin, have U seen the YouTube video? If you had, I'm sure you wouldn't be this calm. Seth and I agree that you should take the high road if this is the only thing they try, but we should at least respond or make a statement.

"YouTube video?" I screech. "What YouTube video?" I start punching numbers on my phone to dial Laney. Austin has parked the car and is staring at me curiously. It takes a while to get through to Laney, since I have to keep hitting IGNORE to Sky's messages so that I can press SEND on my phone.

"I knew you didn't know what I was talking about!

Don't you ever read TMZ?" Laney is yelling as usual, but not because she's mad. Construction still isn't done on her Malibu beach house, and I can hear the hammering in the background. "You can play all sweet and nice in your statement and spin some crap about not caring, but if this happens again, those two girls are FINISHED. You must go on YouTube and see what they—NO! HELLO? Not there. I said *there*! Why would I want the same tile that I have in the kitchen? I thought we—"

"Laney," I try to interrupt. "I'm about to go into Disneyland." Austin just looks at me worriedly. "I'm not pulling up YouTube on my phone! I don't want to see this. I'm having a nice day with Austin and want to be left alone. I just want to know what you're talking about. Please," I add nicely since I know I sound a little bratty.

"Remember the YouTube video you shot with Sky at the premiere?" Laney asks. I hear her walking and her heels are click-clacking across the empty floors. A door slams and wherever she is now is much quieter. "The one you shot for Tom and *FA*? The girls apparently spoofed it on YouTube."

I see another message pop up on my phone.

SKY'S CELL: K!!!! U have 2 call me. I'm not sitting on this! TOO MAD!!!!!!!!!

This is what Sky's so worked up over? "Laney, it wouldn't be a Tuesday if someone somewhere didn't have something to say about me. Who cares about YouTube?"

Laney is quiet. Unusually quiet. Laney is never quiet. And that's when I feel a pit in my stomach that I haven't felt in a long time. "Laney?"

"I wouldn't normally care about YouTube either," she says finally, "but this is over the top. They don't just mock you and Sky, they completely rip you both to shreds. They're wearing wigs to look like you too — bad wigs, but still. Lauren plays you and talks about how she's always in trouble with the press and how her downfall is everyone else's fault, not her own. She has two big, fake front teeth, which is silly because your veneers are gorgeous. I mean, Julia had hers done by the same dentist! Anyway, Ava is Sky, and she has this long, equally horrible wig and keeps complaining about not getting as much attention as you do. Then they joke about how both of your careers are washed up now that *FA* is over."

Oh.

I see.

Maybe this is a little worse than I imagined.

My cheeks flush as if Austin can read my thoughts. "Laney, tell me the truth. Is it that bad?"

Laney pauses before she speaks. "Kaitlin, they've taken all of your insecurities and publicized them to the world. And their video is so mean-spirited that, of course, the press is eating it up. The clip has gotten over a million hits in the last twenty-four hours." She sighs. "It's not good."

I swallow hard. The video sounds like a fender bender you can't look away from. I want to see the clip, even though

I really don't. I could pull it up on my phone right now, but do I want to? Do I really want to torture myself?

"Laney, let me call you right back," I tell her. "Let me see it myself."

I turn to Austin. "I need ten minutes, and then I won't say another word about this all day." I quickly explain what's happened.

"You really want to watch it?" Austin looks surprised as he fiddles with his car keys. A miniature lacrosse stick dangles from the bottom. "Why torture yourself?"

"Because it's going to eat me alive if I don't," I confess. I pull up YouTube on my iPhone and find the clip. Austin leans over the seat and I turn the volume up high so we can hear it. My heart is pounding as the video quickly loads. I'm so freaked that every sound is magnified, from kids screaming giddily as they walk by to Austin breathing in my ear.

And then there it is. Lauren and Ava, normally so (I hate to admit this) gorgeous, look cartoonishly awful in clownish makeup and rat-teased wigs.

Lauren introduces herself first. Lauren as me, I should say. "Hey, *FA* fans! It's Kaitlin, the one-hit-wonder from the most dull soap opera in the world! I'm the one more famous for my tabloid articles than for doing a decent movie. I'm so boring that no one wants me for another TV show." Ava pretends to sob.

Ouch. "She's one to talk," I sputter angrily, and bounce up

and down in the leather seat, which makes squeaking noises. Laney's right. This is cruel.

"I'm Sky!" Ava tosses the hair on her beat-up wig. "I'm a nobody who is more famous for hating Kaitlin than for doing anything worthwhile."

I wince. That's Sky's biggest nightmare come to life. I keep hitting ignore to the texts from Sky that interrupt the video, but I can see now why she's so upset. The jabs get nastier and nastier, and I feel worse and worse about myself as I watch. Lauren and Ava talk about how we got Alexis fired (not fair), how we killed *FA*'s ratings (so not true), how the two of us were turned down for our own spin-off show (an offer wasn't even on the table!).

When the clip finishes, I sit there, stunned. Why did they have to do something so mean? I've left them alone! Couldn't they have done the same? Having them tossed out of the *PYA* party might have been the worst mistake I could have made. Now the girls are never going to leave me alone. Not when a fight with me can get them the press they so crave.

Austin is quiet. "Are you okay?"

"Yeah."

I think. It's just a YouTube clip, but…in this age, YouTube is more popular than *90210*. Is Laney right? Should I be worried about this? I quickly call her back. "I saw it," I say when she picks up on the first ring. "What should we do?"

"You have to comment," Laney insists. "I'll contact your

favorite reporter at *Hollywood Nation*, and you can do a quick interview."

"Okay, but tomorrow," I beg. "I'm off today. I'll do it when I arrive in New York."

"Fine," Laney says. "I'm just glad you're not fighting me about this."

"I don't want to play their game," I admit, "but they're not giving me much choice. I'll make a statement, but I'm not stooping to their level."

Laney sighs. "There is nothing wrong with going a little postal once in a while. This thing would die the minute some other star did something heinous, but not now. Kaitlin, they're promising new Sky and Kaitlin videos will be posted in the coming days! Alexis Holden is going to be in the next one. She's apparently their BFF now."

"So I heard," I tsk. Alexis is just as awful as Lauren and Ava. She was an *FA* guest star who tried to get Sky and me tossed off the show during its final season so that she could stay onboard. What is with mean girls? Is there some secret code word they have to help them find each other and team up? "I'll take care of it, Laney."

"Good," she says and I hear her open a door. The hammering sound is back and it's louder than ever. "I'll touch base with Sky's publicist too. I have to go. The contractor is about to put *beige* tile in my entranceway when I distinctly asked for stone." Click.

I type quickly.

KAITLIN'S CELL: Watched video. Understand Y UR upset. I
   promised Laney I'd make a statement.
SKY'S CELL: That's it???? I'm making 1 2, but we have to do
   more!
KAITLIN'S CELL: They're not worth it. Saying more will only
   fuel the fire.
SKY'S CELL: L & A must go down!!! They're evil, K.
KAITLIN'S CELL: Y, but not worth our time. They're...

They are evil. They're worse than evil. When I think
about what they've done, I can't believe it. They act all sweet
and friendly when a camera is pointed at them, but when
the light is off, their claws come out. Thankfully whatever
they do usually sours fast, and the press forgets about them.
Sweet and sour. They're like candy!

KAITLIN'S CELL: Just forget about them. L&A are like
   Skittles. Sweet @ first, but when U have too many, your
   stomach sours and U feel sick.
SKY'S CELL: LOL! Good one. Like that a lot. But we need to
   do MORE. We need to do our own video and

I don't read the rest. I shut off my phone. If anyone important needs to reach me they'll call Rodney or Austin. The
rest of the world can wait.

"Are you sure you're okay?" Austin asks, and touches my
hand.

"It's not even worth talking about." I open the car door

and the warm air hits me in the face. "Today is about us. Let's go have fun."

And that's exactly what we do. We ride the Matterhorn Bobsleds ride two times, Splash Mountain three, (it's our fave), Pirates of the Caribbean four (two times back to back!). We ride It's a Small World, take the Jungle Cruise, go underwater with Nemo, tackle Space Mountain, survive Indiana Jones and Star Tours, and even spin ourselves silly on the teacups. In hindsight, it might not have been the smartest idea to spin after just having the Mickey ice cream pop, but I didn't hurl, so I consider that a victory. The park is crowded, but our cast member says the park is always crowded, no matter what day you visit. Even though there are a lot of people, we manage to see and do everything we want to tackle. Austin brought his camera, and we get tons of pictures. It helps to have Rodney with us to do most of the camerawork. Besides Mickey at my quick photo shoot, and the gang we snag at the character breakfast, our Disney cast member makes sure we get pictures with the Beast, Ariel, Stitch, Buzz, and Woody before we go our separate ways.

By the time we're nestled at our table for dinner at Blue Bayou I'm exhausted, and my feet are killing me. Thank God Austin told me to wear sneakers. If I hadn't, I would have had to buy those hideous pink Mickey Crocs they seem to sell every fifty feet. I'm sucking down my second Sprite and finishing off my New York strip steak while Austin tackles the fish. We've rush ordered dessert so that we can make it outside in time for the evening fireworks. I take a breather from my meal and look around. The Blue Bayou is my favorite restaurant in Disneyland because it's so romantic. Not that I've been here on a date before, but I've always wanted to. The restaurant is indoors, but you feel like you're outside on a clear moonlit evening watching boaters (on Pirates of the Caribbean) float by.

"This has been the best day," I tell Austin. "Thank you for thinking of it." Of course, being a total cheeseball, as I say the words, I start to get teary.

"Burke." Austin puts down his fork and takes my hand. "What's the matter?"

"Nothing," I choke, and try to fix my makeup with my free hand before someone sees and snaps my picture. I can see the headline now: "Kaitlin Burke and boyfriend break up at the Happiest Place on Earth." I look into Austin's eyes, which seem darker in the softly lit restaurant. "I know I'm being ridiculous. We've talked about this a dozen times! We'll be fine. I'm just going to miss you. A lot."

"I'm going to miss you too." Austin squeezes my hand tightly. "A lot."

I smile. "Maybe it will be good for us," I tell him. Look at Will Turner and Elizabeth in *Pirates of the Caribbean: At World's End*. After he gets shackled to *Flying Dutchman* duty, he only gets to leave the ship once every ten years, and still, Elizabeth is waiting for him ten years later with a kid in tow. Sure, I hated the third film after they sort of killed off Will, but waiting for your true love is romantic, especially now that it applies to me. "And it's only a few months."

But what if after those few months, Austin doesn't feel the same way about us anymore? What if absence doesn't make the heart grow fonder?

"We'll talk every day," Austin insists. "We can Skype too. Just promise me one thing."

"Anything," I swear.

Austin is smiling, but he looks sort of grave too. "I don't want to pick up every tabloid there is and find pictures of you all over the city with *that guy*."

That guy is Dylan Koster. My costar in the play. He and Austin met when Dylan and Emma Price flew out to test with me. Austin thought Dylan was into me, but I didn't see it.

I give him a look. "You have nothing to worry about. He's my costar, not my New York City tour guide."

Austin grins. "Good. Then we have nothing to worry about. It's only a few months," he reminds me for the umpteenth time. "And like we were saying, this is a good dry run for college. Who knows where we'll both be next year."

I move the remains of my steak around with my fork. "Absolutely." Does he have to bring up next year already? I'm having a tough enough time with *this* year.

"Here you go." The waitress—excuse me, cast member—brings us our dessert. We both ordered crème brûlée. "I know you asked for the check, but there is no charge," she says. "Your cast member took care of everything. When you're done with dessert, head over to Main Street. You have fifteen minutes before the fireworks."

As I thank her and sign an autograph for her daughter, Austin figures out a tip. Then I scarf down dessert. I do not want to miss the fireworks. That's the most romantic part of the day! Austin must feel the same way, because he eats his dessert in three minutes flat, and then we spring up from the table. Rodney, who has been eating at the table behind us, leads the way and keeps autograph seekers at bay. (I've signed happily all day, but right now I have somewhere I need to be!) We make it to the spot on Main Street that our VIP tour guide told us about just as the park lights begin to dim and the music starts. Rodney seems to disappear, even though I know he's probably close by, and I feel Austin wrap his arms around my waist just as the first firework explodes over the cloudless night sky.

"When you get back August twentieth, let's promise we'll come back here and do this all again," Austin whispers in my ear. "We'll celebrate our perfect summers and our reunion in the fall."

I turn around. "August twentieth? You remember the exact date?" I ask, touched.

Austin blushes. "Of course. I've said it a hundred times, but I'm going to say it once more: I'm really going to miss you, Burke."

"I'm going to miss you too," I tell him, but this time I don't choke up. I don't know if it's the music crescendo, the voice of Jiminy Cricket over the loudspeaker, or just being in Disneyland, where everything is always perfect, but suddenly I feel okay. I really do believe Austin and I will be fine.

Austin smiles at me. "So it's a date, then?"

"It's already on my mental calendar." I point to my head and almost poke myself in the eye.

Satisfied, Austin leans in for a kiss. I know we're being watched. I've been hearing parkgoers around us whisper things like, "I think that's the girl from *Family Affair*," or "Isn't that Kaitlin Burke?" They're taking pictures too. But I tune them out. The only one I'm focused on is Austin. I close my eyes as Austin kisses me, and I can hear Rodney.

"There's nothing to see here, folks," he says gruffly. "You can move along."

Let them snap away, I want to say. But my mouth is too busy to actually say that. I'm making the most of my last few minutes with my boyfriend.

Monday, June 1

NOTE TO SELF:
Flight to NYC: 11:15 AM tomorrow.

Celeb Scoop!

SKAT* and LAVA* Face Off!

* (Our new nicknames for Sky Mackenzie and Kaitlin Burke (SKAT) and Lauren Cobb and Ava Hayden (LAVA)

Includes an exclusive interview with Kaitlin Burke and Sky Mackenzie!

by **Penny Rosebud**

Kaitlin Burke can't catch a break. Just when it looked like the paparazzi princess had finally handed over her crown, a melee at the premiere of her new flick, *Pretty Young Assassins,* puts her back on the hot seat. According to several witnesses, Kaitlin Burke and Sky Mackenzie, Kaitlin's *Family Affair* and *PYA* costar, had a meltdown when Lauren Cobb and Ava Hayden turned up at their party. "Ava and Lauren started trading insults with Kaitlin and Sky," says a witness. "Whatever they said must have really ticked off Kaitlin

and Sky because the girls had Lauren and Ava tossed out."

Kaitlin, Lauren, and Ava were tight up until a few months ago when Kaitlin's new hard-partying ways caught up with her and landed her at Cedars Sinai. The hospital stay came on the heels of Kaitlin's *Sure* photo shoot where LAVA showed up and allowed Ava's pooch to pee on a priceless dress. Kaitlin has since admitted the difficult times caused her to have panic attacks.

Crashing is certainly LAVA's style, and they did the same at the *PYA* premiere. "Everyone knows that Kaitlin had a falling out with

Lauren and Ava," says an event planner. "The girls were *not* on the guest list. They must have wormed their way inside. Those two would show up at the opening of an envelope. As soon as the studio saw what was happening, they wanted the girls out of there, but Sky took care of that first."

Yes, Sky, Kaitlin's onetime nemesis, now appears to be her savior. Sky knows what it's like to be on LAVA's "not" list. She had her own parting with the pair a year earlier, when the two dropped Sky like a hot potato. "It was interesting seeing Sky stick up for Kaitlin, but then again, those two seem sort of friendly these days," says someone who was on the scene. SKAT are so chummy that they even took time out of their partying to shoot a YouTube clip for Tom Pullman, their *FA* producer. (He reportedly sent a cameraman to the affair to get the girls to do a final plug for their beloved TV show.)

The clip was a hit—getting over two million hits—thanks to the jokey nature of the pair, who tease each other throughout. Maybe that's why LAVA decided that spoofing the clip was the easiest way to get back at SKAT for having them kicked out of the *PYA* premiere. Their own YouTube clip, mocking Sky and Kaitlin, began airing yesterday. Wearing wigs and fake teeth, the two make fun of *FA* and its stars. Their clip has been viewed so much that the pair promise future videos will begin airing right away.

"I think it's pitiful that a ridiculous video like theirs would get this much attention," says Sky, who phoned us to chat about the nasty news. "But it just goes to show you how badly some people are starved for attention. If the best job they can get is an unpaid YouTube clip, then let them have it."

Will Sky and Kaitlin retaliate? Both girls say no—for now. "When there are so many more important issues at stake in the world, I'm sorry something like this is taking up so much of our nation's attention," says Kaitlin. Does she agree the clip is over-the-top rude? "I think it was unnecessary," says Kaitlin, "but it's a free country. If making a clip like that makes them happy, then that's their prerogative. I've got more important things to think about — like starting my play."

Kaitlin is currently in New York rehearsing for her Broadway debut in the teen drama *Meeting of the Minds*. Sky has filmed a pilot about a group of teens living in Alaska that is tentatively titled *I Heart Snow*. The show begins filming in Vancouver this summer. On Lauren and Ava's agenda? More videos. "The girls know that a fight with stars as big as Kaitlin and Sky is a way to keep themselves in the public eye," says a source. "They're going to milk this incident as much as they can."

It sure seems that way. "We're so pleased that people like what we've been doing," said Ava when asked for comment at the Verizon Wireless party at Shelter where she was picking up three new phones. ("Calou, my dog, has his own line.") "We love making our fans happy."

THREE: *Welcome to New York*

"Is that the last of them?" I wipe the sweat from my brow and pull my long blond hair off my neck. Matty and I have been unpacking boxes for the last three days and if I never see another piece of packing popcorn it will be too soon.

He makes a face and fans himself with one of my New York guidebooks. "I think there are a few more in the hall."

"How can that be?" I say, my voice jumping an octave. "Are they Liz's?" I told her I'd unpack her stuff, since she has finals and doesn't arrive for three more weeks, but I'm already regretting that decision. Thank God this apartment we rented came furnished, or we would have had even more stuff to unload and put together. As it is I feel like my whole life is in boxes. Clothes, pictures (of me and Austin, of course, plus *FA* cast pics and shots of Liz and me on vacation), my camera equipment, Austin's lacrosse jersey (which is my new pajama top — I'm so glad he agreed to part with one! I may never give it back), my driver's ed stuff (because I fully plan on *finally* going for my license when I get home), my MacBookPro, iPod, Bose docking station…you name it, I've brought it with me. Now I'm kind of wishing I'd packed lighter.

"They're yours," Matty yells from the hall. "Do you even have room for this stuff?"

I look around my new room. It's smaller than my one at home, but not as tiny as I thought it would be. One wall is exposed bricks, which is very cool, but my favorite thing is my almost floor-to-ceiling window. We're on the tenth floor, so I have a view of some other rooftops, a Joe's Pizza, a movie theater, and (thankfully) a lot of blue sky, which is one thing I'm already missing about Los Angeles. I have to purposely look up to see what the weather is truly like here — even the smaller buildings are at least six stories high and squished together. I also have to take a cab to find a large patch of grass. Every inch of real estate is used in New York, and greenery is hard to come by.

On the upside, city living is posher than I would have imagined. Every time I've traveled to New York, my hotel room has been small, so I figured an apartment would be the same, but the place Mom and Dad rented is pretty spacious. After much family deliberating, we chose to sublet (new term for me!) an apartment in Tribeca that has a doorman and private security, its own indoor pool, a gym, and a laundry room. Since our housekeeper, Anita, stayed back in Los Angeles to take care of Casa Burke, Mom hired a cleaning service and is having a personal chef come in a few nights a week to cook (Mom's specialty on either coast is still take-out). The apartment is set up railroad style. There are two floors and the rooms go from front to back. In the front is the living room; behind it is the decent-sized kitchen and eat-in dining room, and behind that is a rooftop patio. The floor above it has four bedrooms connected by a narrow hallway — Mom's and Dad's, Matty's, Nadine's, and mine and Liz's. (Rodney is actually staying at his brother's place uptown, which worked out well.) From what I can tell, the location of our place is perfect. It's only a ten-minute — twenty with traffic — ride to the theater, and just a long walk to the West Village, which has the best shopping and is home to my beloved Magnolia Bakery (they make the most amazingly sinful cupcakes in the world).

"Kate-Kate!" Mom flies into my room carrying her datebook and her BlackBerry. Her Bluetooth is on her diamond-studded ear. "I was just wondering if your calendar was open on June eighteenth for a private Chanel dinner at MoMA."

I've already decided that the downside to an apartment in Manhattan is how close in proximity Mom is to me at any given moment. Our house in Los Angeles is so big that I can easily move from room to room without her catching me. But here, there are not a lot of places to hide. I glance at Matty who is decked out in moving clothes like me — cargos and a bleach-stained William Rast (JT's line!) T-shirt — though I'm pretty sure the bleach was intentional on JT's part. "Um…" I grab a box that Matty is carrying into the room and put it on my bed to start unpacking it. Anything to avoid Mom.

Mom sighs loudly. "You promised you'd do some events before the show starts! You only have a few weeks before you're shackled to that stage."

"Gee, Mom, shackled?" Matty teases. He pulls a teddy bear Austin won me on the Santa Monica Pier out of the box, and his green eyes jump playfully. "She's not in prison. She *wants* to do the play, remember?"

"Yes, yes." Mom sounds distracted. I can't believe that even on a day when we're all just unpacking her foundation is flawless, let alone that she put any on. Mom's definitely planning to stay in, though — she's wearing one of her old PB&J sweatsuits, which according to her are so three seasons ago. If that's so, then why does she still have them?

"I'm just trying to squeeze some social obligations in before she starts," Mom tells Matty. "Now, I spoke to Nancy Walsh — you know her, dear, she's the wife of Tom Walsh, the real estate mogul."

"Not exactly." I wink at Matty, and he tries not to laugh.

Mom keeps talking. "She's very big on the social scene and she's been kind enough to coach me on the season's must-do events, which reminds me that I forgot to tell you the most divine news." She claps her hands excitedly, and her Black-Berry tumbles onto the hardwood floor. She scoops down and picks it up, her permanent French manicure scraping on the varnish. "I'm going to be one of the new chairs of her Darling Daisies committee!"

Matty and I look at each other. What the heck are the Darling Daisies?

Mom crosses her arms impatiently, zipping her PB&J track top up and down menacingly. I can see she's wearing a Juicy tank underneath, despite the fact that Matty and I are always teasing her that she's too old to wear Juicy. "The Darling Daisies committee raises money to plant flowers around New York City to beautify the landscape," she says, as if this is something we should already know. "Haven't you noticed the sweet saplings that are springing up everywhere? We're doing the same with flowers."

I haven't noticed the saplings, but that could be because I've been too excited about other cool living-in-New-York things. Like the fact that I can walk to Starbucks for a Strawberries and Cream Frappuchino rather than wait for Rodney to drive me. And how there is a deli every five feet in the city, which means I can run down and pick up Fruit Loops for breakfast without Mom knowing. ("It's pure sugar, Kaitlin! You'll bloat.")

"The Darling Daisies sound life-changing, Mom," Matty mocks her, and runs a hand through his short dirty blond hair.

"Anyway, Kate-Kate, with that new job of yours you won't be able to attend many of the Daisies fund-raisers, but we can squeeze in a few now and, of course, you'll be able to make a few events in the Hamptons on weekends." Mom glares at me, raising her recently threaded right eyebrow thoughtfully.

"I have matinees and evening performances, Mom," I

remind her, wiping my hands on my little jean cutoffs (It's not even worth telling you the designer, since I've had them since before they were cool).

"Not every day! And you're off on Monday." Mom isn't going to give up easily, so I decide it's best to go back to unpacking. I pull my framed Carrie Fisher (aka Princess Leia) autograph out of the box. Why exactly did I think I needed this in New York?

"We're going to do some lovely dinners," Mom gushes. "There are a few charity events coming up, a Polo match in the Hamptons that sounds to die for, and, of course, the Ivory Party."

"You mean the White Party," I correct her.

"This year it's all about the *Ivory* Party." Mom's long blond hair is styled just like mine. ("We look like sisters!" she always tells people.) "Nancy says it's going to be better than the White Party in every way."

Matty looks up from the *Star Wars* alarm clock he's just unpacked for me. "Didn't Diddy's White Party move to Los Angeles anyway?"

Mom rolls her eyes. "Figures he'd move it to Los Angeles when all the best people are in New York for the summer."

"Can I go, Mom?" Matty pleads.

"Of course, sweetie." She puckers her lips slightly at him, like he is still five. "It's been much easier booking *your* schedule, since you don't have anything till July. Nancy said her daughter is very excited for your show, by the way."

"I'm hearing that a lot," Matty says, trying to sound modest even though he's not. His eyebrows raise hopefully. "Is she a fan of mine?"

Mom hesitates, looking away with the green eyes we got from her. "No, but she did say how much she loves the cast as a whole. Anyway, back to the Chanel dinner —"

"I'll go," I say, hoping it will get Mom off my case. No one says no to a Chanel event. "Just leave me a list of things you want me to go to, and I'll star the ones I like, okay?"

This seems to make her happy, because she takes a call about some costume gala this weekend and leaves the room just as Nadine pops in. "You done yet?" she asks, looking around at the room's modern furnishings. The previous owner's taste is different from mine — stark, minimalist, with modern chairs and plastic headboards on the bed. It makes me feel like I'm in a twisted version of *Alice in Wonderland*. I warmed the room up a bit by bringing my Ralph Lauren comforter from home, some stuffed animals, and loads of personal touches.

I groan and fall backward on my bed, landing on my R2-D2 pillow. "I'm never going to be done," I complain. "Just send the rest home."

"I would, but the box in the hall says *Kaitlin's underwear drawer*. You sure you don't need that?" Nadine tries not to smirk. Matty snorts.

I bite my lower lip and cover my face with R2-D2. "Never mind."

"Just leave it for later." Nadine grabs my hand and pulls me up. "Rodney is waiting downstairs. We're going on another field trip."

I slip on some Havaianas and follow her dutifully through the rest of the minimalist apartment, which has touches of Asian influences. The whole building is "green" (very Cali), so the people we're subletting from have used a lot of sustainable materials, like a bamboo floor, and have put a compost bin in the limestone and steel kitchen.

Nadine's "Getting to Know Your New City" field trips have been so much fun! Tuesday night we had a late dinner at Houston's because Nadine knows I'm obsessed with the chain and I love the spinach dip. (I'm so relieved there's a location in New York.) On Wednesday we went to MoMA, and I stared at Claude Monet's *Water Lilies* for almost twenty minutes. Then we had frozen hot chocolates at Serendipity. On Thursday Nadine took us to the Central Park Zoo and then to Dylan's Candy Bar to stock up on chocolate-covered Oreos (I also bought this cute Dylan's dispenser with a little silver scoop and filled the whole thing with watermelon gummies for Austin). Friday included a trip to the Statue of Liberty, which Dad tagged along for, and then dinner at South Street Seaport.

"Where are we going today?" Matty asks. "The American Museum of Natural History? That *Journey to the Stars* movie is supposed to be awesome."

"Dad wanted to see that on Sunday," I remind Matt. "I'm

coming with you, but I'm skipping the planetarium and sticking with the dinosaurs exhibit."

"Today's excursion might be Kaitlin's favorite," Nadine says with a sly smile. "I'll tell you about it after I get you guys out the door."

"Can we get something to eat first?" I ask, letting her lead. "I'm starving." I quickly grab my tan Gap spring trench coat with my free hand. It's a bit cooler in New York than it is in Los Angeles in June, which is fine by me. Seventy degrees is gorgeous. I still slip on some oversized Chanel sunglasses, though — seems like all the New York celebrities do it, and I like the way they make me look mysterious.

"We'll grab a quick bite in midtown," Nadine says. "We're not having dinner till much later." I look at her quizzically. "We have reservations at Dos Caminos at eleven-thirty PM. First up, the Empire State Building."

Nadine is so organized, even when it comes to sightseeing. I've been obssessed with seeing the Empire State Building ever since I saw *Sleepless in Seattle* back in the fifth grade. (Yes, I know it's an oldie, but it's on TBS all the time and I love it!) I was kind of disappointed to learn from Nadine that select windows don't actually light up red on Valentine's Day, but I still want to go.

We wave goodbye to Mom, who is still on the phone. From what I can make out, she is making plans for me to attend some *Teen Vogue* high tea for teen stars. When we're finally in the elevator, Nadine tells us the big surprise.

"You got tickets to *Wicked*?" I freak. I've seen the Los Angeles production several times but haven't made it to the one in New York yet. I have a list of shows I want to see before I start my own, and *Wicked* is at the top of the list.

"I called the production office and they hooked you up," Nadine says proudly, and then puts on the Gucci sunglasses I got her for her last birthday. "I told them you were a big fan. They even offered to give you a tour backstage. They do them on Saturday mornings, but they could set up a private one for you if you like."

Matty high-fives our already favorite doorman, Andrew, on our way out of the lobby. He's an adorable old man who takes his job very seriously, wearing an outfit that looks sort of like a policeman's, complete with a hat. Andrew made us show our ID every time we came or went the past few days — Mom was peeved that he did not know her star children — before he remembered we were new tenants.

We move through the revolving door, where Rodney is waiting at the curb, and the noise level increases. It's considerably higher than it is at home, but I'm starting to like the sound of taxis honking — just not at one in the morning when I'm trying to sleep. Rod is in his standard outfit (all black even in June) with black sunglasses, his brown head shaved so close it's shiny and a frown on his face as he nurses a soda and cradles a Twix in his right hand. Rodney is never without a snack.

"What's wrong, Rodney?" I ask as I slip into the air-conditioned car behind Matty and Nadine.

"I still feel weird not driving while we're here," he grumbles, and closes the door for me. He goes up front next to the driver.

"I'm mad that Mom won't let me take the subway, but what are you going to do?" I tell him. My biggest pet peeve with Mom so far is that she won't let me go underground. She'd rather I hoof it, take a taxi, or use a car service (her preference). "There is not enough Purell in the world for me to let you go *down there!*" she declared when I mentioned getting a MetroCard. Nadine just rolled her eyes at her. She's been taking the subway everywhere, and she says that nine times out of ten it's the quickest way to travel.

"Rod, Seth hired a car service for off hours, and the theater hired Kaitlin one for workdays," Nadine reminds him gently. "It's easier if you don't have a car here. Where would we park?"

"They have garages," he says gruffly, and takes the second Twix out of the wrapper.

"I know, Rod," I say, looking at Nadine worriedly, "but I'd rather not have you waste time trying to park when I need you by my side." New York streets are much more crowded.

Rodney appears to mull it over. "You're right." I think I even see him smile a little, because the sunlight hits his prized gold tooth, making me flinch. Satisfied, Rodney chats up today's driver (unlike Rodney with me in L.A., the driver we have here changes every time). "Hey, how is the mileage on this thing? Are you from the city? Do you know where the nearest Whole Foods is? I need to get my protein shake mix."

Nadine's schedule is dead on, as usual. My camera has been living permanently in my coat pocket this week, so we take pictures of our group at the top of the Empire State Building (where I also pose with tourists) and of me insisting we all stop in Macy's and buy something decent to wear to a Broadway show. (I hate how people dress down these days to see theater!) I buy a cute BCBG chiffon taffy-colored, pleated dress to wear, Matty gets Ralph Lauren khakis and a navy polo shirt, and Nadine even splurges on a Calvin Klein cream sleeveless organza dress that's on sale for $65. Rodney sticks with his own clothes despite our begging him to try on a Michael Kors suit.

Finally, I have a tourist take a picture of us all dressed up outside the Gershwin Theater before we see *Wicked*. The show is incredible. I've seen the touring production before, but there is something about seeing that time dragon clock and Elphaba flying and Galinda pouting here on Broadway that kicks the magic up to a whole new level. The play flies by and it's all too soon that I'm clutching my *Wicked* book and staring at the sign on the wall above the exits that says *You're Now Leaving Oz. Fly Carefully.*

The streets are packed as people spill out of shows on several blocks at the same time, and everywhere you look tourists are smiling and laughing as they walk along or jump into taxis or waiting limos. It's nice to see so many people in one location that aren't a corral of paparazzi. In Los Angeles, you never see this large of a crowd together unless you're leaving Dodgers Stadium or the Kodak Theater. "Can we walk to the restaurant?" I ask Rodney. The high I have from seeing the show has me feeling all wound up and gooey. "It's so nice out."

Rodney looks around skeptically. Other than a group of young girls at twelve o'clock—I heard them debating whether to ask me for an autograph—I don't think anyone else notices or cares that I'm here. It's one of my favorite things about New York so far. The anonymity is a nice change.

Nadine laughs. "Kate, it will take too long if we walk. This is just like the other day when you wanted to walk from the apartment to Topshop—it's too far when we're in a time crunch. We have dinner reservations in forty-five minutes."

I keep forgetting that the city is bigger than it seems. With so many stores near our apartment, it feels like everything is within walking distance, which is not the case at home. I guess it's not the case here either.

"I'll tell the driver to meet us a few blocks down," Rodney compromises.

The crowd gently pushes us toward the neon bright lights of Times Square. It's impossible not to slow down and look up at the flashing screens and ads here, even if I know I'm walking too slow for locals. I can hear people around us discussing dinner plans (everyone eats late in this town!) or chattering about the plays they've just seen. I can't help but think that they'll be doing the same thing about my show in a few weeks. Will they like the play with me in it? Will they miss Meg Valentine, who originated the part of Andie

Amber? It's dizzying to even think about what their reviews will be.

"Kaitlin, look!" Matty says, pulling at my arm as he points up. "It's both of us!"

Strangely enough, Matty and I have billboards right next to each other. Matty's is a cast photo from the upcoming *Scooby-Doo*. The picture is dark and smoky and the cast is smiling, oblivious to the fact that there is big, green, icky monster lurking behind them. Well, oblivious except for Matty as Velma's boyfriend and the CGI Scooby he and Shaggy are holding. It's a really cool print and I stare wistfully at the tagline: THE SCOOBY GANG — SAYING BOO THIS FALL ON THE CW. Even though the CW is continually struggling, it seems to have all the coolest shows, like *Gossip Girl* and *90210*…I so want to be on that network.

Next to *Scooby* is a poster of the *Meeting of the Minds* cast, with me front and center. We shot it at a quick one-hour shoot a few weeks ago when I flew in to meet with the whole cast, who thankfully seem pretty cool. I mean, it's hard to tell at an event where you're smiling, not talking, the entire time, but Ben, who plays my brother, was really nice. I stare up at the poster and read and re-read the words over and over. "With *Family Affair*'s Kaitlin Burke starting June 26th." I take a photo of the posters with my camera, then snap another with my iPhone and send it to Liz and Austin.

HOLLYWOOD SECRET NUMBER THREE: I don't know about Broadway show posters, but when it comes to movie and TV posters, everything you see on that one-sheet is deliberate. Studios market their shows and movies very carefully and posters are no exception. Every word, every actor name and their placement (the biggest star's name goes above the title), and each image is carefully thought out. A studio will use a good review, even if it's by a no-name outlet or critic, to full effect. They'll enlarge the quote and put the unknown critic's name in small print. Sometimes studios will even deliberately use an image that reminds people subliminally of another movie they liked. *The Women* had a poster with a ton of writing that looked just like the poster for *27 Dresses*, on which Katherine Heigl is wearing a dress made out of words. I guess they hoped women seeing the poster would get the same fun feel, but they didn't (*The Women* bombed). A Renée Zellweger movie that was dead on arrival looked just like the poster from *Sweet Home Alabama* with Reese Witherspoon—black dress, sitting/standing near luggage. Studios who try this should be forewarned: If you think the press won't notice the coincidence, you're mistaken and in for a bashing.

But right now, all I can think about is the fact that I'm here. I survived the end of *FA*, got myself a new job I'm excited about, and now I have a billboard in New York City. Okay, so maybe I've been on one before for *FA* or a film, but I've never been singled out as the reason to see a project.

It's surreal. I'm standing in Times Square staring at a picture of myself in Times Square, and Matty is doing the same thing. I hug my brother as he continues to look up at his doppelgänger.

"I think I'm going to like this town," Matty says, hugging me back, but never taking his eyes off, well, himself.

I couldn't agree more.

Friday, June 5th

NOTE TO SELF:
Mon: Mtg w/producers, cast of show and rehearsal. 12PM.
Next Sat.: dinner w/ Laney.
**Ask Nadine 2 ship dress 4 prom home!
Send Austin care package w/ Dylan's Candy Bar loot & cast
   t-shirt from *Meeting*.

Sunday, June 7th

By Haley Patterson

Hot on the heels of Ava Hayden and Lauren Cobb's second brutal YouTube clip in less than a week dissing Kaitlin Burke and Sky Mackenzie comes a dirty ditty from the rival camp. Fans are atwitter, literally, about Sky's postings on her Twitter account, MySpace page, and Facebook, not to mention her official website.

"Want to know where Ava and Lauren can stick their videos? In their bony asses! xoxo Sky and Kaitlin," said the post on Twitter, which Sky's publicist confirms is the real deal. Over at MySpace and Facebook, Sky has put up a Top 25 Reasons We Can't Stand Ava Hayden and Lauren Cobb list. Among the gems: "Because they pair leggings with flip-flops. That is SO eighties!" Or "Because lavender lipgloss went out in winter '08 but they continue to pucker up in purple." And this gem: "Because the two haven't had a hit anything EVER, which means their 15 minutes never even started." Our personal fave: "Because the two are like Skittles. Sweet at first, but if you eat too many, you want to barf."

While Sky's camp has been more than forthcoming in confirming that the statements are legit, Kaitlin's camp has been keeping mum, which isn't surprising. The former *Family Affair* co-stars always ran hot and cold, and it would seem unusual that the two would team up for anything, even disses. Still, as one friend of the pair muses, there's always a first time. "The two of them are really mad about how far Ava and Lauren are taking this thing. I wouldn't be surprised if they came back swinging. Hard." Stay tuned.

MEETING OF THE MINDS

<u>Time and Place</u>
Modern day. A high school cafeteria.
NOTE: References Americanized for Broadway
production.

SCENE 1
Several tables line the stage. The walls are filled
with posters from recent pep rallies, yearbook
ads, and flyers from a spring production of *Guys
and Dolls*—pictures of LEO and JENNY are on them.
Several students are eating lunch at tables and we
can overhear their conversations. LEO and JENNY
are at one table with friends, and BECCA, ANDIE, and
JORDAN are at another.

BECCA:
I'm thinking of leaving for Chapel Hill a month
early. I was going to try to get a summer job and
make some spending money.

JORDAN:
Becca, you have four years to ditch us for Chapel
Hill. I thought we had plans here this summer.

BECCA:
I love you guys, but I can't handle another eight
weeks of being ignored. Pete Summers is having

a graduation party tomorrow night and I'm not
invited. The only reason I know about it is because I
overheard Jenny Waters talking in the bathroom.

JORDAN:
Like you'd even go to Pete Summers's party if you
were invited, which you're not seeing as how he
doesn't even know we're alive.

BECCA:
He would if we spent Friday nights at the Hill
instead of at your house doing Wii Fit.

JORDAN:
Andie, will you back me up here and remind Becks
that Wii Fit is what got her into that size six
Calvin Klein for prom? Andie? Come in, Andie!

ANDIE:
Sorry.

BECCA:
Get your fill of him now, Andie. This is your last day
to stare. Tomorrow, Leo Sanders will be history, a
memory, a yearbook photograph of a guy you crushed
on for four years.

JORDAN:
She gets the point, Becks. Leo doesn't even know Andie
exists. Tomorrow we graduate and after that Leo and

Jenny will head off to Berkeley together. They'll grow long hair, stop shaving, and go eco-friendly while our Andie will head off to Penn State and crush on some new Poli-Sci dude she'll never talk to either.

ANDIE:
Guys, you know I can hear you, right?

JORDAN:
That's the point.

BECCA:
We want to spare you another four years of anonymity. Like someone more on your level next time, Andie.

JORDAN:
Yeah, don't aim so high. Does the next guy have to win Class Thespian, Best Smile, and Most Popular? No. He just needs to trim his nose hairs and breathe.

ANDIE:
You guys, is it so wrong to want more? Just because Leo is all of those things and I'm just...I'm just...

BECCA:
A nerd with a perfect 4.0?

ANDIE:

I was going to say someone who prefers Monet to
Moët. Just because I am that doesn't mean we don't
have anything in common. Leo is into the arts, and
literature—he got an A on that English Lit paper
about *Angela's Ashes*! He loves Steve McQueen, like
me, and hates the beach, just like me, and he thinks
the fog is freaky, just like me. (laughs to herself)
One time he got stuck in it at his lake house and he
thought he ran into Bigfoot, but it turned out to be
a cow that got loose from a nearby farm.

BECCA:

How does she know all this?

JORDAN:

She hangs on his every word in class. I think she
takes notes.

ANDIE:

Oh, and he tutors inner-city kids, just like me.

JORDAN:

Leo tutors a special ed kid in Spanish so he can stay
on the football team! That hardly qualifies him for
giving back to the community.

ANDIE:

My point is, there is more to him than what we see at
school, just like there is more to me than what people

here see on the surface. I do yearbook, I tutor, I'm in the English Honors Society, but there is more to me than my yearbook entries. I like karaoke, rock climbing, pool, volleyball, and the smell of freshly cut grass. If Leo and I had the chance to talk, he'd know these things.

JORDAN:
Yeah, but he's never taken the time to, Andie.

ANDIE:
Because we've never had the chance! He's in his circle, and I'm in mine, and we just go around and around.

BECCA:
And it's going to continue that way because we graduate tomorrow. Face it, Andie, it's over. I love you, sweetie, but this crush has got to end. You're out of chess moves.

JORDAN:
Becks is right, Andie. Leo is a loser. He doesn't deserve you. You're better off without him. There. I've said every romantic cliché I can think of, but the end result is just like the movie version of the bestselling book: Andie, he's just not that into you.

ANDIE:
How can he not be into me if he doesn't know me?
(*Andie stands up.*)

BECCA:
(*panicked*) What are you doing?

ANDIE:
Something I should have done a long time ago:
talking to Leo.

JORDAN:
Andie, this is suicide! Come back. I don't want to wear
black on graduation day.
(*Andie walks over to Leo's table. His friends are
talking, but Leo looks up.*)

ANDIE:
Leo? Hey. I'm Andie Amber. You don't know me even
though we've had the same history class together
for four years. We talked once. I lent you my purple
highlighter in science class when you needed
something to write with because you forgot your
backpack at home.

LEO:
I remember you. Hi, Andie.

ANDIE:
You do? I mean, hi.

JENNY:

(whispering to Leo) Snoresville! Tell her to go away.
She's giving me a headache.

ANDIE:

You never gave me the highlighter back.

LEO:

Sorry. I'll buy you another one if you want.

ANDIE:

That's okay. It doesn't matter.

JENNY:

Do you have a point to make?

ANDIE:

Yes. I have something I've waited four years to say
to Leo and I can't wait another day because we don't
have another day. So I'm going to say it now, okay?
Out loud, before I lose my chance.

FOUR: *The Welcome Wagon*

"You couldn't let this thing just die, could you? You had to go and make it worse! They're never going to back down now!"

I'm on the phone with Sky — yes, Sky — and I haven't come up for air in at least ten minutes. I think we've had maybe six phone conversations between us during the last decade and I've already spoken to her three times this morning as I get dressed and ready to go to my first rehearsal with the *Minds* crew. My room is finally free of boxes and looks more like a real bedroom. All of my pictures, posters, and pillows have been carefully placed around the room. I'm wearing my iPhone Bluetooth while I talk so I can pick out what I'm going to wear today. Shockingly, Sky is letting me speak.

"My mom is freaking out that I'm going to wind up back in the hospital!" I vent. "Laney is worried that I'm going to damage my already fragile reputation, and *Access Holly-wood* has been calling Nadine all morning begging for an exclusive."

"Don't forget *Celebrity Insider,*" Matty reminds me. He's

sitting on my bed drinking a banana smoothie. We're going to take a car uptown together. I have my first rehearsal for the show, and Matty has a photo shoot for *Teen Vogue*. He's wearing Diesel jeans and a plain white Hanes tee. Even though they're going to dress him at the shoot, he's worried that they'll do some behind the scenes feature where they say what the star arrived in and he doesn't want to wear anything "uncool." *Teen Vogue* is featuring him as a fresh face in a fall issue for *Scooby*, and he's so excited I think he might spontaneously combust. Either that or his head is going to explode, but that was going to happen someday anyway. His ego is sort of swollen.

"*Celebrity Insider* called too!" I repeat. I hold up two different sweaters for Matty's approval — A DKNY turquoise knit one that I could pair with a white linen ruffle shirt and Nanette Lepore indigo wide-leg pants or a black Tahari wrap sweater with short sleeves that screams New York. Matty points to the black top. I give him a thumbs up, then wave him out so I can change. I quickly throw my Bobbi Brown lipgloss and my notebook in my snakeskin Orion Wrap bag. Orion is this new brand that is huge right out of the gate and this is their must-have first bag. They sent it to me and it's become my bag of choice for city living. It's big enough that I can fit my makeup, a book, and my iPhone but small enough that I don't feel like I'm carrying a sack of potatoes.

"K, would you stop whining?" Sky interrupts me. "I did you a favor, and you haven't even said thank you." I hear her sniffle.

"Thank you? Thank you?" I say in outrage. "You're getting me in trouble. Again! You are absolutely pulling a Britney on me, aren't you? I bet you didn't even talk to your publicist first. And I can't believe you used that line about Skittles! That was a private text."

"If I hadn't put your name on those things then Ava and Lauren would think you're a total doormat, which you are, but since your name is linked with mine I had to do something! Your 'Let's take the high road' Gandhi texts just weren't cutting it," Sky says in a high-pitched voice that I assume is supposed to be mine. "You're too peace, love, and understanding. You have to get fired up and strike back at people sometimes! I needed to say those things on Twitter! And Facebook! And my blog! I was doing damage control for *us*. You should hear what they said to me at—*BEEP*—Hershberger's on Saturday! I almost jumped off the massage chair and—*BEEP*—her neck!"

"Sky? It's Laney," I say, staring at the caller ID. "I should take this."

"I've got a—*BEEP*—I'll see you in a few days," Sky tells me. "I'll be in town for the upfronts and…"

The upfronts! Sigh. Oh, how I miss those! HOLLYWOOD SECRET NUMBER FOUR: Some people get to see next fall's shows before the rest of the world. Every spring, the five major networks roll out the red carpet in New York City and fly in their biggest talent to show off their new schedules to advertisers, media elites, and network affiliates. They put on this big production to do it, throwing parties and airing clips from their newest shows. It's basically a schmooze-fest, but it's also a lot of fun. This is one of the few times a year you get to hang out with fellow network stars under one roof. It's where I met Patrick Dempsey (so love him), tripped over Jennifer Garner's (adore her) cute black stilet-tos at a party and, according to my mother, embarrassed her in front of George Clooney eons ago when he was on *ER*. I was little so I don't remember this, but Mom claims I asked him why his hair was gray. Anyway, back to the upfronts: You do interviews with the press and appear at the main event, but mostly it's one big party filled with gift suites, cast photo ops, and fan pictures. I used to beg Tom Pullman, our *FA* cre-ator, to send me every year. Now Matty gets to go for *Scooby*, and Sky for her pilot.

"...so I was thinking Bubby's for brunch," Sky is saying. "K? K! HELLOOOO?"

"What? Yeah. Sure," I agree to I'm not sure what. "What was the question?"

Sky lets out a deep, long sigh. "Brunch. With me to dis-cuss Project Destroy LAVA. You in?"

Brunch? With Sky? Even though I find the idea odd, I find the next thought that pops into my head much odder: I actually want to go. "Okay," I tell her. "As long as you stop calling them LAVA. Call me when you get to town."

"Or sooner," Sky says quickly. "Who knows what — *BEEP* — next, you know? Gotta hop, K. More later." *Click.*

I switch over to Laney. "I'm so sorry. I —"

"I've got the most fabulous news!" Laney nearly bursts

through the phone, she's so loud. This is the most upbeat I've heard her since Fergie asked her to be a bridesmaid at her wedding. "You'll never guess! Seth and I were FLIPPING! He's going to call you, so play dumb because I'm not supposed to open my mouth, but I had to tell you first. Ready?"

A new TV show?

That's the first thought that pops into my head, which surprises me even more than wanting to have brunch with Sky. Is that what I want? A new TV show? I finally have a schedule that allows me to do things like Broadway. Do I really want to spend all those hours on a set again? Maybe I'm just thinking about TV shows again because *Family Affair* had its finale Sunday night and because the upfronts are next week. That's got to be it. "Tell me."

"Lorne Michaels just called Seth!" Laney trips over the words, they're coming out so fast. "He wants you and Sky to host the season finale of *SNL!*"

"*Saturday Night Live?*" I repeat her words just to be sure. That's the only *SNL* I know of, but I'm so shocked I have to double-check. "He wants me to host the show?" I start doing laps around my room to calm down. Me? *SNL?* I've always wanted to host. I wonder who the musical act is? Ooh, imagine if it's Lady Gaga? I so want to meet Lady Gaga!

"You and Sky," Laney reiterates. "I guess the trash-talking that maniac did on all her websites was a good thing because Lorne says your little brouhaha with Ava and Lauren is the 'it' topic du jour! People are salivating over you two like a good piece of Kobe beef! They're dying to see you and Sky pummel the girls, and Lorne figures they can write some great skits. He wants the writers to cook up one where the two of you pretend to be Lauren and Ava, and you're dressed as Skittles. Wouldn't—*BEEP*—hilarious? God, I'd love to see their faces when it airs."

I check my call-waiting. It's Seth. "Laney, Seth is beeping in."

"Fine, let him tell you the rest," Laney sounds miffed.

As I switch over I can't help thinking that Sky was right about getting your inner anger out sometimes. Her rants got us the gig on *SNL*. Now I feel guilty for yelling at her. She is *so* going to make me apologize after this.

Still, doing skits bashing Lauren and Ava makes me nervous. It will just set them off more, and this whole circus will continue. But this is *SNL*. You *don't* turn it down. And besides, their skits won't be out and out mean. They'll be funny mean, which I guess is better.

"Hi Seth!" I try to sound breezy. "Just running out the door for rehearsals. What's going on?"

"She already called you, didn't she?" Seth laughs. "She always does this to me. Don't deny it, Kaitlin. Just tell me how you feel. Excited, right?"

I exhale. "Yes. SO excited! I can't believe they want me!" I stop pacing. "Seth, how can I do this?" I bite my lower lip. "Won't I be doing the play by then?"

"Since the season finale is late this year, you'll still be in rehearsals," Seth explains. "I'm going to call the production office to confirm, but we think we figured it out. We're sure

Meeting will cooperate and you should be fine. It's going to be a lot of hours, but you can't pass this up. This is huge, my shining star!"

"Okay!" I say giddily. "I'm in!" I wiggle into my sweater while I'm still talking, pulling it over my Bluetooth, then grab my Orion bag and head into the hall. "Send Nadine all the details. When do I meet with them? Do I get to go over the skits? Will I get to do one with Andy Samberg? I love him! Ooh, maybe Justin Timberlake will come on and do a skit with us! Can I ask for Andy and Justin?"

I'm still talking as I practically float out the door and down the elevators with Matty, who is staring at me curiously. I scribble him a note to explain what's happening as I continue to chat with Seth about the logistics of hosting, what I need to do before then, and how I should call Sky to discuss details. If only Seth knew I was just on the phone with her. Matty shows Nadine the note and then she turns and shows it to Rodney and then he shows it to our doorman, Andrew, and before I know it we're all doing the happy dance.

"Seth's right, this *is* a big deal," Nadine agrees a short time later as we crawl up Broadway in traffic on our way to the theater. The car moves and stops, moves and stops, then the traffic opens up for a minute and our driver hits the gas, then the brake, and we move and stop again. The whole dance makes me feel like a bobblehead sometimes! We've just dropped Matty off at the Sheraton Midtown, where the rest of his cast is staying for the upfronts, and we're slowly on our way to my stop. At least in New York, there are other ways to get around if we have to ditch the car. I can ask the driver to let me out so I can walk, which is great because when I'm walking I see shops I didn't even know existed. The other day I was heading back from a fitting for my costumes and I got out of a taxi right in front of the original Kiehls. I got so much stuff that I had to get in another taxi to go home, which meant more traffic, but I was so busy trying out my new loot, I didn't care. Last night when our cab was idling between 36th and 34th Street on Broadway for over fifteen minutes, Nadine and I jumped out and took the subway. (Shh! I've already gone on it twice with Nadine and it was fine. Sure, a little hot down there, but it was easy and so fast! And crazily enough, no one even looked twice at me.)

"Think of the exposure you'll be giving the production and yourself," Nadine continues. "I bet a bunch of casting directors will come knocking after this."

"Do you think they'll still knock when they find out Sky and I were only asked to host because of this catfight with Lauren and Ava?" I worry. "*SNL* only picked us because of Sky's angry rants on Twitter. I'm nowhere as nasty as she is. I'm just along for the ride and I kind of feel guilty about it."

"Who cares?" Nadine makes her point loudly. Loud enough to be heard over the sound of horns honking at the intersection. Two cars are blocking our path in the opposite direction and our driver has his hand firmly pressed on the horn. I'm already so used to the melody of horns — and police sirens, bright lights, and ambulances, not to mention drivers yelling in English and their native languages. "The point is you're hosting *SNL*," Nadine tells me. "No one watching knows why they asked you. They just know you've been picked and that's a good thing. And as for Sky going postal on Lauren and Ava, I personally think it's about time."

I stare at her wide-eyed.

"I'm serious," Nadine says defiantly and smoothes her red hair with her nail-bitten fingers. "I think Sky might be right. Sometimes being a jerk actually works."

"Um, maybe," I say, looking at Nadine like she's crazy. She just agreed with Sky. Is hell freezing over? "I should tell Liz and Austin." I look at my watch. It's eleven-thirty AM, which means it's eight thirty AM in Los Angeles. They're both probably in first period. I try Liz first — she's late for school and in the car with her dad. She screams so loud that her dad yells at her and she has to go. Next I call Austin and he picks up on the first ring.

"Hey, Burke. Where are you off to?" Austin's deep voice almost causes me to stop breathing. Just when I think I'm getting used to not seeing him, I hear his voice and it sends me into a tailspin all over again.

"Sorry to catch you in class," I apologize.

"I'm not," Austin says quickly and I pick up on the sounds in the background; lots of guys' voices, balls bouncing, and squeaking sneakers. "We're on an assembly schedule today so I have gym, which as you know, I don't consider a class."

I picture him grinning as he stands in the middle of the gym in nylon shorts and a tank top that shows off his biceps. I want to ooze onto the floor. His arms. I want to see Austin's smooth, muscular arms, which are usually wrapped around my waist...

"But I do have to get back to a basketball game Murray is beating me at, so...," Austin hesitates.

Oh! That's right. I'm on the phone. No daydreaming about my boyfriend when I'm actually talking to my boyfriend. I have to remember that. "I just got a call from Laney. Well, Laney and Seth," I correct myself. "Guess who is the host of the season finale of *SNL*? Me! And Sky, but me! I'm going to be on *SNL*!" I'm practically bouncing up and down on the black leather seats. I'd be doing that anyway with these potholes now that the traffic has cleared. Nadine and I are slipping and sliding into each other. Rodney's in the front seat and he keeps staring down the driver, trying to yell at him telepathically. (I told him the first week to let them do their job without all his "constructive criticism" and staring them down through his shades. Their job is probably harder than it looks, and it looks hard.)

"Nice, Burke!" Austin exclaims. "You'll finally get to meet Andy Samberg."

"I know!" Austin remembers how much I like him. He really does pay attention when I talk. Or ramble. Which I do a lot. "I wish you could be in the audience," I say wistfully. "I'm going to be so nervous."

"No you're not," Austin insists. "You'll be perfect. Think

of *SNL* as a dry run for the play. That's live too, in case you forgot. The difference is with *SNL*, millions of people are watching you." He chuckles. "Okay, I'd be nervous too. But I'll be tuning in to cheer you on."

I feel my body being pulled forward and I put out my hand to avoid smushing my face into the padded black leather back of the front seat. We're slowing down. I look outside and see we've reached the theater. "Thanks." I feel anxious now that we're here. "I'll call you later, okay? Go beat Murray to a pulp."

"I will," Austin promises, and then he's gone.

I take a deep breath — partially to calm down from thinking about kissing Austin, which I think about a lot now that I can't, and partially to keep me from hyperventilating about what I'm about to do: go into my first rehearsal for *Meeting of the Minds*. The play I'm going to be starring in. In just a few short weeks. Yowza.

Nadine gets out of the car first, followed by Rodney, who is still grumbling. "What kind of driving was that? We're crawling and he's weaving in and out of lanes and making tight turns, squeaking by pedestrians…"

"Rod, they drive like that here," Nadine reminds him for the umpteenth time. "They've got to keep up with the taxi drivers and move, move, move."

"Still, if I was driving us around, I wouldn't do that." He stares longingly at the back of the Lincoln Town Car that just dropped us off.

"I keep telling you, you've got more important things to

do than chauffeur." I rub his huge arm. He hands me a green Sharpie and nods to two tween girls who've just spotted me. They dart over, speaking in such a high register that I can barely understand what they're saying. I glance at him. "You've got to keep me safe. Usually from myself." I sign the girls' T-shirts, take a picture with them on their camera phone, and then I head into the theater.

The Limestone Theater isn't much to look at from the outside, but the lobby takes your breath away. It was built in the 1930s and from what I read online, it's been restored twice since then. The first time they did away with all the vintage touches; the second time, when old school became new school, they put them all back. There are gilded gold moldings throughout, carved stone pillars, plush red carpeting, high vaulted ceilings, plaster walls, and heavy wood doors leading into the actual theater. What I love best is the painted murals on the walls. They seem art deco, which doesn't quite jibe with the rest of the Renaissance decor and Greek statues, but it still works. The lobby is quiet — there is no performance on Mondays — but I can picture what the place must look like before a sold-out show. You can almost hear the voices of people finding their seats. I pull the closest heavy door open and step into the cool, partially dark theater. Rows and rows of velvet-lined seats greet me in the cavernous room. (I think Nadine said the house holds 1,100 seats between the main level and the balcony.) The decor is even more elaborate inside, with lots more gold leaf on the walls and carved stone on the balcony boxes. The stage looks huge from here and there are long, thick red velvet curtains pulled to the sides. I can see the fifty-person orchestra pit which is partially exposed to the audience, in front of the stage. Only some of the lights are on, but the stage is still completely lit up and I can see the exposed black bricks of the backstage area. The show's background is missing at the moment.

There's a bunch of people standing around on stage and they all turn to look when the door closes behind me. I take a deep breath to keep from passing out. Broadway is a world I know nothing about and as excited as I am to try it, I can't help feeling like the awkward new kid in school. What if I can't keep up? What if I don't fit in? What if they hate me?

"Kaitlin! Welcome!" Forest Amsterdam, the show's director, flies up the aisle toward me and puts my fear on hold. In a weird way, Forest is a newcomer just like me. Forest and I are the only two Americans in this production (he took over the direction when the show moved to New York). The rest of the actors are from the original London cast. Unlike me though, Forest is an old pro at Broadway. He just finished a traveling tour of *The Little Mermaid* and before that he worked on *God of Carnage*. "It's great to see you again," Forest says cheerfully. His face is pasty white, which is fitting for someone who has spent hours in the theater, but his bright smile and gray eyes are warm as he shakes my hand. He's wearing a baseball cap, like he did the last few times I met him, and I still don't know what his hair — or lack thereof — looks like, but I do know he's taller than me, and maybe even thinner. He's clean-shaven though, which is a one-up on most of the Hollywood directors I've worked with. "Have you been settling in okay?" he asks. "We wanted to give you a few days to get a feel for the city before we started hounding you."

"I'm great," I tell him, and smile equally big, even though I'm freaking out. I've been side-eyeing the stage, which looks HUGE even up close. "I'm unpacked and I've been getting acquainted with my new neighborhood. I've already found the closest Starbucks and the best pizza place, and taken a twenty minute walk to Magnolia Bakery. I'm addicted to their cupcakes," I admit, embarrassed.

Forest laughs. "Who isn't? You've got to try Crumbs, though. We'll have to get some of those in for rehearsals to keep your sugar level up." He jots a quick note on the pad he's carrying under the arm of his untucked navy blue dress shirt, which he is wearing over worn-in jeans. "The script — has it been treating you okay?"

I nod. "I think I have my part memorized." I pull the pages out of my bag. "I made some notes where I have questions," I add nervously. Is it okay to have questions on a play script? That's the norm for movies, but I wasn't sure what the protocol was for theater. Maybe you're not allowed to touch the dialogue. "I wanted to see how Meg did a few things."

Meg Valentine is the actress I'm taking over for. She originated the role of Andie Amber in London and here in New York, and her reviews were stellar. She's the only original cast member to leave the show. It's tough to slam one out of the park with a teen play, but this one sparked Seth's interest because of the plot. The whole story takes place in a high school on the last day of senior year. Andie gets up the guts to confess her love to Leo, who she's loved from afar for four years. Her confession sparks a trend that affects everyone in the lunchroom and pretty soon everyone, even the teachers and principal, are confessing something—their fears for the future, their dark side, their insecurities. And, of course, what it means to love someone who has never even known you existed. Teens in London thought the show was the second coming of *The Notebook*. They became addicted and repeat ticket sales were through the roof—partially because of Dylan Koster, who plays Andie's love interest. Dylan is a huge star across the pond, and has his first movie coming out in the States this year.

Forest takes my hand and squeezes it tight. "No mention of Meg's name again," he says. "This is your part now and I told you—we want you to make it your own. It's your turn to get the critics in a tizzy! They're going to love you."

I'm glad Forest has so much confidence in me because I'm still worried about how I'm going to pull this thing off. And I have to pull it off because if I don't, my already precarious place (according to Mom) in the Hollywood Food Chain will be in even more peril. Thankfully this is a great part. Andie is a cut-up, a klutz, a talker, and full of heart, just like the show.

"Come say hi to everyone." Forest leads me to the stage while Nadine and Rodney take a seat in the back row of the theater. "Everyone, you remember Kaitlin. Kaitlin, this is everyone."

"Hi." I feel so awkward, like it's the first day of school. What should I do? Shake everyone's hand? Make small talk? I don't want to say or do the wrong thing. How do cast introductions work on a play?

Thankfully, the cast takes care of those questions for me. Everyone introduces themselves and shakes my hand. The cast is small, only about twenty people, and I make my way down the line talking to everyone. No one talks about the play. Instead they have Hollywood questions, mostly about celebrities. (Is Miley really as cute and bubbly in person? Do I consider myself a BFF of Taylor Swift too?) I'm so busy chatting, I don't realize Forest is waiting to introduce me to two other people.

"And of course," Forest is saying, "you remember Riley and Dylan. These two are going to be your right and left hands on stage."

"How have you been, lovely?" Dylan has this adorable British accent. "Ready to have a go with this thing?"

Yowza. Was Dylan this gorgeous the last time we met? I was in the middle of my Lauren/Ava phase when we rehearsed, and at the time I couldn't think of anything but shoes, shopping, and sweets to keep me awake after all those late nights. But now that the fog has lifted, it's hard not to notice just how good-looking the guy playing my love interest actually is. He's taller than me by at least a foot, and has the frame of a linebacker, but the face of a dark-haired cherub, with green eyes that suck you in.

I sort of lose my train of thought for a moment and have to send my brain a signal to react. Say hi, I will myself. Stick out your hand and shake his. I do. His grip is warm and steady. Instead of saying hi though, I sort of squeak.

"I saw *PYA* at the cinema over the weekend," Dylan adds. "You whipped Sky Mackenzie's arse, which you probably wanted to do for a while." He winks at me.

Why do accents make a guy extra attractive? I'm a sucker for accents, which is good, because Andie, my character, is supposed to be head over heels for this guy. Dylan being this cute will do well for my character motivation. Although, I guess Dylan won't be using his accent during the show. Forest told me all the actors are using American accents for this production.

"She's not so bad, actually." I find myself finally speaking and I'm talking nicely about Sky of all people. "Especially when we're not working together and I don't have to hear her gripe about our line counts." Both Dylan and I sort of laugh, and I hear someone clear their throat.

"Stop hogging her," Riley interrupts, and elbows Dylan. "Can I say hi too?" Riley hugs me tightly. "You've certainly been up to bits and bobs, no? Your name is all over the papers. Which is good, if you like that sort of thing, which I guess you do. It suits you."

"Nice to see you again, Riley." I smile warmly, even though

inside I want to shrivel up and disappear. Riley I remember. Her stage name is Emma Price. Apparently she has these huge fears about people knowing her real name so she uses her middle name for professional purposes. Emma, Riley, whoever she is, had a way of making me feel very small and inferior about tackling the theater the last time we met. I chalked it up to jet lag—I distinctly remember her telling me how much she hates long flights, and the flight to L.A. from New York is a long one she didn't want to make. Forest made her and Dylan fly out with him to audition with me. But maybe it wasn't the time change. Maybe this is just her.

"Forest just told us your smashing news—you're hosting *Saturday Night Live* in a few weeks," Riley says. While I look smart casual for today's rehearsals, and the rest of the cast is dressed down in jeans and tees the way you normally would be for a practice run, Riley looks like she's headed for a day at the office. She's wearing a fitted white dress shirt that is tucked into a navy pencil skirt. She's also got on heels. I look down at my cute and comfy black Dolce gold-studded sandals.

Wow, Seth works fast. "Yes, I'm honored." God, I sound like I'm accepting an award. Riley makes me so uncomfortable! "I mean, I can't wait. It seems like such a fun show."

"Well done!" Riley claps. "That row with those wankers really paid off for you." She smiles thinly and I can't help thinking Riley looks like a cat who swallowed a canary. A pretty cat with pale skin, long light brown hair that falls to her narrow waist, and brown eyes that view me warily. "I'd love to do that sort of show while I'm here, but of course, I don't have enough paparazzi coverage to warrant it. I did get to present Sunday night at the Tonys with Meg Valentine. We didn't see you there. Weren't you invited?"

I blush. "I wanted to watch from home," I lie. Okay, so the truth is I wasn't invited, but the American Theatre Wing apologized profusely for the oversight. Laney laid into some poor executive on the phone this morning. Being so new to the Broadway game, I didn't even realize the Tonys were happening last week. Laney should have, but I suspect she was too busy dealing with a high profile client who is looking for a new nanny — she caught her husband with their current one (which means she's also looking for a good divorce lawyer).

"Really?" Riley looks mildly amused. "I've never heard of anyone turning down a Tony Awards invitation! Did you get many invites to important award shows when you were on your soap opera?"

I ignore the dig. "Only the Oscars," I say smoothly.

"Riley, be nice," Dylan scolds. He looks much more relaxed than the ice queen. His jeans are as worn in as Forest's, if not more so. There is a hole near his right knee. He has on black tee with a picture of John Lennon on it. There's a bleach stain near the bottom, which I suspect is real, unlike the one Matty had on his shirt today. "Just because she's a Hollywood actress doesn't mean she's going to give you fleas." Dylan looks at me, covers his mouth, and loudly whispers so that Riley can hear. "She doesn't think you celebrity types over here have the chops for the stage."

"Bollocks, Dylan! I didn't say that," Riley tells him, ignoring me. "I said that *most* Hollywood stars who do theater are doing it because they're in a career slump and they need a boost. Producers jump at the chance to hire them to get their seats filled, all the while never caring how much the tosser's inexperience is dumbing down their play." Her voice is growing louder and I become aware that others are listening. "I know this isn't the case with you, Kaitlin, darling," she emphasizes. "But in so many cases the play would work perfectly well with another stage actress, one as qualified as Meg was, but instead, the producer hires the Hollywood arse who doesn't know the playing area from the center queue or what the box set is. Then the rest of us trained thespians, who have been doing this sort of thing our whole lives, have to spend ten weeks sorting it out with someone who will never see the inside of a theater again after this run, especially after the papers that heralded their debut pan them." She inhales then, having not taken a breath during her entire "speech." Wow, she really is a trained thespian.

I'm sort of stunned into silence. My face burns and I stare at the floor. I can't think of a witty zinger to sling back at her, partially because what she just said is something I've been worried about. Did Forest hire me to fill the house? Did I snag the lead role just because I'd drum up press? If

Sky were here, she wouldn't let Riley get away with a long-winded speech like that. But I'm not Sky and right now all I feel is embarrassed.

"Brilliant, Riley, tell us how you really feel about Kaitlin being here," Dylan says dryly and I look up at him. He winks again.

"I didn't say Kaitlin," Riley insists, looking around. "Did anyone hear me say Kaitlin's name?"

"Unlike you, I like the idea of a paparazzi princess — that's what they call you, right?" Dylan asks me, but doesn't wait for an answer. "I like the idea of sharing the stage with one. It's like being on one of those roller coasters at EuroDisney. They dip, and turn, and you're never sure where they're going, but you like the ride."

"I think you've found the right paparazzi princess then." I smile back. "I'm a big roller-coaster enthusiast." Dylan smiles and I notice the cute tiny gap between his two front teeth.

"Riley, may I have a word?" Forest's voice interrupts our conversation and we all turn to look at his stony face. "Now?"

Riley turns and walks past the director, who follows her offstage and into the wings, where I can hear him whispering heatedly. I wish I could hear what he's saying, but I'm almost positive I know: He doesn't like the way she's behaving. And that makes me smile, because even if Riley doesn't like me, I know Forest does. And so, apparently, does Dylan. The other cast members are quiet too. You can tell that Riley is their queen, if only because everyone seems a little frightened to get on her bad side. I take the moment to address them.

"Look, Riley's sort of right," I tell them without flinching. "I've never done this before. I don't know what the playing area is. Or the center…" I look at Dylan questioningly.

"Queue," he whispers.

"Center queue." I bite my lip. "I do know that I'm excited to be here. I hope you guys can show me the ropes. And I promise to work hard. I'm dedicated to making this the best performance I've ever done. I'm just asking for a shot."

"This, people, is the attitude I'm looking for." Forest walks over and gives me a hug, all the while keeping his eyes on Riley, who is staring glumly up at the rafters. "Kaitlin is going to make a superb Andie," he says affably, and fixes the pencil hanging behind his ear. "And we're going to help her every step of the way, aren't we? I'm counting on all of you to help, since I'm not around at every rehearsal."

Oh God, he's not? Forest is my biggest supporter. How am I going to do this without him?

"Remember: the better she does the better we look," Forest adds. "So let's give her a hand and make her feel welcome."

Forest starts clapping and I feel my face flush as people join him. They're all smiling and Dylan is whistling and even though I'm embarrassed, I'm touched. It's nice to feel wanted by everyone. Or should I say almost everyone. Riley is barely clapping. But that's okay. I look at the others and smile gratefully. After crazed paparazzi (Glad you're back in Cali, Larry the Liar!), bitter guest stars, and socialites gone mad, winning over Riley should be easy.

I hope.

Monday, June 8

NOTE TO SELF:
Ask Nadine 2 buy theater terms dictionary!!!
Brush up on my British-ese.
Study script!!!
Rehearsals: T–F w/ cast: 11-2:30. Me only: 2:30-4.
Sat. nite: charity dinner 4 Operation Read America
Sun. nite: party 4 *Scooby*
SNL Mtg: Mon. AM w/ Sky *brunch w/ Sky after
Wed. the 18th: Chanel charity dinner.

Kaitlin and Sky's Meltdown-o-rama!   June 11th

Do our eyes deceive us, or were Kaitlin Burke and Sky Mackenzie arm in arm in Hell·ay last night, acting as chummy as Drew Barrymore and half of Hollywood? Dressed in matching outfits that make Britney Spears's tour clothes look timid, with their hair teased higher than the Captiol Records building, the pair hit the Sunset Tower Hotel for dinner and then went dancing at MyHouse, stopping at each location to take dozens of photos for waiting paparazzi who were already salivating over the pair's previous mishaps that evening. At the Sunset Tower Hotel, they caused a scene in the middle of dinner by spraying a bottle of champagne on other guests. At MyHouse, they made Zac Efron flee in terror after they repeatedly tried to kiss him in front of a steamed Ashley Tisdale, who is pals with Zac's love, Vanessa Hudgens. "Kaitlin and Sky were out of control!" says a witness. "They were loud, rude, and didn't care who was watching. It was so out of character for them. Well, for Kaitlin, at least."

Hmm...gets us *Hollywood Nationers* wondering. How were SKAT (our we·so·love·it abbreviation for Sky and Kaitlin)—both in the Big Apple for work—in Los Angeles for the night? And why would the recently redeemed Burke be up to mischief?

THE L.A. LADIES WERE IMPOSTERS!

"Ava Hayden and Lauren Cobb thought it would be a hoot to dress up as Kaitlin and Sky and cause trouble," admits a supposedly close pal who fears "they'll kill me if they know I blabbed. The two were furious when they heard that Kaitlin and Sky were benefiting from all this publicity instead of them. They can't believe Sky and Kaitlin are going to host the season finale of *Saturday Night Live*! That didn't fly. Now they're trying to get payback."

Others back up this source's claims, as do the pictures posted here, which distinctly show LAVA (Lauren and Ava's new nicknamae courtesy of *HN*) playing dress-up. (Who could miss Ava's tattoo of her dog Calou on the inside of her wrist?) "I knew it wasn't Kaitlin and Sky," said a waiter at the Sunset Tower Hotel. "Kaitlin was just in a few weeks ago and couldn't have been sweeter. I feel so bad for that girl. Lauren and Ava are really out to get her."

Don't we know it—and we can't wait to see what happens next!

FIVE: *Pucker Up*

I bet Giselle doesn't have these problems. I should have been
in a car heading to the Waverly Inn for the Operation Read
America event fifteen minutes ago. Instead, I'm dealing with
a dress crisis (Sky just stole the Vera Wang Lavender Label
steel-belted one I was going to wear because she liked it better than her Nicole Miller bustier mini) and trying to put on
makeup while I ignore my ringing phone (I'm sure it's Mom
wondering where I am). Then the doorbell rings.

"Tell them to go away!" Sky barks. She's hogging the bathroom mirror as she applies her third coat of berry lip gloss.
Matty is jumping behind her trying to get a look at himself,
but Sky doesn't budge.

I run out of my bedroom with only one leg in my Spanx
(don't let the stars fool you. Everyone in Hollywood wears
them) and hop to the front door. When I look through the
peephole I scream. That sends Nadine, Matty, and Rodney
running. (Sky doesn't move from the bathroom mirror.) I
pull open the door.

"SURPRISE!" Liz yells. She's wheeling a piece of carry-on Louis Vuitton luggage and is wearing a plum tie-dyed Free People tube top that flares out at her waist, slim black linen pants, and her favorite Elie Tahari black leather slingback wedges. Her thick curly hair is piled on top of her head with chopsticks poking out. Not exactly a travel look, but that's Liz.

The two of us jump up and down, hugging each other and squealing so loud we sound like the seals at the Central Park Zoo (which I visited again yesterday. They're so cute!). We're bouncing so hard on the hardwood floor that a Pottery Barn frame slides off the Asian hall table and lands on the floor with a thud.

"The people below us are going to start banging," Nadine warns and picks up the framed photo of Matty and me in Turks and Caicos. She puts it back on the table.

"Who cares?" I trill. Let them bang all they want. They banged for half an hour the other day when Mom was doing her Wii Fit aerobics at full volume. It's only been two weeks since I've seen Liz, but it feels like a decade, and I can't help being excited.

"Daddy flew in for the weekend, so I came with him to see you and start unpacking, but I head back Monday for finals," Liz tells my shoulder. She finally lets go of me too. "Are you happy to see me?"

"Nope!" I tease. "Of course! I have so much to tell you."

She rolls her luggage over to the couch and leaves it there

while she looks around the spacious living room, with its floor-to-ceiling views of lower Manhattan and cool dark leather couches. "Nice digs."

"Mom wants to buy this place," Matty tells Liz. "The Realtor says it's over two million dollars, so I think Mom's backed off."

"She also wanted to buy a home in the Hamptons last weekend that was ten million," Nadine chips in. "She abandoned that idea too."

"Well, either way it's nice," Liz agrees. She looks at me. "So? Tell me! How is the play going?"

"Really well." I look down at my hanging Spanx and pull them off, crumpling them up into a ball and hiding them in my fist. I'll put them back on in the privacy of my room. "Rehearsals have been exhausting but amazing. It's harder than I thought it would be."

"And Riley?" Liz reads my thoughts. "Is she still acting as if you're Britney Spears trying to do Shakespeare?"

"Yes." I sigh. "'Kaitlin, that take was spot on! Spot on if you were going for comedic effect rather than drama. That is what you were going for, right? Interesting. Not exactly what I'd expect the character to do, but okay. Jolly good! Cheerio!'" I use my fake British accent—the one I perfected when I posed as a British exchange student at Liz's school a while back—and take some liberties with what Riley actually said, but the idea is still the same. Riley makes me feel like I'll never be able to handle the stage. She's always second-guessing the way I say my lines, and making little comments about how Meg — a *real* thespian — did things, or questioning my knowledge of theater (*"Wicked* is good but so commercial," she said with a sniff when I told someone my favorite Broadway show. "Have you see *Waiting for Godot?* No? But it's a classic! I thought *everyone* in theater had seen that.") I will not play the crazy pampered celebrity role she so wants me to and complain (even though Sky and Laney think I should), but it's been tough biting my lip.

"Yesterday was the worst," I tell the group. "I ordered lunch for the cast every day this week — sort of a thank-you for the all the rehearsals they're doing with me — and everyone thought that was cool. Everyone but Riley. Yesterday I ordered pizza, and Riley wouldn't touch it. She said, 'None for me, thanks. I can't handle all the cheese. It makes me bloat, but from the looks of things you don't mind as much. You should think about another costume fitting, darling, just in case. Well, guess I'll be off. Need to take the tube uptown. We don't all get car services like you do, you know. Cheerio!'"

Liz giggles. "Troll. Does she really say 'cheerio'?"

I grin. "No, I just threw that in. It sounds better that way."

Sky coughs. Loudly. "We're going to be late, K. Get your Spanx back on and let's go." She stares down Liz and stomps her snakeskin stilettos impatiently on the hardwood floor. Sky's hair is pulled back in a tight bun and her long yellow-gold earrings hit her in the cheek as she shakes her head.

"What are Spanx?" Matty asks, looking bewildered. He's dressed in a white shirt, black pinstripe vest (very Justin

Timberlake), and black pants. Rodney said he looked like a waiter. Hee hee.

Nadine shoves him toward the still open door. "It's top-secret girl stuff." She turns to look at me. I'm still only wearing a fluffy pink robe. "Finish getting dressed and let's go. You're really late."

I head back toward the bedroom to finish getting dressed, then realize Liz is still standing in the same spot she was a few minutes ago, staring straight ahead, her arms crossed. "What's the matter?" I frown.

"What is *she* doing here?" Liz points one purple painted finger shakily at Sky.

"We have an Operation Read America dinner tonight at the Waverly Inn," I explain. "Sky and I are doing the kissing booth."

Sky grabs my arm. "K! Get dressed! You can have your geekfest later." She looks at Liz. "She can hang here and watch *The Real Housewives of New York City* or something else lame."

Liz grabs my other arm. "Nooo…I'll come with you," she says defiantly.

Sky snaps at her. "There's no room at our table."

"Sky." I use a warning tone.

"They'll squeeze a chair in for me." Liz is snippy. "Maybe your father can't get a table there, but Daddy eats there when he's in New York all the time."

"Liz." I use the same voice. Obviously Liz and Sky can't stand each other. Never have. Their dads worked together at Liz's dad's entertainment law firm, and some deal gone bad led to bad blood. Sky's dad has since started up his own firm and is always trying to poach clients from Liz's dad. If that wasn't bad enough, there's the fact that besties always defend each other, which means since I used to hate Sky, Liz hates Sky, even though now Sky and I sort of get along. "We can all go. I'll tell Nadine to call ahead and add another person."

Liz smiles triumphantly while Sky scowls. I hurry off before they erupt again so I can finally get dressed.

* * *

I think this outfit is better than my original one. I'm wearing a BCBG kelly-green pleated jersey halter top dress and Roberto Cavalli black peep-toe slingbacks. I left my hair down and curly basically because I had no time to do anything else with it. Fifteen minutes later we were all on our way to the Waverly Inn in the West Village. That's where the Operation Read America event is being held. It's my first time at the hotter-than-the-equator eatery and I can't wait to see inside.

Vanity Fair's Graydon Carter is a co-owner of the tiny bar and restaurant, and people say he eats here several times a week in his usual banquette. He also supposedly looks at the seating plan and the reservation system, which keeps track of clients and how many times they've dined, whether they've complained about their meal or berated a waiter. I guess he likes keeping the joint sort of exclusive and mysterious. You never know who you're going to run into. Even though tonight is an event rather than a dinner reservation, I plan on staying on the restaurant's good side so I can come back with Austin. The car rolls to a stop in front of the green barn door entrance, which is on the ground floor of a townhouse.

As we step out of the car, Liz yanks my arm and stares at my feet. "Kaitlin Burke, are you wearing FLATS?" I blush. "You never wear flats to events!"

"That's because we drive everywhere in L.A." I remind her. "Here I do a lot of walking. I had to walk fifteen blocks in my Manolos the other night. My feet haven't stopped aching since." Nadine warned me not to wear heels everywhere, but I didn't listen to her. I thought she just wanted me to look like one of those businesswomen we see power-walking by us in the morning in a suit and Uggs or sneakers. I told Nadine I was willing to suffer for fashion and wouldn't succumb to rubber soles. But that was before my driver got stuck in a jam on West 4th Street for forty-five minutes and I decided to hoof it home instead. It was torture! The upside to walking around New York is that it's almost impossible to get lost. I love how the streets are linear and most blocks are numbered and it's amazing how you can stand at the end of Fifth Avenue and stare all the way uptown.

"I don't care how much my feet hurt, I am never wearing flats," Liz declares, and wiggles her plum-manicured toes. "You're not wearing flats to the Junior Prom, are you?" Liz asks me as we head toward the door. There are no paparazzi lurking out front, so it's a short, uninterrupted walk. There's no red carpet either, since *People* has an exclusive on the event and plans for the evening were sort of hush-hush.

"K, don't forget we have our *SNL* meeting on Monday," Sky interrupts.

"I remember," I tell Sky, and then to Liz, "I'm not wearing flats to the prom."

"Good," Liz says. "Austin and Josh rented a limo, but we still have to make dinner reservations. What time is the flight back on Sunday?"

Sky is still talking as well. "I told them we want a skit with Andy, and of course, he'll say yes because it's us. You'll work with Andy even if it's a twisted skit, right, K?"

"Yes, I want to work with Andy," I tell Sky, and then to Liz, "Noon."

Liz's turn again: "Have you called Allison since you got here? She's going with Murray, of course."

"What are you wearing on Monday, K?" And Sky's: "I do not want both of us to show up in Stella McCartney."

I stop short right in front of the door. This paparazzi-free walk should have been easy. "Are you guys going to try to talk over each other all night, or are you both going to grow up and actually talk to each other?"

The pair look at each other quickly and then back at me. "Talk over each other," they say almost in unison.

I look at Nadine, who seems rather amused. Matty just shakes his head. "Girls," he mutters.

"Kaitlin! Sky! So glad you're here!" Olivia Thompson, the

Operation Read America coordinator, rushes over to us from where she's standing with the guest list at the door. She's wearing the program's logo T-shirt, which is a black tee covered in red lipstick marks, and has on dressy black pants. Her frizzy graying hair is pulled back in a bun and her long, narrow face has just a hint of makeup. In her hands are two pairs of red wax lips on sticks. "These are for you," she says as she hands us them. "You can use them in the booth. Some of the celebrities felt more comfortable giving kisses if they had the lips as a filter."

"I don't need a filter," Sky insists. "As long as the kiss-ee is hot."

Olivia looks flustered. "Well, this is a charity event, so I'm not sure who you'll get during your fifteen minutes, but we've been doing a lot of hush-hush publicizing and we have a great turnout. Lots of people are in town for the upfronts. We're so fortunate Graydon let us do this sort of event here," she says, looking around the crowded room. "He doesn't usually do them at the Waverly, but then again, he is old friends with the program's director. Maybe that's why so many stars volunteered for tonight." I stand on my tippy toes to see inside the dark interior of the hot spot.

Sky nods. "You're lucky I'm here, Olivia. I would have been hard to come by if I wasn't in town promoting my upcoming show." Liz snorts. "It's one of the most talked-about shows of the fall season."

Olivia frowns slightly. "What is it again?"

I steer Sky through the cracked open door before Sky can berate her. "Thanks, Olivia," I call out. "We'll be sure to get to the booth by eight-twenty-five for the eight-thirty spot." I push Sky toward the dining area. The rooms are tiny, lit with low-watt lamps that make the brick walls glow, and there are small tables, red chairs, and banquettes throughout. Adding to the homey feel are tons of tchotchkes, like old books and pictures of the Brooklyn Dodgers, and there is an unlit fireplace in one corner.

"Let's get some food before we get to work," I tell the others. "I hear the truffle mac and cheese is excellent."

"Ugh, you can't eat and kiss," Sky sounds disgusted. "Haven't I taught you anything?"

"That's what mouthwash is for," Liz argues. "Have the mac and cheese. I saw a waiter with mini chicken pot pies."

"Ooh, I want one of those!" I rub my hands, and my two green beaded bracelets knock together.

"K! We are on *SNL* in two weeks!" Sky reminds me. "You don't want to look bloated."

"Now you sound like Riley," I tell her. "Do I look bloated?" I ask Liz.

"Kaitlin could never look bloated," Liz insists. "Maybe you're the one who needs Spanx, Sky."

"Who are you calling bloated?" Sky snaps, her long beaded earrings swinging angrily again.

"The first half of SKAT." Liz rolls her eyes and looks at me. "How dumb is that nickname, by the way? They're using it everywhere."

Sky glares at Liz. "I like it."

"It's better than LAVA," I agree. "I think it's funny, actually."

"It means we've reached Brangelina territory," Sky insists, and Liz rolls her eyes.

But before Sky can get in a full-blown tirade, the most unlikely of heroes steps in.

"Katie-Kate! Katie-kins!" My mother glides toward us. She looks unbelievable in her white J. Mendel pantsuit. Her hair is long and curly, and from the back you'd think she was eighteen. Spending so much time in the Hamptons doing charity work has really relaxed her. Sort of. Dad is wearing a navy suit and tie (wrinkled shirt again underneath, poor Dad) and he looks bewildered by all the flashbulbs popping as *People* swoops in to catch our mini-reunion. "Honey, you look darling!" Mom gushes, and then in my ear whispers, "The green dress is pretty, but why is Sky wearing the Vera Wang? I thought it really brought out your glow."

"I'm going to get something to eat," Nadine growls. We've only been here a few weeks now and Mom is already getting on Nadine's nerves. I don't think Nadine quite anticipated what it would be like to live in the same house as us.

"Lizzie, so glad you got here in time. You remind me of the sixties in that top," Dad tells my best friend, and hugs her. "All ready for the move next week? Your father told me you're counting down the hours till you come to New York full-time."

"What move?" Sky asks everyone.

"Didn't K tell you?" Liz asks her with a sly grin, tugging

on her triple-beaded pendant necklace. "I'm moving in with the Burkes while I attend an NYU summer class."

Sky looks as if she just had a rancid cube of cheese (although that would require her to actually eat cheese, which she doesn't). She taps her Prada shoe on the floor. "Gee, Mendes, I would think you'd be the type to bunk at the dorms with the little people. Isn't that the best way to get a feel for the college experience? I know that's what I did for two nights when I was shooting the hit Lifetime movie *Coed College Courage*." I grab Liz's arm to keep her from tackling Sky in front of a packed room of celebrities.

"How are the Hamptons, Dad?" I ask.

"Good." Dad beams. "Lots of polo matches, things for your mom's charity."

"Any job opportunities?" I ask hopefully.

"No producing projects yet, but I'm sure I'll find something." Dad sounds chipper, but I feel bad. He hasn't worked since I did *Off-Key*, and I think he's bored.

"I have to interrupt. There is someone I've been dying for Kaitlin to meet," Mom says and pulls forward a wafer-thin forty-something woman with a deep tan, toned arms, and white blond hair. She's wearing the most gorgeous white Gucci suit, what I'm sure are real diamond pendant earrings, and a chunky gold necklace. On her ring finger is a diamond bigger than anything Harry Winston has ever lent me. This woman could double for one of the moms from *The Real Housewives of New York City*. "This is Nancy Walsh, wife of Tom Walsh, the New York real estate mogul."

"Well, I wouldn't say *mogul*," Nancy drawls, and touches my mother's arm lightly. "Okay, maybe I would." She smiles at me. "Kaitlin, it is a pleasure. Your mother told me you're very eager to be part of the New York social circuit while you're in town."

I don't recall saying that. I look at Mom out of the corner of my eye, and she raises her eyebrows menacingly at me. A double eyebrow raise mean serious business, so I nod at Nancy and smile.

"It's going to be quite tricky, dear, with that theater schedule of yours, but there are events during the day and on Mondays that you can attend. You'll have to jitney out to the Hamptons, but it's worth the effort if you want to be seen in the right places."

"Which we do, Nancy," Mom tells her seriously. "We want to make an impact while we're on the East Coast. This may be a short trip, but my husband and I are enjoying it so much that we've talked about adding a second residence here. I had no idea charity work could be so rewarding."

Here we go again. Nadine and I look at each other. Mom I could see, but Dad would never want to live here. He needs sun, sand, and big green areas to golf. I'm enjoying my extended stay, but I'm not sure I'm up for dual residencies. I really miss our private pool in this heat. And I am craving greenery. There are all these sweet little trees dotting the streets, but it's not the same as the tall rows of palm trees you see all over Los Angeles, or the lush, fountained parks and yards.

"Sweetie, I...," Dad starts to say. Mom doesn't let him interrupt.

"Kaitlin is exploring many options outside theater and who knows? One may take her east before she knows it. A lot of shows are filming here these days. My son, Matthew, is doing *Scooby-Doo* in Los Angeles, but we just heard they're planning to shoot three episodes in New York."

Nancy takes a sip of her white wine and smiles knowingly. "It is the place to be, as they say." She looks at me. "And we'll make sure you're seen, Kaitlin. I've given your mother a list of important events that you must say yes to."

"And she will," my mom responds for me.

"Your mom is cochairing some events," Nancy adds, "so I'm sure we'll be seeing a lot of each other this summer. My daughters Sabrina and Seraphina are huge fans and can't wait to see *Meeting of the Minds.*"

"Kaitlin will be sure to bring them backstage," Mom tells Nancy. Nadine is standing behind Mom and she looks like she wants to scream.

"That would be lovely." Nancy beams. Wow, her veneers are blinding! "I must say hi to Margaret Beatrow—you should too, Meg. Join me?"

"Of course!" Mom air kisses me on both cheeks and gets glimmering pink gloss on my cheeks. "Katie-kins, I've got to dash, but I'll try to make it over to your booth if I can spare five minutes. Bye, girls!"

"I should keep an eye on her." Dad winks at me. "You never

know what she'll sign me — or us — up for without asking." I grab his tie and straighten it before he walks off.

"Good idea, Mr. Burke," Nadine calls after him. "Keep us posted." Nadine turns to us. "*People* wants a few photos and a short interview about the play, but be prepared to answer questions about Lauren and Ava. Then you guys should eat before heading over to the booth. You only have twenty minutes."

"She means *us*, Liz." Sky pokes Liz in the back, right above the new tattoo on her left shoulder. (It's the Japanese symbol for life. Liz is really proud of it, even if her dad was furious.) "Not you."

"Obviously," Liz snaps as she slides into a red leather banquette and dips a fork into the gooey mac and cheese already waiting. "I can't imagine having to defend myself to *People*. That's more your area of expertise, Sky. Kates, I'll make sure I save some bananas Foster for you. I hear it's killer here."

Sky's lip curls into a snarl and I pull her over to the reporter. Just as Nadine suspected, they ask our opinions about Ava and Lauren's latest video (Sky blasts the girls while I stand meekly in the background, afraid to say anything that might set the Paparazzi Twins off even more) and they ask us to give some tidbits about our upcoming turn on *SNL*. I talk a little bit about my play and the reporter tells me they're planning to review my turn in it in a few weeks. I'm not sure if that makes me excited or more nervous. Then talk turns to Sky's show.

"I'm just honored to be a part of such an amazing cast and I can't wait to get to work on such an important, highly life-changing program," Sky says, sounding as if she's accepting a Nobel Peace Prize rather than talking about her role as a ski bunny/sorority girl.

"So there is no truth to talk that your show's creator, Grady Travis, has battled the network over budget concerns?" the reporter asks.

Sky looks momentarily flustered and picks at one of the small crystals on her manicured thumb. "No. No, we're ready to roll in a few weeks. Up to Vancouver. I still have to find some chic cold-weather ensembles. They do have clubs up there, don't they?"

The reporter frowns. "I thought the production was moving to Los Angeles now. At least that was announced earlier today on the network website." She sticks her tape recorder closer to Sky's open mouth.

"I...I'm not sure what you're talking about," Sky says and starts tossing her hair all about like she always does when she's nervous. The reporter sneezes when Sky's hair brushes her face.

"Bless you! Los Angeles? For a show about Alaska?" I ask.

The reporter sneezes again as Sky's hair whacks her face another time. "Grady was peeved too. Rumor is he's going to pull the show altogether if they don't reconsider Vancouver."

Sky stops swinging. "What? That's impossible!"

Uh-oh. I've got to get her out of here before she says something she regrets. "Look at the time," I tell the reporter. "We really should use ChapStick before our lips get action at the booth. Will you excuse us?" I pull Sky through the crowded room back out to the covered garden. Her body is limp and easy to drag.

"She's got to be wrong, right, K?" Sky sticks a powder-pink thumbnail in her mouth, biting down, which is something I've never seen her do before. "I mean, yeah, I'd rather be in Los Angeles, which is where I *thought* we were shooting originally, but now I'm kind of psyched for Vancouver and the show may not fly at all? We just had a cast round table at the upfronts! Grady was thrilled about the show. He can't pull it."

"Calm down," I tell Sky and sit her down in a chair near the booth. I hand her a ChapStick from a large fish bowl.

The kissing prep table is covered with lip-quenching products, mirrors, and perfumes. All things to help a star be more kissable if they choose not to use wax lips. Not that some of us need help in that area. There's a line for Zac Efron's table that wraps around the restaurant. To take Sky's mind off the show, I wave Vanessa over and we talk about upcoming L.A. parties. Then Sky and I apologize about a zillion times for the poseurs that tried to liplock Zac at MyHouse the other night. She knew it wasn't us, of course, but it still makes me mad that Lauren and Ava tried to make her think otherwise.

Sky looks fornlornly at the mirror in front of her. "I *need* to be on a show, K. I have to have a show to go back to. What would I do? I have to work. I have to. I love working! I love TV! I can't imagine the new season starting and not being a part of it. Not having a cast to be part of or a soundstage to show up to every day. Can you?"

"Um, I sort of have to," I joke, but I look down and pull a little at the hem of my dress. It still hurts to think about.

"That's right!" Sky's jaw drops. "You don't have a TV contract. Just this little summer thingie."

"The summer thingie happens to be Broadway," I say indignantly. "Now stop worrying. You can call your agent tomorrow. Right now we have some kissing to do."

Sky takes a deep breath and reapplies her gloss in the mirror for the zillionth time. She makes a few practice fish kisses at the mirror. "You're right. I have to be professional. I'm sure there are tons of people waiting to pucker up to me."

"Exactly." We head over to the booth, or should I say table. There is a large sign behind it that says "Read My Lips." Clever when you remember this is for a reading organization.

Liz meets us at the table, and I see Sky scowl.

"Thank God you're here, Lizzie," I say quickly. "Sky is going to have a huge line, so you can help us do crowd control."

Liz practically chokes on the French fry she's eating. "I doubt that. I'm here to take pictures of you being naughty." Liz side-eyes Sky. "If you ever tick me off, Kates, I can use the photos for collateral." I have a feeling that's a thinly veiled threat toward Sky, but I don't say anything. Liz pulls me aside. "Did you tell Austin you were doing this?"

I shake my head, and Liz's smoky eyes drop. "Should I have?" I squeak.

Liz groans. "Kates, you're doing a kissing booth! You know, kissing other people. Austin would want to know."

"I'm kissing people for charity!" I insist. "That's different." I bite my lip. "Right?"

Liz stuffs another fry in her mouth. She mumbles, but I watch her mouth and can make out everything she's saying. "I'm not saying you shouldn't be doing this, I'm just saying your boyfriend, who is thousands of miles away, might want to know before he sees the photos in *People*. If I were you, I would call him ASAP."

Liz is right. I'm such an idiot! This is something I should have told Austin about. Not the cute little Rebecca Taylor tank I scored half off at a sale. But in my defense, it's not like I've kept tonight from him. We haven't talked in three long days. We keep missing each other's calls, and then with the time change we never get to talk at night. We text, but I'm starting to see it's really not the same thing.

We didn't talk today either. It's almost as if...no, I couldn't have...forgotten to call him. I'm getting frustrated. Already. And we've got a *long* time apart to go.

"I'll call him as soon as we're done," I promise Liz.

"Do you have your wax lips, girls?" Olivia walks over and holds out a few extra pairs. I hold up mine, and Sky grabs a pair from Olivia this time. ("Just in case," she tells me.)

I'm still feeling a little anxious about this Austin snafu, but the *People* photographer is waiting, so I push the thoughts aside. The photographer takes photos of Sky and me hamming it up. I hold my wax lips by my butt and Sky kisses them. Then we pretend to hold our wax lips up and let them kiss. Sky even has her wax lips kiss a photo of Ava and Lauren that a fan brought.

"I'll start the clock NOW," Olivia tells us when we're finished with pictures. She clicks a little electronic timer. "If you have a longer line, we can always add time, okay? Have fun!"

We do! We kiss a bunch of cute, chubby babies, some nervous teen boys, and some stuffy society types. Some of our celeb friends pop over too, like Channing Tatum, Jimmy Fallon, and Chace Crawford (who I don't think either of us minded kissing). As I hand a baby back to his mother, I look up and see Dylan. He's wearing a crisp white button-down shirt that is unbuttoned at his neck, a black vest, and dark denim pants. He smiles and my palms start to sweat, which is so weird.

"Not shabby, Burke," Dylan says, and before I can say hi, I realize what he's said and freeze.

"What did you call me?" I ask, momentarily stunned.

Dylan's smile fades. "Burke. Isn't that your last name?"

I nod slowly and then try to compose myself. "Yeah. It's just. Nothing." I laugh it off, but I start playing with my bracelets anyway. "My boyfriend calls me Burke."

Dylan nods. "I guess that's why you look like you've seen a ghost! Sorry about that. I bet you're itching to get back to L.A. next week and see him."

"I am," I admit. "What are you doing off tonight?"

"Understudies are getting their due," Dylan tells me. "Since our lovely leading lady doesn't start for a few more weeks,

Forest is rotating in the second players and giving us blokes a few nights off. Did you get my message on your mobile?"

I nod. "About dinner at the Monkey Bar on Monday night? Yes."

"Can you go?" he asks. "I want to check out some of these scene-y haunts, and I thought you might too."

My heart beats a little faster, and I blush. "I do," I can't help saying. And it would be totally fun with Dylan. Then I think of Austin again. "But I have to check my schedule."

Dylan nods. "Sure. We can run lines beforehand too, if you're free. I know you're a bit worried about the second act. I made some notes on a script for you. I would have brought it tonight if I'd known you'd be here."

Dylan is really sweet. "Thanks. That's so nice."

"No problem," Dylan says and fingers a button on his vest. "I'm here with Riley tonight, but I lost her by the mob at Zac Efron's table."

I start to frown. I can't help myself. Dylan laughs.

"You're not a fan of Riley's, I know. She's giving you a rough go, huh?" Dylan asks.

"No, not really," I lie. But she is. If I have to hear, "Maybe you do it in the movies that way, but, Kaitlin, in theater we stand like *this*, so our voices carry. I thought you would have known that" one more time, I may cry.

"She's tough, but I promise she's a cub once you get to know her," Dylan says. "She and Meg were fierce mates. She just misses her."

"*Who* is this?" Sky drapes herself over my shoulder. "K, aren't you going to introduce me?"

"And me?" Liz grabs Dylan's hand. "Hi. I'm Kaitlin's best friend, Liz. We'll be seeing each other a lot this summer, seeing as how I'm in town for a writing and directing workshop at NYU."

"A university girl." Dylan's eyes twinkle. "Cool."

"I'll be in town too for various things as well," Sky coos.

For two girls who have boyfriends, they sure are worked up over Dylan. They're all over him! Not that I can blame them. He's a dish. A very, very hot dish.

I make the introductions. "Sky, Liz, meet Dylan. Dylan, meet Liz and Sky. Sky was my costar on *Family Affair*. Dylan is my colleague in *Meeting of the Minds*."

"Lucky you." Sky runs her big brown eyes over Dylan and shakes his hand. "Are you here for a kiss?"

Dylan looks at where he's standing — at the front of the line — and laughs. "I guess so, since I'm queuing. Which one of you wants to go first?"

"Queuing?" Sky asks.

"Oh, you Americans say *in line*, right?" Dylan asks.

Sky and Liz can only manage nods. They've turned into mush.

"*Queue, line*, who cares." Sky is massaging his shoulder, and Dylan looks a little uncomfortable. "Do you want a kiss? I'm ready!"

I can't help but blush. I feel strange kissing Dylan. We share one kiss in the play, near the end of the second act, but we haven't rehearsed it yet, and I feel weirdly glad about that. I don't want to get practice in now.

"There you are," Riley says as she pushes her way to the front of the line. "Oh, hi, Kaitlin." She sees me and smiles coldly, which goes well with the ice-blue halter top she's wearing with skinny black trousers. I wouldn't expect the blue to look good with her pale coloring, but it works for Riley, not that I would tell her that. "What are you doing here?" she asks. "I thought Forest might have had you make a go of the show for practice tonight. All the second-string players are performing. I guess he didn't think you were ready."

"This must be Riley." Liz looks at her sharply.

"You think?" Sky seconds. "What gave it away? The bony butt or the frigid attitude?"

"Excuse me?" Riley asks. "These two are cheeky. Are they your friends?"

"Yes," I tell her, raising my chin proudly.

"Were you referring to both of us?" Liz asks, pointing to Sky. I shoot her a look.

Riley nods. "It's so nice to have friends in town. Mine are across the pond. I can't be distracted. Theater is a lot of work and I like to concentrate fully on my character development."

"I'm sure Kaitlin does too, Riley," Dylan says gently and winks at me.

"Absolutely," Riley agrees. "She's devoted so much of her time to studies," she tells Liz and Sky. "And she'll get it, I'm sure, eventually. Right, Kaitlin, dear? Like the lingo." Riley starts to chuckle. "Sorry, Kaitlin, I don't mean to laugh. It was just so charming that time you thought the ABTT was an ABBA Theater fan club!"

I color slightly. How was I supposed to know that the ABTT was the Association of British Theatre Technicians? This is all new to me, and quite frankly, I don't see what any of it has to do with whether or not I can actually act. And yet, I've never been so unsure of my acting.

"EWW." Sky crosses her arms over her bustier top, crushing the silk and making me cringe, and stares rudely at Riley.

"Excuse me?" Riley asks, trying to smile, but not succeeding. "Was I talking to you?"

"Thank God, no, but I'm talking to you," Sky says. "Just for a sec, of course. I don't really like you. And I don't like you picking on K for not knowing some stupid tech term. Like, who cares? Let me ask you something: Do you know what a honeywagon is? Or what dress to camera means?"

Riley looks flustered. "No…"

"Those are movie set terms," Sky says smoothly and starts whipping her hair around again like a sword. It hits Riley in the mouth, and she practically chokes. "Something you'd know nothing about since you've never actually been on a movie set, have you?" Riley shakes her head slowly. "I figured as much. Must be tough living on theater wages too, from the look of that Marc Jacobs knockoff top."

HOLLYWOOD SECRET NUMBER FIVE: Riley may have her theater terms, but we movie actors have our terms too. A honeywagon is a discreet term for the crew's portable toilet truck. And dressing to camera means placing an object or a person in the best spot to be seen on camera. There are tons of other terms that would take all year for me to tell you, but some of my favorite are: Doris Day Parking (the best parking spot on the lot), Perrier meeting (a meeting that only lasts till a person's Perrier is gone), twin Ts (or twin peaks—a shot that is framed from the chest up), and shower curtain (a large, clear sheet used to soften lights). Take that, Riley!

"I'm tired, Dylan," Riley says stiffly as she stares down Sky. Sky doesn't even blink. "Doing eight shows a week and giving it your all takes a lot out of people who are serious about their commitments."

Liz is staring at me, her eyes drilling into mine. She's telepathically telling me to come back at this girl, but I can't. I'm not sure I'll ever feel less awkward around Riley, even after my (hopefully) positive theater reviews come in.

"Dylan can't yet," Sky tells her, and pulls Dylan toward her by the collar of his white shirt. "First he has some kissing to do."

Before Dylan can protest, and without her wax lips as a buffer, Sky plants one on my stunned costar. The kiss seems to go on forever and Riley stands by, looking flustered. I watch the kiss in awe. Finally Sky releases him. "K, your turn."

I look at Dylan's green eyes and feel a flutter in my stomach.

"I think you gave Dylan a long enough kiss for both of us," I say nervously.

"I agree." Riley seconds. "Dylan, let's go."

I lock eyes with Sky. She can sense the same thing that I'm feeling now. Riley has a crush on Dylan. And letting Sky know that is Riley's worst nightmare. Sky holds on to a stunned Dylan and plays with his collar while he blushes. "Not until he kisses K! Don't you want to, Dylan? It's for charity."

"Don't bully him, Sky," I tell her.

Liz stares at Riley crossly. "Kates, you can't skip Dylan. He's a paying customer."

While everyone argues over us, Dylan and I make eye contact. He actually doesn't look uncomfortable — he's smiling at me a little, and I can feel my ears flush red. I look away.

Is Liz crazy? Kissing babies is one thing, but kissing Dylan is another. Austin would freak. Then again, kissing Chace Crawford wasn't much better. I'm already doomed. I look up again. Dylan looks amazing tonight. My breath catches in my throat.

Riley stares at my friends in horror. "Dylan, we're holding up the queue. Let's go."

"I, um," Dylan looks at me still with that lopsided, good-natured smirk. "I guess it's good practice for the show, right? And it's for charity."

"Right," I say, sounding professional. Riley glares.

Sky pushes me forward. "Kiss him," she demands.

The *People* photographer has caught on to the chaos and moves in for a close shot. Great. Just great.

"Hurry up, K, we have a line waiting!" Sky insists, her voice growing louder and more impatient. "It's just a kiss!

Do you think Trevor cares who I kiss?" Her face goes blank. "I *mean*, do you think Trevor cares that I kiss someone for charity? No."

Sky is right. This is for charity. One kiss can't hurt, right? I grab my wax lips and stand on my tiptoes. All I can see are Dylan's eyes. I close my own and feel my wax lips ripped out of my hands.

"What are you, two? You have to kiss him onstage anyway!" Sky insists. She grabs me by the arm and steers me around the table, which was the only barrier between me and Dylan. She shoves me toward Dylan, and he catches me. His arms linger around my bare shoulders, and I can barely breathe. "No wax lips."

"But —" I protest. My skin is starting to feel prickly.

"I'm not sure about that," Liz says worriedly. "The photographer —"

"It's okay, Kaitlin," Dylan looks down at me. Wow, he is tall. "You don't have to if you don't want to."

"It's not that," I start to explain.

I am momentarily blinded by the first flash and then another and then another. Sky is yelling in my ear, Liz is pulling on my arm, and Riley swears under her breath (a British term I shouldn't repeat), but I'm mesmerized by Dylan's eyes. They're really nice and his dimpled grin is so cute. I don't think, I just act. I grab Dylan's vest lapel, pull him in close, and lay one on him. And…

Wow. Really wow.

His lips are softer than I imagined and feel different.

Different from Austin's is all I can think, but my heart's racing anyway. Dylan leans into the kiss and doesn't pull away.

This is nice. Really nice. My shoulders relax and…OH MY GOD! WHAT AM I DOING?

I let Dylan go, but the camera flashes continue to pop. My face is beet red. I hope you can't tell in the photos. Actually, I take that back. I hope you can, for once, so Austin will know I didn't like it.

Even if I did.

Sky looks satisfied. "There! Was that so hard?"

Dylan smiles at me and I try to smile back, but inside I feel all weird and squishy, like I do if I eat ice cream too fast or eat too many Oreos.

I feel…guilty.

"Next!" Sky says. "Bye-bye, RI-LEE! Bye, Dyl!"

"See you Monday?" Dylan asks, his face totally calm and relaxed, as if he kisses other people's significant others every day of the week. Oh yeah. I guess we both do. We're actors. "At rehearsal? Then maybe Monkey Bar?"

"Rehearsal, yes," I tell him, and stop myself there. "See you then."

"K, snap out of it," Sky says, as I watch him walk off. "We have paying customers waiting."

"Right, right," I agree. I wipe my lips with a baby wipe and quickly apply more ChapStick. And then apply ChapStick again. I rub it on my lips harder and harder.

"Are you okay, Kates?" Liz asks worriedly.

"I ine," I mumble as I continue to rub my lips with

ointment. And that's when I realize what I'm trying to do — erase Dylan's kiss from my lips, as if that were possible. And even if it were, there would still be proof — in the *People* photos. I've got to call Austin and explain. He already thinks Dylan has a crush on me. He's going to *freak out*. I'm kissing Dylan and I'm not at work! What if the photos, like, show how into the kiss I was? For just a second, of course, but what if?

What if Austin can tell I enjoyed that kiss?

"K! Come on!" Sky insists and throws my wax lips at me. "Get back to work and start kissing!"

"Sorry!" I smile at the next payee apologetically. I pick up my wax lips and prepare to plant a kiss on the nervous-looking guy, but all I can think about is Austin.

Saturday, June 13th

NOTE TO SELF:
Call Austin ASAP.

SCENE 6
In line in the cafeteria.

JENNY:
Amy! Amy! HELL-O? Amy!

ANDIE:
(turns around) Are you talking to me?

JENNY:
(impatiently) Yes!

ANDIE:
I'm *Andie.*

JENNY:
Whatever. Listen, *Andie*, whatever it was you were
trying to say to my boyfriend back there, you can
save your breath. Leo isn't interested.

ANDIE:
I didn't think he was, Jenny. This is more about me
than it is him. I don't want to start the rest of my
life having regrets. Sort of a *carpe diem* on my last
day as a minor, you know?

JENNY:

Carpe what? Leo didn't even know you breathed the
same air until today. Even if he did, you don't belong
with our crowd and you know it.
Don't embarrass yourself.

ANDIE:

(lowering her voice) You're the one who should be
embarrassed. I saw you. Last weekend. With Thomas
Lopez at the Bait Shack, and I don't think he's part
of your crowd either. Unless you started accepting
members from the Spanish Honor Society all of a
sudden.

JENNY:

You...you...I would never hang out with Thomas Lopez.
And if I were you, I wouldn't dare say another word
about something you know nothing about. Got it? *(gets
bumped in the back)* OW!

JORDAN:

Oops. Didn't realize I was standing so close to you.
Hey! That shade of Jell-O looks really good against
your orange tan.

JENNY:

(shrieking) It's Golden Summer! And you just got
Jell-O all over my new shirt! I was going to wear this
to Leo's graduation party.

JORDAN:
Guess you'll be wearing something else then, won't
you?
*(Jenny stalks off and Jordan and Andie burst out
laughing.)*

ANDIE:
What was that about? I've never heard you open your
mouth to their crowd before.

JORDAN:
Maybe you've inspired me. We do only have twenty-
four hours left here, you know. How bad could Jenny
make things for me?

LEO:
Andie?

ANDIE:
Leo! Hey.

LEO:
Do you have a minute?

JORDAN:
She actually has eleven till next period. *(Andie
nudges her.)* I think I'll take my Jell-O to go.

ANDIE:

(smiling) I have eleven minutes.

LEO:

So I heard. Then maybe we should start talking. But
first, this conversation is going to need ice cream. I'm
getting the fudge pop. What can I get you? My treat.

ANDIE:

Okay. The strawberry fruit bar, please.

LEO:

You got it. *(hands bar to Andie)* So...you wanted to
tell me something?

ANDIE:

Yes, and here it goes...

SIX: *It Ain't Over Till the Fat Lady Sings*

"Amy! Amy! HELLO? AMY!" Riley takes her cue and bounds out onstage in a violet tank top and khaki cargo shorts. Her tone is impatient with me, just like the one she uses in real life.

My line! "Are you talking to me?" I ask, sounding confused. I'm wearing black Bermuda shorts and a fitted white Juicy tee that says "Juicy loves drama." We haven't worn costumes for rehearsal yet, not that our stage clothes are really binding. Riley wears a cheerleading uniform and I'm in jeans. "I'm Andie," I say and enunciate loudly the way my acting coach taught me.

This is really fun. Acting on stage is just like rehearsals for *Family Affair*. We always ran through everything before shooting. Except on stage, your first take is your only take — when you've got an audience I mean. And I think I'm going to like that a lot. It's live and anything can happen.

Riley shakes her head at me. "Kaitlin, I was supposed to say 'yes' before you said 'I'm Andie.' Remember?"

She's right. I know she is. Just like she was right in the last scene when I accidentally cut out one of her lines by skipping her. "Sorry."

"I know you are," Riley says patiently and fiddles with the tiny purple pearl earring in her right ear. "This is very different from cinema, I'm sure. If you trip me up, then I trip up Karen and she trips up Dylan and it's all rubbish. Do you see what I mean, lovely?"

I shake my head, aware that the rest of the cast is watching me, including Karen, who plays Jordan. Everyone looks uncomfortable, as they usually do when Riley berates me. I just wish I knew if it's because she's being obnoxious or because I'm such a rube. Forest isn't here today. It's just the cast members. Whenever Forest's not in the house, I get more anxious around Riley because she tends to make a spectacle of the fact that I don't know theater the way she does.

"Now did you watch that video on stage direction on the American Theatre Wing website I told you to?" Riley questions. I nod again. "We don't want to have what happened yesterday, do we? When we queue up in the cafeteria, I'm behind you, not in front of you. Something like that can mess up the show's whole aesthetic."

"Riley, come on now," Dylan tells her. He's wearing an outfit similar to his character, a black tee that shows off his fit upper torso, tight jeans that are torn at the knee, and black Converse. Running his hand through his dark, short hair, he looks tired of having to talk her down for the millionth time today. "Kaitlin is working her arse off."

"I know she is, Dylan." Riley crosses her arms over her chest and I notice the small ruby ring on the middle finger of her right hand. "Everything I tell her is for her own good. I don't want her going on stage opening night, messing up like she continually does, and feeling like a total wanker. She should shine!"

"You're right," I tell Riley, blushing, and ducking behind my hair a little. But why does she have to constantly bring up every little thing I do wrong?

"Now let's try that again, shall we?" Riley claps her hands. She's somehow taken over Forest's role when he's not around. ("I do have the most experience, having been on stage since I was two.") "Let's take it from the next line."

Riley rolls her shoulders back, shakes her head, and takes a deep breath. She even closes her eyes and I try not to snort. Yesterday she caught me laughing at her "mental preparation," as she calls it, and I got a ten-minute lecture on theater etiquette.

"Whatever," Riley drawls in a dead-on American accent. I have to admit, Riley is good. "Listen, Andie, whatever it was you were trying to say to my partner back there, you can save your breath. Leo..."

"Boyfriend," I interrupt and Riley just blinks. "You said 'partner.' Isn't it 'boyfriend'?" Everyone is looking at me. I look at Dylan. He tries not to smirk. Oh no. I probably shouldn't have done that.

"Bugger! Kaitlin's right," Riley smiles at me thinly. "It is boyfriend. We say partner in England, you know. It's so hard keeping track of two dialects, you have no idea." She walks across the quiet stage, her white sandals making clomping sounds. "You're so lucky all you've ever had to master is your own accent, Kaitlin. You'd have the hardest time trying to speak like a Brit."

"Actually, I used a British accent in..." Dylan coughs and I shut up. I've learned his cues to navigate Riley's wrath. Right now, he's inconspicuously trying to signal me to close my mouth. Which I do. "You're right, Riley." I smile patiently trying to glue my lips shut to keep from screaming.

"You're lucky you have me, Kaitlin." Riley strides back my way and puts her arm around me, turning me slightly to face the others. "On the stage, there is no 'I,' only 'we.' We work together or we all fail. When I was in *Gypsy*—you've seen *Gypsy*, haven't you?"

I don't look her in the eyes. "I haven't."

Riley gasps and drops her bony arm as if I'm on fire. "Kaitlin, it's another classic. I saw *Gypsy* when I was just a wee one. It was the second play I saw after *Jesus Christ Superstar*."

My voice is even smaller. "I haven't seen that either."

Riley looks around at the others. Some actually look surprised too, I notice as I lift my eyes ever so slightly to peek at the others. Some just roll their eyes. "Can you imagine? These are staples every trained theater actor has seen! You should really see a local production, Kaitlin. It's so important to view others' works for your craft."

"I just got tickets to see *Rock of Ages* for this week." I look at Riley hoping this will appease her. Instead she looks at me like I've just suggested she watch *American Idol*.

"*Rock of Ages* can't compare to *Jesus Christ Superstar!*" She's so shocked she's stuttering and she looks to the others for support, but no one gives her any. "That's like, that's like, comparing *Gypsy* to *Mary Poppins!*"

"I liked *Mary Poppins*." I'm beginning to realize I can't win. "I saw it the other night." I'm trying to see as many plays as I can before I start my own show.

"A Disney show!" she laughs. "Oh, Kaitlin, whatever will we do with you?" She looks at her shiny silver Movado watch. "Loo break! We'll reconvene in fifteen minutes."

Karen and Riley head off to the bathroom and I collapse cross-legged on the dusty scuffed-up floor, knowing I'm dirtying my Rebecca Taylor shorts, but I couldn't care less. All I want to do is hear Austin's voice. I dial his number and wait patiently till I hear him pick up.

"Hi, you've reached Austin," I hear him say.

"Austin! Hey, it's me," I say quickly, excited to finally catch him. "I haven't talked to you in two days…"

"You know what to do at the beep," he says. "I'll call you back soon. Promise." *BEEP.*

It's a message. A new message that I don't recognize, which is what confused me. "It's me." I can't help sounding glum. "Call me, okay? Miss you." I hang up and shove my phone into my overstuffed snakeskin bag. (I'm carting around a change of clothes for the meeting I have with Laney later.) Why did he change his message since yesterday?

"Chin up, mate." Dylan joins me on the floor, not minding that his battered jeans are getting dirty too. He offers me half of his Cadbury bar, and I look around for Riley ("No more cupcakes, Kaitlin! Theater is about being dedicated to your body!") before I take it. He has them shipped over here from the UK because he swears the Cadbury sold in the States tastes different. "What's that saying you guys have? Riley's bark is worse than her bite?"

I laugh. "That's it. I hope you're right."

Dylan is sitting right next to me and our knees are touching. He smells a little like pineapple. Maybe it is CK One cologne. And even in just a faded Ed Hardy tee, I've been sneaking looks at him all rehearsal. His biceps peek through his tee. He must work out a lot.

"It's too bad *Meeting of the Minds* already opened." Dylan snaps me out of my thoughts. "You could really use the Gypsy Robe."

"I read about the Gypsy Robe," I tell him excitedly. It was in one of the books I read about the Great White Way. HOLLYWOOD BROADWAY SECRET NUMBER SIX: The ritual of the Gypsy Robe occurs on the opening night of a Broadway musical right before the curtain goes up. The whole cast and members of the production get together on stage and form a circle. In the center is a performer who is supposed to be a representative of Actors' Equality and a former recipient of the ritual from the last musical that opened on Broadway. The performer holds a gorgeous decked-out robe that has memorabilia from past Broadway musicals all over it. The recipient of the robe is usually someone from the chorus who has performed in the most Broadway shows and embodies the qualities of the Broadway "gypsy"—someone who is dedicated, is professional, and has a seasoned career. The hope is that the robe brings luck and charm to the play's opening night.

"I don't think it would work here, though," I tell Dylan, tracing my pointer finger along the floor. "This isn't a musical, this is my first show, and I'm not in the chorus."

"Bollocks, you're right," Dylan says with a laugh. He rests his head on his knee. "You don't need it anyway. Everyone likes you, and you're going to be brilliant on opening night."

"You think?" I know I'm fishing for it, but this is the sort of reinforcement that I shamelessly know I need right now. I pluck at the fabric of my cotton shirt, fretting. I'm freaked out enough about being on stage without worrying how I'm going to sound. I was hoping Austin would say the same thing, but he's been out of reach the past few days. I know he's just busy with finals and getting ready for lacrosse camp, but I really feel how much I miss him.

"I know," Dylan tells me firmly. "Rehearsal is done in an hour, and I was going to take the tube uptown to get some lunch. You interested?"

"Yes," I tell Dylan regretfully, "but I have a meeting with my publicist. She's in town with another client who is doing the talk shows."

Dylan smiles, knits his forehead, and looks down at the painted black stage. "Maybe tomorrow then," he suggests.

"We can even stay after to go over a few more scenes if you like."

"I could really use the help." I struggle to get up and Dylan offers me his hand. He pulls me up and I find myself looking into his green eyes again.

"Happy to," Dylan says and gives me the most amazing grin. Huh, look at that. He actually has two dimples, not one. It makes me blush, oddly, and I feel the heat move over my face.

"That would be great." I feel my iPhone vibrate, and I run for my bag. "Will you excuse me a second?" Dylan nods. "Hello?"

"Hey, stranger." Austin's voice growls in my ear.

"Hey!" I'm so excited I practically scream. "I mean hi. And *you're* the stranger. I haven't spoken to you in two days."

"Well, it feels like a lot longer," Austin tells me. "But I'm really sorry, Burke. We had those two meets in San Diego and we wound up staying overnight and by the time I went to call you, I realized it was too late."

"It's okay," I say. Did I even know about those two meets? I can't remember either way. Then again, I didn't tell him about the charity kissing booth, which I have to do now. Eek. "I just wanted to hear your voice."

"Does it sound good?" Austin teases.

"Yes!" I laugh.

"So what is it you wanted to talk about?" he asks. "I'm all ears."

Okay, here it goes. "Do you remember me telling you

about that Operation Read America event I went to the other night?"

"Um…did you tell me you went to an Operation Read America event the other night?" Austin laughs. "Sorry. I can't remember."

I'm a tinge annoyed. I did tell him and I talked about it for like an hour because it was at the Waverly Inn and I was really hoping to bump into Graydon Carter. But now is not the time to point that out. "That's okay. It was this event for charity and they had this kissing booth with the stars where people paid money to kiss celebrities."

That gets his attention. "Go on."

"And Sky and I were two of the kissers," I continue nervously. I can't think of a time I've ever been this nervous to talk to Austin, ever. "We wore wax lips and we kissed babies and it was all for a good cause." God, I sound like Laney. "Anyway, I just wanted you to know because you might see some pictures in the tabloids."

"Huh." Austin sounds sort of quiet, but my phone is a little fuzzy. Oh wait, that's the air conditioner unit blowing backstage.

"And well, one of the people I kissed was…"

Say it.

"…Dylan Koster. You know, my costar."

"I know who he is." Austin's voice sounds strange, almost as if he is about to laugh. Or maybe cry.

"The pictures are probably online already and *People* will

have some this week." I can't stop talking. "It was great publicity for the play and he was a really good sport. Oh, and I also kissed Chace Crawford and Jimmy Fallon."

"How was Jimmy Fallon?" Austin asks.

"Funny," I squeak. "He wanted to kiss my elbow." Now it's my turn to let the dead air hang between us. "I've been trying to reach you for days so I could tell you. Are you mad?" I finally ask.

Austin takes a while to answer me. I hear him sigh on the other end. "No." He sounds like he is choosing his words slowly. "I don't *like* it, but I know it's work. Sort of. I'm glad you told me though."

I feel like I could exhale for a whole minute, I'm so relieved. "Of course. It was nothing, but I didn't want you to think it *was* something so I thought I should tell you about the nothing."

Did that even make sense?

"Glad you did." Austin still sounds off. Or maybe it's just me being paranoid.

I've got to change the subject fast. "All ready for the dance?"

That topic perks Austin right up. "Limo is booked, dinner reservations are made, and I've already picked up my tux."

"My dress is already in L.A.," I tell him. "And Paul and Shelly are coming to the house to do my hair and makeup."

"Sweet." I'm paying attention to every word Austin says to hear if he's still mad, but he sounds okay again. And I know he is when he says: "Burke, I can't wait to see you. Liz told Josh your flight gets in at three. Make sure you sleep on the plane okay?"

"I will," I promise. He's so sweet to worry about my beauty sleep. "I'll be well rested for the dance on Friday." I hear Riley on stage so I better go. Any second she's going to come looking for me. "I'll try you later, okay?"

After we hang up, I feel a little better. At the same time, I'm a little sad. The only thing we got to talk about was the silly charity kissing booth. I didn't even ask him who won the meets in San Diego! I didn't get to tell him about Riley, or Mom driving me nuts about the Hamptons, or ask how his family was. That's what I'm thinking about during the last hour of rehearsal. Thankfully nobody notices my mood change. I'm still a little blue when we say our goodbyes and I head outside to the waiting town car.

When I open the car door, I hear wailing that would rival any passing cop car siren. I look inside and see Nadine in the backseat with her arm around Sky. Her long black hair is sort of frizzy and her nose is all red and her skin is blotchy. Very unlike Sky, who never steps outside without at least concealer and bronzing powder. Even Rodney looks worried about her.

"What happened?" I ask.

Nadine's face is grim. "Sky's show got the ax." That makes Sky cry harder. "I mean, it was put on hold. Indefinitely." Sky begins to hiccup. "She showed up at the apartment looking for you and insisted she come meet you here."

I slide in next to Nadine and put my arm awkwardly around Sky. She pulls the shoulder of my tee and uses it as a tissue. I guess she can't risk getting anything on her one-of-a-kind Nicole Miller magneta silk sundress. (I know it's one of a kind because she tells me every time she wears it.) I let the my shirt-as-a-tissue thing slide. "Sky, I'm so sorry." I rub her back. "What happened?"

"Reporter…"—*sniff*—"…was…right!" *Snort.* "Grady is fighting with the network…"—*snort*—"about location, budgets, EVERYTHING! He threatened to pull the plug, so they…"—*SOB*—"…did it for him! We're off the schedule." She buries her head in my shoulder, sending snot all over my tank top. Eww.

"I don't know what to do," Sky continues, starting to get hysterical. She looks up at me with big, dark eyes, her chandelier earrings dangling as the car moves. "What do you do when your career is in free fall?"

"I don't know."

"You *must* know. Yours has been in free fall for a while!" Sky snaps.

I look at Nadine. She's trying not to laugh.

"If you're going to get snippy then you can cry to someone else." I sound sterner than I intended and Sky starts to sob again.

"I'm sorry, K." Sky takes a compact from her small Gucci clutch and examines her face. She grabs a tissue from the box Nadine is now holding. I guess Nadine doesn't want her cute multi-print Gap boho top becoming a tissue either.

"I'm just mad and you're the only person I could think of who would actually listen to me. You're too nice to say no." Nadine hands her another tissue.

"Call Laney and ask her if we can reschedule," I instruct Nadine, then turn to the driver in the front of the black town car. "We need to go to the Upper West Side. The Shake Shack."

"Yes!" Rodney exclaims. "I've been dying to go there."

Sky pops up again. "What the heck is the Shake Shack? I'm in no mood to take some weird Zumba dance class, K!"

"It's a burger and milk shake place, Sky." Nadine tucks a lock of Sky's black hair back behind her ear.

"They say it's out of this world," I add. "Come on, it will cheer you up."

Sky buries her head back in my chest. I take that as a yes. I pat Sky's shoulder gently, wondering how my life got so weird.

Forty minutes later (It's a long wait!), Sky and I are deep into vitamin creamsicle shakes, made with frozen custard and ice cream, and the fattest burgers you've ever seen. We both got sides of fries, of course. Sky demanded Rodney stand guard outside the corner shop's door so that the paparazzi can't capture her eating "a gazillion calories in one sitting." Nadine offered to stand outside and eat with him — anything to avoid hearing Sky cry some more. Thankfully, Sky appears a little calmer now and the color has returned to her cheeks. She sucks hard on the straw of her shake, and her pink lipstick leaves a mark on the straw.

"I told you food can fix anything." I dip another fry in my ketchup.

Sky rolls her eyes and stares at the glass ceiling. "A shake does not fix my employment problem. But it does taste good. Thanks." She gets quiet and looks down at the table. Then she takes another bite of her burger. "I needed this."

"You're welcome." I smile. "You're going to be fine. You'll get another gig before the week's out."

"Not on TV." Sky's voice cracks. "The fall schedule is set, and for the first time in over a decade I won't be on it."

"You've got *SNL* coming up," I remind her. "That will be huge for both of us. And then maybe you'll do a movie for the fall. You're always going on and on about all the offers you have coming in. Pick one."

"True." Sky moves the fries around her plate with a long fuchsia fingernail. "But it's not the same thing and you know it, K." She looks at me. "I miss *FA*." Her eyes begin to well up.

Now my eyes start to tear too. "Same here," I say hoarsely, digging my fingers into the bottom of the green bench I'm sitting on.

"I miss being part of a show that I loved—even if I pretended not to some of the time." Sky is on a roll. "I didn't realize how much I'd miss it, you know? Until it was gone. And I'm not saying this to send you off the deep end again, but I feel like the only one who could possibly understand any of this is, bizarrely enough, you. Does that make any sense?"

I nod. "More than you know," I tell her. "Believe it or not, I even miss fighting with you. At least you were always up-front with your insults." I tell her about how badly Riley has been making me feel. Sky is pretty worked up about "the British tart," as she calls her, and says a bunch of other things I shouldn't repeat. Still, hearing Sky say I'm being too hard on myself about being a first-time stage star makes me feel better.

I raise my milk shake.

"What are you doing?" Sky asks, suddenly alarmed. She fumbles for her Burberry shades and puts them on to avoid being noticed.

"Toasting us."

"With milk shakes?" she says, flabbergasted.

"Go with it, Sky." I arch my eyebrow (they look great now that I've had them shaped at Eliza Petrescu, aka the queen of the arch). I raise my paper cup higher. Sky does the same, even though she has a puss on her face. "To us finding something that makes our future as bright as our past."

"Nice, K," Sky mocks me.

"It was on the back of my fortune cookie wrapper at Shun Lee Palace last night," I say. "But it's true. I hope we both find the next *FA* of our lives — whether it's TV, movies, Broadway, or none of the above. But I hope, maybe, as we're looking for those things," I say tentatively, "we can do it together." I almost cringe, waiting for Sky to make some sort of witty jab at me. But instead she sort of smiles.

"It's a deal," she says. And then we clink on it.

Wednesday, June 17

NOTE TO SELF:
Pack 4 L.A.
Have Nadine ck. w/Paul/Shelly about hair/makeup time.
Fri. Flight 2 L.A. 11:55 AM, JFK Airport.
Prom pickup Friday @ 6 PM.

**SNL* week starts—Monday @ 10AM!

PSSST . . . Everything you're not supposed to know about Tinseltown's Faves!
by Nicki Nuro

Will Kaitlin Burke Sink Her Broadway Show?

She wowed us on *Family Affair*, smoked the big screen in *Pretty Young Assassins* and is known by fellow stars as one of the sweetest actresses there is today. Is there anything Kaitlin Burke can't do?

Maybe Broadway.

Sources close to the *Meeting of the Minds* production are worried that Kaitlin's first part on the Great White Way may be her last. While Kaitlin is working hard at rehearsals and is wonderful with both the cast and the crew (she recently delivered pizza for the entire cast after they finished a rehearsal), some say she just doesn't have what it takes to do live theater.

"She has no clue how to take direction or connect with a live audience, and her stage presence is way off," says one. "If she doesn't improve, I fear the show may end its run early. There is no way people will pay to see Kaitlin butcher the role that Meg Valentine made famous."

Could celebrity be getting in the way of Kaitlin's work ethic? Since moving to New York, Kaitlin has been on the scene a lot. She recently attended an Operation Read America event at the Waverly Inn, has taken in several plays like *Wicked* and *Mary Poppins,* and has been seen on the town with costar Dylan Koster (see picture at right of Kaitlin and Dylan's kiss at the Operation Read America event). "Kaitlin is lovely," Dylan said when he was reached for comment. "And she's going to be brilliant in the show."

Biased opinion? Guess we'll just have to wait and see for ourselves.

SEVEN: *It's Good to Be Home (Even if It's for Less than 48 Hours)*

The hot, gooey cheese drips off my slice of pizza, and splashes of oil drip onto my vintage *Star Wars* tee. Oops! Thank God for Shout wipes.

"Ugh! Watch that grease," says Paul, my former *FA* hairdresser. "I don't want any oily fingers ruining my masterpiece. How do you eat that stuff and stay so thin anyway? If I even look at fried dough my stomach poofs up and Jacques reminds me of my unused gym membership." He pats his taut midsection, which is in direct proportion to his well-toned tanned arms and long legs.

I giggle. "I highly doubt your stomach bloats after one slice."

Liz is sitting next to me in her melon C&C California V-neck hoodie finishing her own slice, and she agrees wholeheartedly. "Even if it did, this slice would be worth the extra twenty minutes on the elliptical trainer."

I stare at my slice lovingly. Nadine ordered takeout from

Liz's and my favorite pizza place in Los Angeles, A Slice of Heaven, so that we had something to nosh on while we got ready at my house. We were starving after the almost six-hour plane ride. We got our usual—a Sicilian pie with extra cheese, peppers, and broccoli, and large Sprites. I've already had two slices and am starting on my third. With the Food Police (Mom) back in New York, I can eat what I want without hearing the words "fittings," "photos," or "cellulite."

HOLLYWOOD SECRET NUMBER SEVEN: People always want to know how it's possible for celebs to gain a few pounds when they have trainers, personal chefs, and money for any vegan/organic/gluten-free diet they want to try. My latest trainer, Olga Emegen, isn't afraid to tell the cold hard truth to anyone who asks: you can work celebrities to the bone, give them all the perfectly portioned packaged meals in the world, and tell them every workout and diet trick in the world, but you can't watch them 24/7. Even celebs have moments of weakness—like now—and Olga is not here to stop me from having this third slice of pizza. Or from gulping down that gooey chocolate chip cookie Dylan bought me the other day at rehearsal. She can't hold my hand—or rather slap it—every minute of the day. And celebs, just like everyone else in the world, are human. We have cravings too.

I hear a small click and look up. Nadine has just taken a photo of me in mid-bite on her camera phone. She smiles at me mischievously before tucking the phone back into her faded Gap jeans. "I think I'm going to save this for future blackmailing purposes. If we don't like those SAT scores that are due any day, this picture will guarantee you go back and take them again."

"Some chaperone you are," I mumble. I couldn't believe Mom and Dad let me fly back to Los Angeles with just Nadine and Rodney. Mom said I was old enough to do it, but I suspect the real reason neither of my parents accompanied me for the quick trip was that Mom's Darling Daisies committee has some charity dinner this weekend at the Time Warner Center. I've never seen her so excited to work on something for free before.

"I'm sure Kaitlin got a great score," Shelly boasts. She's my former TV makeup artist so she's a bit partial. She's doing Liz's makeup first while I get my hair done and Shelly is so short she has to use a step stool to reach her. She takes Liz's empty plate and hands it to our housekeeper, Anita. Then she starts Liz's makeup by dabbing a little under-eye concealer and applying loose powder as a base. "You need a stronger moisturizer. The L.A. sun is doing serious damage to your delicate skin." I try not to laugh. Shelly has always worried about my skin too. She's a mama bear–type, plush body and all. I'm glad Paul and Shelly were free to do our hair and makeup for the prom. They're both doing a ton of day shoots and are fielding offers to go on staff for some new fall shows.

"Kates was studying hard at the end for that test and I'm sure it paid off," Liz says as Shelly starts to sweep a purple shadow, the same shade as Liz's cashmere drawstring pants, over her lids. "I don't know what she worked on harder — fixing her image, spending time with Austin, or studying. I know Nadine would like us to think it was studying."

"I did all three." I resist the urge to wipe my greasy fingers on my brown Torn stretch terry pants and instead look in the mirror that Paul has placed on the kitchen island. Thank God Mom isn't here to see the mess we've got going on. Anita, our housekeeper, who has had more than one run-in with Mom, promised to have everything back in order before she flies back in two weeks for her standing date with Botox. (Shhh!) "Sometimes I do have my act together."

Just being back in Los Angeles makes me feel more in control. I know it sounds odd, but I breathe better here (which is strange considering all the smog). Maybe it's all the hills and the grass and the palm trees or the luxury of having a pool in my backyard (something I sorely miss in New York). One thing I don't like so much is how isolated Los Angeles can make you feel. In New York, you can meet a new person every ten seconds. In L.A., the only way you talk to strangers is if your car overheats on the freeway during rush hour traffic and someone rolls down their car window to talk to you. Which is to say, you don't.

Paul begins to pull strands of my honey blond hair into a twist and then back into a loose bun. We're going for my friend Taylor Swift's look. The dress I picked is just as ethereal. I went with this fitted ivory strapless Diane von Furstenberg dress that has a mermaid tail. There is a ruffle accent that trails from the top of the dress all the way to the bottom. It's simple but, I hope, elegant. Liz, as she is Liz, went with something flashier. She's rocking a glittery gold Betsey Johnson strapless knee-length gown. The bottom is made of tulle. Liz calls it her fairy godmother look.

"I miss seeing you guys every day." I watch Paul. "It's just not the same."

"We miss you too, darling." Paul sticks a pin in my hair. "There is one upside to the show ending. You don't have to deal with Sky anymore." He makes a face. "That princess has pulled some royal flushes over the years, hasn't she?"

"She's not so bad." I stare at my hands. I got a French manicure last night. "She's mellowed." Everyone stops what they're doing and stares at me. "I'm serious! Come on, guys. You know she was a real help with the Alexis thing. And she defended me after my meltdown this spring. She's sort of changed." Liz laughs. "Okay, maybe not changed. She's still snippy, but she's not as bad. I sort of get her now."

Liz rolls her eyes. "I think you're fooling yourself."

"Maybe Kaitlin is right," Nadine agrees and grabs a slice of pizza from the box. Thank God Nadine ordered several pies. Rodney makes a grunting sound behind her, and without looking she hands the piece back to him and grabs another for herself. "I felt a little bad for her the other day."

"Bad for Sky? What's wrong with you guys?" Liz practically jumps out of her chair she's so annoyed. Shelly tsks and puts a hand on Liz's black styling cape to keep her from getting lip liner all over her face. "Did you forget all the crap she's put Kates through over the years?"

"I know, but she was really beat up over her show being canceled." Nadine looks up from the copy of the *New York Times* she's reading while eating. "She actually had a milk shake, a burger, *and* fries and then broke into Kate's extra Sugar Sweet Sunshine cupcakes stash that Rodney hid in the car."

"I thought we might need a late-afternoon snack," he explains, and looks a little embarrassed.

Shelly smirks. "You're eating your way through New York's cupcakes as well, I see."

"Shel, there are so many places better than Sprinkles," I inform her, tilting my head for Paul. "So far I've had Sugar Sweet Sunshine, Magnolia, and Crumbs. Someone said I have to try Butter Lane and Buttercup next, which I completely plan on doing."

"Actually there is a box here from someplace called Buttercup." Nadine slips off her stool at the kitchen island and grabs something from the floor. "Anita handed it to me when we walked in." Nadine walks over with a large box addressed to me. "It was sent all the way from New York, and I know who sent it," she adds mischievously.

"Mom?" I wonder.

Rodney's laugh is loud and it echoes through the large room. "Do you think your mom would send you cupcakes?"

"Sky?" I try again. "She wanted to check out Buttercup with me. We were talking about it the other day after my rehearsal."

"Nope." Nadine shakes her head and her small green beaded earrings jingle. "You're going to die when you see who it is."

"Sky won't give you room to breathe," Liz feels the need to tell me, even though she's busy having lip liner done.

"Love the SKAT nickname." Paul nudges me, and for some reason I think he means it. "LAVA is lame."

"She's only hanging out with you because she has no job," Liz interrupts again. "You know that, Kates."

I don't say anything. When Liz is on a roll like this, I have learned to let her go. Instead I motion to Anita for scissors. There is no name on the return address, so I have no clue who sent the package. I bust open the box and reach inside a dry ice–filled container to find a dozen perfectly wrapped cupcakes that are only slightly smushed. I have no clue how they made it to L.A. like this, but I'm happy to see them. I start passing them out. Rodney is the first to grab one. At the bottom of the box is a sealed notecard.

"You two are done being long-suffering costars." Liz is still talking as she reaches over to grab a pink-frosted cupcake. "I don't understand why she can't disappear like all costars do after they stop working together. Just pretend you're going to be chummy and then never return the person's calls. Is that so hard?" She stops for a second as Shelly finishes her face with a quick spray of glitter. Liz glides off the bar stool and begins tenderly eating her cupcake while Shelly stares at her in horror. She's going to need her lips redone for sure, which is fine because Paul has to finish my hair before he does Liz's. He's almost done — he's just adding a few little faux diamond hairpins in the back. "Instead of disappearing, Sky has practically followed you to New York and moved in," she says with her mouth full. Shelly watches as Liz ruins her lip-gloss. "She hung out at our apartment all last weekend while I was in town and she goes ON and ON about herself. It's all I could do not to throw my new textbooks at her to knock her out so we could have a few minutes of peace and quiet!"

"Someone sounds a little jealous," Paul sings in my ear.

"I heard that!" Liz sounds steamed and she makes Anita, who is wiping down the counters, jump. "I am not jealous." She looks at me. "Kates, you *know* I'm not jealous."

"I know," I tell her, avoiding the piercing stare Nadine is giving me.

"We just got through a jealousy thing with me and Mikayla, and I am not jealous," Liz tells everyone. "I cannot stand Sky Mackenzie. My problem is that I can't believe Kates would want to spend time with a girl who has made her life hell ever since I've known her."

"We have to host *SNL* next week," I remind Liz while Paul pushes my head down for one last pin.

"And then you promise she'll be gone?" Liz tosses her wrapper in the stainless steel garbage pail. "She'll vacate her permanent spot on your couch and leave? Check out of the Soho Grand and torture Los Angeles again instead?" Shelly pulls Liz back over to her makeshift station and fixes her lipstick.

"I'm sure," I tell Liz, even though I'm not. I vaguely recall one of Sky's crying sessions where she mentioned New York summers being good for her psyche. I felt too bad for her to suggest her psyche try Florida instead.

"Next!" Shelly says as she releases Liz and Paul frees me up to go to Shelly's chair. I glance at my hair in the mirror. It's so soft and romantic. I don't know how Paul gets it to stay up and look so effortless at the same time.

I rip open the notecard and see a handwritten message inside.

Thought you might like a little bit of New York while you were back in Los Angeles. I knew you wanted to try this place. Next pick is on me—you promised to try fish and chips. (Remember your British slang: chips are French fries and crisps are potato chips.) Have a great holiday and try not to worry about the theater. You're brilliant as Andie and I won't stop saying it till I convince you so myself.
Cheers, Dylan

"They're from Dylan." I'm so surprised I can barely speak. I can't believe he mailed me cupcakes all the way from New York. That is so sweet.

"What is a Dylan and where can I get one?" Paul sounds intrigued.

"He's Kate's absolutely gorgeous, incredibly nice love interest in *Meeting of the Minds*," Liz gushes. I give her a look. "What? He's not all of those things?"

"He is, but he's just a friend," I stress.

A friend who sends sweets to me three thousand miles away. No biggie.

"I know that and you know that, but does Dylan know that?" Liz asks. "Because something tells me Dylan would like to be more."

"Muh too," Shelly agrees as she licks white frosting off her second confection before starting on my makeup.

"He was so cute about sending you a care package, Kates, that I didn't want to say no," Nadine apologizes. "He knew you wanted to try Buttercup and he asked me for your home address so he could send you some. He said he was worried that you were going to stress all weekend about the show. He thought these might help."

"They are quite good," I admit, and decide to move them up in my unofficial New York cupcake ranking.

"Are you going to save one for Austin?" Paul innocently bats his eyes. He's so bad. He's always trying to cause drama!

"No." I frown for a moment, but can't for long because Shelly needs to put lip moisturizer on me. "Austin is already bent out of shape about Dylan as it is. This would drive him nuts."

"Ooh! A love triangle." Paul is beginning to loop around Liz's dark curls with more flamboyance. "I only wish I were in New York with you to see how this plays out."

"It's not a love triangle," I insist a tad huffily. Shelly tuts at me, fussing that frowning will ruin my foundation.

"Maybe we should talk about something else," Nadine steps in. "There are a few things I should tell you before I let you go off to the ball and forget to remind you about a curfew." She winks.

"The limo is paid till three AM." Rodney looks up from eyeing the last chocolate buttercream. "I spoke to the driver this morning and I'll be riding shotgun."

Nadine reads off her BlackBerry. "It's the rest of the weekend I'm worried about. I know you're going to want to spend every waking moment with Austin till Sunday at ten AM when we leave, and I understand that, but I've been having a tough time pushing a few people off, especially since your mom keeps calling and reminding them you're here." She grabs her bible, the notebook that has all of my schedules and info in it. (Nadine has a BlackBerry, but she likes writing things by hand too.) "Seth is begging for an hour for coffee in the afternoon tomorrow. He has some scripts he wants to go over with you."

"I promised Seth too." I shrug. "I already told Austin and he's going to come with me. That's fine."

Nadine crosses it off her list. "Great, so that just leaves…Laney."

The room collectively groans.

"She swears she just needs a half an hour," Nadine begs.

"You *know* that will never happen." I try to laugh, but it's hard when Shelly is applying bronzing powder. "When she was in New York two weeks ago, our half-hour coffee was a three-hour chatfest."

"'And then I told Angelina that the "it" spot to adopt children from is Darfur, and she said I was brilliant and why hadn't she thought of that before?'" Paul mimics.

"I know it's hard to rein her in, but she said there is something—and I quote—'absolutely crushingly important' that she needs to discuss with you." Nadine smiles. "She wouldn't say what it was."

"Can't it wait till Sunday night? A conference call maybe?" I plead. "I have so little time with Austin and we really need to catch up. You know we have the hardest time finding time to talk on the phone."

"It doesn't help that all boys are bad at phone conversations." Liz's head is down as Paul uses the curling iron to give her tiny curls by her neckline.

"All boys but me!" Paul tells her.

"Please, Nadine." I bat my eyes at her. "I'll see her when she's in town next."

"Aww...Nadine, how can you refuse?" Shelly asks.

Nadine sighs. "Fine. I'm going to hear about this, but I'll call and lie. Say you're doing meetings with Seth or something."

"Watch what you say," I warn. "She can find out anything from anyone."

"WHO CAN FIND OUT WHAT?"

I nearly jump out of my skin. Anita, who was washing dishes, screams and picks up a soapy frying pan, spraying bubbles and water everywhere, but ready to hit the intruder, who is whipping around the corner into the room from the door next to her.

The intruder stops short at Anita's cast iron weapon and screams. In less than two seconds she has her Mace out and is ready to mist the room. Thankfully Rodney grabs the can before she can strike.

"ARE YOU PEOPLE TRYING TO GIVE ME A HEART ATTACK?" Laney bellows, pulling her arm away from Rodney. "WHY ARE YOU ALL HERE?" She clutches her beige Chanel purse to her chest and takes big gulping breaths. Anita, realizing who it is, quickly says something in Spanish and then rushes to make Laney a cup of tea. Paul scurries over and fans Laney's face with a handheld mirror and strands of Laney's long straight hair begin to fly around.

"YOU'RE GOING TO HAVE TO FIX MY FLYAWAYS," Laney tells Paul, who stops immediately. "I JUST HAD MY HAIR BRAZILIAN STRAIGHTENED."

"But your hair was already straight," Liz can't help reminding Laney. Laney glares at her.

"Laney, why are you yelling?" Nadine wants to know.

Laney looks at her, ready to bark, and then reaches up and touches her ear. And then the other one. "Oh, sorry." She plucks the Bluetooth headsets out of each ear, exposing three-carat diamond studs underneath.

"You have two?" Paul sounds incredulous.

"I have two lines." Laney drops the Bluetooths in her purse. She sees me and smiles. "Kaitlin, there you are! When I didn't hear back from Nadine, I got worried your flight was delayed. It's not like Nadine not to call me back." She clicks her tongue and Nadine colors slightly. Laney's starting to pull herself back together, smoothing her ruffled sleeveless DKNY top and navy blue sailor-style pants.

"That's my fault, Laney," I apologize. "The phone has rung nonstop since we landed, and I made her turn her work line off."

Laney looks from Nadine to me skeptically.

"But you found us, so what do you need?" I brighten, trying to pull her out of her cranky mood. "We can chat while Shelly does my makeup. I have the junior prom tonight."

"Oh, that school thing, right." Laney waves a poppy-red manicured hand dismissively as she pulls up a chair so close its almost impossible for Shelly to get near enough to apply my mascara. "So we're all set for *SNL*, no? I have great news — *TV Guide* wants to shoot a cover on set of you and Sky for next week's issue. Fun, no? *Entertainment Weekly* and *People* all asked to do features as well. The *SNL* press girl says you two are getting more inquiries than Justin Timberlake did when he hosted last time."

"Ou on't ay," I mumble as Shelly applies peach MAC lipgloss.

"Can I say yes to all?" Laney pulls out her BlackBerry. "I'll send Nadine a list. They'll work around your rehearsal schedule for both the play and the show. It's going to be a crazy week."

"Ell e bout tt," I agree and then when my lips are free, "Well, I'm glad you found me so we could discuss these things. I'm sorry I don't have time to do lunch like you wanted. I am meeting with Seth, though."

"Good, good." Laney nods absentmindedly.

Uh-oh. "What is it?"

"There is something else," Laney admits, readjusting the ruffled collar of her blouse. "Something that we found out this morning. It's nothing major, but I know you're going to be upset, and your mother and I still worry about your fragile state and those panic attack things you used to get."

I grab Laney's hand and squeeze. It feels funny to do that — to be the one that is kind of mothering rather than the one who is falling apart. "I'm fine. Lay it on me. What did Ava and Lauren do now? Dress up as Sky and me again? They are going to freak when they see what we have in store for them on *SNL*. I'm sure they're planning something good." I laugh, but Laney looks serious and pulls a printout from her bag.

"This came over the wire this morning," Laney says. "It was posted on Hollywood Insider.com."

I grab the page and read it quickly. It's an article about me being on Broadway. An unnamed source says I'm not cut out for theater. I squirm slightly.

Am I really that bad? I'm not that bad, am I? Forest would tell me. Dylan says I'm doing really well. The only one who still thinks I have a ways to go is Riley. It doesn't take a rocket scientist to realize she's probably the website's source.

"I've already contacted Liz's father about threatening to sue if they won't take the article down, but you should know the piece was picked up by TMZ, People.com, and Eonline .com too." I hand the page to Liz, and Nadine, Paul, and Shelly read it over her shoulders.

"You don't have to take things that far, Laney," I say even though I'm pretty glum about it. "I'm sure this is just the first of many stories like this. I'm not mad, just a little embarrassed."

"Why?" Laney wants to know. Now that she knows I'm not going to hyperventilate, or pass out, she looks much calmer. Even her high cheekbones seem to have relaxed, if that were possible. "This is complete fluff. Don't let it get to you, sweetie. As I always tell Jennifer — bad press can be made good press if you use the attention to your advantage."

"I know." I hedge a bit. "It's just…"

"It's just what?" Liz busts in, mad for me. "You're worried the source is right, aren't you?" I don't say anything. "Kates! You know, you make this easy for her, don't you?"

Laney sighs and brushes her straight blond hair away from her eyes. "We really have to do something about your self-esteem issues."

"My self-esteem is fine," I insist. "Everywhere but in theater. Riley keeps telling me I don't know what I'm doing," I blurt out. "It's hard not to feel a little green."

"You were green when you did your first Disney Channel movie and what happened?" Laney works up steam. "You had huge ratings! Same goes for your film roles! You have to start somewhere and look where you're starting — Broadway. They don't hire you for a Broadway show if you can't perform."

"You're right." I don't know if it is jet lag or what, but I'm suddenly too tired to discuss this. "Don't worry about the article, Laney. I'm fine. You can tell Mom that."

"Good." Laney taps a long red nail on her BlackBerry decisively. "I'll call off the dogs." She slides her Burberry sunglasses back over her eyes and grabs her bag. "Enjoy your little dance! I'll see you in New York next weekend for *SNL*."

I reach for the last cupcake and take a bite. Wow, these really are good. Who cares what some unnamed source says? Laney's right. I can do this. I'm working hard to get ready for Broadway. Tonight, all I want to think about is Austin.

*   *   *

Forgetting about Riley and her Great White Way pasty face (hee hee, I just came up with that one) is a lot easier when you have a mug as gorgeous as Austin's to gaze at. When he turned up with Josh at my house with the most glorious pink roses I've ever laid eyes on, I forgot about everything else and I flew into his arms so fast, I practically knocked him over (which might not have been the best idea considering the thorns on the rose stems. Thankfully Rodney stopped the cut on my arm from bleeding all over my dress). Austin was wearing a tux, of course, with a bow tie, and his hair was lightly combed back 40s-style, leaving his forehead kissably free. Even his soapy scent smelled better than I remembered it. We must have kissed for ten minutes before Liz tugged on my arm and told me we had to take pictures and get in the limo or we'd be late to pick up Rob Murray, Allison, Beth, and her date.

"You look beautiful," Austin tells me for the millionth time as we walk hand in hand through the marble floored lobby of the Santa Rosita Sheraton Hotel where the junior prom is being held. There are mirrors everywhere and I can't help check us out as we walk by. We look so cute together. "I still can't believe you're here. I mean, seeing you, it feels like you never left, but you did."

"I was thinking the same thing." I look at my pink Christian Louboutin shoes, feeling pleased, and then take another peek at his strong profile. Okay, so it's only been a few weeks since I've seen my boyfriend, but seeing Austin feels like slipping on my favorite Gap trench — comfy, gorgeous, and just perfect. Nothing's changed. I look down at our intertwined hands and smile. Okay, maybe I am holding on a little tighter than usual, but that's because I'm getting in as much contact as I can in my less than forty-eight hour trip.

"Next couple," a voice commands and the two of us stop what we're doing and look up. We're next for our junior prom photo. There are about a dozen pearlized blue and silver balloons and a teal crepe backdrop with the words SANTA ROSITA JUNIOR PROM written on it in metallic ink.

"Yes!" I can't help but blurt out and Austin looks at me curiously. "I've always wanted a prom picture." I feel a little bashful about it with all my professional shoots. "It's not like I'll ever have my own prom to go to. This could be my only one."

"Don't forget the senior prom," Liz chimes in behind us. "You can get another couple photo with a bad background at that shindig too." Josh laughs.

"Make fun all you want, but I'm excited." I look at the package options and tell the photo guy, "We'll take D."

"You really think you need an 8×10, two 5×7s, and eight wallets of you and Austin in formal attire next to art-class crepe paper?" Josh asks me.

"No offense, Burke, but aren't some of the red carpet shots we've gotten a better backdrop than this?" Austin looks at me.

"D." I'm being stubborn, but this is important to me. "Premieres are about my work life. This is about *our* life and this is the kind of picture I want to remember."

"Aww, guys," Liz gushes, holding her hand to her heart. "That's so sweet."

"D it is then," Austin pulls me over to the backdrop. He wraps my hands around his waist and then he wraps his hands around mine. We stand nose to nose. "Make that two Ds. We want two poses." He winks at me and the photographer gets ready to shoot.

CLICK.

For once, I don't mind the flash at all.

*   *   *

After we've danced to "Love Story," "Say," and "The Climb," it's time to take a break from the dance floor. Austin grabs us two glasses of punch and we sit down at our table. Only Rob and Allison are sitting there and they're deep in conversation so I don't interrupt.

Clark Hall went all out for the decorations. Allison and Beth were on the committee and they made sure the place felt less like a boring windowless conference room, and more like a tropical paradise. There are fake palm trees covered in little white lights dotting the corners of the room. Blue streamers cover the ceiling and the strings hang over the dance floor (Beth told me they were trying to go for that under-the-sea feel), hitting the tops of some of the guys' heads. There are grass leis covering the food and drink area and the DJ is wearing a coconut-covered hat while he spins. On every wall is a mural of the tropics from the classic setting sun on the sand to a look at the ocean floor complete with scuba divers. (Pictures of Principal P. and Mr. Hanson hang where the scuba faces should be, which is pretty funny.)

Looking around the room, I see a lot of familiar faces: Austin's teammates, Allison's and Beth's friends, even my enemies—Lori and Jess, who tortured me when I was enrolled here, smile huge and wave every time I turn their way. I manage a small smile, which takes a lot of effort.

"So tomorrow we're hiking up to the Hollywood sign, then having lunch at Slice of Heaven again, then we're meeting with Seth for coffee, swimming at my house, and going out to dinner in Santa Monica," I tell Austin.

"Is that all?" Austin replies with a wry grin.

Being with Austin makes me feel like I never left. We have no trouble with conversation when we're together. It's the phone that is a major problem.

"Is that too much?" I twirl a heavily hair-sprayed lock innocently.

"Absolutely not," he says and offers me a bite of coconut cake. "You are going to love the hike to the Hollywood sign." Austin smiles, excited. "A bunch of us did it two weeks ago and the view was amazing."

"I didn't know you hiked it already." I frown. Our plan was to do it together.

"Didn't I tell you?" Austin asks. "It was the day after the meet against Southside. If we won, Coach said we could have the next practice off and do the hike, remember?"

"No." I shake my head. I didn't even know he had the meet against Southside. The guys have been riled up about them all year. They're number one in their division. "Maybe I forgot," I lie. I would have been all over the Southside meet if I had known. Then again, it's not like Austin has asked me yet about play rehearsals. He knows how worked up I am about Riley and performing live. Doesn't he? I know I told him how anxious I am about doing a good job. At least I think he knows. "Between rehearsals, meetings, *SNL* stuff, and my quest to find the perfect cupcake, I'm beat."

"I thought you were waiting for me to try some of the cupcake places," Austin points out. "I just read about one called Buttercup."

"Never heard of it." I look at the packed dance floor. "I've only tried a handful of others. They're my sanity savers. That and Shake Shack."

Austin groans. "Burke, we were supposed to go there together too."

I'm surprised. I so don't remember that. "I'm sorry," I apologize. "I went with Sky the other day after she had this meltdown about her show getting axed."

"How is team SKAT?" Austin's mouth twitches.

"You've heard the nickname too?" I marvel.

"Hayley told me," Austin admits. "I didn't realize you two were around each other enough to warrant a joint name." Austin keeps getting more and more surprised. "I thought she left after that charity kissing booth thing you did. You know, the one where you kissed Dylan." He gives me the strangest look.

I blush. "She stayed in town. I told you."

"I think I would have remembered you talking about Sky." The two of us stare at each other.

I guess we haven't talked all that much since I've been away. It's not all my fault. I call all the time. I think about blaming the time change again, but I can't blame that for everything. Things feel tense for a moment, but I shake it off. "I guess we do have a lot of catching up to do." I smile. "We can do it this weekend."

"Are you sure we'll have time with everything else you crammed in?" Austin jokes, although I'm still a little stung.

"Don't forget we're also viewing our favorite *Clone Wars* episodes," I remind him and he laughs. Yes, the series is technically a cartoon, but Austin and I both agree it is far superior to *Star Wars: Episodes I, II,* and *III.* The only thing that makes me sad when I watch them is how much I like Anakin. It's like in *Wicked* — I so don't want Elphaba to be the "bad" girl. I don't want Anakin to become Vader either.

"I've been TiVo'ing them for you." Austin livens up. "I even waited to watch the last three so I can't give anything away." Oops. Were we supposed to wait? I think I watched the last one with Matty. I'll keep that to myself too.

"So, Kates, are you going to come to Texas and see us play this summer?" Rob yells across the table.

"Absolutely." I grin, relieved for the interruption. "I hope you guys have some games on a Monday. I can't get off any other day of the week."

"I'm sure we do." Rob combs a hand through his long brown hair. "We have about half a dozen games a week. Practices for six hours a day in that sticky Texas heat. Man, I don't know how we're going to do it all and still impress the scouts."

"You'll manage." Austin gives him a huge smile and puts his wing tips up on an empty chair, going adorably boyish at the talk of camp. "This guy has more stamina than anyone."

"Thank God you two are roommates," Allison says more to me than to the boys. "You can keep each other in check. I don't want either of you passing out on some muddy field from heat exhaustion."

"Can that happen?" I worry.

"Nah, they have us practicing early and then very late in

the afternoon," Austin promises. "During the heat of the day we're off."

Good. The last thing I want to think about is Austin being hurt and me not being able to get to him. He's always been able to get to me.

"The girls can't handle the fire so they have to go easier on us guys too," Rob says with a slight roll of his eyes, making Allison nudge him. "Sorry! But it's true. If it was an all-guys camp, they'd have us out there all day and night. Toughen us up. They're afraid the girls will faint."

"I had no idea you were such a Neanderthal." Allison sounds more than a little annoyed, but I've zoned in on another detail.

"*Girls?*" I ask no one in particular. "Did you say 'girls'?"

"Yeah, Burke. It's a coed camp," Austin explains. "Didn't you know that?"

"No." I shake my head slowly. Ugh, I can't believe we're back to this.

"I know I told you," Austin insists, but he looks slightly confused. "Didn't I?"

"I think I would have remembered if you told me the camp was coed." I keep my voice light, but it's hard to keep the edge out. Austin definitely notices.

"Maybe it was during the same conversation that you told me you had kissed other guys at the charity event," Austin says smoothly. I notice Allison raise her eyebrows.

God, does he have to keep bringing that up? It was a charity event! I glare at him.

"The camp is completely coed," Rob says, oblivious to the tension. "They've got coed dorms, coed eating areas, field trips. If I had known, I would have had us pick a different camp, man."

"Do you have a problem with girls playing lacrosse, Murray?" Allison snaps.

The two start to have a heated discussion, but I tune them out. "Coed dorms?" I exclaim. Are they crazy?

"Burke," Austin says, softening a bit and grabbing for my hand. "This camp was the best one around. Coach picked it for us because scouts attend it more than any of the others in the area. Some of these guys have gotten scholarship offers right there on the field. It's a great opportunity."

"I know." I sigh, even though all I can do now is picture girls swarming to Austin's room. How could they not? Look at him! And I'm going to be hundreds of miles away. No, thousands! I think.

"SPARE ME!" I hear Allison's voice rise over the music, interrupting us both. She throws back her chair and stomps off.

"Al! Allie, wait!" Rob begs and hurries off after her.

Whoa. I do not want our night to end like that. I have too little time here to get into an argument over this. And besides, Austin's right. He trusts me, I trust him. Everything will be fine. There are girls here at school and I've never worried about that. I'm being paranoid because we're so far apart, and that's silly because it's not like Austin is worried with me being in New York. I can be big here. "I'm sorry about the kissing booth," I tell him gently.

"And I'm sorry I didn't tell you the camp was coed — even though I swear I did." Austin puts his arm around me and pulls me close. I can feel his heart beating. "Not that it matters, Burke." He touches my chin. "You know I only have eyes for you."

"Same here," I agree, and we kiss. Again.

"You'll see how fast the time goes," Austin says when we finally pull apart. "I'll be in New York in two weeks for your premiere and then you'll get to Texas to see me and before you know it, we'll both be home."

"You're right. It's only a few…months." I gulp. Geez. We still have two months to go. This separation feels too long already.

"Exactly," Austin says cheerily. "Ready to get back out there?" he asks as we hear Ne-Yo pump through the loudspeaker. I nod and then he takes my hand and spins me back onto the dance floor.

Friday, June 19

NOTE TO SELF:
Have Nadine ck A's lacrosse camp enrollment. How many
    girls??!!
Meet A at 9:15 AM.
Seth at 2:30 PM.
Flight back to NYC: Sun. 10AM.
Mtg. @ *SNL:* Mon. 3 PM.

KAITLIN'S SCHEDULE — Week of June 15th

FUTUREPREZ: Kates, UR schedule is PACKED this week so I've put together this itinerary. Print a few copies — 1 4 car, 1 4 dressing room, 1 4 home. I will have extras. Driver has copy 4 addresses. Hope it helps! — N

MONDAY:
10 AM — Rehearsal for play
3 PM — Meeting for *SNL*. 17th Floor, 30 Rockefeller Center, Lorne Michaels's office. Discuss your thoughts for the show and any skit ideas
5 PM — Your mom's charity dinner at the Brooklyn Botanic Garden (I know, I know, you don't want to go. I don't think you have a choice!) Private event so give your name at the gate.
***NOTE: Liz is officially an NYC girl now. She'll be unpacking all day, but she wants to meet up for dinner. Place TBA. She'll call you.

TUESDAY:
10 AM — Rehearsal for play
2 PM — Photo shoot for play coverage
3:30 PM — Interview with Dylan and Riley for *Seventeen*
5 PM — Fittings for *SNL* followed by photo shoot for *SNL*.

WEDNESDAY:
10 AM—Rehearsal for play
2 PM—*SNL* weekly read-through (Audition for skit ideas that were greenlit on Monday. Warning: meeting could last up to three and a half hours. You will then meet with the writers and the producers to discuss which skits will be used going forward.)

THURSDAY:
9AM—EARLY! Rehearsal for play
1 PM—*SNL* rehearsal for larger skits followed by shooting promos (approx. 2 to 4) to air for *SNL* prior to recording. (LONG REHEARSAL)
9:45 PM—Interview with *Playbill* for *Meeting of the Minds* followed by interviews with *People, Entertainment Weekly*, and *Teen Vogue* (that interview will be done with Sky for *SNL*).

FRIDAY:
10 AM—Rehearsal for play
2 PM—*SNL* Blocking—aka where you'll be standing, etc., in each skit followed by more rehearsal
7 PM— Photo shoot for *Teen Vogue* with Sky (*Time could change if your rehearsal runs long for *SNL*)

SATURDAY:

10 AM—*SNL* run-through

4 PM—Arrive back at *SNL* for final prep, last costume fittings

7:45 PM—Dress Rehearsal for *SNL*, Studio 8H, followed by brief meeting with Lorne Michaels to see final skit run-through

11:35 PM—Live Show

2 AM—*SNL* after-party. McCormick & Schmick's Seafood Restaurant.

SUNDAY:

Rest! Yay!

EIGHT: *Live from New York, It's Saturday Night!*

SKY'S CELL: K!!!!!! Where R U??????????

KAITLIN to SKY'S CELL: In a fitting. WHY????

SKY'S CELL: Spoke 2 PR. Thought it would be cool 2 tweet during the live SNL broadcast tonite. What do U think?

KAITLIN to SKY'S CELL: We have like 2.5 secs 2 change hair/costume/makeup. How R U going 2 do that?

SKY'S CELL: Trust me. I can.

LIZ'S CELL: Kates, I M on my way! How R U holding up?

KAITLIN to LIZ'S CELL: Good! Thx. How did project go?

SKY'S CELL: Getting coffee. Need?

KAITLIN to SKY'S CELL: Yes, please, double shot of espresso.

LIZ'S CELL: GROAN! So tough. Spent 4 hrs. in Washington Sq Pk trying 2 get perfect 1-min. footage of pigeons being pigeons. SO WEIRD.

KAITLIN to LIZ'S CELL: I'm sure URs will be GR8!

AUSTIN'S CELL: Hey you. Just touched down. Ready 4 2nite?

KAITLIN to AUSTIN'S CELL: HEY!!! There U R! Tried U all

morning, last night too. Glad U R on the ground. Getting ready. Nervous. Excited.

SKY'S CELL: Got U X-LG coffee. 2 shots espresso. Will pass 2 Rodney.

MOM'S CELL: Kate-Kate, Matty wants 2 come backstage. How do we do that?

KAITLIN to MOM'S CELL: Send him 2 security. Ask 4 Rodney.

AUSTIN'S CELL: Sorry. So busy. Last minute stuff. Crazy week. Sorry didn't check on U more. U will rock.

KAITLIN to AUSTIN'S CELL: Yeah, busy week 4 me 2. Real busy! Still tried 2 call U...

AUSTIN'S CELL: I left U 2 messages 2...

KAITLIN to AUSTIN'S CELL: Sorry. Just stressed. Miss you, that's all.

AUSTIN'S CELL: Miss you 2.

DAD'S CELL: Kaitlin, this is Dad. Mom upset. Security won't let Matty through. Can you come out and talk to them? I'm sure you're busy, but Mom is worried that she is being, and I quote, "disrespected in a way a host's mother should not be disrespected." I'm not sure what to END MESSAGE

LIZ'S CELL: And Suz, this girl in class, was there doing it at the same time and I was so nervous we would have the same footage.

AUSTIN'S CELL: Miss U 2. Will talk 2 U before U go on.

LIZ'S CELL: U'd think they'd give us all different assignments? No?

MOM'S CELL: SO RUDE! Security said to wait outside. I said, "Do you treat Justin Timberlake's mom this way?!" Tried to stop Andy Samberg, but he looked at me like I was crazy! I don't like his attitude, Kaitlin. I hope you're not doing a skit with him.

DAD'S CELL: Dad again. Sent last message too early. Mom is getting a little wild. Waving her arms madly, upset. Can you come out here? PLEASE.

MATTY'S CELL: K, need 2 get backstage!!! MOM IS EMBARRASSING ME! SAVE ME!

SKY'S CELL: K, don't like wig 4 skittles #. Come down here so we can change it.

LIZ'S CELL: I would have done cockroaches if I could, U know?

AUSTIN'S CELL: UR hard to reach so in case I don't talk to U later, Love U. Knock them dead.

KAITLIN to SKY'S CELL: Love U 2!! Thx 4 being here 4 me.

KAITLIN to AUSTIN'S CELL, LIZ'S CELL, MOM'S CELL, MATTY'S CELL: NO WAY!!!! I WON'T CHANGE AGAIN. U R 2 MUCH! STOP WORRYING ABOUT THIS STUFF!

KAITLIN to ALL: Oops. Sorry. Crazy message meant 4 Sky. All others ignore. 2 much texting @ once.

"What was that message about?" Sky yells as she barrels into my fitting 2.3 seconds later. She looks ridiculous — which is what we're going for — in an oversized Skittles bag with just her long legs sticking out. Her hair is classic Ava in a big, blond bouncy curls way. She taps her yellow tights and black tap-shoed foot in aggravation. "You love me? Um, eww!"

I burst out laughing. "I'm sorry. It's just I've never been screamed at by a monster-size bag of candy before." Clara, the seamstress crouched at my feet who is finishing my own Skittles costume, can't help but giggle.

"Do you think you look any better over there?" A small smile escapes Sky's lips despite the obviously annoyed tone of her voice. When she walks over and her cellophane wrapper crinkles as she moves, I lose it completely. Tears are running down my face. "Stop! You'll ruin your makeup!" Sky barks.

"Sorry." I wipe my eyes. "You just look so funny. You are the last person I ever thought I would see looking like this." Sky crosses her arms. Or at least tries to, but her costume is too bulky for her to reach the whole way. "Okay, I'll stop. But as for your original question, no, I don't love you. That text was meant for Austin."

"That's a relief." Sky gives me a strange look. "I mean, I know I'm awesome and you've been having a lot of fun with me in New York, but that's not the way I roll."

I roll my eyes at her. "It was too much at once. Everyone was texting me, I got annoyed with Austin, and my mom was flipping out about not getting backstage. I freaked."

"Your mom is taken care of." Sky waves me off. "I saw her on my way over here and made them let Matty in. She was really grateful. Although I think your brother and father may have been more so, just to get her out of their hair." Sky plays with her wig, pulling strands slowly. "I did, however, maybe, just sort of, leave Liz out there and claim I didn't know her."

Thankfully Clara has finished her work, because I dart forward with a sound like crumpled trash. It's going to be hard not to crack up every time I move in this costume.

"Sky! Why did you have to do that?" I ask, annoyed, and she follows after me as I head down the hall, the two of us crinkling and crackling as we go.

"Because it's fun." Sky shrugs her hidden shoulders with a crumpling sound.

"Do you two have to torture each other?"

"She's the one who purposefully ordered me chicken and broccoli for dinner from Yummy Noodles last night when I distinctly said *tofu* and broccoli." Sky sniffs. "Do you have any idea what the meat could have done to my delicate digestive system?"

"Kaitlin?" Parker, one of the pages working on the show, comes running up to me. "I saw Liz outside and let her in early to go to her seat. She has tickets for the dress rehearsal and the live show, right?"

"Yes, thank you, Parker." I smile gratefully, and Sky sighs loud and deep.

"No prob." He falls in with us walking down the hall toward the stage. "You guys ready to run through this number one more time before dress rehearsal?"

"I have a wig issue," Sky starts, but I cut her off.

"We're ready." Parker must sense the tension because he takes his cue to head off ahead of us. "Your wig is fine," I say through clenched teeth.

"The hair and the costume together make me look poofy," Sky pouts and tries smoothing down the costume to shrink it. It doesn't work.

"That's the point," I remind her. "You're playing Ava, not

yourself. Do you think I like my wig?" I point to the mega-teased dark brown wig I'm wearing that is supposed to make me look like Lauren.

"Yours is worse," Sky agrees happily.

I sigh. "Let's go."

Ten minutes later the two of us are singing and tap-dancing on stage in our giant Skittles costumes. A tiny, yappy Pomeranian — standing in for Ava's equally yappy dog, Calou — howls along on command next to us. The song is absolutely hysterical, if I do say so myself. The writers came up with this biting ditty that makes Lauren and Ava sound like total paparazzi-crazed airheads, which, well, they are. Our number is supposed to be a Skittles commercial that Lauren and Ava have signed on to do because they're cash-strapped now that their reality shows have bitten the dust. The funniest part about the bit is that Lauren and Ava don't realize that the song they're singing is not just about the candy, it's about themselves. At the last minute, legal made us change the name of the candy from Skittles to Skirtles to avoid any lawsuits from the candy company. I wouldn't want my product compared to Lauren and Ava either.

At the end of the skit everyone on the soundstage actually gives us a huge round of applause, which only gets me more pumped up for tonight. I know I'm trying to be nice and calm and not be catty like they are, but I have to admit, it is fun to slip into the girls' barely worn shoes for a few minutes. And Sky kills as Ava. Afterward, we get ready to do our dress rehearsal in front of a live audience.

HOLLYWOOD SECRET NUMBER EIGHT: *Saturday Night Live* is actually taped in front of a dress rehearsal audience and then airs live in front of a different studio audience a few hours later. The dress rehearsal audience sort of serves as last-minute testers of each skit — if the number gets no laughs, or bombs, then it could be pulled entirely. Every number can get tweaked up till the last second on the show. On occasion, encore showings of an episode are different from the original broadcast that airs that night. If something goes majorly wrong during the live broadcast — a musical act goes off the deep end and does something censorable, a comic curses, or a number plays better in dress rehearsal — it may be replaced with the dress rehearsal version in later showings.

For the most part, our sketches get a ton of laughs, especially one where we play our *Family Affair* characters as eighty-year-olds living in a celebrity assisted living center. The two of us think we're our characters, not ourselves. The one sketch that bombs and winds up getting dropped is a number where Sky and I play karaoke singers who perform at a fried chicken pizzeria (don't ask). Our digital short with Andy Samberg — possibly my favorite thing we've done all week — has Sky and me playing his dream girls. All in all, I'm feeling pretty good as I head off to grab something quick to eat in my dressing room with Liz and my family before we get ready for the live show. Then my phone vibrates with another text.

DYLAN'S CELL: Hey, lovely. The bloke at the door will let me slip in before live show starts. Going to dash from our show. Good luck! UR going to nail the Skirtles number.

KAITLIN'S CELL: Thanks 2 U! U ran play and *SNL* lines w/ me all week. How can I thank U?

DYLAN'S CELL: Lunch tomorrow? My treat.

KAITLIN'S CELL: You treated the other day! My turn. Least I can do 4 all UR help.

DYLAN'S CELL: Don't mention it. C U later. I will be the bloke in the jumper. Heard the studio is cold. Don't want 2 freeze my arse off!

"Who is that?" Sky asks, hearing me laugh. She peeks her head nosily over my shoulder as we keep walking down the hall. We've both changed out of our costumes and are in comfy C&C California drawstring pants and tees. I'm in a green tee and black pants; Sky is in a peach tee and tan pants. We both got the outfits at an L.A. gift suite. I can't remember which one. "Is that Dylan again?"

"So what?" I sound defensive. Why? "He was just checking up on me. I think it's nice." I wish my boyfriend would have found more time to do the same. I barely spoke to him all week even after we had the most amazing weekend in Los Angeles. Austin knows how much *SNL* means to me. Why is he acting so distant?

"Dylan is into you," Sky clasps her hands and makes googly eyes at me.

"No, he's not!"

"He so is," Sky counters. "You've been practically joined at the hip all week in between rehearsals, which has been so annoying, by the way."

"He knows I have a boyfriend." I'm getting flustered. I know she's right that we've spent a lot of time together.

"That doesn't stop everyone," Sky points out. "Some guys go after girls who are taken, you know. And who knows? Maybe you're sending him mixed signals."

"I am not!" I tell her hotly.

"Are you *sure* you're not, because that kiss at the charity booth seemed sort of hot." Sky is actually wagging a finger at me now. "Plus you get this goofy smile on your face every time you talk about him."

"That's just because he's been such a good friend." He has! Dylan's got the play to worry about and yet he's spending all his free time making sure I'm not too overwhelmed. He even brought me lunch at my *SNL* rehearsal yesterday because he knew I didn't eat at the play rehearsal. He remembers every little detail I tell him, from what show I watched on TV the night before to what book I'm trying to read during my car rides (the latest Jodi Picoult. So sad).

Sky won't let up. "I think you *feel* something for him."

"I don't feel anything," I protest. I try walking ahead of her, but she reaches my dressing room at the same time as me.

"Look, K, I've been in a lot of relationships…"

I interrupt her. "Really? I haven't noticed," I snap.

"And one thing I know is when people are into each

other," Sky says, looking at herself in a mirror and primping her long, black hair. "You've got a thing for Dylan whether you're with Austin or not. That's what this all boils down to — Dylan is here and is giving you the attention you crave, and Austin's far away and is barely picking up the phone. It's not your fault. It was bound to happen. I'm sure Austin will be the same way when he goes to camp and..." A catering person walks by with a tray of goodies. "Oh look! Brownies! See you in a few, K!"

I'm left standing in the hall feeling anxious and worried.

DYLAN'S CELL: Are you going to the after-party? Want some company?

I stare at my iPhone in alarm. Dylan's just being friendly, right? I thought that's what we were. Friends. But is Sky right? Am I sending Dylan the wrong signals? Why would I do that? I'll ignore his text for the moment and worry about the after-party later. I can't get myself worked up before the show. Everything's been going so smoothly up until now, even with my crazy week. I survived Mom's charity event and a ton of photo shoots and interviews, and made it through double rehearsals every day. Even Riley didn't bother me too much, probably because I was too tired to get upset about her nitpicking. ("Forest, didn't you tell Kaitlin to stand *six* feet from the desk, not eight?") I can't worry about what Dylan is or isn't feeling. Instead I call my boyfriend. He picks up on the first ring, but I can barely hear him because there is so much commotion in the background. Loud music is playing and people are laughing and talking.

"Burke? Can you hear me?" Austin yells over the noise. "Let me find somewhere quieter to talk." Two seconds later, I hear a door shut and the noise is more muffled. "That's better. Hey, are you still there? Listen, sorry about before."

"I'm sorry too." Hearing his voice makes me feel instantly calmer. We seem to be saying "I'm sorry" a lot since we've been apart. "I'm sorry I forgot to call. Sorry I didn't tell you. Sorry, sorry, sorry."

"Where are you?" I ask. "Are you at a party?"

"Sort of," Austin admits. "Most people moved in earlier this weekend and tonight they're having a get-to-know-your-roomies bash in the common area. The dorms here are pretty nice. People seem cool too. The best part: Murray and I have our own bathroom, so we're pretty stoked."

"I would be too." I try to picture what Austin's new home away from home looks like, but I can't. I realize I never even asked to see the camp brochure he kept mentioning to me. I will have to Google it later.

"So it's got to be almost time for you to go on," Austin continues. "Mom is taping it for me. She was worried the camp wouldn't have a TV set up yet, but there is one. It's just, um, overrun at the moment, but I spoke to my RAs and they're letting me use the one in their room, so I'll be cheering you on live, even though you can't hear it."

"Thanks." I'm touched. "Knowing you're watching will keep me on my game."

"You're on your game even if I'm not watching," Austin tells me. "Liz texted me to say you killed at the dress rehearsal. Especially your Skirtles number. I can't wait to see it."

"Hey, you even got the new name of the candy right," I point out. I check my watch. I haven't made it to dinner with everyone and there is still so much I want to go over before the live show. I don't know whether I'll have time. "You do pay attention."

"Always, when it concerns you," he says, and I grin.

"Kaitlin?" It's Parker again. I cover the phone and nod at him. "We need you on set for a moment to check lighting again."

"Sure. I'll be there in a second." I take my hand off the microphone and go back to Austin. "I've got to go."

"AUSTIN! COME ON!" A chorus of male and female voices shouts, and I hold the phone away from my ear to keep from going deaf.

"I'm on with my girl, guys," I hear him say. "I'll be a sec."

Aww…his girl. And he said that in front of other girls! "You've got to go too," I tell him. "Call me after if you're up, otherwise I'll call you in the morning."

"Knock 'em dead, Burke."

"Thanks." I smile. "I will."

The next forty-five minutes before the show are a blur of final checks, costume stuff, and last-minute notes. Before I know it, Sky and I are standing backstage while the opening skit — a political number that we aren't in — plays out. I look over my outfit one last time. My hair is down and I'm wearing a lilac Laundry by Shelli Segal satin pleated dress with Prada peep-toe heels. Sky has on a BCBG smoke sateen bead-detailed mini dress. Her long hair is pulled back in a ponytail. I'm obsessed with her black Miu Miu slingbacks with the tiny bows on the top.

Then it's our cue and we walk next to each other through the doors and down the steps and stand in front of the applauding audience. Even though the lights are blinding, I can see Liz and my parents, Nadine, Rodney, Matty, and, in the back corner, Dylan. I try not to get distracted and just remember my lines.

"You might recognize Kaitlin and me from our show, *Family Affair*," Sky begins, getting a ton of applause at the mention of *FA*.

I take a breath before my first line. "Or you don't recognize us from the show, but you know us from your favorite gossip tabloid," I tell them. "Which is why we're here. To set the record straight. You see, we don't really hate each other." A few people chuckle.

"Absolutely not." Sky shakes her head emphatically. "Total falsehood. We're like sisters."

I frown slightly. "Sisters who occasionally fight," I clarify, looking directly at the audience. "But still, you can't believe everything you hear."

"Even if it sounds sort of true," Sky adds. "Like that story about Kaitlin being hospitalized." I stare at her in mock horror. "It was true, but not because she was suffering from exhaustion." Sky puts a hand over the side of her mouth that

I can see and whispers the word "lipo." People laugh. They're getting it! And they seem to like it!

I put my hands on my hips. "Exactly," I say. "Some stories are exaggerations, like the ones about Sky being a total control freak." I cover my hand over my mouth now. "SO TRUE," I stage whisper. "AND SO IS THE STORY ABOUT SKY COLORING HER HAIR. SHE HAS GRAYS."

After a few more barbs, the two of us start clawing at each other, pulling off pieces of each other's clothing that are meant to rip on cue. Finally Andy Samberg and Seth Meyers come out and pull us off each other. I'm dangling in Andy's arms, my legs flailing, while Seth holds back Sky. When they remind us about the cameras, we calm down and compose ourselves—sort of. We're still bickering as they go to the commercial break, and the audience loves it. And I love doing it! Who knew saying things to Sky that I've always said could play so well for a crowd? But it works, and Sky and I, I guess after years of working together, know each other's rhythms and know exactly how to play each line and each expression.

The whole show works that way and then it's time for our curtain call and the whole cast is onstage saying goodnight. But it doesn't feel like goodnight. If anything, I'm more awake at 1:30 AM than I've ever been. No wonder they do an afterparty. When the show officially ends, I hug the cast members and pose for a few pictures with the audience while my family, Nadine, Liz, and Rodney wait patiently to congratulate me. I look up and notice Dylan is with them and he's holding a HUGE bouquet of gorgeous summer flowers like lavender and sunflowers. He's talking to my mother.

"Kaitlin! You were fabulous!" Mom gushes. I've never seen her so happy. "Brilliant! I just e-mailed Seth. This should do amazing things for your résumé," she adds in a whisper. "I'll get on him about that tomorrow morning, but just great! Wasn't she great?" she asks the group.

They all murmur their agreement, including Dylan, who is staring at me, smiling.

"These are for you," he says shyly.

Mom clutches her heart. "Isn't that sweet?"

"Thanks." I take the bouquet from him and breathe in the heavenly scent of lavender. Wow. "You didn't have to."

"I wanted to," Dylan insists. His teeth are so white. Blindingly white. I don't think I noticed that before. "You were brilliant. Spot on. Didn't I tell you?"

"You did." I laugh. "What about the…?"

"Skirtles number?" he finishes my sentence. "You sorted it out. It was excellent!"

"Thanks." I feel weirdly shy all of a sudden. I feel my phone vibrate. It's Austin. "Excuse me a second. Hey," I say to Austin. "What did you think?"

"It was great!" Austin sounds so proud and I get all gooey. "Burke, you are a true comic. Who knew?" It sounds so loud where he is. "I saw almost all of it."

"Almost all?" I frown.

"Yeah, they kept pulling me away. I can already tell dorm

life means a total lack of privacy. I missed the Skirtles number, but I'm going to YouTube it as soon as it's up."

"Oh." That was the one number I wanted him to see. He knew that. "Okay."

If he can pick up on the disappointment in my voice, he doesn't say anything. "Have a great time at the after-party, okay?" Austin, sounds like he's rushing me off the phone. "I'll call you tomorrow." He's gone before I can even say goodbye.

"So to the after-party?" Dad interrupts. "We can come, right?"

"DAD," Matty groans. "Please don't." I giggle.

"Sweetie, I don't want to go to that." Mom sounds uneasy. "Let's head home. I have an early appointment with the Daisies. Nadine and Rodney will take the kids."

"We won't be too late." Liz winks at me.

Matty and I breathe a sigh of relief.

"Are you going too, Dylan?" Mom asks him.

"Can't leave the lady without an escort, can I, ma'am?" Dylan is looking at me intently.

"And I do need an escort," I joke, sounding much more excited than I intended to. Nadine looks at me oddly. So does Liz. "I mean, of course, he's coming. We're all going. One big happy group! Um, we're going to leave in a little while. Let me get changed and I'll meet you out here."

"Great." Dylan smiles again, revealing those dimples. "I'll be waiting."

"Super!" I say dumbly, a nervous grin plastered to my face. I head back to the dressing area to grab Sky and get my stuff, but all I can think about is this new mess I've somehow created.

Geez, maybe Sky is right. I might have a *teensy* crush on Dylan. And Dylan might like me back.

And if he does, what do I do about it?

Saturday, June 20

NOTE TO SELF:
GO TO SLEEP! Stay there all day Sunday. ☺

The New Queens of Saturday Night—
Kaitlin Burke and Sky Mackenzie!

Week of June 22nd

by TV Tome Critic Brayden Woods

If you caught *Saturday Night Live* this past weekend—and many of you obviously did, since the ratings spiked 21 percent—you might have been surprised to find yourselves laughing *along with* and not *at* the week's hosts.

After being both praised and reviled in the tabloids for years, teen TV queens Kaitlin Burke and Sky Mackenzie of *Family Affair* turned the tables on America by poking fun at themselves. From the moment their opening monologue started—a hilarious bit about the two who famously hate each other claiming they don't hate each other even as they were griping at one another—we knew we were in for a rare treat.

The girls didn't disappoint in the ninety-minute show (if you count out a weak game show skit about airhead cheerleaders). They cleverly mocked their octogenarian selves in an *FA* nursing home skit, played obnoxious paparazzi in another, and proved they could sing in the best skit of the night, a Skirtles commercial in which they played their enemies, socialites Ava Hayden and Lauren Cobb.

The *SNL* writers struck gold with that ditty, but they can't take all the credit. The idea stems from a blog Sky and Kaitlin wrote likening Ava and Lauren to Skittles candy—sweet but when you get too much of them, you feel sick. The foursome have been fighting via the media for a month now and it seems as if everyone has a side, with Team SKAT (which stands for Sky and Kaitlin) T-shirts popping up on teens from Times Square to the Grove.

Lauren and Ava must have had a meltdown over that skit, since it captured their TV personas perfectly. Sky was brilliant as the notoriously paparazzi-obsessed Hayden, using hair flips to her full advantage. And while Kaitlin made a worthy Cobb, she sparkled even more in a skit where she played a 1950s B-movie queen heroine fleeing from an army of ants. The best parts of the show were when the pair were onscreen together, proving to this TV critic what so many of us already know—like each other or not, the two belong back on TV together. Television producers, hear my plea: cast Sky and Kaitlin on a sitcom before someone else snatches them up.

SCENE 8:

School courtyard. Basketball court is in the
background. A few park benches line the stage.

LEO:
Andie, wait!

ANDIE:
(crying) You don't need to follow me, Leo. It was
a stupid idea to begin with. I never should have
told you.

LEO:
(catching up to Andie) Hey. It wasn't stupid.
Actually, it was probably the first honest thing
someone has ever said to me at this school. I've spent
four years here and so much of it was bull. We're
all so busy being a type that we don't know who we
really are. You know who you are, Andie. I like that.
I may not have seen it before today, but I like that.

ANDIE:
You do?

LEO:
I do. And I want to try something. If you'll let me.

ANDIE:
What is it?

LEO:
This.

(Leo leans in very slowly and kisses Andie very softly at first. Andie responds by kissing Leo back and wrapping her arms around his neck.)

NINE: *The Calm Before the Storm*

"This is it, people!" Forest tells us. "I want to go over one last scene before we call it quits for the day. Kaitlin? Dylan? I think we need to give THE MOMENT one last go."

THE MOMENT is exactly what moment you think it is, and even after rehearsing it for weeks, I still can't help getting all jumpy beforehand. My hands get clammy, my forehead sweats, and I feel like I'm going to pass out from nerves. Dylan walks across the stage toward me.

"Peppermint?" he offers. We had a full dress rehearsal yesterday and today we can wear our street clothes. Dylan's wearing a cool green polo shirt that brings out the color of his eyes even more (if that's possible) and frayed khaki cargo shorts.

I cover my mouth and breathe into my hand "Does my breath smell?" I shuffle my feet uncomfortably. I have on cute plaid Coach ballet sneakers that go well with my hot pink Gap tee and my new super fit Lucky capri jeans.

He laughs. "Your breath is like roses, darling, relax. These are for me. You want?"

I shake my head. Someone is testing the lights and a bright one blinds me for a moment. Then the lights go dim — too dim — and I feel like I'm on a romantic date.

"Take it from the beginning of the scene, Kaitlin," Forest says, without looking up from his notes. He's sitting on a crate near the edge of the stage. Did it just get hot in here? All we need is for them to pipe in John Mayer, and I'm done for.

I nod. Dylan and I both exit stage left and then I run back onstage and Dylan runs after me.

"Andie, wait!" Dylan uses his American accent. He even sounds charming as an American. How does he do it?

I start to cry. "You don't need to follow me, Leo." I literally shake, my character is so upset. "It was a stupid idea to begin with. I never should have told you." I turn toward Dylan after he starts his little speech about honesty and then it's my turn again. I almost forget to say my line. I'm looking so deep into Dylan's eyes, trying to concentrate on Leo rather than think about how good Dylan looks, and I catch myself just in time to hear Dylan say "but I like that."

"You do?" I ask Leo. I start snapping my pink beaded bracelet absentmindedly. Remember, Kaitlin. This is Leo, not Dylan talking. I feel my heart begin to speed up. The kiss is seconds away.

"I do," Dylan says softly. LEO. I mean Leo says softly! "And I want to try something. If you'll let me."

My breath catches in my throat. "What is it?" I practically whisper.

"This," Dylan whispers back. He puts one hand on my back, pulls me forward and with the other hand on my chin he leans in and kisses me so lightly I barely feel it. I close my eyes and lean into the kiss, my lips melting into his. Dylan smells like peppermints, I think, and peppermints smell delicious. From far away, I hear "Excellent!"

"Amazing!" Forest says as I unwind my arms from Dylan's neck and step back. I feel sort of wobbly and Dylan actually grabs my arm to steady me. "You two are superb together. Such chemistry. Don't you think so, people?"

I didn't even realize the rest of the cast was watching us. I was in a total zone, but there they are. They're standing offstage and they walk out toward us. A few people mumble their agreement.

I can't look at Dylan. I feel guilty kissing him, which is weird because I never feel guilty kissing another actor. It's just work. And yet…there is something about kissing Dylan that doesn't feel like acting. What am I saying? I try to block the thought out of my mind and picture Austin.

Since Forest is here for today's final rehearsal with me before I open, I kind of figured he'd say something to all of us before we leave. And he does. "I want to thank all of you for putting in so much time and effort the past few weeks," he says, smiling like my dad does when I do something particularly wonderful, like win a Teen Choice Award or tell him he can produce my next film. "I know it was a lot of hard work — having you all come down here on different days and times to work on things you've already perfected, but this was a time to make your work gel with someone else's and I think the results, as you can see, have really paid off." Forest walks to my side and puts an arm around me, throwing me his famously dimpled smile. "Kaitlin, I think you're ready."

"You do?" I can't help but ask sort of nervously and sort of excitedly at the same time. Hearing Forest say that means a lot. I flush from embarrassment, knowing the others are looking at me. I pull down on my Gap V-neck nervously. "I mean, thank you. I owe it all to you guys." Dylan winks.

It's Wednesday afternoon and we've just finished a full rehearsal from start to finish. Usually we work on select scenes or sometimes Forest has me come alone and go over dialogue with him. It's been a grueling process. More practice than I've ever had on film. With a movie, the bulk of my rehearsal is done on my own, sitting in a trailer memorizing my lines. Then we do several takes and shoot the scene for real. I know my character's motivation and purpose and who she is, but I've never known a character as well as I've known Andie. Forest has pushed me to think about every aspect of Andie, from her walk to her facial expressions to the way she carries her school books. ("Everything you do on the stage brings another layer to your performance," he once told me. "Remember that.") It's amazing to think something I've worked so hard on will only be seen by a select group of people for the next eight weeks and after that it won't exist anymore. Well, at least not with me in it. Forest already said the next actress they hire will keep the part for at least a year.

"This is a big week for all of us," Forest tells the small group that includes the company, Dylan, and Riley. Her pink cardigan is a surprisingly good choice on her, and I love how it hangs long in the front and she has it knotted at her waist over an ivory tank top. She's pulled her hair back messily in a bun, held in place with a chewed pencil. I've always wondered how to do that, but I obviously can't ask her.

"I think we've gotten a lot of interest from the press and media outlets thanks to our new star," Forest continues, reading from a clipboard. "The articles some of you have been part of have helped ticket sales tremendously. And I think your work at the Broadway Cares event last week really said a lot about our family. I'd like to keep that momentum going."

"You want us to join the Broadway softball league?" Dylan jokes. He's sat down on the stage and is leaning back on his elbows, his body stretched out in front of him. He looks like he could fall asleep at any moment. "I'm not sure I'd be much help in that area. My expertise is in football — or, as Kaitlin calls it, soccer. Or maybe we could play cricket."

Forest laughs. "I have a better idea. We just found out this morning that *The View* wants us on the show to perform a select scene."

A murmur of excitement rises through the group. I've sat on the ladies' couch before and it can be both intimidating and fun at the same time, but I have a feeling I'm the only one here who has. Riley is talking a mile a minute to anyone who will listen about her love for Elizabeth, who coincidentally happens to be my least favorite. Figures.

"What scene?" someone asks.

Forest looks from us to one of the producers. "Andie's breakthrough — the scene with Andie and Leo."

Uh-oh. This won't go over well. I sneak a peek in Riley's direction. Riley's face is as pink as her sweater.

"That's a brilliant scene, Forest," Riley agrees, surprisingly. "*But* don't you think Kaitlin would fare better with more company onstage? Kaitlin works best when she has a group to support her."

That's a backhanded compliment if I ever heard one.

"*The View* wants Kaitlin." Forest is completely unapologetic. "She's a face America knows and she's giving our show a face. The scene I picked is Kaitlin's best moment." He looks at me. "It truly is. Your emotions are raw and your words run deep, and it's a valuable showcase for your work."

I can feel Riley watching me, but I don't look up. Instead, I examine my new sterling silver Tiffany necklace. I fell in love with the starfish pendant the other day when we strolled into the famous jeweler after practice and I bought Nadine and me matching ones on the spot.

I still don't know how to deal with Riley's veiled jabs. To get out my frustration I've started taking Zumba classes. Liz comes too. She couldn't find a kickboxing class that worked with her new schedule, so the two of us have been taking Zumba, a Latin dance and music cardio class that includes merengue, salsa, mambo, rumba, and calypso. I may not be really good at any of the moves, but it's a lot of fun for releasing steam.

"The good news is that the rest of you can take the next few days off from rehearsals," Forest says to obvious excitement. "Get out of here! Get some color!" People start to disband, not waiting around for Forest to change his mind. I wait to hear what Forest wants me to do next. I usually stay after all the others. "And Kaitlin, you can too, if you want. Friday is your big day and we want you well rested."

This Friday is D-Day. I stare at the empty chairs in the darkened area of the theater. Friday night I'll be standing here, on this stage, in front of over a thousand people. I think I might throw up.

"Maybe I should go over that scene for *The View* one or two more times," I tell Forest anxiously. "I'm not sure I have Andie's emotions just right."

"You have them," he insists with a smile. "And think of *The View* on Thursday as good practice." I open my mouth to say more, but he stops me. "No buts. Take a few days off. Think about Andie all you want — from home." He grabs his stuff and heads offstage. I start packing up too, throwing my Vitaminwater, a wrapper from a Fiber One bar, and my notebook in my bag. I don't even realize Riley is standing there till I turn around, which of course, causes me to jump.

"Congrats, Kaitlin, on *The View*," she manages. She fiddles with her sweater, pulling the cardigan tight around her small frame.

"Thanks." I swallow, bracing myself for what she's going to say next. She will say something, I'm sure.

"I've always wanted to be on one of those silly American talk shows. So mindless but fun," Riley adds. "Right up your alley, I suppose. Have fun." She grabs her bag and starts to head offstage, hesitates, then turns back. "Some advice: during your big scene on the telly try not to look so pained, okay? You still tend to look like you need to go to the loo every time you emote something serious. Have you noticed that?" I shake my head before I can stop myself. "I thought you would have sorted it out by now, but I guess not. Bye!"

"Don't let her get to you." I hear Dylan and I turn around. He runs a hand through his close-cropped hair and I watch the action almost as if it is in slow motion, then I turn away quickly. Austin. Think about Austin. "She fancies your gig on *The View*. Totally jealous."

"You think?" I'm afraid that slow-mo thing will happen again, so I don't dare look at him. "I don't think she's jealous of anyone. It's hard to be jealous when you think you're the finest theater actress alive."

Dylan chuckles. "True. So are you still having that nightmare where you're onstage naked?"

"I didn't have it last night, actually." Dylan knows all my fears about live theater. The naked acting gig is my latest nightmare. I think Dylan was actually amused by the idea. He gets a twinkle in his eye whenever I bring it up.

"Good." Dylan surveys me. "Forest is right. You were worried about bits and bobs, but it's all good. You're ready. We can get together before then if you really want to rehearse some more, but you don't need it. We should celebrate. Maybe over lunch tomorrow? There's this great restaurant near my flat."

I know I should say no, but I don't want to. Hanging out with Dylan is fun. "Lunch it is, then."

My phone is vibrating and I pray it's Austin. I missed our scheduled phone call last night. We decided to set up a time to talk since we've been so bad about spontaneous chatting. I was busy shopping last night at this cute little boutique Nadine and I found I didn't hear my phone. I look at the caller ID. It's not Austin. "It's Sky." I sigh. "I should really take it."

"Absolutely." Dylan's sympathetic face makes my heart flutter. "Don't want to leave her hanging. She's cheeky."

"See you tomorrow." I hurry out the side door to the theater where Rodney and Nadine are waiting with the driver and answer the phone. "Guess what? I'm going to be on *The View* on Thursday!"

"K, I have no time for chitchat," Sky snaps, whispering. Her voice is echoing slightly and it sounds like she's hiding in a closet (it wouldn't be the first time), although I can hear faint music in the background. "This is important! I need you to listen instead of going on and ON and on about mindless details that I could care less about."

Ah, I'm talking to *that* Sky today. "Fine. What's going on?" I ask, and wave to Nadine and Rodney as I slide inside the air-conditioned car, which is a sharp contrast to the humidity outside. New York really is sticky. Thankfully all the tall buildings cast big shadows so the sun doesn't beat down on you. Still, my choice of denim capris doesn't seem like such a good idea all of a sudden. It's a good thing I texted Nadine earlier and asked her to bring my T-Bags teal floral batwing-sleeved dress to change into. "And why are you whispering?"

"I'm in the bathroom at Geisha," she explains. I hear a toilet flush. "My agent is waiting for me at the table to give him a decision. I told him to come prepared with three offers."

"Didn't you make that demand last night?" I feel a huge rush of panic. She's got options already? "I told you, the offers are going to come flying in after Saturday's show. Laney and Amanda told us that."

"I can't take that chance," Sky huffs. I hear a door slam and heels click clacking across a floor. "I want an offer today! And of course, my agent said the same thing as yours. Give it a week, but I don't want to. I want a new job now. So I'm thinking — how do you feel about *Dancing with the Stars*? Or *Celebrity Apprentice*? I have offers from both. Hold on, K!" Her voice drops and I assume she's talking to a bathroom attendant. "Do you have any Aveda hairspray instead of this Suave garbage? My hair only responds to natural oils."

"Sky, have you eaten a bad spicy tuna roll?" I'm completely flabbergasted. "You would never take an offer from either of those shows in a million years!"

"Yeah, but I could start working like tomorrow on

their new seasons." Sky sounds a bit crazy. "Back on a set! Tomorrow! K, I need to get back on a set."

"Calm down," I tell her sternly. "And listen: You are not taking either of those shows. Do you hear yourself? *Dancing with the Stars?*"

Nadine looks up from her BlackBerry, which her short, stubby pink nails are typing away on, and looks at me oddly. "Sky?" she mouths. "Has she lost her mind?"

"Stay calm and wait a few days, do you hear me?"

Nadine butts in, waving her freckled arms wildly. I love that coral scalloped flutter-sleeve top she's wearing. It looks like Juicy Couture, but that's impossible because Nadine would never — oh, that's mine! I think I remember her asking to borrow it. She's meeting a friend for lunch later. "Tell her to think of the other offers you two have that are bringing in exposure," Nadine's voice tumbles out in my ear. "That Funnyordie.com clip you were asked to do sounds like a riot."

"It's decent money, K!" Sky sounds desperate.

HOLLYWOOD SECRET NUMBER NINE: Just because you're a star doesn't mean you make money on a reality show. There are some where you can make an okay paycheck. Like — I can't believe I'm going to say this — *Dancing with the Stars*. Seth told me he had a client who got an initial payout of $125,000 to appear and then between $10,000 and $50,000 for every week he survived elimination. But there are shows like *Celebrity Apprentice* where stars get paid next to nothing. Same with *The Bachelor*, which I hear only covers housing while a person is off doing the show. Too bad there isn't a celebrity *Bachelorette* yet. Sky would love that gig. Maybe Ava and Lauren need reality shows, but Sky does not. I remind her of this and she starts to decompress.

"Okay, I'll wait." I hear another door open and then much more noise. She must feel safe enough to go back to her table. "I don't know what I was thinking. If *you're* not taking an offer like that, then I certainly shouldn't."

"Mmm-hmm." I roll my eyes. Nadine can't hear what Sky is saying, but she laughs anyway. From my expression she can tell it's something quintessentially Sky. As soon as I hang up this phone, I am pulling my hair into a loose side pony-tail to help beat the late June heat.

When that's done, I sit back and let the air-conditioning continue to cool me down. Thank God Sky didn't ask where I was going. If I had told her I was meeting Liz, she would have wanted to come too — just to torture Liz. That's what the two of them seem to like to do best. Get on each other's nerves. But my loyalty still lies with Liz, and today is a best-friend outing.

We pull up to Tortilla Flats on Washington Street and I hop out. Liz is already sitting outside at one of the Mexican joint's rickety sidewalk tables. I sort of wish we were sitting inside, but I know it's too nice a day to do that. Besides, last time we were here this loud group of women sat for hours at a table and we could barely hear ourselves think. The inside of Tortilla Flats is so much fun to look at. It's tiny, cramped, and sort of dingy, but it has the coolest decor. Every inch of the walls and ceiling is covered with Ernest Borgnine memorabilia, eccentric framed photos, twinkling lights hanging from the ceiling, and streamers. Liz sees me and waves, but her face looks too tired to actually smile. Her ensemble is the one making all of the statements today. She has on a bright green slip dress that is big and boxy and flows in the light breeze. I kiss her cheek, excuse myself to go to the bathroom (that car ride was too long!), change into my T-Bags dress, and then rejoin Liz.

"Hey!" I make my way to our table. "Why the long face?"

"I hate another one of my teachers." Liz grumpily munches on a tortilla chip. She dunks another into the salsa and it crumbles, which only seems to aggravate her more. "He called on me in class and I got the answer wrong and he asked me if I got it wrong on account of the fact I was too busy partying with celebrities to do my homework! I wasn't going to let it slide, of course, so I politely asked what he was referring to and he mentioned the photo of me out with you at the *SNL* after-party. As if that has anything to do with my class attendance! It was a Saturday night."

"What is with people hating celebrities?" I hand her a menu. I already know what I'm getting. We've been here twice already and both times I got the queso dip to start and the cheese enchilada platter. "He's just jealous because he wasn't invited to the *SNL* after-party and you were."

"I don't think so." She shakes her head, and her large hoop earrings whip around like they're going to fly off. "They hate Hollywood people."

"Who does?"

"Everyone." Liz's face crumbles, her peach-glossed mouth slipping into a frown. "The other people in the workshop—who make little comments about me being from Holly-WOOD land. And the teachers act as if *I* think I deserve more props because I'm from there and my dad is in the business. I just want a fair chance, you know?"

I nod. I so know. It's exactly how I feel about trying Broadway. I pray the critics this Friday night judge me on my actual performance, not the number of articles I've headlined in *Hollywood Nation*. "How'd you do on your pigeon piece?"

"I got a B," Liz says stiffly. Her face is flushed and I can't tell if she's mad or just hot. Her curly hair is down and frizzing all over the place. I'm trying to resist the urge to hand her a hair elastic.

"That's good, no?" I try to sound upbeat. I already know the answer: It's not when you're Liz and you expect straight As. She just glares at me. "The next one will be an A. Did you find a subject yet?" She shakes her head. "Forget their feelings about L.A.! Prove them wrong about Hollywood land or whatever they call it. I can be your next subject if you want. You can follow me around the day of the opening. Believe me, I'll display a whole range of emotions that will knock their socks off."

"That's not a bad idea," Liz admits, grinning for the first time today. "I'll show them what Hollywood is really like. It's harder than they think!"

"Darn straight!" I laugh.

"This workshop is tougher than I thought it would be." Liz sighs and plays with the half a dozen gold bangles on her wrist. "Maybe I'm wrong about NYU. What if I can't cut it?" Liz asks seriously. "There are some great writing programs and directing workshops on the West Coast too, you know. Maybe I should look at some colleges near home."

"Did your brain just fry from the hot salsa?" I sound startled, I know it. "You've wanted to come east forever!"

"Now that I'm east, I'm thinking I'm more of a West Coast girl," Liz says longingly. "Do you think that's bad?"

"I'm definitely a West Coast girl," I realize. I love it here, but it's exhausting! "But I haven't loved NYU forever either, the way you do. Hey, at least you're trying it now rather than calling your dad freshman year and begging him to let you come home."

Liz grabs another tortilla chip. "Good point."

We wind up staying at Tortilla Flats for almost two hours and then head over to the Tory Burch boutique to do some shopping. We both pick up the same playful blue-and-white floral pleated skirt. Liz gets a pair of funky three-inch-high beige sandals, and I pick up a green and white striped harbor shirt that I'll wear to one of the dozen Hampton events

Mom keeps hounding me about. I curb my shopping there. I finally paid off my credit card bill from my shopping disasters last spring with Lauren and Ava.

"Dessert?" Liz hoists her shopping bag over her bare shoulder. "We worked up a sweat trying on all that stuff."

"I guess if we made the long walk to Magnolia Bakery and then back to the apartment, we would burn some calories," I put in quickly. "Let's do it."

"I spoke to Josh before you got to lunch," Liz tells me as we walk. "He says he spoke to Austin this morning."

"At least someone did," I let slip. Liz gives me a surprised look. "Sorry. I'm just frustrated. Our schedules are so opposite that we barely have time to talk, and then sometimes when we do talk we're griping about not talking enough."

"You're seeing him this weekend and that will make up for all the bad phone calls." Liz puts her arm around me, but it's hard to walk this way.

"I guess." I shrug. "I want to talk to him the way we've always talked, you know? I want him to know about Riley and what it's like being in this huge, cavernous theater and having to learn how to project my voice and wear a mic the whole time. But we barely have time to talk as it is and when we do, he doesn't ask about the show."

"So bring it up to him," Liz suggests.

"He should bring it up," I say stubbornly and feel myself start to speed up. Liz's arm slips off my shoulder. That's another thing I've noticed about living in New York. I sort of speed walk everywhere. You can't help yourself. Everyone tends to move fast. At least I've started wearing the right shoes for all this walking. I have a new pair of Havaiana flip-flops that I leave in my bag and take everywhere. "Shouldn't he? I mean, Dylan asks me how I'm feeling all the time."

"Kates," Liz warns. "Watch yourself there."

I blush. "There's nothing to worry about. I love Austin. I just miss him a lot."

"You guys will be okay." Liz sounds so sure of herself. I wish I was. "When does he fly in? Friday?"

I nod. "His mom and Hayley are meeting him here. Mom suggested they stay at the Soho Grand, which I'm not sure is the Meyers' style, but at least it's really nice. Sky promised to look after them since I'll be so busy on Friday." Liz raises her eyebrows, but I let it go. "They don't leave till Monday afternoon, so during the day I'll have loads of time to show them around." I pause. "Except for Saturday when I have a matinee. And the night performances, but other than that."

"Other than that, you're totally free." Liz grins. "This is going to be some schedule, but hey, at least you have your days free. We can take more dance classes."

"Absolutely." I pull my hair down and then put it back up again in a normal pony. The side one was too annoying. "That's about the only thing that works with this schedule. That and meetings with Seth and Laney about my next big move, which between us, I have to say, I want to be something on TV."

"Really, Kates?" Liz sounds excited. "That would be awesome."

"Seriously? You don't think I'm crazy after complaining all those times about my schedule and workload?"

She shakes her head. "You were glowing Saturday night. TV is your thing, Kates! Look how much fun Matty is having." Liz lowers her eyes. "Don't get mad, but sometimes when he's talking, you look a little jealous."

"I am!" I say ruefully. "That's why it felt so good to do *SNL*. Being back with Sky and trading lines like that, acting so funny, it was fun! I need a new character to focus on. Someone a little lighter than Sam."

"She was a bit melodramatic," Liz agrees, and I pinch her. "Well, she was!"

Ten minutes later, we're standing in front of the miniscule Magnolia Bakery. I stay outside and try Austin on his cell while Liz gets two iced coffees and two cupcakes to go. It's not like I need an excuse to call him, but I'm feeling a little guilty about complaining about him to Liz and besides, I forgot to ask him where it was his mom wanted to have brunch on Sunday. I look at my watch. It's an hour earlier in Texas, so Austin should be on his lunch break. The phone rings and rings.

"Hello?" A girl answers, shouting over thumping music. "Hello?"

"Sorry, I must have the wrong number," I tell her apologetically, and prepare to hang up.

"Wait. Are you looking for Austin Meyers or Rob Murray? If so, you're in the right place."

"Oh." I hesitate. Who is this girl answering their phone? "I'm looking for Austin."

"A! Phone for you!" she yells.

A? She's calling *my* Austin, A?

"He's down the hall," another voice yells back.

"He's not here right now," the girl says. "Call back in five." She's giggling. "Carl, stop! I'm on the phone! I said, 'I'm on the phone!'" She laughs harder. "Sorry. He's tickling me. These L.A. boys are too much."

"Can I leave a message?" I snap without realizing it. "Tell Austin his *girlfriend* called."

Fine, it's childish, but I'm playing the girlfriend card. I'm staking my claim.

"I didn't know A had a girlfriend," the girl says, causing me to get even madder.

"It's Kaitlin," I tell her, trying to stay calm. "Can you just tell him I called?"

"No problem, Katrine," she says, and then she hangs up before I get the chance to correct her.

Tuesday, June 23

NOTE TO SELF:
The View: Thurs. @ 11. B there @ 9:45 AM
Dinner w/ parents, Matty @ the Met 4 Mom: Thurs. 6:30 PM
Friday: opening night! B there @ 5 PM.
Austin & family get in @ 2PM. Have Rodney pick them up @ JFK.

Find out who that girl was who answered "A's" phone!

Scene 10

After Andie and Leo are caught kissing, Jenny is
furious. She chases Andie back to the cafeteria to
confront her. Jenny's friends and Andie's friends
quickly take sides, and soon a riot starts. The class
bell rings, but nobody moves. Andie has jumped up on
a table to avoid the cheerleaders.

ANDIE:
(screaming at the top of her lungs) STOP!

*(The crowd grows quiet and looks up at her. Andie is
a bit unsettled.)*

ANDIE:
Good. Um, thanks for listening.

JORDAN:
Wow, Andie, who knew one day the queen bees would
actually listen to what you had to say?

JENNY:
We're not listening! We're waiting till she climbs
down so we can grab her.
*(Chorus of "Yah!" The girls try to grab Andie's legs.
Becca and Jordan step in to stop them, and hair
pulling ensues.)*

ANDIE:

Wait! Wait! Don't you think this is a bit crazy? What
are we doing? This is the last day of school and
even today we can't find a way to get along for five
minutes?

JENNY:

Not when you're kissing other people's boyfriends!

ANDIE:

He kissed me. *(Jenny moves to grab her again.)* Okay,
okay, not that I stopped him. But that's not the
point. The point is we all used to be friends and
now we can't even say hi in the halls. Remember first
grade? Jenny, you used to come over to my house every
Monday after school. And Jordan—you and Katie
took gymnastics together. Sara, you can pretend you
didn't, but you used to play soccer with Becca. What
happened to us? Why did we get so caught up in who
is popular, who is not, who lives on the west side of
town and who lives east of the river, who drives a
Beamer and who has a '90 Nissan Sentra?

JORDAN:

That would be me and I'm proud to say that car drives
quite well. *(pause)* When I'm not having it serviced.

ANDIE:

We should be supporting each other, not trying to find ways to tear each other down. What's the point of doing that?

JENNY:

There is no point. It's just fun to point out the obvious, like Jordan's terrible roots.

JORDAN:

It costs money to have my roots look this bad! You should know; yours are worse.

JENNY:

This is your last chance, Andie. I want you to leave. Now. And don't even think of showing up in a cap and gown tomorrow or you really will have to pay for trying to humiliate me by kissing my boyfriend. It's your choice. What's it going to be?

ANDIE:

I'm staying and I'd like to see you try to stop me.

TEN: *Opening Night*

It's so quiet in the theater, you could hear a pin drop. I hear someone cough, but I tune out the sound. My eyes are on Riley—aka Jenny—and this is one of the biggest moments in the play. I'm trying not to think about that fact, though—or the fact that the audience is jammed with people I know tonight. My parents, Matty, Liz, Sky (who acted indignant when I asked if she wanted a ticket. "Of course I want a ticket!"), Nadine, Rodney, Laney, and Seth are seated in a box on the right-hand side of the theater. In the second row, center, are Austin, his mom, and his sister, Hayley. A few rows behind them are my friends Gina, Taylor, Miley, and Vanessa. Page Six said Lauren and Ava were going to crash the show, but Forest set up security to keep them out in case the rumors were true. Someone told me Kelly Ripa is here, but I haven't seen her. The *Gossip Girl* cast is supposedly here as well, but I'm trying not to think about that either. The most important thing I have to do right now is concentrate on the moment.

I'm standing on top of a cafeteria table trying to avoid a mob of angry cheerleaders. My voice is strong and a little angry: "We should be supporting each other, not trying to find ways to tear each other down. What's the point of that?"

Oh wow. I said that differently than I have in rehearsal. I usually say it softly, as if it's a delicate reminder of the truth. But tonight I'm fired up. I guess going live will do that to you. I was so nervous all day. I only had a banana for lunch. Nadine forced me to eat a power dinner with lots of protein (I had lemon chicken, which I love, and a big side of broccoli) and a huge bottle of water so I'd stay hydrated. Then I worried I drank too much water and I was going to have to pee during the first act. But I've been fine. So far. I was so anxious about tonight that I showed up at the theater two hours before the curtain went up. Liz and Nadine offered to hang backstage with me, but I told them I was too nervous for guests.

I haven't even seen Austin yet — well, up close. (I can see his gorgeous face in the audience, though.) Rodney dropped his family off at the hotel around three thirty, and they had just enough time to grab a bite before they came to the theater. I told Rodney to bring Austin backstage during the brief intermission, but Austin called me before the curtain to wish me luck and tell me he would see me after the show. "I don't want to break your concentration," he insisted. "I want you at the top of your game, Burke." He was so sweet it almost made up for the fact that we hadn't talked in the three days before he arrived.

I've been such a wreck about opening night. Dylan was sweet and took my mind off things by taking me to do karaoke somewhere in Koreatown after the show two nights ago. We had so much fun that I stayed out the second latest I ever have in New York so far (two-thirty AM. The SNL after-party stills holds the record at four AM.). Rodney was with me so Mom didn't freak out. After karaoke I was much calmer about tonight. I still had some minor meltdowns, but when I couldn't reach Austin, Dylan talked me off the ledge.

"I can't do this," I flipped out on the phone this morning. "I don't know what I was thinking. Live audience? LIVE? I can't go on live! What if I blow a line? What if I forget where to walk? What if I'm just plain awful?"

"You won't forget a line," Dylan's voice was calm. "You can sort it out, Kaitlin. You're brilliant as Andie. You're ready for Broadway."

"You really think so?" Talking to Dylan this week has been like taking a huge swig of water after spin class. Or catching your breath after a long walk. I feel better instantly.

"I know so," Dylan insisted. "I can't wait to say 'I told you so' after the curtain drops."

So that's what I'm doing right now. Trying to do the best job I can so that Dylan can say "I told you so" later.

"There is no point," Riley spits. She's wearing a cheerleading uniform and she thrusts her pom-poms in my face.

"It's just fun to point out the obvious, like Jordan's terrible roots." Someone else has a line and then Riley says: "This is your last chance, Andie. I want you to leave. Now. And don't even think of showing up in a cap and gown tomorrow or you really will have to pay for trying to humiliate me by kissing my boyfriend. It's your choice. What's it going to be?"

My turn. "I'm staying," I shoot back, shuffling my feet on the plastic table. I'm wearing a casual pink tee and loose-fitting no-name jeans I normally wouldn't be caught dead in. "And I'd like to see you try to stop me."

And scene! The curtain drops. End of act one.

The applause is deafening, even from backstage. I'd give anything to peek through the curtain and see what people are doing. I can hear people whistling and clapping, and I can't help feeling pleased. They liked it! They liked the first act with *me* in it!

When you're on a film set and you spend months making a movie, you never know how it will be edited or whether anyone will actually care to see it when you're done. It can be hard to find your motivation. But playing off the audience's reactions, like I've been doing tonight, is different from anything I've ever experienced. When they laugh, or they clap, or I catch a glimpse of someone's face and see their expression, it pushes me to want to emote more.

I rush back to my dressing room for a quick touch-up, a costume change — a major bathroom break — and another huge gulp of water.

"Kaitlin!" Forest swings into my dressing room and hugs me. Tonight he's in a suit and tie. (Usually he's in jeans and an untucked dress shirt.) "Excellent first half. Just as I expected. How do you feel?"

"Unbelievable." The words spill out of my mouth and tumble over each other. "I've never felt like this when I've acted. Thank you, Forest." I'm getting choked up. "This has been…"

"Now, now, don't ruin your makeup." He holds up his hands to stop me just as the makeup artist rushes in again. "Keep it up. I know you will. We'll celebrate after, okay?"

Dylan swings by my door next and I freeze. "Great job out there, treacle." I know now that's the British term for *friend*. "Did I tell you so?"

"You did." I hug him on impulse. Dylan's really been there for me this week and I can't thank him enough. Dylan hugs me back and neither of us moves. I'm very aware that Dylan's hand is on my lower back.

A voice over the backstage loud speaker crackles through my small dressing room. "FIVE MINUTES."

"I should…" I should what? Oh yeah, get ready!

"Me too. Got to hit the loo. And remember to keep my mic off." Dylan gives me a lopsided grin. "See you out there."

I take a few deep breaths to center myself. I'm not sure what has me more worked up: act two starting or Dylan, but I can't think about the latter right now. Instead I head to my spot on stage across from Riley. The curtain is down and our mics haven't been turned back on yet. She smiles at me.

"You're doing splendidly," she says. If I could, I would practically fall through the curtain and into the orchestra pit. "Of course, I wouldn't have ended the last scene the way you did. It was a row, but I pictured Andie having a more delicate touch. What do you think?"

Riley likes to pose the question as if I have a choice, but I don't. She's usually right. She's been at this a lot longer than I have and no matter how uncomfortable she makes me, she usually has a point. "I didn't think of that."

"No matter." Riley waves her hand away. "There is always tomorrow night for improvement, even if the critics have already made their decisions."

Groan. The critics. Does she have to keep reminding me they're watching? I've never acted in front of a critic before. Whenever they reviewed *FA* or one of my films, obviously I wasn't there to see their reactions. It's sort of unsettling to know there are people in the audience paying attention to my every line and emotion.

Riley laughs. "Bollocks! I didn't mean to upset you. You can't help it if your insecurities show on stage. It is your first time up there and, well, no one compares to Meg Valentine so don't you worry! I'm sure your press will be lovely." She looks pensive. "Just maybe tone down your attitude in this next scene. It's a tad overcooked, don't you think? Anyway, break a leg!"

Oh God. Maybe I am bad at this. Maybe I don't have what it takes to be up here. Maybe…I feel a hand on my shoulder.

"She's being a proper arse," Dylan whispers in my ear.

"You're brilliant. Give the second act all you've got." I blush at the feeling of his breath on my neck.

Dylan's right. All I can do is my best—whether critics are watching or not. No one calls "cut" in a play. No one asks to "do that take again." No one has a meltdown and berates a crew member. You keep going no matter what happens.

The second act flies by and I can't believe it's time for me to stand in the middle of the stage and take a bow. I'm holding hands with Dylan and Riley and the rest of the cast, and the audience is going wild. There are even people standing! A standing ovation! I look for Austin and see he's whistling. Then I look up at my family and friends and see they are smiling and clapping. Dylan is handing me a huge bouquet of flowers, since it's my opening night, and I bow again to even more applause.

What a rush! I feel like the First Lady!

And then the curtain falls again and everyone backstage is hugging and congratulating me and my head is completely spinning. I thank everyone for helping me get through my first night, even Riley. ("Don't worry! I'm sure you'll be stronger tomorrow!") I hug Forest, talk to everyone in the chorus, and make my way to the dressing area to change into my party dress (a fuchsia Plastic Island with spaghetti straps and a silk chiffon tiered bodice). On my way, Dylan stops me.

"You were brilliant! We should celebrate," he says with a cute grin. He's unbuttoned his shirt and I'm trying not to stare at his abs.

"I can't," I manage to say. "My —"

The word *boyfriend* gets caught in my throat. Whoa. What's that about? Why did I hesitate to say Austin's name?

"My boyfriend." Oh good, I've said it. "He's here and we're going out with my family." I still feel weird, though, and I can't look Dylan in the eye. That is so odd. What is happening to me? I know Dylan and I have been spending a lot of time together, but my heart belongs to Austin even if he's not here with me. Right?

RIGHT?

Dylan nods and looks at me wistfully. "A raincheck then. Have a great time."

"I will." Why do I feel all tangled up inside? There's no time to dwell on what I'm feeling. I have to get changed. Rodney is waiting for me to take me out the side door where fans will be waiting.

HOLLYWOOD SECRET NUMBER TEN: If you want to get up close and personal with your favorite actor, seeing them in a Broadway show might be one of the best ways to do it. Most actors emerge from a side entrance of the theater—never the front doors where crowds are—and take a few minutes to sign autographs or pose for pictures before they jump into a waiting car. They usually do this night after night after every show they perform in. Seth told me it's a great way to appear as down to earth as the rest of the cast. I like to think of it as a way of giving back to the fans who shell out anywhere from forty to sometimes two hundred dollars for a ticket.

Rodney has my arm as we open the side door and people start screaming. I can't help but smile. I was a little worried no one would be out here tonight, but the area is crowded with teens and adults. Some news outlets are out here too. I smile politely and wave to them, but my focus is on the fans. I scribble my name on as many *Playbills* as I can, take a few pictures, and then I'm in the car.

"Surprise," Austin says when I slide in pretty much on top of him, my chiffon dress gliding over the seats.

"What are you doing here?" I squeal and envelop him in a huge hug.

It feels good to hold him and as soon as I do, any insecurity I have about this increasing weirdness with Dylan seems to melt away. He's here! Austin is *here*. And if he's here, everything is going to be okay. It has to be.

"Rodney snuck me in," Austin says. He's wearing a navy suit and a yellow tie for the occasion and I couldn't be more touched. Plus, he fills it out perfectly. Liz and I were just complaining that no one dresses up for the theater anymore and it seems like such a shame. I remember coming to New York with my mom when I was seven for a *Family Affair* event and she took me to see *Beauty and the Beast*. I had on this poofy red dress and little black satin shoes and I felt like such a big shot sitting on a booster seat in the theater. I reach out to touch his tie, just wanting to be close to him. "Burke," he says, looking at me seriously with those big blue eyes of his, "you were incredible. I know I missed your calls a lot this week and I feel stupid because I know how stressed you must have been getting ready for tonight."

"It's okay," I say even though two hours ago it wasn't. I don't want to talk about bad things right now. "I know you're busy too." He's busy, but I've still managed to leave him encouraging messages about camp.

"It's not okay," he insists. "I've been a bad boyfriend, but I'm here now and I'm going to make it up to you. You looked amazing up there." He leans in to kiss me.

If I was at all unsure before, I know for certain how I feel right now. When Austin kisses me it feels like we haven't been apart at all even though it's been two weeks. I reach up with my right hand, my oversized silver clutch bracelet sliding up my arm, and touch his cheek. Austin's fingers interlock with my other hand. I'm starting to feel so much better. Anything I was thinking about Dylan before must have been in my head. Austin is the only guy for me.

"So tell me everything," I say when we come up for air. "How are the scrimmages? Do you like the camp a lot? What are your coaches like?"

Austin chuckles. "I know we haven't talked a lot this week, but I want to hear about *you* tonight. Did you feel like you were going to throw up?"

"No!" I swat him. "I was feeling faint, but in a good way. It's such a rush. Now tell me about your dorm mates. Who do you hang out with?"

What I really want to ask is if there is a girl who has been hanging out in his room when he isn't there. But I don't. Nadine, Liz, and Sky—amazingly she agreed with Liz and Nadine on this one—said I shouldn't bring it up. They said that I was overreacting and that the girl was surely a friend and Austin adored me (well, Sky didn't say that, but she did say he was that school boy I didn't shut up about). I know he adores me. I just hate that I can't see what's going on when I'm so far away.

"Murray and I pretty much stick together," Austin gives in. "The other guys seem cool. Some of them have been playing much longer than us. There are a few that are on more than one team. It never even occurred to me to be on a school team and a local one. Who has the time?"

I play with the uneven hem of my dress, feeling the purposefully frayed edges of the fabric. "You practice every afternoon. When would you work with another team?"

"I know!" He sounds incredulous. "But I guess that's what I have to do next year. I'm lucky the local league had room for me, you know? They even okayed the fact that I'll miss the first week of practice since I'll still be at camp."

"You signed up for the other league?"

"Yeah, I told you about that." Austin gives me a strange look. "One of the coaches is a coach at the summer camp so I had an in."

"No you didn't." I know I'm being argumentative, and ungracious, but I just can't stop it from coming out of my mouth. Things were so perfect a second ago!

"I could have sworn I did." Austin scratches his head, making his hair look even more tousled than it was a second ago. "It was during that call where you told me about the *SNL* review that said you and Sky should do a sitcom."

"I didn't tell you about that." I swallow, trying not to get annoyed. Austin is bringing up all the things that annoy me on the phone. "I wanted to, but you were half-asleep when I called."

"Oh, I must have read that on my own then." Austin plays with the band of his gold Citizen watch. "All my scrimmage scores are online to read too, by the way, in case you were wondering about how I was doing."

I'm always wondering how he's doing! Geez!

Okay, Kaitlin, stop.

Austin is here for a short time and I don't want to fight. I want to have a good time together. "I'll check them out," I say even though it kills me.

That seems to make him happy because he stops bickering too. "I can't believe I'm with you in New York City." He takes my hand. "And I'm here all weekend. Thanks for setting stuff up to do while you're working, but like I told my mom and sister, during shows, I'm going to be at the theater."

God, his eyes look amazing in the glow of the city lights.

"You can't watch me all weekend," I protest, even though I find the notion incredibly romantic. My boyfriend sitting in the front row, staring at me and only me on the darkened stage. Sigh...I think Broadway is making me more mushy.

"So," he says, and rubs my hand, "that was Dylan, huh?" He doesn't look at me when he says it, but then when he finally does look at me, he's sort of serious.

Sigh. Why does he have to bring up Dylan now? Just hearing Austin say Dylan's name makes me feel guilty, which is weird because I haven't done anything wrong.

I think. Is it wrong to have all these strange thoughts running through my head?

"The guy playing Leo?" I try to sound nonchalant. Austin nods. "Yeah, that's him. He's cool. He's been helping me with my lines."

"As long as that's *all* he's helping you with." Austin stares at me long enough that I can tell he means it. "He'd better not be hitting on my girl."

Is Austin jealous? No way. He's not the type. "I don't think so," I assure him, even though a tiny voice at the back of my head is screaming *Dylan is interested in you!*

"So *Hollywood Nation* has this one wrong — he doesn't have a major crush on you?" Austin asks slowly.

They wrote that? How did I miss that article? Nadine usually always shares that sort of stuff with me. "There is nothing going on there," I protest a little too strongly, and Austin looks at me oddly. Okay, even if Dylan is interested, I'm not. I just think he's cute and charming and very considerate. Which is allowed. I think. But I don't say any of that out loud. "My heart belongs to you." Wait. Did I just say *that* out loud? That was sort of corny. I blush a little, but it actually seems to be the right thing to say, because his full lips turn back up into a smile.

"Good." Austin doesn't have dimples like Dylan but his smile is even better. "So let's go over this again — I'm watching you work all weekend." I attempt to protest, but he puts his hand on my lips and levels his blue eyes on mine, tucking his chin in like he's administering a scolding. "That's why I'm here, Burke, to see you. In the morning we'll do some tourist stuff, and we can have dinner between your two shows tomorrow and brunch on Sunday. Burke, I want to be with you as much as I can. After this weekend, I won't see you…" He stops.

"You won't see me for at least a month," I finish glumly. We both looked at our calendars and realized the next few weekends — well, Mondays and Tuesdays for me — are crazy for both of us. Austin has back-to-back games and some aren't on campus. I have events that Mom booked in the Hamptons and here in the city. The first chance I'll have to go to Texas is the end of July. Then both Austin and I head home to Los Angeles in August.

"But I'm here now." He kisses me again.

While we're kissing I feel a vibration on my leg. I pull my phone out of my jacket pocket, and stare at it strangely. My phone isn't even on. "It must be yours." Austin pulls his own phone out of his suit jacket and looks at the screen before breaking into a wide smile. Then he starts texting.

"Is that Hayley?" I ask casually. "Tell her I swear we will find time to hit Bloomingdale's while you guys are here."

"Actually, it's someone from camp." Austin is still texting.

"This girl Amanda I'm friends with. She wanted to know how your show went."

Amanda? Hmm…"She didn't happen to answer your phone the other day when I called, did she?"

I know I said I wouldn't bring it up, but I can't help myself. Austin gave me an in!

Austin looks up, confused. "When did you call and I didn't answer?"

"The other day." I try to sound nonchalant. "I wanted to check on brunch reservations, but this girl answered and she acted like she didn't know who I was."

Austin nods. "If it was Amanda she was probably confused," he says. "She's been hanging out with us a lot. She just broke up with her boyfriend, Kevin, who's also at camp, and she's been pretty upset about it. We can't get her off our couch." He laughs. "But if it was her, I don't get why she didn't know you. I talk about you all the time." He looks worried, which makes me worried. Is he worried because there is something going on or worried because he thinks I'll be mad? He's not flirting with this girl or spending a lot of time with her, is he? Because that is so wrong!

It's wrong, but isn't it the same thing I'm doing with Dylan?

"I'm sure she didn't hear me right," I say quickly, feeling bad now for even bringing it up. "Besides, she knows who I am now, right?"

His phone buzzes again. Austin reads the text and laughs.

"What?" I ask, a frantic edge to my voice. Oops.

"Amanda again. She said something funny about camp, but it's too hard to explain."

Oh. A camp thing. Between Austin and Amanda. The A-Team. Fun.

Chill, Kaitlin. Don't act like a jealous girlfriend.

Austin texts back quickly and then, to my surprise, turns off his phone. "But that's enough for tonight. Tonight is about your Broadway debut." He puts his arm around me and I lean into his shoulder, feeling content. "And I can't wait to celebrate."

Friday, June 26

NOTE TO SELF:
Sat. AM: Empire State Bldg., St. Pat's, lunch @ Shake Shack
Matinee then dinner res.—where in midtown??? Nadine,
   help!!!
Sun. AM: Res. at Bubby's w/ A's fam, my parents, Matty, Liz
Matinee then dinner—Gramercy Tavern following show (is it
   still open??)
Mon. Off!
Tues–Sat.: B @ theater 5:30 PM–6 PM. Wed. matinee @ 2.

Kaitlin Burke Goes Broadway!   Tuesday, June 30th
**A totally biased review by self-professed #1 Burke fan,
Carly Asiago, age 16**

No one was more excited to see Kaitlin Burke take the stage than
me, but there were plenty of others in the audience who seemed
pretty stoked to be there too. Kaitlin had a huge turnout for her
debut, including her parents; her brother, Matty; security, Rodney;
assistant, Nadine (sorry I don't know all their last names); cute
boyfriend, Austin Meyers, with his mom and his sister, Hayley; and
some of Kaitlin's friends, like Vanessa Hudgens and Taylor Swift,
who gave me an autograph. Kelly Ripa was also there with two of
her three kids. But let's get to the show itself.

The story is AWESOME. They totally nail how it feels to be in high
school and deal with peer pressure. I love how they talk about the
different high school cliques and what it's like to be an outsider.
Kaitlin actually cries on stage at one point, has to kiss a boy (Leo,
played by Mr. McHottie Dylan Koster), and has to display a huge
range of emotions that are really tough to do. I don't care what
the *NY Post* says about Kaitlin's lack of stage presence—this girl
can act and she wasn't wooden at all. Kaitlin expresses all her
emotions perfectly, just like she did on *Family Affair.* I especially
liked the part when Kaitlin (I mean Andie) realizes that her crush
on Leo is really just a high school crush and it might be too late for
them to have their chance now that high school is over. That was a
hard part to watch, but completely true because sometimes when
you love someone you have to let him go because you know it will
never work out. I would suggest that the critic from the *Post*

go back and watch Kaitlin again. That guy from *Newsday* too who said, "Kaitlin shows potential but needs to work harder at commanding the stage rather than fearing it." If they had seen Kaitlin the second and third night—like I did—they would have seen how much more comfortable she was up there. Everyone has opening-night jitters. I know I did when we performed *Spring Awakening* last year at my school.

So in conclusion, I just want to say that Kaitlin is a great actress whether she's on TV, in movies, or up on stage. I'd watch her do a Tide commercial if it was the only way to see her! But for now she's here, in the flesh, performing every night for New York. If you're a Kaitlin fan, you don't want to miss it. Get tickets now!

SCOOP PATROL

Friday, July 3rd

Ava Hayden and Lauren Cobb Get Their Revenge!

The Gruesome Twosome—Lauren Cobb and Ava Hayden's nicknames given to them by Sky Mackenzie on Twitter—got their own *SNL*-type revenge last night when they hosted a Kaitlin Burke and Sky Mackenzie Boofest. "Boofest was our way to pull apart Kaitlin and Sky's work in the same harsh manner that they did to Ava and me," said Lauren Cobb, at the event.

The pair invited thirty of their closest friends to the Hollywood Forever Cemetery in Los Angeles to join them in bashing SKAT's work. Against a backdrop of mausoleums and tombstones, LAVA aired a key *Family Affair* episode, a pirated scene with both girls from *PYA*, illegal video from *Meeting of the Minds* (which was confiscated by cops after its airing), and Sky's now never-to-be-seen fall pilot.

During each video, LAVA took the mic to critique the actresses' work and invited the others to boo or throw trash at the screen. Ava even took to throwing tomatoes whenever either girl was shown. Others, like party boy Finn Grabel, just heckled. Alexis Holden, who was also on the guest list, felt it was only fair that Kaitlin and Sky receive the same treatment they dish out. "Ava and Lauren were mortified by the girls' appearance on *SNL*," said Alexis. "What they did was so cruel." Added another partygoer, who wanted to remain nameless: "There are so many people who can't stand Kaitlin or Sky either so it was nice to give them some payback. If you know what I mean. We even had some folks in New York—who shall remain nameless—who wanted to be here, but couldn't. They said they'd definitely join

us the next time we get together. Everyone got the biggest kick out of watching Kaitlin do a scene from her Broadway show. She's awful! I'm sure this will be her first and last stage appearance."

In the spirit of bashing, the girls also handed out Team LAVA tees, courtesy of www.starslikeustees.com, as part of the night's Boofest gift bag. "We got a lot of support and positive feedback from tonight's event," said Ava, holding her dog Calou, who was ripping a picture of Sky and Kaitlin to shreds with his teeth. "If those two want to get nasty, we can be even nastier. This feud is far from over."

ELEVEN: *Reality Bites*

"Sweetie, do you really think you should order *that?*"

That would be the Waz-Za, the waffle with the brûlée top that is on the menu at Norma's, this eatery inside the Le Parker Meridien on West 57th Street that has the world's best breakfast. The restaurant itself is pretty boring by restaurant standards — no actual windows to speak of, nondescript tables, and boring white tablecloths. But the menu is mouth-watering. Nadine and I found it one morning after we went to Broadway Dance for a few classes. That day we had the PB&C Waffle 'Wich, which is this to die for chocolate waffle with peanut butter and toffee crunch filling. But today Mom is here, and my dreams of eating carbohydrates are about to go up in flames.

My dad comes to my defense. "Meg, she's at the gym every day, let her eat in peace." Mom closes her mouth, but flustered, she raises one hand to the collar of her white Versace tank shirt and plays with a small pearl brooch there. Mom may be eating a fruit platter, but that's only because she's been so busy with the Darling Daisies committee that she has almost no time for her pilates, yoga, or yogalates. She does look tanner than ever thanks to so much time spent in the Hamptons. She's been spending half the week and weekends out there — leaving Nadine to chaperone me and Matty while she and Dad golf, hit Barefoot Contessa for dinner, and do charity stuff. I, on the other hand, am glued to the city limits with my work schedule, which is fine by me. I'm free most days till 4 PM so I have had plenty of time to sightsee, visit museums, and take spinning, Zumba, or cardio dance jam with Liz (when she's not in film class) and Nadine. I have to admit, seeing Mom less has made my stress level go way down. I'm not being barked at on a daily basis by anyone other than Riley.

"I'll have the Waz-Za," I say sweetly to the waiter, handing him the menu. I play with the collar of my yellow silk Alice + Olivia pleated dress.

"Hell, I'll have it too," Laney surprises me by saying. Laney pats her taut midsection, which is hidden under a gray herringbone cropped Johnson blazer and a light white tank top. Laney even has on a skirt today — a knee-length black pencil one — which is a rarity. "I'll pay for it with my trainer when I go home in two days."

Laney and Seth have been doing business in New York all week after my opening night. Both have several other clients in town doing morning shows or shooting movies and Laney has been busy dealing with what she calls "avoidable client nightmares that are giving me a permanent migraine." I keep telling her she has to drop clients who are named after famous cities or pieces of fruit. Thankfully though, having Laney and Seth in town gave Mom the opportunity she was dying for—a chance to powwow about my life post-Broadway. It's something I've been thinking about a lot, but pretending not to because the unknown still freaks me out. A lot.

"Laney, you need some sun. You're so pale." Mom clicks her tongue. Mom is dressed in a white tank top and white pants and even has a wide-brimmed white hat, which she took off when she sat down. She's all about white these days. "You have to join us in the Hamptons and have dinner with us at Laundry. Their crab cakes are to die for. I keep telling Kaitlin how much she'd love them if she'd take a night off." Mom raises her eyebrows menacingly, but I try to ignore her.

"Meg, you know she can't take any time off from the show," Seth reminds Mom gently, and rocks his sunglasses back on his head. Those shades are never far from Seth's eyes. "She signed a contract."

"Would it kill her to ask for one Saturday night off?" Mom protests. "It's July fourth weekend for goodness sake. No one is in town!"

"Except tourists," Dad points out. "Lots of tourists for those Macy's fireworks. Do you know what type of barge they put the fireworks on?" he asks Seth, who shakes his head. "The firepower on that barge is incredible and the boat they use to haul that stuff must be massive. I'm thinking of a duel engine motor yacht. Jimmy Harnold has a forty-two-foot Motor-yacht Fast Trawler that we were on last weekend. That boat can cook." Dad smiles widely, his teeth almost blinding me. They look so white against his tan skin, offset with a rumpled green Polo. With no car in New York except for rentals, Dad has been spending a lot of his time in the Hamptons looking at boats and their engines. He's seriously considering getting one when we get back to Los Angeles.

"Even the tourists know that the real scene is outside the city," Mom sniffs. "Everyone will be in the Hamptons this weekend except my daughter."

"Mom, I am sticking to my schedule." I point my fork at her. "My goal is not to miss a single performance. I'm eating well, sleeping a lot, exercising…doing all of the things I'm supposed to do when on stage. You heard what Kristin Chenoweth said the other day at the Calvin Klein luncheon."

"Yeah, yeah, get lots of sleep and rest," Mom clucks. "But you can't do that all the time. You could come out Saturday for a few hours for the Sun at the Shore house party, but you won't, or on Sunday for the Mercedez-Benz Polo Challenge, but you won't. It's only a three-hour car ride, if that! So you have to travel a little. Who cares? You'd be completely relaxed once you got there."

Nadine rolls her eyes at me, but neither of us says anything.

"Meg, I think she's being wise to rest up while she's in town," Seth continues, readjusting the yellow pocket square in his Theory suit. "Laney and I have been talking and we both agree — Kaitlin is in the best position she could be in right now. Everyone is still buzzing about her *SNL* stint and her Broadway reviews aren't shabby."

"If you ignore the *Post* and *Newsday*," Mom points out.

"But look at *Time Out New York* and TeenVogue.com," Laney reminds her and beams at me proudly. "They both said Kaitlin's voice is fresh, witty, and full of the spunk you need to compete with a live audience. Kaitlin is getting raves compared to what happened when Julia took the stage several years ago."

Laney is right. My reviews could be much worse. Even the *New York Times* said I wasn't an atrocity (I'm paraphrasing), which is positive considering what they've said about some stars who've hit Broadway. All in all, I'm pretty pleased with the reviews I'm getting. And the best one so far has come from Austin: "You're glowing when you're up there and that makes me happy because I know how happy you're making the people who are watching." Aww.

We had such a good time together last weekend. We vowed to be better about keeping in touch too. Austin and I promised to not miss our scheduled phone call before bed each night and we swore that if something was bothering us, we'd speak up rather than let things simmer. (That last one was my suggestion. Nadine read it in a relationship book. She thinks reading self-help books will help her find a "normal" boyfriend. Her word, not mine.)

"My point is, this is when we have to strike." Seth takes his Ray-Bans off his head. He stares at me intently.

"Everywhere I go someone is asking about *you*. People are talking about you. The play, *SNL*, your thing with Lauren and Ava...you're hot."

"So why not up her exposure in the Hamptons?" Mom tries again, almost pleading. "Darling Daisies is having an event this Saturday that Kaitlin would be perfect for. They're practically begging for an appearance. Kaitlin, would it kill you to do take the trek out and come back the same day? Or Sunday? Please? Please? I know you said you'd come out Monday to Tuesday, but no one worth seeing will be there on Monday. Sunday is the 'it' day this summer."

"The Hamptons have an 'it' day?" Seth's mouth twitches.

"She's begging," Nadine whispers. "You might be able to get anything out of her if you say yes. Hint. Hint."

Nadine's right! "Can I visit Austin next weekend?" I blurt out. My bargaining skills are clearly sorely lacking, but I can't help it. "My night off? Nadine will come with—"

"Absolutely not." Mom freaks and clutches her short strand of pearls to her neck. "I told you we could pop over for a visit in August before you head home, but visiting a boy unsupervised? Can you imagine the press? Austin's mother would not approve either, and you know it."

"Nadine will be there," I say, digging my fork into the tablecloth in aggravation. "What's the difference if it's Texas or New York City? You're not here watching me!"

Our waitress smiles politely as she places my food in front of me. I grab the little syrup pitcher and pour on a huge river of liquid, then cut off a giant piece and chew angrily while

I glare at Mom. I tap my foot anxiously and my coral Christian Dior mules almost slide off.

Mom sighs and takes a small dainty bite of a slice of cantaloupe. "You can have anything else." She seems to be mulling it over. "I'll let you go shopping at Blue & Cream or get a massage at the Naturopathica Spa when you come to the Hamptons. Sweetie, you would love it. Can't you at least think about it?"

Laney coughs and elbows me. Her fork clanks to the floor and I reach down at the same time as she does to retrieve it. She grabs my shoulder and looks at me quickly. "Just get it over with and she'll get off your back for the rest of the summer," Laney whispers. "I'll work on her about Austin."

Wow, Laney, thanks! We both sit up and Laney smoothes her napkin on her lap and then takes a sip of her iced tea while Mom stares at her suspiciously.

"Okay, I'll come to your event on Saturday," I give in and Mom shrieks and claps happily. "But I am not coming out Monday and Tuesday as well. It's too much."

"Fine," Mom agrees. "It's at 11 AM. We could have a car pick you up at seven and you'd be back by four-thirty at the latest. It's going to be a wonderful day. Darling Daisies teamed up with Sun at the Shore and we're having the Jonas Brothers and Selena Gomez plant seeds! You can do it too."

I side-eye Laney and she nods ever so slightly. "Fine," I mumble and take another yummy bite of my breakfast to wash down my distaste.

Mom is so happy she starts gobbling down her breakfast

and even swipes half of Dad's butter-laden English muffin off his plate.

"As I was saying," Seth tries again, sounding weary, "Kaitlin's career is having a good moment. I think we should strike now."

"I have offers?" I'm slightly excited even though I have no idea what he's going to say. I wipe my sweaty palms on the pleats of my short dress.

"Several coming in and several more have been mentioned," Seth tells me. "I have scripts for you to read and I'm not talking about teen slasher garbage. *Good* scripts. Coming-of-age movies and some headlining vehicles. You even have an offer to do a Judd Apatow film. Seth Rogen asked for you personally."

"Imagine that." Dad is glowing. "I've been hoping to get him for some of the productions I'm working on."

Seth doesn't reply to that, but smiles broadly as he announces his next tidbit. I have a bad feeling Dad's production company dreams may be over before they even really started. No one is calling him back. "I even have a pay or play offer." Mom gasps and drops her spoon in her decaf coffee with skim and Splenda with a loud clink.

HOLLYWOOD SECRET NUMBER ELEVEN: Pay or play offers are pure gravy deals in Hollywood. When an actor, director, or producer is offered this, it means that you're wanted so badly for the project that they'll pay you regardless of whether the movie ever gets made. They'll even pay you if you get replaced before production begins. It's a big deal.

"What's it for?" I ask breathlessly.

Seth brightens. "It's sort of a *Gossip Girl* meets *90210* meets *Greek* meets *Ugly Betty* set in a *Supernatural* meets *Lost* meets *Survivor*-type environment."

Mom says "We'll take it" at the same time Laney, Nadine, and I say "I don't get it."

"It is confusing," Seth hesitates, as always ignoring Mom over me. The man's a pro. "But worth reading the script. It tripped me up a few times too, but it sounds like groundbreaking material."

"Groundbreaking material that covers several shows that have already been done," Nadine mutters under her breath, and I giggle.

"I'll read the script this week," I promise and Seth pulls it out of his bag and slides the large manuscript over to me.

"There's something else I should mention." Seth sounds a bit unsure this time. "It's a cable TV show. A sitcom, actually, about six college freshmen who become tight and wind up best friends. It's tentatively titled *Little Fish, Big Pond* — get it?"

"I've heard of this." I lean forward, being careful not to let my yellow dress get bathed in maple syrup. "Gina mentioned it. Everyone wants in on this pilot. It's for mid-season. I heard Scarlett read for it. And Miley and Selena. Everyone wants it!"

"Well, they're looking for two girls to play roommates who battle but become good friends and they're thinking of two people in particular." Seth squirms slightly. "You and Sky."

Mom and Laney start laughing so hard that I think

food is going to come flying out of their noses. Even Dad chuckles in between bites of his Mexican omelet. Nadine and I look at each other. Nadine raises one eyebrow hopefully.

I don't know why, but the idea makes my heart race. My gut reaction is that I like the idea. Sky and I back on TV together doing something totally different from *FA* could be a lot of fun. I had a great time doing *SNL*, and Seth is right — Sky and I have good comic timing together. I'd love to play someone less serious than Sam. Could a sitcom with us as roommates actually work?

"Are you crazy?" Laney scoffs. "Those two are fire and ice. Don't get me wrong." She holds a palm up apologetically at me. "You two were superb on *SNL*, but your days of being a twosome are over. It's like Lauren and Ava. Enough is enough already! I have been exhausting myself calling around and complaining about their ridiculously lame Boofest, and now I'm dealing with their latest YouTube slandering. Yesterday those two fools actually invited paparazzi to film them filming their latest video spoof of you and Sky." I find myself actually stopping and thinking about what she just said, it's that confusing. "They had that dog of theirs, Calou, play Sky! They put a little wig on the poor thing."

Dad bursts out laughing and we all look at him. "Sorry. That sounds sort of funny." Mom shoots him a dirty look.

"The bottom line is I'm sick of this Team SKAT versus Team LAVA garbage and Lauren and Ava's D-listness." Laney slaps her hand down on the table, her oversized gold cuff emphasizing her point. "Kaitlin and Sky together are in danger of going the same way — we've been there, done that."

"I don't know about that," Seth disagrees. "Together the two are magic. Their comic timing was impeccable. Lorne Michaels and I were chatting about it the other day. He thinks both of them have a future in comedy."

Really? I'm about to ask more about this when Laney tsks.

"I say it's time to move on to something new," Laney insists. "Besides, those two always get along for three days, then brawl again."

"I agree," Mom interjects before I can get a word in. "I don't trust Sky. I know she's been spending a lot of time here lately, but that's just because she's out of work. As soon as she gets something new, she'll be back to being evil again. I don't want Kate-Kate dealing with that again. We don't need any more..."—Mom leans in close and whispers—"panic attacks."

Everyone murmurs their agreement.

"Is it an actual offer, Seth?" I ask tentatively.

"Not official," Seth tells me, "but we're in talks. I've read a rough draft of the pilot and I laughed out loud twice. That's two times more than I usually laugh when I read first drafts of sitcom pilots." He winks at me. "But I wanted you to know and keep it in mind."

"It sounds great," Nadine says to me. Mom glares at her.

"I think that's a pass." Mom shrugs.

It used to bother me so much when she'd do this, but it's beginning to seem funny to me.

"Can I read the pilot?" I ask without skipping a beat. Mom looks at me. Laney's and Dad's jaws drop. Nadine looks pleased. "I just want to read it," I try to assure them. "Sky and I are getting along fine — and for more than just three days, Laney. We've reached a new level of understanding." They're still looking at me. "I'm just saying I wouldn't be opposed to working with her again if the project was worth it."

"I don't like it," Mom protests.

"It's going to be a disaster if it happens," Laney echoes.

"I don't want you stalling out and getting water in your engine, sweet pea," Dad agrees. I'm assuming that's a boat analogy. I'll have to decipher its meaning later.

"I'll get it for you, Kaitlin," Seth says with a smile. "You read it — you all read it — and then tell me what you think. I think Sky's agent is getting a copy this week as well."

The rest of breakfast is more of the same. Laney enthralls us with tales of a client's recent book tour and a story about how the celeb author flipped out when a bookstore didn't have enough Sharpie colors for to her sign with. Mom talks about meeting Kathy Lee Gifford and how Kathy Lee swore Mom would make a good *Today* show host fill-in. (Nadine spits iced tea all over the table when Mom says that.) Seth laments the state of the film industry as a whole during a recession and Dad regales us with tales of being on a boat with Beyoncé and Jay-Z last weekend. Finally we pay the check — or I should say Seth does — and Nadine and Rodney and I split off from the group and head uptown to Broadway Dance to take a class. We both jump on our phones as soon as we're in the car — Nadine to confirm a dinner reservation I have for that night with Sky, and me to call Austin. I know it's not our scheduled time to talk, but I need his opinion on the thought of me working with Sky again. Am I nuts for remotely considering this? Is Sky even interested? Am I interested? The last thing I want is to sign on to a project and to be back in Sky Terror Level Orange territory. I dial Austin's room and let the phone ring three times.

"Howdy!" A girl starts giggling and laughing, which annoys me instantly. "I mean, hey! It's A and R's room."

"Hi, Amanda." I try to sound very grown up and worldy. "It's Kaitlin. Is Austin there?" I've tried to delicately tell Austin how much it bothers me to hear Amanda answer the phone, but he's either oblivious or he doesn't care. I don't want to get too crazy either since we're on such good terms after his New York weekend. I'm trying not to sound jealous, but it's hard when Austin keeps bringing Amanda up and telling me what a big help she is. Amanda is from Texas and went to the camp the year before so she knows the ropes. Camp tour guide or not, I am not happy about having her play phone cop.

"Oh, hey, Kaitlin," Amanda sings. I hear someone snort in the background. "Austin just ran down to the café to get us some drinks."

"Can you tell him to call me back?" I ask, trying to sound

pleasant even as I yell over two cabs honking at each other in the midtown traffic. "It's important."

"Sure thing! Listen, can I ask you something?" Amanda says as someone else whispers something I can't understand. "What's your last name?"

I pause. Maybe she already knows and is just teasing me, but if she doesn't know, then maybe she should. Maybe she'd back off. "Burke. My name is Kaitlin Burke."

The phone is silent. "So it *is* you! We saw your picture in A's room. Pam and I were looking at it earlier and she said that's that girl from *Family Affair*, but I said nah, A would have told us that. He just says 'Kaitlin.' He never brags about who you are. So you live in Hollywood and stuff?"

"And stuff," I answer importantly.

"Really?" Amanda sounds skeptical. "Austin doesn't seem Hollywood enough to date a celebrity, even if he does live in L.A. He's so...normal."

"He's so nice!" I can hear someone else in the background. That must be Pam. "Austin is cool. Not Hollywoodish."

"Starstruck is not in his vocab," Amanda continues.

Okay... "I know that. I love that about him." Amanda and Pam start to giggle. "Do you have a point?" I can't help but snap. I don't need my boyfriend described to me.

More whispering. What are they, two? "Our point is he's too good for you," Amanda says firmly and Pam snorts.

"Well, that's not your decision to make." I'm getting loud and my ears are getting hot with embarrassment and anger. "It's none of your business either. Tell Austin I called. Better yet, don't. I'll text him. I *am* his girlfriend, so I don't need to go through you." I hang up, pressing end angrily.

Nadine frowns. "Bad call?"

"Bad call."

And I'm not sure it will be the last one either.

Friday, July 3

NOTE TO SELF:
Tell A U will call his cell from now on.
Tonite: Dinner w/ Sky at Butter—11:00 PM. Lame, I know!
Sat: Hamptons pickup 7 AM. Sun @ the Shore party. Car
    back: 1 PM.

TWELVE: *Hitchhiking Hamptonites*

"This is the life," Liz murmurs. She's lying on a massage table in the middle of a large tent on the grounds of a multimillion dollar mansion that the New York City club The Cave rented for the summer in the Hamptons. They've dubbed the house the Sun at the Shore. On weekends it turns into a vacation outpost for celebrities, debutantes, and Hamptons socialites, and today they've partnered with Mom's Darling Daisies committee for an event. "This aromatherapy shiatsu massage makes me feel like I'm home."

"Liz Mendes, if I didn't know any better, I'd say you were homesick," I tease. I'm sitting in a massage chair next to her while someone from Pinky Toes, who The Cave brought in for today's event, gives me a pedicure (I went colorless for my manicure, since my nails need to be nude for the play anyway). For my toes, I picked a deep Bordeaux color to match the Tadashi pleated chiffon V-neck dress I'm wearing. "Weren't you the one who said New York was your future and Los Angeles was your past?"

"I changed my mind." Liz gets worked up, her arms swirling round and round, sort of like the print on the yellow and brown one-shouldered Grecian T-Bags dress she had on before her massage. "I miss my car and grass and the beach and…"

"In case you haven't noticed, you're *at* the beach," Sky gripes. For a moment I forgot Sky was even with us because she and Liz haven't snapped at each other for the last 3.2 minutes. I guess their relaxation treatments only go so far. Sky is getting a mani and a pedi at the same time. Two girls are working on giving her such pale nude nails and toes you'd think she didn't even get them done. Sky says that's the point. She'd hate to have her nails overpower her outfit (a mosaic Alice & Trixie long halter dress).

"It's not the same!" Liz props herself up on her elbows, knocking her masseuse backward. The woman was massaging her arms when Liz swung them forward to start making her point. Again. "If you spent any time at Venice Beach like me and my boyfriend do, you'd know that the beaches here are very different. And if you're a surfer, like Josh, the Pacific Ocean rocks."

"Are you a surfer?" Sky wants to know. "Because I thought we were talking about *you*."

"I am talking about me," Liz stammers. "I like the Pacific Ocean too."

"You said Josh."

"I meant me!"

"You didn't say you."

"I shouldn't have to!"

"Nadine," I call her phone quickly. "911!"

Nadine and Rodney are just outside the tent getting something to eat from Uncle Jimmy's Backyard BBQ. They are one of the caterers of today's party. They also have Cold Stone Creamery, The Juice Bar, Baja Fresh, and a number of other eateries on hand. I would never admit this to Mom, who is running around with the Darling Daisies having celebrities plant flowers, but this whole scene is pretty serene. Well, it would be if Liz and Sky would stop bickering.

"Why are you still here?" Liz is raising her voice now. Her curly hair is pulled off her face with a headband and she looks positively fierce. "Don't you have meetings to get to in Los Angeles? Oh, wait. Maybe you have none because no one wants to hire you!"

"And maybe you suck at your little summer workshop not because everyone is mean but because you can't direct or write!" Sky retorts.

Liz gasps. "How dare you!"

"How dare *you*!" Sky fires back. Our masseuses and manicurists just stare in confusion. We're lucky the tent can only hold about six people at a time for treatments or this would be more embarrassing. The only other clients in here are Liv Tyler, who looks amused, and one of the guys from Metro-Station. He just ignores us.

"Guys, you're causing a scene." I give a fake smile to the growing group of onlookers.

"I'm tired of her being around," Liz laments, pointing at

Sky. "I've had it! This was supposed to be *our* summer and Sky has totally crashed it. No one even invited her! She's mean, and you don't even like her. Tell her!"

My face colors. That is a bit harsh. Sky looks at me, her face beet red, which could be sunburn since she did refuse the Neutrogena SPF 45 I offered her earlier.

"Yes, K, tell her the truth." Sky's voice is strange, and she plays with her raven pigtails. "Tell Liz that I'm the only one who truly understands what you're going through. I get you and our Hollywood lives, and as an outsider, she doesn't have a clue."

Liz looks at me, and my face burns more. I pull my hair off my neck and fan myself. Maybe Nadine has an elastic band. They both have points, I know. Do I really have to choose?

Liz hops off the table, clutching a towel around her torso, and gets in Sky's face. "*I'm* her best friend."

"And *I* worked with her for over a decade," Sky retorts. "I've known her way longer."

I know I should be doing more to squash this, but I'm a bit mesmerized by the whole thing. Sky trying to claim she's the better buddy? I never thought I'd see this day unless it was part of a script. I look around and notice people are starting to peek their heads into the tent. Our masseuse is whispering heatedly to someone on the other side of the entrance. Next I see a photographer with a large camera and I duck.

"Guys! PAPS," I hiss as Nadine, Rodney, and Matty finally come running in to see what's happening. "CUT. IT. OUT."

"I'm leaving." Sky actually sounds upset. "I need tanning time." She passes by me and whispers so that only I can hear, "You should have stuck up for me."

"Sky, wait," I beg.

"Good, go!" Liz hurries to grab her dress and her bag and change in the makeshift dressing room in the back of the tent. "I'm going. I promised Meg I'd plant some begonias."

"What? You're going too?" I can't believe it.

"You shouldn't have let her talk to me like that," Liz huffs. "I need some air."

I look at Nadine, Rodney, and Matty. "Why am I here again?"

"Forget those two!" Nadine waves them away. "They'll get over it. You're here because your mom made you come, but the real reason you should be in this tent is to celebrate that SAT score of yours. You deserve some R&R." She hugs me, and she smells overwhelmingly of sunscreen. Nadine hates her pale skin getting any color whatsoever.

Last night, I got my SAT scores in the batch of mail Anita forwarded from home and I almost flipped out. I got a 492 in math, a 605 in English, and a 650 in writing. I left a message with Mom and Dad to share the good news, but they didn't call me back. Whatever. Nadine says this will go a long way in helping me with colleges, should I choose to go. Liz, Nadine, and I stayed up late and had a celebratory pajama party. We were going to keep the party going today since I don't perform tonight till the 8 PM show. How come the paparazzi can't print something like that?

"You're right." I cheer up a little, feeling proud of my accomplishment. When I think about how much stress I was under and all the craziness with Lauren and Ava this past spring, I can't believe I even managed to take the SATs. "I do deserve a little fun."

"You're not having fun if they're fighting," Matty points out. "Couldn't you get them to stop? I don't need to be seen with people acting like that. It's not good for my rep. I want to be known as the problem-free Burke. No offense."

Nadine and I look at each other. Matty is dressed in white linen pants and a shirt, like he's a genteel rapper. The clothes hang loose on his boyish frame. His shades haven't left his eyes since we arrived early this morning. He thinks everyone is looking at him or wants his autograph. Matty lowers his shades slightly. "See that girl over there?" We look and see a teen waving animatedly at Matty. "She's been stalking me all day. How cool is that? Maybe I'll make her morning and go say hi."

"Yes, go make her morning, Matt." I purse my chapped lips (I forgot to put sunblock on them). "We'll catch you later."

Nadine and I apologize to the Pinky Toes folks and head back outside in the bright sun. Rodney trails behind us with his Cold Stone sundae. The Cave's mansion is directly ahead of us and it is incredible. Everything inside and out is white, even down to several dozen lounge chairs and beach umbrellas. They have a large infinity pool that people are lounging at and a DJ is spinning nearby. The pool is only a short distance to the beach, which you can get to by following the tall reeds dotting a small path through the bushes.

"Matty is right about one thing," Nadine says a few minutes later. "Liz and Sky both adore you and can't stand each other. What are you going to do about it?"

"I don't know." I feel thoughtful—this is a complete surprise for me. "I guess hang out with them separately. I feel guilty lying to either of them. Yesterday Sky and I were getting lunch and Liz called and I didn't say who I was with. And then Sky asked who I was on the phone with and I lied to her too! I know I'm a coward but I don't want to fuel the fire. I like being with both of them. Even Sky! She's right about us knowing each other well. And Liz is right that she's my best friend. I just feel guilty about Lizzie because we had this huge fight a few months ago about Mikayla."

"That was different though." Nadine shakes her head, her gold diamond studs glittering in the bright sun. Nadine looks so cute in that ocean blue Laila strapless dress I lent her. She takes a small filet mignon toasted bread bite from a passing waiter. "You weren't really fighting about that girl from NYU, you were fighting about not being there for each other."

"Still." I take an appetizer of my own. "What do you do when you have two friends you like and they don't like each other?"

Before Nadine can answer, a woman rushes at me, her face covered in a white mask that smells like sour cream. Her hair is covered in a shower cap. I shriek and jump back.

"Hi, sweetie!"

"Mom?" I stutter as someone takes a picture of me looking horrified. The woman leans in and smiles.

"Of course it's me, silly!" Mom laughs. "I'm wearing a daisy face mask made with fresh daisy blossoms." She touches her face gently with one baby-pink manicured finger. "It's age-defying, Kate-Kate. You have to try one. You wear it for twenty minutes. We just gave one to Christie Brinkley."

Nadine is covering her face behind my shoulder and trying not to laugh. "I don't think I should, Mom," I say as gently as I can, looking around. "I can't have my skin break out before a show."

We've obviously reached the Darling Daisies area of the event. There is a large flower bed where stars are on their knees on gardening pads and they're using hoes and planting seeds. Is that Katie Holmes? Whoa.

"Suit yourself." She fixes the shower cap, which looks like it might blow off in the breeze. Mom is wearing a fitted pale blue linen dress to go with her shower cap motif. She smiles at another woman walking by in the putrid-smelling mask. "The First Lady is stopping by later, and we're told she'd love a daisy mask. You'll miss her though since you have to go back for your *show*."

She says the word *show* as if we're talking about the plague. I smile sweetly and finger the purple chiffon on my dress. "I'm here now, Mom. What can I do instead?"

That seems to appease Mom a bit because she changes the subject. "I need you to go plant some seeds, Kate-Kate."

"Mom, did you get my message about my SAT scores?" I ask, and beam at Nadine.

"Yes," Mom says, sounding excited. "Thank God that is

finally over with and you can stop worrying about school." Nadine glares at her. "Now go plant, and then are you going to stay and have some lunch? We're having a daisy salad with strawberries."

For some reason, the word *lunch* makes me smile. Lunchtime is twelve-thirty — which is normal for most people, but it's only been the last few months that I'm on a semi-normal schedule.

HOLLYWOOD SECRET NUMBER TWELVE: On set, lunch is usually not held during lunchtime. Lunch could be held during normal lunch hours, but it could also be served at six PM. It depends on what the halfway point through the shooting day is. If you start work at eight and you are ending at four, then yeah, lunch is probably at a regular time. But if you start shooting at one PM and end at eleven PM, then lunch is probably at six PM even though that's technically dinner. Also, "lunch" is the only meal served on a set. Breakfast is usually served from a truck, and crafty has lots of snacks, but lunch is the only real meal. Of course, since it's the only real meal, there is unwritten protocol about how you line up to get food. Cast lines up ahead of the crew, then the crew lines up ahead of any background people. The director can cut and go first, but usually he bands together with the crew. At least our *FA* director Tom Pullman did.

Thinking about Tom makes me think about *FA* and my smile turns into a frown. I miss my show.

"Stop frowning, you'll get frown lines," Mom scolds me.

"That daisy facial would do wonders for that, you know. Dylan, will you tell her how wonderful it is, please?"

Dylan? My Dylan?

I don't mean "*my* Dylan," just the Dylan I know. Oh, forget it.

I look up. The only person near Mom that could fit that description is a guy in a white polo shirt and wrinkle-free navy shorts who is wearing a face mask like Mom's. Oh, no.

"Dylan, tell me you didn't!" I can't help but laugh.

"Of course he did." Mom sounds a bit offended. "He even took pictures for me with that little friend of his."

Now I'm full out laughing and so is Nadine. Mom throws her hands up in disgust and stomps off. Dylan's face is covered in drippy goo with tiny flecks of flowers and it's dripping onto his shirt. At least it's white.

"Laugh now, but my skin is going to look bloody great," he says to me, putting his hands on his hips and striking a pose.

"It's been twenty minutes," a woman in a daisy apron chirps, and she starts scrubbing Dylan's face right in front of us, which just makes me laugh harder.

"I'm sure it will," I say, trying to compose myself now that the woman is giving me nasty looks. "How did you get roped into this one?"

"Your mom spotted me," he admits. "She said it would help her out if I would do it so I agreed to be a good sport. How could I say no? The woman fed me dinner the last few nights."

Dylan has been hanging out with me in the afternoon, which means he's around when I have my early (four-thirty PM) dinner before the show, so Mom has been feeding him too. Matty seems to think Austin wouldn't like Dylan eating with us, but as I told Matty, Austin isn't around to gripe. He's not even around to talk to! Our pledge to make nightly phone calls at the same time seems to have dissolved in little over a week. Now whenever we do talk, one of us is blaming the other one for not calling. Or we flat out forget. I've been with Dylan so much this weekend, I forgot to even try reaching Austin.

Wow. That makes me a terrible girlfriend, doesn't it?

"I'm so sorry," I tell Dylan in between giggles.

"Don't be," he says. "This stuff tastes great." He takes a finger and swipes his left cheek and then sticks the finger in his mouth. "Seriously, try it."

"Eww." I make a face. "I'm not eating off your chin!" Nadine is laughing so hard now she can't control herself.

Dylan swipes a dollop from a nearby container. He holds it out to me. "Don't pull a face like that until you try. Come on, darling. Take it."

Skeptical, I wipe my index finger along the length of his and stick it in my mouth. Nadine coughs. Of course, someone catches a picture, but I don't say anything. Wow. That's not bad. "Peppermint?"

"And lime," says Dylan with a smile. I'm starting to see his face now that he's almost completely wiped clean. He touches his cheek. "Hey. Your mom is right. My skin is baby soft."

I can't help but commend her. "She knows her products."

Nadine, finally composed, grabs my elbow. "I'm going to grab a daisy mojito. I'll be right back. Kaitlin, we have about two hours before the car comes."

"I'll go too," Rodney says. "I could use another sundae."

"Gotcha." I look at Dylan. "So you decided to take a day at the beach yourself, huh?"

"Yeah, I'm heading back in a little while with Riley." He shifts uncomfortably. "She hired a car for us."

I love how Dylan has all these cute British phrases I've never heard before—like hire a car instead of rent a car. Or waiting in queue instead of waiting in line. Or bits and bobs when he means this and that. He sounds so cute. I sigh. Keep it professional, Kaitlin!

"It's nice Riley is here too," I lie. I certainly don't need another lecture about how I can improve my performance or my Broadway education.

"Liar," Dylan says, watching me, and a rogue white blob drips down his face.

"You have a little spot on your cheek." I grab a wet wipe and scrub gently at his face. Our faces are kind of close and when I lock on his green eyes, we stare at each other. I quickly look away even though Dylan is still staring at me. I feel very hot all of a sudden. Must be the ninety-degree weather.

"Kaitlin, I know you have a partner and I'm not the type of bloke to get in the way of that," Dylan starts to say, sounding all soft. "But I can't help feeling a connection between us."

Oh, no. He trails off as the wind picks up, sending my hair all over my face. He brushes my bangs away and I take a deep breath, barely moving.

I will myself to turn away, even if he is giving me goosebumps. "Dylan, I—"

"Oh! Sorry! I don't mean to interrupt such a private moment. Wait. Dylan?"

We both turn around. Riley's hair is spilling around her face and bare shoulders, her pink embroidered cotton dress swaying in the breeze. She looks as confused and uncomfortable as I am. I feel like I was just caught doing something very wrong. Why aren't I pushing Dylan away more? I love Austin.

But Austin is not here and he's never around, a little voice says.

Still! He's my boyfriend. I love Austin. Dylan is cute, but that's it.

So then why do I feel so confused?

"I didn't know, I mean, I..." Riley trails off, sounding the most unsure I've ever heard her. She looks down, her hair creating curtains around her face. "I didn't know you and your partner broke up, Kaitlin."

"We didn't." I say it so fast I don't even take a breath. "Austin and I are still together."

"Oh, I see." Riley's tone turns sort of chilly, which isn't normally how Riley sounds. She may have a lot to say about me, but she always says it pleasantly. Right now she actually sounds upset. "I guess you two were just rehearsing your lines for the love scene in the show. That's why you look so chummy."

"Riley." Dylan starts to walk toward her, but she backs away. I look at Dylan oddly. His face is strained.

"No, don't let me interrupt this moment for you two." She sounds shaky. "Kaitlin needs all the help she can get with that scene. I'll see you later, Dylan. The car is coming around two PM. Later, Kaitlin."

I look at Dylan and his face is all twisted and bothered. What's up with that? Could there be a history there I don't know about? I'm so curious I can barely hold my tongue.

"I should look after her." Dylan seems flustered so I don't push it. "Can we finish this later? I really want to talk to you about—" I manage to nod and he takes off without even saying goodbye.

I push what just happened will Dylan and Riley out of my head and look for Nadine and Rodney. I walk over to the Darling Daisies area and see Mom is busy talking Katie Holmes's ear off about daisies. Katie looks miserable. Matty is holding court in a nearby cabana with a group of giggling teen girls. I decide to look for Liz and/or Sky instead. Both of them like to lounge, so they might be by the pool. On my way there I stop a few times to talk to people I know or to people eager to introduce themselves. I'm actually surprised to see so many stars in town. I had no idea this many people spent time in the Hamptons. I run into Vanessa and she tells me about that shop Mom loves, Blue & Cream. Ashley is with her and she raves about the Hampton Social @ Ross concert series. It's an exclusive concert series where people pay big bucks to see acts like Billy Joel or the Jonas Brothers.

It sounds like there is a ton to do and it almost makes me wish I had more time to do it. Maybe I can squeeze a full weekend in before we head home in August.

There's still no sign of Nadine, Rodney, Sky, or Liz anywhere, so I sit down by the pool for a minute and decide to have one of those cool-looking peach iced teas the waiter is serving. Then I lean back on the lounge chair and close my eyes. I have a good hour or more before I have to leave and I am sort of exhausted from the drama of this morning. I guess there's no harm in lying here for just a few moments. It feels as though I've barely closed my eyes when I feel something cold and wet dripping on my chest. I jump.

"Oops!" Lauren Cobb is standing over me with an ice cube. She's wearing the tiniest dark brown bikini I've ever seen. Ava is standing next to her with her hair in a turban, and she's wearing a pink terry beach cover-up over a teal bikini. Calou is in her arms. He's also wearing a pink bandanna. He growls at me. Both girls have on large, oversized Chanel sunglasses that I suspect are brand-new. There is a gift suite here and I saw a sunglasses station. Two of their posse are wearing TEAM LAVA T-shirts (they have a picture of two Barbies on them that look like Lauren and Ava). "Super sorry. Did I get that on your last-season dress?" Lauren asks.

My mood darkens. What are these two doing here? And why the heck are they at the same party as me? There are nine million events going on in the Hamptons on any given weekend. The two of them stare at me like I'm a rat and they're snakes. I've seen them do this to others when I used to hang out with them. I notice they have the paparazzi with them. Of course. But I'm not getting into an altercation. Not at Mom's event with her people here. And besides, I'm trying to be so good and avoid being as obnoxious as they are. But if there was ever a time to forget my vow, it would be now.

It takes all of my willpower to say, "It was an accident." I grab a towel and dry off.

"Not." Lauren sounds like a horse when she laughs. "I did it on purpose and it felt good." She high-fives Ava and they both smile for a nearby camera.

I roll my eyes. "I have to get going." I scan the crowd for Sky and Liz, but still don't see either of them. Nadine and Rodney are MIA too. Where are they? It's almost one-thirty — I guess I actually fell asleep for a bit — and we have to leave by two PM. I should call Nadine. I start texting her.

"Back to Manhattan for your little show, right?" Ava sounds giddy and I'm not sure why. "How's that going?"

"Great," I boast, not looking up. "Couldn't be better."

"Bet you're being little Miss Goody Two-shoes and getting there early every night," Lauren adds and looks at Ava.

"I've never missed a performance," Ava mimics my voice.

"That's right." I ignore her sarcasm. "Bye, ladies. Don't forget to wear sunscreen. I wouldn't want you to look like lobsters by tonight." I start walking away.

"Why don't you stick around and see for yourself?" Lauren asks.

"I'm working," I call over my shoulder. "I'm leaving for the city now."

"No, you're not," the two of them say and burst into giggles.

I slowly turn around. "What are you laughing about?"

"You." Ava is barely able to get the words out. "You're stranded."

"If you've done something to my mother's ride, you've screwed up." I shrug. "We're not heading back together. Nice try, though."

"We're smarter than that." Ava is totally cool. "We canceled *your* car. Just now. Saw the driver waiting out front and told him you weren't leaving. We told him you were canceling."

"That's impossible." I try to remain calm, but I'm freaking out. "There is no way the driver would have believed you."

"He would if someone posing as you called him to confirm the cancellation." Lauren's eyes are big and misleadingly innocent. "Your ride is gone. And good luck getting another one on July Fourth weekend. Especially with half an hour notice. That's how much time you need, right?" She walks toward me slowly as the color drains from my face. "To get back in time and be ready for your little performance. Oops!" They laugh even harder.

I'm too upset to zing it back to them. Instead I race off to find Nadine. I do two laps around the party, looking like a crazy person, I'm sure, before I actually spot her. She's walking toward me with Matt, Rodney, Liz, and Sky, who strangely look similar in their long summer printed dresses. Neither are talking to each other, but they're not yelling either.

Nadine sees my face and her jaw drops. "What's wrong?"

"The girls—" I don't stop for a breath. "Canceled my car," I get out. "Lauren." *GASP*. "Ava. They're here. Nadine, I won't make it back in time." Everyone's faces are stricken.

"Where are they?" Rodney growls.

"That's impossible." Nadine fumbles, and her hand reaches around in her bag for her binder and her BlackBerry. "I have a confirmation number. The car has been here since one. I ordered it early just in case." She starts dialing while I stand there, panicked.

"I'm with Rod. Where are they?" Sky growls. "I'm going to give them a piece of my mind!"

"Me, too!" Liz's chin tightens. Any second I expect the pair of them to pick up lightsabers and tear after the Gruesome Twosome. "They've gone too far this time."

"I'm going to find Mom," Matty says, and runs off.

"I did not cancel the car!" I hear Nadine yell into her phone and my heart sinks. They really did it. I look at my watch. If I leave right now, I'll make it. If I don't, I won't have enough time to prep, but I can still get there. I need a car right away.

Nadine grunts angrily. "They did cancel your car, but don't panic. I'm going to call a few other car services right now." Nadine sounds worried, even though she's not saying it. "DON'T MOVE."

"Kaitlin, it's going to be fine, don't freak." Liz touches my arm.

"Yeah, we'll get you back there in no time," Sky adds. She

looks at Liz out of the corner of her eye. Liz eyes her too. Neither says anything.

"I'll call some people too," says Rodney, and starts to dial. "We'll get you there."

"If I miss the show on this short notice, Forest will kill me!" I'm trying not to hyperventilate. "My understudy can't perform on Saturday night. That's the most important show of the week! People are paying to see me."

Liz's phone rings and she grabs it. "Uh-huh. Yeah. Are you serious? NO! You tell her! Okay. Okay!" She hangs up and looks at me nervously. "That was Matt. Your Mom is MIA. Something about driving to get more daisies for the facials. She's not answering her phone."

"I'm dead." I want to pass out. I knew the Hamptons were a bad idea on a work day! Why did I listen to Mom?

"I called three car services, but no one has anything available till four-thirty PM," Nadine says, wincing as she says the words.

"No one is free," Rodney adds. "Everyone is out already."

"This can't be happening." I sink into a nearby white wicker chair. "This cannot be happening. I can't miss the show. Why would I think I could do a one-day trip? I'm going to kill Mom!"

"Hey, cut yourself some slack." Sky puts a hand on my shoulder and I wince as her spiky black beaded bangle scratches me. "Nadine says Dylan was out here too."

"DYLAN! OF COURSE!" I yell, startling everyone, as well as a couple kissing on a lounge chair nearby. "I'll get a ride with him. I'll be right back." Before rushing off, I turn and hold up my palms to them. "Don't move!"

I race to the front of the house where all the cars are lined up with the valet. Dylan was leaving at two as well, so if I can catch him, I'm saved. I run up and down among the town cars and Priuses, but I don't see him. Just when I'm about to turn around and head back to Liz and Sky, I see a girl in a stiff pale pink dress.

"Riley!" I run toward her and grab her shoulders. "Thank God you're still here." I practically hug her I'm so relieved to see her. "I need a ride back. These girls canceled my car and we were supposed to leave by now. I can't get another car this quickly. I need a ride with you. Is that okay? I'll just call Nadine and tell her." I start to dial.

"No." Riley's voice is so quiet, I almost think it was the sound of the wind howling against the side of the weathered shingles on the house.

I look up, confused. "What did you say?"

"I said no." Riley sounds eerily calm. "We don't have the room. The car is full."

"But it's just you and Dylan!" I protest.

"It's a small car." Riley's mouth starts to turn up in a little smile.

"Riley." I'm trying to be patient, but I'm going to lose it any second now. "I know you like Dylan, okay? And it looked like something was going on between us before but it wasn't."

Riley's chuckle is high and off-pitch. "Rubbish! You can lie to yourself all you want, but you're as into Dylan as he is into you." Her face twists slightly. "I should know since Dylan and I were once partners. Then I dumped him for some tosser and I instantly regretted it. But it was too late. He met you at auditions and you were so lovely that the wanker was smitten. He never looked back." She looks so sad I almost feel sorry for her.

"I'm sorry, Riley." I know how I would feel if I were in her (less than desirable) brown Easy Spirit sandals. "Maybe you can still fix things with him. I'm not interested in him that way. I swear! You can tell him that, okay? Take him to lunch or something. Get him alone." Riley seems to be mulling the idea over. "But right now, I have something more important I need to worry about. I need a ride. If I don't get in the car with you, I might not get back at all."

But instead of changing her mind, Riley actually starts to walk away. "Riley!" My voice is so panicked it comes out like a squeak. Even some of the waiting drivers turn around.

Riley waves. "Sorry, darling. You gave me a brilliant idea there. If I don't take you back to the city with us, then I have Dylan all to myself to tell him the truth. Thanks, treacle."

"Riley, please." I'm begging now. "This is for the show. You wouldn't mess up the show, would you?"

"I would never mess up the show," Riley says evenly. "And with you not there, I won't be. Your understudy is superb."

I start to panic. "I'll call Dylan!" I blurt out. I don't want to use this card, knowing now how she feels, but I have to. I'm desperate. "He'll take me. He won't leave me here."

Her smile is sort of creepy, just like the gap between her

two front teeth. "That might have worked if he actually had a mobile with him." I feel my stomach lurch and I know it's not from the weird daisy salad I tried. "He forgot it at his flat. Didn't he tell you when you were getting cozy by the beach?" I start to blush. "Well, got to go. And don't think of following me and begging either. I'll tell Forest you can't make it."

I burst into tears and crumble against the valet stand. One of the valets has been watching our spat and he hands me a tissue. My entourage comes running.

"What happened?" Sky asks. "Didn't you get a ride?"

"She wouldn't take me," I sob. "She refused." I fill them in quickly, in between huge gulps and blowing my nose. The valet continues to hand me tissues as I sob. Liz and Sky offer words of encouragement while Nadine continues trying every number she knows.

"You'll get back." Liz pats my back soothingly.

"They can't start without you," Sky agrees.

"We'll make sure you get there," Matty adds.

"We won't let you miss the show," Nadine tells me, sounding both delirius and determined.

Rodney is still on his cell phone and he's asking everyone at the party if they have a car we could borrow...for six-plus hours since that is the amount of time it would take to get the car to Manhattan and back out here. Without traffic. Groan...

"Excuse me, miss?" I look up at the valet and I realize he looks a lot like Matty. "Did you know this house has a heli-pad? Maybe you could take a helicopter back to Manhattan.

The owner does all the time and I believe it's only a half hour ride."

I stop sobbing and look at the others. Sky breaks into a smile.

"Where is the owner?" Nadine asks, grabbing the valet by his white Polo.

"He's out back," says the guy, startled. "Cecil Caren. He's the short, pudgy guy in the Cave tee. He loves that show you guys were on, by the way."

"He does?" Sky asks.

"Actually his daughter Tabitha does," the guy says. "Never missed it."

"Guys, let's MOVE!" Nadine barks, her eyes wild. "Kaitlin, get your game face on. Sky, prepare to schmooze! Rodney, prepare to intimidate! We're hitching a ride on a helicopter to Manhattan."

Nadine charges off and the rest of us follow, as fast as our legs will take us.

Saturday, July 4

NOTE TO SELF:
Cost of a helicopter ride per person to Manhattan: approx.
    $550
Actual cost of helicopter ride to Manhattan: 1 day of shopping
    with Cecil Caren's 12-year-old daughter.
Getting to the *Meeting of the Minds* theater before Riley:
    Priceless

Scene 11:

Andie runs into an empty hallway and throws her
books on the floor. She screams at the top of her
lungs.

JORDAN:

Whoa. She's going to go all Carrie on us.

BECCA:

Or we're going to have to get her on Dr. Phil ASAP.
Andie, sweetie, are you okay?

ANDIE:

No! *(shouting)* I don't know what I'm doing. I don't
know what I was thinking telling Leo the truth. Me
giving Jenny lip? Am I crazy? You don't take on the
cheerleading squad.

JORDAN:

Some might disagree with that.

ANDIE:

I shouldn't have tried to change things. You don't
buck the system. I am who I am and that's it! I am
never going to be an "it" girl or the girl who gets
the guy of her dreams. I should have stayed safe for

twenty-four more measly hours and then all this
would have been behind me.

BECCA:
Andie, you're wrong! You gave it your best shot. You
dared to do something none of us had the guts to do
for four years.

JORDAN:
You made Jenny speechless. I don't think anyone has
ever done that. Ever.

ANDIE:
And where did it get me? I'm in the same place I was
always in, but now I'm just humiliated and reviled.
Let's face it—Leo didn't kiss me because he wanted to
kiss me. He kissed me to get a reaction out of Jenny,
who treats him like garbage.

BECCA:
You don't know that.

ANDIE:
I do know that. She walked in when Leo kissed me and
he acted all embarrassed. I'm as sure of that as I am
sure that we're going to graduate tomorrow morning. I
just might not be there to accept my diploma.

BECCA:

You can't be serious!

ANDIE:

I can't face all those people again. I feel like an idiot.

JORDAN:

As far as I'm concerned, you should be class valedictorian! You've got guts, Andie Amber. Stand up there tomorrow morning and be proud of your humiliation!

ANDIE:

No, I'm done. I'm going to go back to what I always was—a fly on the wall.

LEO:

Before you just disappear from my life again, can I have the chance to change your mind?

(Andie, Jordan, and Becca jump.)

THIRTEEN: *"Lucky" Thirteen*

"THIRTY MINUTES." They announce over the backstage intercom.

Thirty minutes. I look at the rickety clock on the wall. Okay, that's still enough time. I don't have to leave my dressing room for another twenty minutes and I'm already pressed, powdered, and polished for tonight's performance. I've got plenty of time to talk to Austin during today's scheduled phone call.

If our phone call actually happens.

I can't believe I'm going to say this, but this is my fault as much as it is his. Sometimes I actually forget to call him for a few days. The longer I'm away, the more this seems to happen. I suspect Austin is going through the same thing because sometimes he forgets to call too. But after Riley made that comment about Austin and me being on the rocks since I was hanging out with Dylan, I'm more determined than ever to prove my relationship is solid.

I take a deep breath, dial Austin, and let the phone ring.

It rings three times. I'm about to hang up when I hear some-one pick up.

"Hello?"

Oh wow! He's there! He said he would be and he's really there!

"Austin? It's me!" I say excitedly. He was actually in his room when he was supposed to be and he picked up instead of De-Manda. Yay!

"Hey, Burke," he says sounding all sleepy. "What time is it?"

Wait. He was sleeping during our scheduled phone call? Okay, maybe he was tired. I'm overreacting. It's no biggie.

"Seven-thirty in New York. I go on in a half hour," I remind him pleasantly. "Plenty of time for us to catch up during our *scheduled* phone call." I can't help throwing that in.

"I wanted to talk to you about that, actually," Austin says with a yawn. "Don't you think scheduling phone calls seems sort of forced? Can't we just call when we want to call? I want to call you all the time."

But you don't, I want to say. You don't call and then when I call you're not there. "I hate the schedule too," I admit. "But if we don't set a time, we don't talk. When I'm free, you're busy and when you're free, I'm at work. Then when we do talk, it's for five minutes. The most we get to catch up on is the weather."

"It's sunny here and ninety-five," Austin jokes. "Okay, got to go. Just kidding."

"Ha, ha," I say, but I'm not laughing. Doesn't he see how

serious this is? We need to be in touch more or else we'll just forget about each other and start spending all our free time with other people who are readily available and willing to hang out, and make us laugh, and help us with our problems.

Like I'm doing with Dylan.

That's okay though because Dylan is a friend. Okay, maybe I have a *slight* crush on Dylan. But I don't *like him* like him. I just sort of like him.

NOOOOO!

How can I sort of like Dylan? I love Austin!

But Dylan's here. And he actually takes my phone calls!

I want Austin to take my phone calls!

What does that say about me that I can't handle a few months' separation from my boyfriend? We're never going to survive college!

I fiddle with the picture of Austin that is tucked into my mirror. It's my only personal touch from home in here. It's a picture of us at Disneyland. We're posing with Mickey. Seeing Austin's smiling face makes him seem so real. I should look at this all the time because when I don't...sometimes I actually forget about him.

Paging Dr. Phil! What does *that* say about me as a girlfriend?

"How are you holding up there? Riley still giving you a complex?" Austin asks.

"She hates me." I sigh. "I almost missed the show the other night because she wouldn't give me a ride back from the Hamptons."

"What were you doing in the Hamptons on a workday?" he asks.

"It's a long story." Too long and tiring for this phone call, I want to say. "The bottom line is she left me stranded! She's never gotten over Dylan even though she dumped him and now he likes me and she's mad at me. Like that's my fault."

OH GOD.

Did I just say out loud that Dylan likes me?

I don't have my boyfriend manual handy, but I think telling your boyfriend that another guy likes you is one topic of conversation you are supposed to avoid. "I mean *she* likes Dylan," I backpedal.

"You said Dylan likes you," Austin says, sounding wide awake now.

"Did I say that?" I laugh nervously. "I meant Dylan likes Riley."

"No, no I think what you said is Riley is mad because she used to go out with Dylan and Dylan likes you. Which is funny because that's what I've been saying to you all along, isn't it?" I notice a slight edge to his voice. My heart starts to beat faster.

"I can't control what Dylan thinks," I say defensively. "I know what I think and I don't like Dylan as anything more than a friend."

Liar, liar, pants on fire!

"Anyway, what about you?" I ask. "How was your scrimmage yesterday?"

"It's a long story," Austin says coolly. "I don't want to bother you. I already talked to Amanda. That's okay, right? Maybe I'll tell you some other time."

Is Austin mocking me now? And what's with that Amanda dig? He knows how I feel about that girl! I mean, he sort of knows. I've dropped subtle hints.

Okay, maybe I should change the subject before this gets ugly. "I've got some news. Seth was here last week and he showed me some scripts. One of them was for a new TV show."

Austin is quiet at first. Then, finally, he says, "Did you like it?"

"I did," I say, my voice quickening. "It's about a bunch of college freshmen. Kind of *Friends*-ish. But edgy. There're these two great female characters in it that I just love."

"That's great," Austin says and he sounds like he means it. "So which one are you going to go for? Have they offered another girl one of the parts? Maybe Dylan could play your roommate in drag. Or your boyfriend on the show. I mean, if he likes you I would imagine he would want to stay near you after the play ends."

I can be obnoxious too. "Just like Amanda, right?" I snipe. "Maybe she can move to Los Angeles and play lacrosse with you and then she can answer your phone all the time!"

"That's not such a bad idea," Austin says gruffly. "At least Amanda is honest with me."

"Really?" I bark. "Has she been honest about telling you how much she likes you? Because she's made it obvious to me."

Austin doesn't say anything.

"Doesn't feel so good being hounded about someone you're not interested in, does it?" I ask getting angrier now. As mad as I am, I'm also crying. This is not good at all. Maybe we should hang up and cool off before continuing. I'm about to suggest just that when I hear a girl's voice.

De-amanda.

"I'm on the line with my girl," Austin says. "Can I pop over in a minute?"

At least he's still calling me his girl.

"No can do, loverboy," Amanda says. "We're taking you guys out and we have to go now. Major surprise. We've already got Rob in the car. Tell your favorite B-lister you'll have to chat later."

Hey, I'm not B-list!

"Austin, tell her you need a minute," I insist, sounding aggravated, which I am. "This is important."

But instead of answering me, the next thing I hear is a dial tone.

WHOA.

That had to be a mistake. RIGHT? Austin wouldn't hang up on me and go out with some other girl. I stare at my phone, waiting for it to ring.

Any second now...

Still waiting...

I drum my fingers on my dressing table nervously. I am not calling him. He should call me! He must know the hang up was on his end! Maybe he didn't even hang up. Maybe De-Manda did. In which case, he should definitely call me back. God, I can't stand that girl and I don't even know what she looks like. She probably has a perfect, sporty body. She is so trying to make a move on my boyfriend! MAKE HIM CALL, I will the iPhone. RING, I silently pray. But it doesn't. I keep staring at the main screen, which has a picture of me and Austin at the junior prom on it.

RING! RING! RING!

And then it does.

"Hello?" I say eagerly.

"Sweetie, what is this I found on your nightstand in your room?" It's Mom and she sounds highly annoyed.

"Mom, I can't talk now." And I don't have a clue what she's talking about. What did she find that could have her this worked up?

"Tell the truth, Kaitlin Elizabeth Burke!" Mom says sternly.

Oh, I know what she found. I better come clean. "I'm sorry," I apologize. "I've only had one. Okay, maybe two. But I've been working out every day! My trainer says it's good to treat yourself sometimes. They're less than a hundred calories, Mom."

"What are you talking about?" Mom asks.

"The mini Twix," I say. "You found the bag in my top drawer, right?"

"No," Mom says and tsks. I hear her open a drawer. "But now that I know about them they are disappearing! You don't need chocolate. I'm talking about that TV show! That one you and Seth like. Why are there notes on the copy he gave you? And phone numbers? You are not thinking about auditioning for it, are you?"

Um, yes? Simply put, I love it. I'm particularly into the character Hope, who is sassy, funny, and socially inept. She's the perfect foil for hardnosed Taylor, who is book smart during the day and a social butterfly at night. I could see Sky and me playing these girls. I just have to convince Mom and Dad of that.

"Mom, I really like it," I beg. "It's a great part. If you'd just read it—"

"Are they still thinking about Sky for the other girl?" she asks calmly.

"Yes, but—"

"LANEY!" Mom shrieks and I hear another click on the line, then sudden swooshing and...is that waves crashing? A seagull chirping? Laney doesn't have time for the beach.

"Absolutely not, Kaitlin!" Laney hisses, but her voice is barely a whisper, which means it is a Laney imposter. The real Laney is loud all the time.

"Um, Mom, I think you got your lines crossed," I say. "That is not Laney."

"It is too!" she hisses again. "I'm on a shoot for *Vanity Fair* with Reese and the photographer threatened to have me banned from the set if he heard me on my Bluetooth again. Can you imagine?" she whispers hotly. "Me being banned from the beach! The beach is public! PUBLIC." Her voice rises and she clears her throat. "Public, which means I can't be banned," she finishes in a whisper. "But my answer is still the same if Sky is involved. No."

"See?" Mom says, sounding triumphant. "This is out of the question."

"But you guys have been so nice to Sky while she's been in New York," I remind them. "Mom, you even said you liked her."

"As a person, yes, but as a coworker for you, no," Mom says defensively. "You'll be fighting again in a week and then the stories will follow on *Celebrity Insider* and in *Hollywood Nation*. I feel a migraine coming on just thinking about it."

"But what if…," I start to say.

"No!" Mom and Laney say in unison and Laney says it sort of loudly.

"KAITLIN! THINK!" Laney continues, yelling so loudly that I have to hold the phone away from my ear. "THIS HAS BAD MOVE WRITTEN ALL OVER IT. I DON'T CARE WHAT SETH SAYS! HE'S WRONG!" The next thing I hear is a bit of a rustle. Then Laney's voice is sort of muffled. "Hey! Wait! No, I'm getting off now! YOU CAN'T DO THIS! The beach is PUBLIC!" *Click.*

"I don't want to hear about this again," Mom says. "I've been so relaxed out here in the Hamptons, enjoying a quiet summer, and then I come back to the apartment for twenty-four hours and get stressed. No more talk of this pilot! Do you understand?"

"Mom," I beg.

"Kaitlin, how do you know Sky even wants to do this with you?" Mom asks. "Maybe her people hate the idea as much as we do and you're just fooling yourself." I don't say anything. "When we get back to Los Angeles you can look at something else to do. Anything but another play. They just don't pay." She sniffs.

HOLLYWOOD SECRET NUMBER THIRTEEN: Even if you make twenty million dollars a movie, you will make peanuts doing live theater. Stars who take the stage do it to broaden their acting range and for the prestige that comes with having your name in a *Playbill*. They don't do it for a paycheck. Most stars, even big ones, are lucky to bring home three thousand dollars a week. A lot to the rest of the world, but not those who spend their disposable income on Louis Vuitton luggage.

"If you're set on TV, then we can look at some other shows if you want," Mom continues, "but you are not repeating what's been done before. End of story." *Click.*

I cover my face with the nearest thing I can find — my Burberry raincoat (it's pouring today) and scream into it at the top of my lungs.

I'm so mad at everyone right now! Austin! Mom! Lauren, Ava, Riley! I'm sick of being picked on!

Mom is overreacting! I didn't say I was definitely doing the show, just that I was interested in meeting with the network about it. To be honest, I haven't even discussed the pilot with Sky yet. Part of me is afraid to ask her what she thinks of it. What if she hates it? What if she thinks working together again would be the nightmare it once was? I'd rather not hear her say that.

There's a quick knock on my door and I turn around. "Come in!"

Sky and Nadine march in, looking like wooden soldiers. Their faces are stoic.

I groan. "What is it?" I snap. "I'm in no mood."

"Too bad," Sky says and slams her iPhone down on my dressing table. Great. More phone grief. The screen has a small video on pause. "Watch it," she insists.

I look at them both curiously and then press play. I'm not surprised to see Lauren and Ava's faces staring back at me. They're introducing a clip they call "Lucky Ladies." Then the clip goes animated and it's a cartoon about me and Sky with cutouts of our real faces on animated bodies. We're singing some weird song about what has-beens we are and how Sky's pilot was canceled and all I can get is a part on Broadway for three months. Then they say how *Family Affair* was our last chance at stardom and now it's gone.

Ouch.

"I hate them," Sky shrieks before I even finish the clip. She is visibly upset. "I'm tired of this game. They're cruel. And they're lame. I want out of this twisted drama." Sky looks at me darkly. "Enough with this high road garbage, K. I've done my part bashing them, now it's your turn. It's going to take two of us to take them down."

"I don't know," Nadine says. "Do you two really want to stoop to their level?" She looks at Sky. "I'm mad too! They have to be stopped, but is adding more fuel to the fire going to do it? Kaitlin, you're better than these games."

"K, think about the Hamptons," Sky begs. "They could have cost you your job."

"Forest wouldn't have fired her for missing the show," Nadine insists. "He might have been mad, but he would have gotten over it. It wasn't her fault."

"Exactly," I say, exasperated, "but it still happened. Riley being mad at me because she likes Dylan isn't my fault either, but if I keep letting things slide, then she keeps being condescending and makes me feel like I don't deserve to be here. I'm sick of it!" I yell. Nadine's eyes widen. "I'm sick of De-Manda, and Austin sleeping through phone calls, and Lauren and Ava using me and Sky to get on *Access Hollywood*! I'm tired of being nice. It doesn't get me anywhere."

"Yay, K! You're growing a backbone," Sky says proudly.

"Kaitlin, you beat Riley at her own game when you made it to the show from the Hamptons anyway," Nadine reminds me. "I saw her face when we showed up here. She was flabbergasted."

I shake my head. "It's not enough. I want her to feel the way I feel sometimes. I want her to feel small and powerless for a change." I look at Sky. "And Lauren and Ava too. And Austin!" I add.

"What did Austin do?" Nadine frowns.

"I don't want to talk about it right now." I turn away. "I'll get upset before the show."

"TEN MINUTES," the intercom announces.

"Um, we should go," Nadine says, grabbing Sky's arm. "I don't want Kaitlin getting worked up."

"I'll be right there," Sky says. "I need a minute with K."

Nadine gives me a look. "Okay. Kaitlin, just calm down and think about your performance. I'll be watching in the audience. It's my eighth time seeing you. Could be a record for family and friends."

When Nadine is gone, Sky starts talking at once. "I was wondering if…I thought maybe you…did you…oh hell, did you read the pilot for *Big Fish, Small Pond*?"

"Yes!" I jump up and grab her. "It was incredible, wasn't it? Did you like it?"

Sky looks freaked out. "Chill, K. I didn't like offer you a million dollars or anything. Yes, I read the pilot. So what?"

"What do you mean 'so what'?" I say. "You were the one who asked if I read it first."

"Who cares who is first?" Sky gets huffy. "Like I care that you read it first."

"Whoa, this is not a competition," I tell her. "What I meant to ask is, are you interested? I mean, if they want both of us, are you maybe at all interested in going back down that road with me?" Sky seems unsure and I find myself holding my breath.

But I don't get to hear Sky's answer. My door flies open again and one of the stagehands is standing there looking impatient. "Kaitlin, five minutes. You have to get to your mark."

"Right. Sorry," I apologize.

He slams the door. I look at Sky.

"We'll talk later," Sky says hurriedly, grabbing her Louis Vuitton bag from my dressing counter. "I changed my flight back to Los Angeles. I'm, um, staying in town another few weeks. Just going to enjoy the city." She looks down at the floor.

"You didn't answer me," I try again.

"I probably won't have time to hang out," Sky says. "I can't, you know, hang out backstage waiting around for you. I have a job hunt going."

"Sky," I say, but she slams the door behind her.

It's like a switch that turns on and off with Sky. She just can't admit we're actually friends now, can she? Why can't she tell me what she thinks about the TV pilot?

My door opens a crack and Sky sticks her head back in. "Yes," she says simply.

"Yes, what?" I ask.

"Yes, I like the show even if you are in it," she snaps. But then she starts to smile, just a little, and I start to smile too. "I guess I can survive a few more years with you around. We'll discuss billing later — my name should go first." Then she slams the door again.

She's into it! Sky is just as into the show as I am and is cool with the fact that we could be working together again! We have a shot here. This could work. I need to call Seth.

But first, I have a show to do. I look down at my phone. No missed calls. That gets me crazy again. There's no time to call Austin, but...

I can't stand it. I'm calling Austin. It will just take a second. The cell phone rings twice and then it picks up. "Austin?"

"Nope, it's Amanda," she says. It's loud wherever she is.

"I need to speak to my boyfriend," I tell her.

"Sorry, Hollywood girl, he can't come to the phone."

"PUT HIM ON NOW," I insist.

"Oooh…getting angry, huh?" Amanda laughs.

"Who is that?" I hear Austin's voice.

"Your girlfriend," Amanda tells him. "I told her you'd call her back, A."

"HE wants to speak to me," I tell her. She's in for it now. Austin won't let her push me off. He's probably as upset about before as I am. I wait for him to pick up.

"Tell her I'll call her later," I think I hear him say, but his voice is sort of muffled. It's loud in the background and the connection isn't the greatest. The old walls in this building are so thick.

But I couldn't have just heard him say that. He wouldn't say that. He wouldn't push me off for Amanda!

"HE said he'd call you back," Amanda says smugly. "Bye, princess." *Click.*

I hold my phone in my hand, dumbfounded. What exactly just happened? Why didn't Austin get on the phone? Why didn't he get on the phone with his girlfriend?

The more I think about it, the angrier I get. At Austin, even though I don't know what's going on. At Riley. At Ava and Lauren. At Mom and Laney for dismissing this TV show. I storm over to my spot backstage next to Riley and Dylan.

Sky is right. Being nice gets you nowhere. I can sense Dylan staring at me and even though Riley is watching us, I turn to him.

"Dylan, what are you doing tommorow?" I ask.

Dylan looks flustered. "Nothing. Why?"

"I was wondering what you were doing for an early dinner. There is this Italian place I'm dying to try. Bellavitae."

"Sounds lovely." Dylan smiles. "Do they have good biscuits?"

"I'm sure they make a mean chocolate chip cookie." I don't know that, but I can see Riley starting to squirm, so I keep going. "Would you like to go with me?"

"As your date?" he asks curiously.

I look at Riley. Her face is stricken. Being nice doesn't work, I remind myself. "Yes."

"Brilliant," Dylan says. "It's a date then."

Someone calls Dylan's name and he turns to them.

"Don't you have a partner?" Riley asks quietly so that only I can hear.

"That's none of your business," I snap, not looking at her. I'm enjoying the effect this is having on her. My heart is pounding. "I can't wait to go to Bellavitae with Dylan," I gush. "It's so romantic." Riley doesn't say anything, which just makes me want to upset her more. "Maybe I'll wear that cute little Christian Siriano dress that he made for me. It's so short."

"TWO MINUTES," I hear someone say.

"Oh, and Riley?" She turns to look at me now. "In the second act tonight, when we're doing the scene right before

I run out to the lockers, maybe you could go easy on your attitude." Her jaw drops. "You're sort of overplaying the scene and I'd hate for you to ruin things for the rest of us."

Take that, Riley.

*   *   *

Tonight, I play Andie angrier than I ever have before, but I'm pumped up and the audience doesn't seem to be bothered by it. When I get offstage, I rush to my dressing room and the first thing I do is pick up my iPhone and dial. I don't think. I act.

"Austin, it's me," I say on his voicemail. "Sorry you're so busy with Amanda that you can't take my call. I hope you two are having fun. I'm sure Amanda is easy to have fun with since she sounds like she's been hit in the head one too many times with a lacrosse ball. In case you need to talk to me, I won't be around tomorrow. I'm having dinner alone with Dylan. This sweet little romantic place. Maybe I'll catch you on Monday." *Click.*

Take that, Austin.

Take that, De-Manda.

Now it's time to fry Lauren and Ava.

Saturday, July 18

NOTE TO SELF:
Sunday: Meet Dylan at 4PM

SCOOP PATROL

Sunday July 18th

Kaitlin Burke Calls Hollywood Nation *to Set the Record Straight about Her Feud*

Fresh from the stage after another performance in *Meeting of the Minds* on Broadway, Kaitlin Burke called a reporter from *Hollywood Nation* to talk about the "severe injustice" that is affecting both her and former costar Sky Mackenzie—aka her war of words with Lauren Cobb and Ava Hayden. Until now, Kaitlin has kept the mud-slinging to a minimum. But last night, in this exclusive, Kaitlin was ready to put on a raincoat and let the words fly!

Kaitlin had this to say: "Lauren and Ava are talentless girls with nothing better to do than talk trash about the famous people around them," she said by phone from her dressing room at the theater. "I used to feel sorry for them, but I don't anymore. Those two are gunning for Sky and me and the only reason they're doing it is they have no other way to keep their names in the press. They're dying to be the new Heidi and Spencer, and that's pathetic because those two are equally spotlight-hogging wannabes."

Wow, has Little Miss Nice started sounding like Sky all of a sudden? "Maybe," says Kaitlin. "And if that's true, that's probably a good thing. Sky has never been afraid to express herself and no one messes with her. Well, I'm tired of being stepped on. The Laurens, Avas, Rileys, and De-Mandas of the world better watch out, because I'm not going to take their garbage anymore."

When asked who Riley and De-Manda were, Kaitlin fumbled, and quickly said she had to go. But one thing is for certain, this new Kaitlin is ready to rumble!

FOURTEEN: *Rash Decisions Can Cost You*

Austin hasn't called me back.

That's all I can think about as I get ready for my date with Dylan Sunday afternoon. I try to distract myself with the details, like how I'm wearing my hair (who cares? I'm leaving it down and I don't even care about taming my summer frizz) and what I'm wearing. (Sigh. Like I care about that either.) I grabbed the first thing I could find in my closet: a indigo blue strapless Free People dress with a sweetheart neck and knot center that I've never worn yet. I was going to wear it on a date with Austin, but I wasn't sure if I liked how it hung on my hips. Today I'm too depressed to care.

Date.

I'm going on a date with Dylan.

As in, I am going on a date with someone other than my boyfriend, Austin.

Either Austin and I have just agreed to try some crazy new only-in-Hollywood dating agreement or we're…or we're…

Breaking up.

That's the only reason either of us would go on a date with someone else, right? If Austin went on a date with De-Manda and I'm going on a date with Dylan then we must be breaking up.

Do I want to break up with Austin?

I keep pulling my iPhone out of my bag and staring at the screen hoping I have a missed call from him. But I don't. I still haven't gotten a call by the time I get to Bellavitae, where Dylan is already sitting at a table waiting for me.

The restaurant is just one long room with wide-planked wood floors and beamed ceilings and they have jars of what looks like olive oil and balsamic vinegar lining the walls. Sure it's a little basic, but foodies and stars in the know tell me the dishes are unreal. I hear they have these amazing *Polpettine Fritte* (fried little meatballs) and *Spaghetti Cacio e Pepe* (spaghetti with Pecorino Romano and cracked black pepper). They normally open at five-thirty on Sundays, but I called and they agreed to serve us an hour earlier, so the place is very quiet. Too quiet. I can hear all the voices in my head talking about Austin and I can't get them to shut up.

Are Austin and I breaking up? Is that why I'm here right now?

"Hi," Dylan says, jumping up and pulling my chair out for me. "You look lovely."

"Thanks." I take a seat. I'm very nervous all of a sudden. That's not true. I've been nervous all day. When I told Nadine where I was off to, she barely looked at me. She knows Austin and I had a fight, and that I called *Hollywood*

Nation without clearing it with Laney, but she isn't offering any of her trademark advice. "You look nice too," I say to Dylan.

Dylan doesn't look anything like Austin. His hair is cropped short, and very dark, and his body, while just as fit, is long and lean rather than muscular. I can practically see his taut stomach through the fitted green shirt he's wearing with khaki linen pants. He looks good. Really good. And his green eyes seem to lock in everyone from the bartender to the waitress asking for his autograph. She only melts more when he speaks in that charming British accent of his.

"Would you like something to drink?" Dylan asks me. "We should celebrate. I know we've had dinner before, but this is sort of our first official date, isn't it?"

Date. We're on a date. I'm on a date with someone other than my boyfriend. At least Austin was my boyfriend twenty-four hours ago, before he went on a date too.

The only thing is, I don't know for *sure* if Austin was on a date, do I? He didn't tell me he was on a date. He didn't tell me anything! He didn't get on the phone! The only thing I know is he was out with Amanda. And we had a fight. Our biggest fight ever. Part of that is my fault. I've been wrapped up in my own life and haven't really given a lot of thought to what has been going on in Austin's.

Why am I on a date again?

"Kaitlin?" Dylan looks at me curiously. "I asked if you wanted a drink."

"Sorry!" I laugh lightly and kind of wave my arms around.

I look at my wrist. I'm not even wearing a watch. Huh. I never forget to wear a watch. "I don't know where my head is."

"That's okay. You're here and that's all I want." Dylan looks at me hopefully and smiles. He's got a great one. But it's not Austin's, I realize. And that's the one that makes my heart melt.

I look at Dylan again. He's cute. Very cute. And charming, but...Dylan is my friend (a hot friend, for sure). But Dylan doesn't want to be friends. I know that he wants more and right now I'm taking advantage of that. I've taken advantage of that a lot actually. Dylan's helped me through this Broadway transition and been a shoulder to cry on and I guess I've sort of used him to fill in for Austin while we're apart.

God, how bad is that? I didn't do it on purpose, but now that I think about it, that's what I've been doing. I've been trying to replace Austin since he's not around, and that's ridiculous because he's the only one I really want.

And yet I'm sitting here in his romantic restaurant on a date with Dylan. I asked Dylan out to get back at Austin and to upset Riley. How ridiculous is that? I'm hurting Dylan, who has been nothing but good to me; I'm hurting Riley, who has genuine feelings for Dylan; and most of all, I'm hurting Austin.

We're going to break up over this, aren't we?

Oh my God, I so don't want to break up with Austin!

"Will you excuse me a second?" I try not to sound choked up. Before Dylan can even answer, I head straight for the bathroom. There's an attendant in there, but I barely even smile before I lock myself in a stall and burst into tears. I pull my iPhone out of my bag and dial Austin's number. It rings twice and goes to voicemail.

I don't want to break up. I don't want to break up.

I DON'T WANT TO BREAK UP!

"Austin, it's me," I say softly, pulling myself together, but sniffing and shaking too. "I'm sorry. I'm SO sorry. I know we had a fight, but I don't want to break up. I'm not on a date with Dylan. I mean, I am here, but I know it was a mistake. I was trying to make you mad because you made me mad when you were out with Amanda and didn't take my call. Nothing is going on. I swear. *Please* call me back. We need to talk."

I hang up and burst into tears.

In all my time with Sky, I've never taken her advice before, and I choose now to take it? I'm not a mean person, even if I want to be sometimes. Just thinking about the things I said to *Hollywood Nation* last night gives me a headache. I thought I could take on the Laurens and Avas of the world, but I think Nadine is right. Sometimes you have to take the high road. That is not the road I'm on right now. Right now I'm on a date with a very nice guy just to make other people jealous. And this could cause the relationship I cherish to fall apart. That makes me cry harder.

I must have been in there a while because eventually someone knocks on the door.

"Miss, you all right in there?"

"I'm fine!" I dab at my eyes with some toilet paper. My

mascara must be a mess. "I'll be out in a sec." Which I'm not.

A few minutes later there is another knock.

"Kaitlin, are you alright?"

It's Dylan. I can feel the tears welling up in my eyes again. Hearing Dylan's voice makes me feel more guilty. "Not really."

"Could you open the door then so we can sort it out together?"

I open the door slowly. I wrap my arms around my waist, trying to warm up my bare arms in the blaring air-conditioning. I know I look a little silly perched on the lip of a toilet like I am.

"Kaitlin, it's okay," Dylan says. "I know."

"Know what?" I sniffle.

He smiles. "Us blokes aren't stupid. I know you had a row with Austin. One of the stagehands overheard you so I knew what you were up to. That's the real reason you asked me out on a date, isn't it?"

"You knew?" I stop crying and look up at him. "Then why'd you agree to go out with me?"

"You can't blame a guy for trying." Dylan winks.

I start crying again. "You must think I'm the worst person in the world."

Dylan walks into the stall and puts his arms around me.

I lean into him and continue to sob. "You've been such a good friend to me all summer and this is how I treat you. You're funny and smart and cute, and any girl would be lucky to have you. But that girl isn't me, Dylan. I'm happy with my boyfriend. I really care about him and I was just trying to make him and Riley jealous. I'm so sorry I treated you like a piece of meat."

Dylan chuckles. "There, there. I don't think you're horrid. And well, maybe there was a small bit of me that wanted to get back at Riley too. She dumped me for a complete tosser."

"So you were using me to make her jealous too?" I ask, amused.

Dylan laughs. "Well, bits and bobs I guess. I do like you, but I miss Riley, even if her behavior toward you on this run has been incorrigible."

How could Dylan like her? I guess everyone has different tastes.

My snakeskin bag hangs off my shoulder and I feel for my phone self-consciously, hoping it will ring on command. Of course, it doesn't. I have to talk to Austin. Now. Right now. I can't wait another minute. I'll keep calling till he picks up. He has to pick up.

"Dylan?" I ask. "Would you hate me if I told you I had to leave?"

He grins. "I'd be surprised if you didn't. Tell your partner I said hi. You'll reach him on his mobile eventually. Either that or you'll have to hop on the next plane to see him."

Go to Texas!

Why didn't I think of that?

I give him a kiss on his cheek. "Dylan, you're brilliant. I'll see you at the theater."

I rush out of the bathroom, through the restaurant, and out to the street. I stick my hand out into oncoming traffic and wave wildly for a cab. I've got a plane ticket to buy.

*   *   *

Twenty-five minutes later I burst through our apartment front door with a well-thought out, extremely rational plan of action. Okay, originally it was my Plan B. Plan A was reaching Austin by phone, but he's still not answering.

"911!" I yell. I can yell all I want because Mom and Dad are in the Hamptons again. "Nadine! Liz! PACK YOUR BAGS! Guys? WHERE ARE YOU GUYS? GUYS!"

Nadine and Liz come flying out of their rooms at the same time, doors slamming behind them. Matty opens his door too, his sleep mask still over his eyes. He's wearing a *Scooby* T-shirt. Figures. A fourth door opens and I realize it's the bathroom. A huge cloud of steam precedes Sky, who has my monogrammed towel wrapped around her head. She's also wearing my pink robe.

"What are you jabbering about?" Sky is a total grouch.

"What are you doing here?" I ask, so surprised that for a moment I forget all about my master plan.

"They ran out of hot water at the hotel." Sky pulls my robe tightly around her small waist. "They weren't getting it back for at least an *hour*. Can you imagine? I couldn't wait that long so I called here and Liz said you were out with that cute British costar. What were you thinking?"

I'm not sure what to comment on first — the fact that Liz said Sky could use our shower or about the fact I was out with Dylan. I look at Liz and she sort of shrugs. She's trying and that's all friends can really ask friends to do.

"I know I shouldn't have gone out with Dylan." I sigh. "I screwed up. I was trying to make Austin jealous."

"Did it work?" Sky wants to know.

"He's not returning my calls." I stare at the hardwood floor and feel like I could be swallowed up by it at any moment.

"Shocker." Matty shuffles toward us. He's taken off his eye mask and it hangs on his forehead. His blond hair sticks up all over. "You think you girls are the only ones who can play games. We know how to play them too, you know. Want to mess with our hearts? We'll mess with yours right back. Austin isn't taking your calls, Kates, because you ticked him off."

"I kind of figured that." I sink into the nearest leather couch. It needs cushier pillows that you can wrap your arms around and cry into. Since I don't have any, I tell the gang what transpired last night before and after the show and today.

"I hate De-Manda!" Sky declares.

"Me too!" Liz seconds. "The nerve of her, not to give Austin the phone!"

"*He* didn't take the phone," Matty clarifies, but we ignore him.

"She has been making a play for your man and I don't tolerate that sort of thing," Sky adds. It's hard to take her businesslike tone seriously when she's all wrapped up in plush terry cloth.

"Agreed." Liz is equally outraged and she plops down next to me, her black satin bow-detail 7 for All Mankind halter top billowing around her. It's such a cute top and it looks great with those cut-off Paper Denim capris. Wait, I think those are mine. "She needs to be dealt with," Liz adds.

I shake my head. "No, it's not De-Manda I should be worried about. It's Austin. I've pushed him into her arms and now he's going to break up with me!"

Liz touches my hand, her cool silver bangle hitting my fingers. "Don't say that."

"Why wouldn't he?" I wonder aloud. "We have never had such a big fight before. We've had such a hard time syncing schedules and we've been getting so mad at each other. I guess things just spiraled out of control." I sink lower into the couch remembering it all. "I started spending all this time with Dylan and he was here and great and I guess a small part of me liked the attention and then I wasn't giving Austin or his lacrosse camp any attention..." I bite my lip. "Do you think I'm a horrible person?"

"No." Nadine shakes her head, practical as always. "You're human! And you're not a bad person for finding someone else cute. That's normal. There's not a day that goes by in Los Angeles that I don't marvel at some hot guy's body. But that doesn't mean I pounce on them."

"Trev and I have a simple understanding." Sky is referring to our former *FA* costar who she's been seeing on and off.

"Flirting is okay, but anything beyond that is not. Trev knows that men find me irresistible. I can't help it."

Liz snorts and Sky glares at her. "Sorry."

"You made a mistake," Nadine tells me. "You got caught up in the play, and hanging out with Dylan, and being in New York." She smiles wryly. "This city has a way of changing people. But you didn't do any of it on purpose and you don't want to break up with Austin, so don't!"

I moan. "How do I stop him from breaking things off?"

"You've got to reach Austin and explain things." Liz is absentmindedly playing with her tight corkscrews while she thinks. "This is totally fixable. This isn't as big of a deal as you think."

"It wouldn't be if we were both in Los Angeles" — I point out the obvious — "but we're not. I'm in New York and he's in Texas. You can't have a heart-to-heart with someone who is not in the same zipcode! It's just not the same on the phone."

"Text him!" Liz says.

"No! Send him a Twitter shout-out," Sky suggests.

Everyone groans. HOLLYWOOD SECRET NUMBER FOURTEEN: Sky may do her own Twittering, but not all celebrities do. Some of them are so eager to get in on the ego-obsessed Twitter craziness that they have their personal assistants handle their accounts for them. Are you really surprised? Even some stars' "official website" blogs are handled by outsiders who are paid to write their daily entries for them.

"I'm not about the PDA," I remind them. "And besides, I highly doubt a Twitter shout-out will help things." Liz smirks. "Neither will a text." Now Sky grunts. "I'm not texting and I'm not calling him again." I dig my phone out of my bag and look at the blank screen. "And he's obviously not calling me either. I'm done with technology on this issue. I think we all know what I need to do — go see Austin in person."

A chorus of "What? How? Are you nuts?" follows that statement. Nadine starts rattling off a list of reasons why we can't go (Mom, Mom, and Mom).

"Guys! Think about it." I hold my hands up pleadingly. "I perform tonight and then not again till Tuesday night. I can be there and back and no one has to know! Mom and Dad are away till Wednesday anyway. We can call them from the road."

"Your mom said you couldn't visit Austin alone, remember?" Nadine reminds me.

I smile slyly. "I'm not going alone. You guys are coming with me. Who is in?"

"I'll go," Matty offers first. "We haven't had any road trip time this whole summer and I'm leaving this weekend for work on *my* show."

"As if anyone needs reminding that you have a slot on the fall schedule," Sky snaps. "I'm in too, K."

"Me three." Liz raises her hand wildly. "But maybe we should keep this smallish, you know? I wouldn't want Austin to think he was being ambushed."

Sky puts her hands on her hips. "Are you suggesting I stay home?"

"Austin doesn't know you," Liz points out. "Or should I say, he doesn't *like* what he knows of you. I don't think you'd be welcome."

"Maybe that's the problem." Sky crosses her arms over her chest and juts out a hip. "It's not *who* is welcome, it's who would be best to help Kaitlin through this crisis. Kaitlin needs unbiased opinions here."

"She needs her *best* friend's opinion." Liz takes a step toward Sky and I have the sudden fear that she's going to bust out some kickboxing moves.

"Guys, enough!" I referee. "This is getting old. I should have addressed this a while ago instead of tuning you both out." I take a deep breath and look at Nadine. She nods encouragingly. "You don't like each other. I get it."

I look at Liz. "Sky hurt me, and that bothers you, and I love that you care so much, but I'm a big girl, and I think Sky and I have matured enough that we can handle being friends."

Liz looks away and I turn to Sky, who is gloating at Liz. "Liz treats you miserably whenever you're around because she's my best friend and she watches my back. You can't stand her, Sky, because we're so close, but that is never going to change." Sky opens her mouth to protest, but I cut her off. "I have room in my life for more than one friend. Not everything has to be a competition."

Nadine is grinning so I must be doing well. "I wish you two could get along because I think we'd have a lot of fun together, but I know it's not fair for me to put that on you guys. We'll keep things separate from now on. But this, today, is about me and Austin and right now I could use as much help as I can get. I need you both to get through this," I add quietly.

Liz and Sky look at each other.

"Okay." Liz shrugs.

"Okay," Sky agrees reluctantly.

"Good." I breathe a sigh of relief. "Now we have to take care of the getting there part. Nadine?"

"Already on it." Nadine looks up from her laptop. "But there's a problem. You'll miss the last flight of the night to Texas by two hours. You can't get on a plane till close to midnight. And tomorrow the first flight out is a connecting and you wouldn't get in till like one PM. I should add, the ticket prices are astronomical at this late date."

"I don't care," I tell her. "I'll work off my credit card bill again. I need to see Austin right away. I can't wait till tomorrow! There aren't any other airlines?"

Nadine shakes her head. "I'm checking, but there's not much on here that would work and get you back in time on Tuesday for the show."

"Maybe you should go private," Sky suggests.

"Ooh! Good idea!" I look hopefully at Nadine.

"She cannot go private!" Nadine scolds. "We don't have twenty-five thousand dollars to throw away on a private flight to Texas. We already spent a fortune on gas for that helicopter ride. Her mother would fire me if we booked a Lear jet."

"I can't have that." I sigh. "Private is out."

"There is another flight that could get you in at twelve PM tomorrow," Nadine says thoughtfully. "They only have two seats left. That won't work. Oh! This one might be good, but the connection is too tight. Hmm...the problem is the airport closest to Austin's campus is not the major one and there aren't many flights."

We sit quietly a few minutes, waiting for Nadine to work her magic like she always does. But this time she looks up glumly and says, "Kaitlin, this isn't going to work."

"Okay." My eyes well up with tears. "I'll keep calling him. I guess." I start to cry again. "I'm sorry. It's just I'm so worried Austin and I are going to break up over this. I have to see him and explain things. This can't wait."

"Go private," Sky urges again.

"Sky, it's not an option." Nadine is completely stern on this point.

"Unless..." Liz looks at Sky strangely.

"Liz, don't you start too!" Nadine is aghast at Liz's mutinous look.

"Unless what?" I look from Liz to Sky.

"We could." Sky, cracks a smile. "I never have before."

"I haven't," Liz says. "Have you?"

"I just said I haven't!" Sky snaps.

"Fine. Let's do it," Liz turns to me and grins. "We're going private!"

"How?" Nadine and I say at the same time.

"Courtesy of Kaitlin's entertainment law firm," Liz says smugly. Sky clears her throat. "Despite our dads, fallingout, they kept joint use of the company private jet."

"In this economy, it's smart to be frugal," Sky adds and Nadine bursts out laughing. "Nadine, sharing a jet is cost-effective."

"Whatever you say." Nadine shakes her head.

"Our dads have enough pull that we could get a jet this afternoon and have it ready to fly out tonight," Liz continues.

"Guys, we can't bill this back to the firms," I tell them. "I appreciate it, but I'd feel awful."

"We're not billing it back, per se," Sky explains. "Daddy was having the jet come get me to bring me back to Los Angeles anyway. I'll fly commercial and use the trip for this instead."

"Same here," Liz seconds. "Dad would have flown me back on it after school, but I'll fly back commercial with you. Kates, let's take the jet. We'll leave tonight."

"Are you sure?" They nod. "You have no idea how much this means to me. Okay." I squeal. "We'll leave right after the show and I'll pay both of you back for your commercial tickets." I hug them.

"Guys, the closest airport is still two hours away from Austin's campus." Nadine is looking at MapQuest. "We'll have to rent a car."

"Road trip back on!" Matty hollers.

"This is going to be fun!" Liz looks at me. "Once you and Austin talk things out, of course. I know you're not going to break up. You can't!"

"I hope you're right," I tell her, my heart pounding at the thought of seeing Austin in just a few hours. We can't break up. We just can't. I look around the room. Liz, Sky, Nadine, Matty, and I'm sure Rodney will come too. There is no one else I'd rather have in my corner for this.

Nadine is already on the phone with a rent-a-car place in Texas. "You guys okay with a Taurus?"

"Eww. No. No compact cars." Sky makes a face. "Try for an Escalade."

"What's wrong with a Taurus? God, you're so superficial!" Liz tells her and the two start to bicker again.

Okay, maybe this won't be a fun trip, but I don't care. The goal is to find Austin and make things right. And I will.

Sunday, July 19th

NOTE TO SELF:
Have N pack 4 trip.
Apologize 2 Riley.
Jet leaves at 11:30 PM from Newark.

BREAKING NEWS

Online Exclusive: Kaitlin Burke and Sky Mackenzie Urge the Media to Help Stop the Feud Madness!

Speaking by phone to *Celebrity Insider Online*, Kaitlin Burke and Sky Mackenzie (aka SKAT) made a public plea to squash the escalating war of words between them and socialities/reality TV stars Ava Hayden and Lauren Cobb (aka LAVA).

"We are sick of the drama," said Kaitlin, who claimed she was calling from her New York City apartment (although we heard airplanes taking off in the background). "Sky and I are tired of the back-and-forth between the so-called Team Sky and Kaitlin and Team Ava and Lauren. We just want this whole fight to end," Kaitlin added. "It doesn't matter who started it or why it started. We want the negative energy to go away. No one can win this. We're going to continue to hurt each other. Why? Because we don't get along? We don't have to get along. We can stay out of each other's space and live our lives. That's what I intend to do. I've been doing a lot of thinking and I realize now that nothing good comes of being vengeful and hurtful. You're better off letting some things slide and this is one of them. After tonight, Sky and I won't be answering any more questions about Lauren and Ava's behavior—no matter what they throw our way."

This statement is in sharp contrast to another interview that was posted online just twenty-four hours ago by a less-reputable entertainment outlet. Kaitlin admits the quotes were hers, but says she wasn't thinking clearly at the time of the interview. "I had a rough night and I think I took things too far," she admits. "I apologize for being just as down-and-dirty as Lauren and Ava have been. I don't normally act that way and I regret my behavior. If my statements hurt anyone reading them, I apologize."

Sky was in full agreement with her former *Family Affair* costar on the silent treatment Kaitlin is suggesting. "What good is going to come of this fight?" Sky asked. "Nothing. It's a way to get more headlines and public attention, and K and I are not the type to crave that. Those two keep doing more and more public displays of hatred to try to keep their fifteen minutes of fame going. Well, their fifteen minutes are over because we are not firing back anymore."

Sky was Tweeting while she spoke, saying she was "hoping to get my last two cents in before we shut down this whole discussion completely!" Her Tweets during the midnight hour included: "LET THE HATERS CONTINUE TO HATE. WE ARE OUT OF THIS!" And: "LAVA knows what they've done and they've got to live with that. This star refuses to be dimmed by their callousness." Our favorite: "LAVA, you will not get any more press out of us. We've got bigger fish to fry, you guppies. Go back to the small pond where you belong."

Hearing SKAT on the same page had this reporter wondering: Are the former frenemies now just plain friends? Both skirted around the issue, with Sky even asking, "How did K respond to that question?" But there is one important thing to note: They were together, late at night, somewhere loud (airplanes!), going somewhere else together. Isn't that the sort of thing friends do? Sky laughed when *CIO* suggested that, but she wasn't so quick to laugh off our question about rumors that the pair could work together again on a fall pilot. "I can't comment on that, but you know you'd love it if we would." Kaitlin was equally coy. "If that's true, I'd be pretty lucky," she said, as Sky chided her in the background. "If there's one thing I can say about Sky, it's that at least with her, I know where I stand. With Lauren and Ava I never did. Wait. That was sort of a dig, wasn't it?" she said with a laugh. "I take that back! I'm done hurling insults. Insulting people is not what I'm about. New York was my summer to try new things and I have, but the important thing is not to forget who I was before," Kaitlin added. "I realize that now and that's why I'm stopping this feud craziness. Hopefully *Celebrity Insider* will help us too."

So what do you think? Should we stop the Team SKAT and Team LAVA coverage? Tweet your thoughts to @celebinsider.

FIFTEEN: *Texas or Bust*

"The snack machine had Chex mix!" Sky looks happy as she bounds onto the hotel room bed, shaking the frame and causing Liz to almost spill her Sprite all over her nightshirt. I brace for the impact. "Oh, God, so sorry, Lizzie!" Sky races to her half of the bed in way-too-short black pajama shorts and a pink bedazzled tank that says TEAM SKAT. "Did you get wet? You can wear my new green tank I got at Topshop if you did."

It's amazing what can happen when you spend a six-hour plane flight and car ride with people you normally dislike. Maybe instead of sending a message to Lauren and Ava via Celebinsider.com, we should have asked them to come to Texas with us. It's done wonders for Liz and Sky. Somewhere over Tennessee they bonded over their love of Ryan Reynolds and started trading their favorite movie lines. By the time we crossed the Texas border, Sky had agreed to star in Liz's final class project—a five-minute video that she has to write and shoot within a week.

"Look, it's just a little drip," Liz tells Sky, pointing at her kickboxing T-shirt. "No biggie."

No biggie? Ha! If I had done that to her favorite shirt, she would have squirted her Sprite back at me. I give her a look.

"Chex?" Sky holds out the bag for me and winks.

"No, thanks." All I want is get a little sleep before I see Austin. I wanted to show up at his dorm room tonight when we got in, but Nadine said that arriving at his dorm at five AM might cause a small commotion. So instead we checked into the nearest hotel ("A Doubletree?" Sky scowled. "Eww.") and everyone made me agree to set the alarm clock for ten AM so that I didn't show up "with huge bags under your eyes and a major zit." (Liz. Sky laughed though.) The only room they had left was a two-bedroom suite in a full-on Texas motif so Nadine and I are bunking together and Liz and Sky are in the other bed. Matty and Rodney are already snoring in the other room, but I can't sleep.

"K, if you don't shut your eyes soon, you're going to have a meltdown, and I really don't want to take you to a hospital in Texas." Sky shudders.

"Enough breakdown talk." I sigh. I hug my way-too-fluffy pillow to my chest and lean back against the wood head-board. I pull my custom Ahsoka Tano shirt that Austin had made for me over my mouth. "I'm already"—*yawn*—"freaked out enough as it is."

"Kates, you know Austin is totally going to forgive you once he sees you." Liz smiles. "I called Josh earlier and he didn't even mention you two having a fight. If it was major, he would have told Josh. And if he told Josh, Josh would have told me."

I stare at the picture of the cattle ranch on the far wall, not sure if I buy her logic. "I keep trying to rehearse what I'm going to say to Austin, but the words get all tangled up. I don't know where to start."

"Just make out with him." Sky shrugs. "That always works for me. Then they forget why you were fighting in the first place."

"On that inspiring note, it's time to sleep," Nadine says. She leans over and turns off the light next to me. Sky turns over and flips off the light next to her bed as well. It's dark, but I can already see the sky lightening between the cracks of the window curtains.

"Guys?" I ask through the blackness as my eyelids get heavier. The only thing I can hear is the whir of the air-conditioning unit in the wall and Nadine twisting and turning next to me. It feels like the safest time to admit my darkest fear. "What if all this bickering and all the missed phone calls are a sign of a bigger problem? What if Austin likes De-Manda?"

"You deal with that road if you come to it, which I don't think you will." Liz sounds so calm that I'm jealous.

"But what if we break up?" I almost whisper.

"If that happens, then I'll be there for you." Liz's voice is strong and reassuring.

"*We'll* be there for you," Sky corrects, which makes me a little teary. But I'm too tired to cry.

"We'll all be there for you," Liz amends.

"You're not alone, Kaitin." Nadine is not asleep yet either, apparently. "We've got your back. That's what friends are for."

And that's the last thing I remember hearing before I fall asleep.

* * *

The next thing I remember is my alarm going off at ten AM. Sky hits the snooze three times and then Liz says she's changing the wake-up time to eleven since we don't have a specific time we're meeting Austin anyway. I think about fighting her, but I'm too tired and a little worried that Liz might be right about the under-eye circles. By eleven-thirty we're all up. Nadine's BlackBerry keeps going off and to keep her from hurling it against the wall, I read the latest message to her then immediately regret doing so. It's Mom asking where we are. She had called the apartment twice and gotten no answer. Nadine jumps up to call her from the closet and warns the rest of us to keep our voices down. While Matty and Sky take showers in the two separate bathrooms, and Liz watches *The View*, I check my phone. For some reason it's off, even though I don't remember turning it off. As soon as it powers up, I see the text. It was sent at eight-thirty this morning.

AUSTIN'S CELL: Tried calling all night, but no answer. Call me, okay? We need 2 talk.

"Guys, Austin texted me!" I scream.

"Let me see!" Liz jumps up and reads the text. "He tried calling? When?"

"I know I had my phone on all night, but it was just off." We stare at the screen as the low-battery light blinks menacingly and the phone shuts off again. Liz smacks me in the shoulder.

"Kates, you forgot to charge your phone? You know how quickly iPhones run out of juice!" Liz reprimands and places her hands on her low-rise Juicy Couture cropped denim jeans (she's paired them with the cutest Alice & Oliva yellow silk ruffle camisole). I don't know how I can be thinking about clothes at a time like this. "Austin could have been calling you since we were in New York! When was the last time you looked at your phone?"

I bite my lip. "I don't know." She looks at me. "I was checking during the show last night, but then I guess I got so wrapped up in leaving for Texas I threw my phone in my bag and forgot about it. Don't tell Nadine," I beg loudly and scramble in my bag for the phone charger. When I find it, I quickly plug the phone in to charge. It's completely dead now.

Nadine rushes out of the closet she was in and shushes me angrily and then points to her phone. She's already dressed too (a pale blue Gap V-neck empire top and her favorite white Ann Taylor Loft cargo shorts). I'm the only one procrastinating.

"I am trying to not let on that we're out of state," Nadine

hisses. "I'm trying to throw her off by changing the subject. I told her you have an appointment at the DMV in Los Angeles the week we get back from New York."

"Good one," I tell Nadine.

HOLLYWOOD SECRET NUMBER FIFTEEN: Getting my license isn't really a secret, I know. I've been trying to get it forever and I really am taking the test when I go home at the end of the summer, but how celebrities deal with things like the DMV is sort of a juicy tidbit. Ever wonder why you never bump into Kim Kardashian renewing her license? That's because she probably never waits in line. Certain places, like the DMV in Hollywood or Beverly Hills, have a side entrance, and from time to time they let celebrities use it. You could say it's getting us out of the two-hour line, but the DMV sees it as helping them as well. If a star causes a commotion in line, that would be a lot harder to take care of than letting us cut to the front of the line to get new license plates.

I reread Austin's text twice. "Him texting me has to be a good sign, right? He didn't say anything about the message I left him saying I didn't want to break up. Do you think that means he does want to break up? And then there's this 'We need to talk' part. That can't be good, can it?"

"Oh, God, get in the shower already so we can get you over there and shut you up," Sky barks, as she walks out of the bathroom in an olive green polka dot Walter dress. I'll forgive her attitude because I know she's cranky from the lack of eight hours sleep.

Matty emerges and I do as I'm told. By one-thirty we're out

the door and Rodney is driving the rental minivan to Austin's camp, the Longhorn Lacrosse Clinic, which is held at a local college. I was so nervous about the trip that I didn't give a lot of consideration to what I'd be wearing for my big confrontation with Austin. Luckily I was able to cobble a decent outfit together from Sky's, Liz's, and my stuff. I have on Sky's white Marc by Marc Jacobs cotton chambray pleated top and Liz's royal blue Leanne Marshall linen ruffle skirt. Around my neck is the necklace Austin gave me last Christmas.

I realize when we pull up to campus that I have no clue what dorm Austin is in and there are four. Then Nadine remembers that I sent Austin a care package the first week I arrived in New York—I haven't sent one since. Gulp. She finds the address on her BlackBerry and pulls up the dorm name. We get inside, thanks to a girl who recognizes Sky and me, and make it to Austin's room, but there's no answer. The whole floor is deserted.

"Um, guys? It's midday, there's no one here, and this is a lacrosse camp," Matty says. "Want to take a guess where they might be?"

"The lacrosse fields?" Rodney is hopeful.

"Austin told me they didn't play during the heat of the day," I tell the others.

"That girl said they were on a different schedule this week," Liz points out. "Maybe they're playing. It's worth a shot, no?"

"Let's go." I take off ahead of the group. I can't wait another minute to see Austin.

We don't have to go far to find the fields, which are swarming with players in blue and yellow pinnies.

"How did we miss this?" Liz marvels as we hurry across the grass. The heat is brutal here. I'm sweating already and we've only been outside for a few minutes. I can't imagine why they'd practice in this. Austin said they usually worked out in the morning and late afternoon, but it's almost two and they are all on the field. The question is, with so many guys and girls running around, how am I going to find Austin?

"Hey, aren't you Sky Mackenzie?" A guy with sweaty tousled brown hair leans on his lacrosse stick and stares straight into Sky's eyes. She smiles and sashays her olive green dress side to side.

"Yes I am. Hi, cowboy," she purrs.

Liz laughs. "What makes you think he's a cowboy?"

"We're in Texas," Sky points out.

"This is camp, he could be from anywhere!" Liz is incredulous.

"Do something before they start rolling on the grass throwing punches," Nadine suggests as the two continue to yell at each other. The boy looks on curiously. The girls are actually starting to draw a crowd.

"Hi there," I say, smiling brightly.

And then before I can say anything else, he points at me. "Burke! You're Kaitlin Burke!"

"Yes, I am."

"What are you doing here?" he asks as more people jog over.

"I'm looking for someone, actually," I tell him as I smile at all the newcomers. "I don't know if he's out here though. He told me his group doesn't usually play during the early afternoon."

The guy nods. "None of us do. It rained all last week so we had to do it today to make up for some lost scrimmage time."

That means Austin is out here somewhere. I scan the fields again, wishing I could spot him. "Do any of you know Austin Meyers?" I ask.

The guy motions to someone behind him. "I think she's on the same floor as him." A girl with a long brown ponytail, long side swept bangs, and legs that are longer than Heidi Klum's strolls over. She isn't wearing any makeup, and she's super sweaty, but her tanned skin is flawless and she has the most gorgeous gray eyes. I don't even have to ask who she is.

"Amanda, right?" I ask. Liz and Sky stop fighting and look up.

"Yeah." Amanda looks from my yellow print Coach sandals up to my clean pink manicure and snakeskin bag. Before I can stop myself, I notice her chipped short red nails. She quickly drops her hands to her side and sort of hides them behind her back.

I immediately feel guilty. It isn't hard to tell that Amanda, as beautiful as she is, feels unsure of herself now that the girl she's been toying with is standing right in front of her. And movie star or no movie star, this is a girl-to-girl problem.

"That's the girl?" Sky is loud on purpose. "Deck her."

Amanda shifts slightly and I watch as she keeps pushing her bangs nervously behind her ears. Everyone is looking at us, even though I highly doubt anyone but me and Amanda knows what is going on. But I know. And so does Amanda.

We could go two ways with this. We could scream at each other and make nasty put-downs, both trying to one-up each other for Austin. Or I could rip into her and make her feel insignificant like Lauren and Ava have done to me and Sky all summer, and we did to them on *SNL*, but where did that get us? Nowhere. Where did being mean to Riley get me? It hasn't made her any nicer to me or convinced her I can handle the stage. After everything that has gone down this summer, I finally realize one thing: You really do get more bees with honey. It's time to act mature.

As much as it kills me, I hold out my hand and smile. "Hi, I'm Kaitlin." I keep my tone pleasant and Sky gasps. "It's nice to finally meet you."

"What is she doing?" Sky hisses and I notice Liz start to drag her away. "She should punch her!"

Amanda slowly extends her own sweaty hand. "Amanda." Her voice is soft. She does, however, look slightly relieved.

And I am too. Yes, she's been catty and rude to me more than once, but she also obviously thinks my boyfriend is a hottie, and who can blame her for that one? "I'm looking for Austin. Do you know where he is?"

"He's on the other field." Amanda points in the direction with her stick. "I can take you, if you want."

"That would be great." I follow her through the crowd,

leaving the others behind. I look back anxiously and I see Nadine's face. She actually looks proud. I guess I know how she would handle this situation too.

Amanda and I sort of walk in silence, sticking to a few occasional sentences that are sure not to cause any problems like, "Wow, it's hot here" and "How was your trip to Texas?" Way too soon, or not soon enough, depending on the scattered thoughts racing through my mind, we are at the field and Amanda is pointing Austin out to me. Austin is in full-on lacrosse mode. I can barely make out his face under his helmet, but I know his number, and I keep my eyes on him as Amanda points out other teammates and talks about the scouts that have already come by in the last week.

"He's really good," she says to me.

"I know." I stop when I realize that sounds kind of territorial, even though I don't mean to be. "I mean, I've seen him play at home."

"Right"—she shrugs—"you would, being his girlfriend and all."

I was a few days ago.

God, I hope I still am.

I hear a whistle and then guys and girls start streaming off the field. I see Austin take off his helmet and shake out his wet hair. He is tanner than I've ever seen him and his shirt is so drenched that it clings to the six-pack he seems to have developed since he's been here. He is dirty and sweaty and yet all I want to do is break away from Amanda and throw myself at him. But I restrain myself for the ten seconds, at least, it takes for him to get to the sidelines.

"Austin!" I call his name hoarsely when I can't take it anymore.

He turns slowly and sees me. At first he looks sort of confused, then he breaks into a huge smile and then his face goes sort of blank, which is really confusing.

"What are you doing here?" he asks as he walks straight toward me and stands inches from my face.

It takes all my willpower not to reach forward and kiss him. But I'm too scared. What if Austin doesn't want to kiss me anymore? Part of me doesn't even feel like I deserve him after the way I behaved this summer and if I feel that way there is a chance Austin is thinking the same thing.

Forget waiting for news on *Small Fish, Big Pond*, or my reviews on Broadway. Knowing what Austin is thinking about me being here and what he thinks about the future of us is scarier than anything else going on in my life. I don't want this to be over. Seeing Austin again, right in front of me, I know more than ever what I want, and it's him, and I'm praying he'll give me another shot.

"I came to see you," I say even though I guess that part is obvious. I look at Amanda. "Amanda told me where you were."

He looks from me to Amanda and then his face flinches slightly. "She was very helpful," I add.

"I'll leave you two alone," Amanda says to me. "It was nice meeting you, Kaitlin."

330

"You too," I tell her.

Even though I know there are people watching us, all I can think about is Austin. A hot breeze blows between us and Austin's sweaty blond hair covers his eyes.

"I called you all night and you didn't answer," Austin starts to say. "I thought…"

"Me first," I insist. "I came to say I'm sorry." My voice is squeaky, but I won't cry. "For everything. You were right. I haven't been there for you and you're always there for me. I let my work get in the way and I didn't care about how my friendship with Dylan affected you. I've been a rotten girlfriend."

Austin doesn't say anything at first. His face is scrunched up and he seems to be thinking of the words he wants to say. I'm breathless waiting to hear them. Are they good or bad?

"I thought maybe you liked Dylan." Austin looks so pained. "And instead of telling me you didn't, you kept pushing the topic off the table."

"I should have told you the truth about Dylan." The wind is still whipping and I push my hair off my face. "But I was afraid. We were so far apart and I thought if you knew Dylan was into me that would make you madder. We spent so little time on the phone as it was, I didn't want to spend it fighting."

"I know." Austin's blue eyes are serious. "That's my fault. I should have called you more."

"I should have called you more!" I interrupt, but Austin cuts me off.

"Let me talk, okay?" He sounds gruff, and it makes me

nervous. "I should have called you when I said I would. It's not that I didn't want to talk to you, it's just…" He hesitates. "I hate the phone."

"You what?" I'm confused.

"I hate the phone," Austin admits and his mouth starts to twitch. Is he going to smile? "Hate it. We never talk on it at home. I talk to you for five minutes or we text and then I see you so there's no need for technology to get in the way, but a lengthy phone conversation? I can't stand it. I should have told you that."

He hates the phone. I wish he *had* told me that.

"It's no excuse though." Austin runs his dirty hands through his hair. "I should have made the effort. But then after the stuff with Dylan started happening, I got upset and then when you seemed worked up about Amanda answering our phone it made me think, 'now she knows how I feel.' I guess that's why I let you get all crazy about her."

Austin was getting me back. I guess I deserved that.

"But I shouldn't have done that to you the other night," he admits. "I should have gotten back on the phone."

My throat feels so dry, but I need to make this point clear. "I don't like Dylan. I swear I don't."

"I don't like Amanda." Austin's blue eyes are so truthful, how could I not believe him?

"So does that mean you still like me?" I try to joke, but my heart is aching. "I promise to be a better girlfriend if you'll let me. Do you think you can forgive me? I…" I look at him searchingly and feel the need to say this. "I love you."

332

Austin starts to smile and I feel a rush of relief. "I love you too. You're the one I want to be with, Burke. And I promise to suck it up with the phone calls till you get home."

He grabs my waist and pulls me toward him. I actually hold my breath, almost afraid it's not going to happen. But it does. Austin kisses me. I close my eyes and let the kiss take me away. His lips are soft — if a little chapped — and his kiss feels so nice and familiar. Most importantly, it reminds me of just how things should be and will be again.

Monday, July 20

NOTE TO SELF:
Dinner with A, Rob, & the gang: Longhorn Steakhouse 6 PM.
Flight home: 9 AM Tuesday.
**Send A another care package! Pop Burger could B Good!

SCENE 14:
Andie is cleaning out her locker.
Leo walks up behind her and stops.

LEO:
Do you like sushi?

ANDIE:
(*she looks up, surprised*) I do like sushi.

LEO:
Good. Because I want to take you to this great sushi
place. You'll love it.

ANDIE:
Are you asking me out on a date?

LEO:
I guess I kind of am. Is that okay? Or are you
going to freak out again and wish you never told me
anything?

ANDIE:
I'll be okay. But what about Jenny?

LEO:
I told you before, when you freaked out and ran off.

Jenny knows we were over a long time ago. It's time
to move on. Everyone has to. All we've got is the
future, you know?

ANDIE:
You can't forget the past.

LEO:
No, but you can learn from it and make the future
even better, don't you think?

ANDIE:
I do. At least I hope that's the way it works.

(*Leo grabs Andie's stuff and puts it into her
backpack. Then he offers her his hand.*)

LEO:
Want to go?

ANDIE:
I don't know. This is it, isn't it? The last time here,
at this locker, in this place. It's kind of scary.

LEO:
Yeah, it is. But it sort of isn't. It's sort of exciting.
(*Andie laughs.*) What's so funny?

ANDIE:

I was just thinking that this is my last ever day
here and I'm walking out of school with the one boy I
always wanted to walk into school with.

LEO:

Then let's take the long way out, and check
things out one last time.

ANDIE:

Works for me.

(*Andie and Leo walk toward the back of the stage
together and the stage fades to black.*)

THE END

SIXTEEN: *Back to the Future*

"Kaitlin, they're waiting for you!" The stage manager knocks on my door.

"Got it!" I yell back, checking my reflection in the mirror before making my way backstage in my jeans and T-shirt combo for the last time.

It's been three weeks since I visited Austin in, well, Austin, and the rest of my stint in the play and in New York has been blissfully smooth. I think I've finally gotten the hang of this stage thing, and even though Riley won't give me credit for it, I know I'm improving. She's not even offering me her opinion anymore. Even if she did, I wouldn't listen. I know I tackled something big, new, and scary and I survived. The same thing goes for me and Austin. Everyone else is doing okay too. Liz finished her writing and directing clinic and got an A-minus on her final project, the one starring Sky. Even better, they didn't kill each other doing it! They've sort of taken over the frenemies title that Sky and I used to share. Sky stayed in New York, as promised. She says it was to take meetings, but I know it was to hang with me and Liz. And Liz was surprisingly okay with that. The only ones not still okay with that are my mom and Laney. But we're about to change that.

"Ready?" Sky meets me in the backstage hallway. She's obviously not in costume for a final night's performance so she looks much more appropriate for an audition than I do. Her raven hair is ironed straight and has grown a bit since the start of the summer, almost hitting her mid-back, which is bare thanks to the Versace dress she has on. The green floral print is a bit dizzying, but Sky says she's hoping it puts the people we're meeting with in a complete trance.

I grab Sky's hand. "Are you sure you're ready for this? I mean, we've talked about it, but we haven't *really* talked about it."

Sky sighs. "K…"

"This is a big deal and we both keep skirting around the major issues. You say you like the pilot. You like the character. You like the character I would be playing, but you haven't said whether you think we can survive doing this together. This is a huge deal, Sky."

"K…," Sky tries again.

"Are we sure we want to go down this road again?" I ask. "What if my mom and Laney are right? What if we get on set and two days in we are back to hating each other again? What if our comic chemistry on *SNL* was a total fluke? What if we don't have the chops to do comedy? Or we stink in front of a live audience? What if the show bombs after three episodes and we're to blame? What if—"

"K!" Sky yells and starts shaking me by the shoulders. "SHUT UP!"

"Okay." I'm slightly horrified. She's never this loud.

"I'm in, okay?" She straightens the skirt of her dress. "That's obvious, no? If neither of us wanted to do this, we wouldn't have taken it this far. We wouldn't be meeting with them tonight, two hours before you're doing your last performance in the play, to actually run through some scenes for the pilot. We wouldn't have our agents fly in and finesse the details of the deal. We wouldn't take phone call after phone call with the producers, the director, the network, and the casting folks assuring them that we could work together again peacefully." Sky flips her raven hair. "And I wouldn't have wasted the last two weeks working on the pilot with you when I could have been enjoying the Hamptons with your mom, who despite her dislike of me, actually appreciates my help with the Darling Daisies." Sky smiles wryly. "K, you may drive me nuts, but there is no one I'd rather be driven nuts by."

I grin. "Me either, as bizarre as that sounds."

"We should do this," Sky insists, and squeezes my hand. "It's a great pilot."

"And awesome characters," I add. "A cool director."

"A nice cast." Sky fills in the details. "Cool network, great perks, nice media coverage, good press. Good parking space, not that you have a car to park."

I give her a smarting look. "But the best part, in case you forgot, is that we'd be back on TV again."

"We'd be back on TV again." Sky smirks. "I thought that part was obvious. Seriously, K, sometimes I wonder where your head is."

I hit her and her bony arm makes a light smacking sound. "We'd be doing what we love again — even if the show is only short-term and bombs — we'd be back on a set every day. I thought I had to get away from the daily grind to figure out what I wanted to do, but doing this play made me realize that what I wanted to do was in front of me the entire time. I like being on TV. I'm good at it. Why do I have to transcend and be a movie star?"

"Sweetie, if only someone would say what you just said to Jennifer Aniston," Sky sympathizes. "It's good to know your strengths."

"They're yours too, you know," I point out. "We work well shooting an episode every two weeks. Although I guess this would be every week now."

HOLLYWOOD SECRET NUMBER SIXTEEN: When you watch a sitcom and see in the credits the line: "shot in front of a live audience" that means the show really was taped in front of a live audience. But unlike the morning talk shows that air live in real time, these shows are taped live, but they aren't taped within actual time constraints. It could take hours to film a half-hour sitcom in front of a live audience. Sometimes they have to do scenes over and over from every angle. Sometimes they botch a take. Sometimes the audience laughter is (shhh...) dubbed in.

"Well, I do well no matter how often we shoot an episode."

Sky sounds defensive. "You just bask in my glow." I raise my arm to hit her again. "Okay! You're talented too. Sort of." She links arms with mine. "And I'll help you get even stronger as an actress. Comedy is my specialty. Didn't you see me on *SNL*? I killed."

"Try to rein in the modesty when we talk to these guys, okay?" I deadpan.

We make our way through the backstage area to the side door and then walk onto the street. Because it's so early, there is no crowd waiting to get into the play yet. Just people in the city walking by on their way home from work or to dinner or who knows where. That's the cool thing about New York City. People are always coming and going at all times of day and night so half the time I'm not recognized. I just blend right in.

I'm going to miss it here, and our apartment, and how easy it is to get around, but it's time to get back to Los Angeles. Matty and Dad are already there, since Matty started taping *Scooby*, and every time they call, I get just the teensiest bit jealous when I hear one of them splashing in the pool.

No one recognizes Sky and me as we walk a few blocks down to another building and through the revolving doors, then into the elevator and up two floors to the rehearsal space for *Meeting of the Minds*. Forest said we could use it for tonight's meeting with everyone from *Small Fish, Big Pond*. Or as they're calling it this week, *Small Fries*. (I like that name better.) Seth says this meeting is just a formality. So does Emmett Arrigan, Sky's agent. They claim that we've already gotten the job and they want to see us in person, ask a few questions, and watch us run a few lines. Since they were only flying in overnight and they need an answer by the weekend, I agreed to meet before tonight's performance. That's why I got ready early. I am sticking to my pledge of making every single show and being on time for all of them.

I'm feeling pretty nervous as Sky and I walk the long corridor down to the conference room where we're meeting Seth and Emmett. And part of my nervousness has to do more with the fact that no one other than Seth, Rodney, Liz, Nadine, and Sky knows I'm here. Yep, I didn't tell Mom and Dad or Laney how far I've come with negotiations. I know they'll have to weigh in because I'm a minor, but I made Seth swear that he wouldn't say anything yet. He knows how much they're against me and Sky working together again. They'd FLIP if they knew what was going on tonight.

SWOOSH!

Before I know what's happening, two people jump in front of us and try to grab us, and Sky and I scream. Sky reaches inside her bag for pepper spray and I yell at the top of my lungs and start smacking the people with my snakeskin purse. If they damage the bag that has gotten me through my whole summer here in New York, I'm going to be furious.

"STOP HITTING US! KAITLIN, STOP! IT'S MOM AND LANEY!"

Sky and I stop screaming. I drop my bag and gasp in horror. It *is* Mom and Laney and they're seriously disheveled. Mom's hair looks like a rat's nest. Her Prada sunglasses are crooked and her white fitted blazer is twisted sideways. Laney isn't better off. Her hair was pulled back, but now the low ponytail is a mess and falling out. Any second Sky will accidentally spray her pepper spray on Laney's pretty teal Prada sundress and I'll never hear the end of it. ("Reese and Jake just got me this!")

"You scared us," I scold. "What are you two doing here?"

"I called them." Seth looks guilty as he appears around the corner and removes his shades. He must be sweltering in a navy blue Ralph Lauren suit. It's ninety degrees in the shade today and this is New York City! I know he wants to look professional, but still. "Kaitlin, they need to know what you're doing here or you'll never get this role. Your mom has to sign off. You're better off telling her now than later."

Sky is cheerful. "I'm so glad my mom barely knows what I'm up to, let alone renders opinions."

"This is what I'm talking about, missy!" Mom says to Sky, sounding more and more like an eighty-year-old Hamptonite. "You have no respect for authority or for my daughter. How can anyone expect me to allow you two to work together again? I don't like SKAT! You would hurt her again and I can't see that happen," Mom adds, sounding upset.

"Aww, Mom!" I throw my arms around her stiff frame. "You're actually worried about my well-being." This is a totally new feeling from the parental unit and I'm a little misty just thinking about it. "I appreciate your concern, really I do, but I'm a big girl. I can take care of myself. And this is a great show, Mom. Ask Seth. He'll tell you."

"He already has." Mom sighs. She looks at Laney. "We read it and we both love it. So much so that we're convinced that it will only last two episodes."

"It's too smart for teens," Laney seconds.

"Way to be supportive," Sky chides them.

"If you want to go for this, sweetie, I'd rather be on board than kept in the dark like that little recon trip you took a few weeks ago." Mom raises her right eyebrow.

"You know about Texas?" I squeak.

Mom and Laney nod. "The photos of you and Sky boarding a private plane in the middle of a cornfield were all over TMZ along with the headline, 'SKAT GOES GLOBAL,'" Laney informs me. "You're lucky you made it back to New York on time. But I guess since you did, no harm done." She smiles thinly, which is big for her. "You've been relatively good all summer so I have no complaints." She looks at Sky. "I'll try not to have any about this new yet old working relationship either."

I hug them both and squeal. I attempt to hug Sky too.

"Eww, get off!" Sky freaks out. "No personal affection, K. I hate that."

"We should get in there," Seth cuts in. "They're waiting for us."

"Go get 'em, Kate-Kate," Mom says encouragingly, and Laney winks. "We'll be waiting right here."

I nod, and then with Seth and Sky beside me, I walk through the door and prepare to find out what my future holds.

* * *

Before I know it, the curtain is rising on my last ever performance of *Meeting of the Minds*. My biggest fear about tonight's show is that I won't be able to hold it together. I know I'm saying every line for the last time. It's a little like how I felt shooting the last episode of *Family Affair*, but obviously not nearly as intense since I couldn't care less if I ever see Riley again. The first act runs smoothly and the second is going really well too. Since this really is the end though, I feel like I have to make some sort of peace with Riley.

"Hey." We're in between scenes, in the quick-change area, and I tap Riley on the shoulder. "Thanks."

"For what?" she asks, surprised. We haven't really been talking that much since I went out on my faux date with Dylan.

"For teaching me that I don't need compliments all the time to know I'm doing a good job." It's true. Riley may have thought I couldn't hack it, and my reviews may not have been the grade A I was hoping for, but they were decent, and I know I gave this my all. That, I've learned, can be enough.

Then as much as it kills me, I pay her a compliment. "I know I'm nowhere near the theater actress you are, Riley, but I feel fortunate to have been given the opportunity to do this and work with someone like you. You're really good at what you do."

"Thank you." Riley is stiff. "Good luck to you, Kaitlin."

345

"Good luck to you too." I smile.

Nadine said something to me the other day that made sense of everything that's been happening with Lauren, Ava, and Riley. Not everyone you meet is going to like you, and that's okay. But in the spirit of maturity, I feel the need to say one more thing to Riley, since one thing I didn't do is invite her to my after-party with my family and friends. (I have to have *some* dignity, you know.) The cast already had a cake for me backstage before the show, and I ordered food for everyone before the play last night from Pop Burger, which is this popular mini burger joint in New York City that has sent their burgers to everyone from Jay-Z to Justin Timberlake. Now the *Meeting of the Minds* cast can be added to the list. "Riley?" I try to stop her before she walks away. "I just wanted you to know, Dylan still cares about you."

She turns around. "My private affairs are mine. I don't choose to air my grievances in the rags."

"True, but I thought you'd want to know," I say awkwardly. "In case he doesn't tell you himself. Dylan does still care."

She almost smiles at me. *Almost*—and then she walks away without another word.

The second act flies by and I savor my last curtain call. Forest presents me with flowers and makes me cry. The audience gives me a standing ovation, which means a lot considering who is in the front row—my entire family. Matty and Dad flew in for the night as a surprise, which I realized halfway through the first act. Liz and Sky are here with Seth, Laney, Nadine, and Rodney, who is actually tearing up a little.

This is the first time he's sat through the whole show since he's always with me backstage. Tonight I insisted he watch from the audience and I guess this means he likes it.

Austin is here too. He finished camp last week, but Mom flew him back in to New York as a present for me. I notice he's holding the most magnificent bouquet of peach roses. He whistles and he and Matty yell my name. I take one last bow and then the curtain falls.

Backstage there is a lot of commotion and hugging and chatting. I hug Forest the longest, thanking him for all he's taught me over the last few months. (Who knew I could cry on stage like that, every night without fail?) I trade e-mails and phone numbers with a few of the girls in the chorus and take one last group photo with the cast, then sign a bunch of cast photos. I also gratefully accept one that they've all signed for me as a thank-you. It's going to hang proudly in my room at home.

And then I say goodbye to Dylan. I see him standing there, still in costume, which is a T-shirt and jeans, just like mine, and he looks good. There's just something about that aloof stance of his that makes me sort of swoon. But as Liz says, I also swoon over Zac Efron and Robert Pattinson, and I'm not leaving Austin for them either. (Besides which, Vanessa would just kill me if I broke the friendship code and went near Zac!)

Dylan grins. "Congrats on a good run, mate." He hugs me loosely and I hug him back. "We're going to miss you around here."

"I'm going to miss you guys too," I admit, "but I don't think I'm going to miss the schedule. Working every night is grueling! Yes, having mornings off is fun, but I'd like to be home to catch *90210* this fall."

"What is *90210*?" Dylan asks.

"I'll forgive you because you're British." I laugh, but then I get sort of quiet. "Thanks, Dylan. For understanding about everything."

"You're welcome." He smiles, showing off the small gap between his two front teeth. "You can't blame a guy for trying. You're quite a catch, Ms. Kaitlin Burke."

"As are you," I say and kiss him on the cheek. "I guess I'll be seeing you. Call me if you ever come out to my coast, okay?"

"Will do."

He touches my shoulder awkwardly. And then I'm off to party.

*   *   *

"TO KAITLIN!" The cheer goes up. We're at Babbo, Mario Batali's restaurant on Waverly Place. We've got a private area near the back and everyone is in a festive mood, including me. I've changed into my final New York City splurge, a Badgley Mischka black floral silk cocktail dress. It has a round neck and a scoop back and a darling rosette detail at the front waist.

"Thank you." I hold my champagne glass. (Mom said she'd

vouch for me in the press that she gave her approval for a little glass of bubbly on this special occasion.) "I couldn't have made it through the summer without you guys." I look at Mom, Dad, and Matty. "The fact that you'd all relocate to New York so that I could try something like this still makes me a little misty. And that Seth and Laney thought I had it in me to tackle Broadway, makes me feel good because I know they always have my back. As do my friends." I look at Liz, Nadine, and Sky, who is actually smiling! "And to my boyfriend who stood by me despite everything I did to muck things up." Austin slips his hand into my free one under the table. "This has been an amazing summer. Now it's time to go home."

"We'll be back." Mom looks confident in her white BCBG dress with the black beaded trim around the waist. "I promised the Darling Daisies I'd check in from time to time. I'm even opening a branch in Los Angeles for them. Won't that be fab? We need some of that refined Hamptons spirit on the West Coast and I have more than enough time to run the organization for them." Laney nods in agreement, but I'm not sure she's actually listening. She accessorized her black Donna Karan suit with two Bluetooths again. Something about a Heidi and Spencer issue. Apparently they ticked off Lauren and Ava, who have actually moved on to torturing them instead of Sky and me, which is perfect because those two already have a nickname for the press to use (Speidi). Yippee! I guess Nadine was right about the attention dying down if we just let the story go.

"You can come to New York as long as it works with Kaitlin's new shooting schedule," Seth is saying to Mom.

Yep, I got the show!

The producers echoed Seth's sentiment, that they were just in town as a formality and that they'd want nothing more than for Sky and me to star in the pilot and the show. They were still filling out the cast, but we would be the anchors. Sky and I signed on the spot.

Small Fries, current title, will be starring Kaitlin Burke and Sky Mackenzie and will air this November. I'm back, baby! And I couldn't be happier. Seriously, I'm ready for five AM call times, long shooting days, and this new twist of being in front of a live audience for tapings. God knows, this summer I've had the practice.

"I can't believe we'll both be on the same soundstage." Matty is ecstatic and looks wise beyond his fifteen years in his black Armani suit. His summer tan has already faded thanks to all the hours he's logging on set. Oooh…I can't wait to get pale again too! "Kates, you're going to totally love the studio's cafeteria. They just made a new sandwich in my honor. You know, *Scooby* is getting lots of love."

"Please, that's just until we arrive." Sky waves him away with one long hot pink fingernail. Her orange silk floral Laundry dress is just as playful as her current mood.

"Why isn't there room for you both?" Liz asks and the two are off and running again with their commentary. I think they like it that way.

"So you think you'll be able to handle these two and me

full time when we get back?" Austin wants to know. Now that camp is over, Austin is letting his bangs grow out again, which is just how I like them. He's also back in full-on guy mode with his clothing, ditching the sweats and tanks for great-fitting pants and really nice silk button-down shirts, this one blue. (His sports jacket is lying on the chair next to us.) "Their friendship, which I'm still getting used to even wrapping my head around," Austin continues, "looks like it's going to take a lot of refereeing and I want to make sure that doesn't dig into my time with my girl."

"It won't," I promise Austin. "If they need that much help, I'll have Rodney hire them a bouncer. I'm all yours when we get back next week."

"Good, because once you get back to work, you're going to be pretty busy," Austin says. "I'll bet doing a new show is a lot of hours."

"Yeah," I admit, thinking about that fact. I guess with everything happening so quickly that is the one thing I didn't anticipate. I want to work again and am prepared to, but those hours will probably be long. And I'll be back in the spotlight with the paparazzi, for sure. I guess SKAT is here to stay, which isn't such a bad thing. I wouldn't be surprised if the paparazzi camped outside the studio. Larry the Liar will definitely want a shot of me with my hair in curlers and no makeup. Eek.

Austin interrupts my thoughts. "What's on your mind, Burke?"

"Oh, I was just thinking about our first Los Angeles

outing." I wrap my fingers around his. I don't want to bring the mood down with my worries. I stare at him, wondering if he'll remember our promise to each other at the beginning of the summer. We said we'd return to Disneyland. It was just a casual promise, but I've clung to it the whole time we've been apart.

"Disneyland is a go," Austin says with a lopsided smile, which makes me grin even wider. "Nadine got us tickets a few weeks ago."

"You remembered!" I marvel.

He puts an arm around me. "Of course I did. Are you really surprised?"

"I guess not." I lean into his shoulder. "Disneyland it is. A week from Wednesday."

"Can't wait." Austin kisses my cheek. "First ride definitely has to be Star Tours."

"Definitely."

I'm going home, and future craziness or not, I can't wait to get there.

TO BE CONTINUED...

Like your favorite TV show, we all take a summer hiatus (that's TV lingo for a well-needed short break from filming), but don't worry, I'll be back. I've got *Small Fries* to shoot and with a new TV show, new cast, new network, and a new character, comes a lot of hard work and, knowing me, some freak-outs. I know I'm ready for the challenge...or am I? Is

TV where I really belong? Is Hollywood? Am I finally ready to embrace my inner Meryl Streep and declare acting my lifelong passion or will I watch Liz and Austin fill out their college applications and question my calling again? One thing is for sure, I've got to make a decision about my celebrity life and stick with it once and for all. This time it looks like fate is going to step in to help me make that choice by asking me to picture my life if it weren't set in Hollywood. Will I like that world better than my own? Or will I give anything to get back to my old life and the people in it? There's only one way to find out.

Look for the final book in the Secrets of My Hollywood Life series, coming March 2011.

Acknowledgments

The title alone—*Secrets of My* Hollywood *Life*—doesn't lend itself to a book set in New York, but my fabulous editors Cindy Eagan and Kate Sullivan were as pumped to see Kaitlin's Jimmy Choos click-clacking down Fifth Avenue as I was. This is just another reminder of how lucky I am to work with such amazing editors/cheerleaders. I also want to thank Kate S. for all her notes. Her crystal-clear view of New York helped Kaitlin's NYC feel all the more real.

Thanks too to agent extraordinaire Laura Dail, who always has my back (as well as Kaitlin's) and to Tamar Rydzinski for going over all the little details.

To the amazing team at Poppy and Little, Brown Books for Young Readers—Ames O'Neill, Melanie Chang, Andrew Smith, Lisa Ickowicz, Melanie Sanders, Elizabeth Eulberg, and Tracy Shaw (for yet another brilliant cover design)—it's because of you all that each new Secrets book is more buzzworthy than the last.

I'd also like to thank my family and friends for all they do to help me do what I love to do! (Got that straight?) Mara Reinstein is my first reader/critic/go-to girl on all things from Hollywood to Prada. My mom, Lynn Calonita, and mother-in-law, Gail Smith, make sure the boys are happy and healthy while I type away.

Finally, to my husband, Mike, sons Tyler and Dylan, and Chihuahua, Jack — who are always waiting for me to shut off the computer — thank you for being the best support system a wife, mom, and author could have.

Love secrets OF MY HOLLYWOOD LIFE?

Jen Calonita takes you behind the scenes of stardom
again with her newest novel,

Sixteen-year-olds Charlie, Keiran, Brooke, and Hallie have just been signed up for their own reality television show. They can't even believe it. "You'll be the new *Hills*," the Armani-suited executive tells them, "and the hottest thing on our network." How could they say no? But soon enough, cameras following them everywhere and interfering producers surreptitiously scripting their lives start to affect the four best friends' relationships. Charlie, Keiran, Brooke, and Hallie are about to learn a very important lesson: Friends don't let friends do reality shows.

**Keep your eye out for REALITY CHECK,
Jen Calonita's newest look
at what really happens behind the cameras.**

Coming June 2010.

Lights, Camera, Action!

"Okay, girls, just act natural," Addison tells us with a big smile. "Forget about the cameras. Just pretend we're not here." Everyone keeps saying that, but it sounds impossible. How am I supposed to pretend that there are not *three* cameras surrounding our table right now, all of them focused on us?

We're sitting at the Crab Shack, Hallie's parents' restaurant/ boat dock, for our first-ever taping of *The Cliffs*, and at the moment, I'm so nervous I want to dive off the dock, swim to nearby Shelter Island, and live there permanently. I have my cell phone and my toothbrush in my bag. What more do I need to survive?

"Should we look at the camera?" Keiran asks Addison nervously.

Addison shakes her head and the pencil behind her right ear falls onto the dock. She leans down to pick it up, rests it on her clipboard, and fixes her Bluetooth again. It's been glued to her ear the whole time we've been here and she's had several calls, which she's disappeared to answer. This is the first time I've gotten to see Addison at work, but she seems to be really on top of things. The crew hangs on her every word, and she's been pretty efficient about our time, knowing we can't tape all day.

Unlike the rest of us, who agonized over our outfits for days, Addison is not worried about her work wardrobe. She's wearing a long-sleeved blue shirt, jeans, and sneakers. She doesn't have on anywhere near as much makeup as the makeup artist (yay!) put on us. "I know this first taping is overwhelming for you girls, but I promise, it will get easier," Addison assures us. "Just think of us as the fourth wall to a room. We're not here. Don't look in this direction unless there is something over here other than us that you need to see. In a few days you won't even realize we're around. You're going to become pros fast. You 'll see."

Taping started faster than we could have imagined. Addison actually called the day after the signing to see if would mind getting a day or two in *that week*. I almost fell off my chair I was so surprised, but I guess jumping in headfirst is a good thing. I didn't think we had anything exciting planned for that week, but Addison thought everything I mentioned sounded "super" or "perf." She stressed that Susan wanted us to be as natural as possible, so whatever we normally do together should be fine. We decided our first taping should be at the Crab Shack. Hallie's parents were more than happy to let us shoot. The crew got here early to set up and passed out waivers to everyone (they have to make sure people sign one if they're going to be on camera). By the time we arrived, everyone was ready for us.

"Promise you guys won't mention where I live, okay?" Brooke whispers to me while Addison is still on her call.

"Brooke, we swear, but you know they're going to find out eventually," I tell her. "It's nothing to be ashamed of."

Brooke's house is a stately old colonial, and the barn on her property is fully functional and has a bunch of horses that we all take riding. She has a bigger room than any of us, which seems to be redecorated in Pottery Barn Outlet stuff every two years. What's not to like about Brooke's home sweet home?

"Charlotte," she says stiffly, sounding like my mother. "I'm not a farm girl and I don't want certain people to think I am one."

I know who she's talking about. Brooke's never gotten over Marleyna Garrison's ribbing in ballet class about how Brooke smelled of horse manure.

"Okay," I assure her. "Just relax." I have to admit, I'm alternating between nausea and fits of giddiness. We are about to start taping our very own TV show.

"You're right," Brooke says and breathes a little easier. "This is our starring moment. What am I worrying about?"

"So, Addison, how do we start?" Hallie asks. "Should we tell a funny story? Or talk about boys?"

"Or gripe about homework? Family?" Keiran asks. "Should we avoid sounding negative? I don't want to come off as cranky."

Addison laughs. "Just do what you 'd normally do. Chat. Talk about school, especially since we can't tape you guys there."

The four of us nod. Talk about school. Talk about school.

What about school? Do I mention my possible date with Zac? No, no, that wouldn't be good because then it would be on tape. I'd be talking about him to the world and I have no clue if he'll be around long enough to hear it on TV. Okay, school. Classes? That's boring. Homework? Nah. How much I hate Mr. Sparks? That would just get me an F in social studies. School…

"Ready?" Addison chirps. "We'll go slow and we can always stop when you want."

The girls and I look at each other. Brooke puts her hand out and we all give it a squeeze. "Let's get this party started!"

We've already ordered our usual: mozzarella sticks, clam strips, and a round of Cokes. The order covers the checkered tablecloth. The furnishings at the Crab Shack are pretty cheap—white plastic chairs and patio tables with tacky tablecloths. A large canopy hangs over the fifteen or so tables, giving us some relief from the sun. Food is ordered at the shack window and then your number is called over a staticky intercom so you can pick it up. Definitely not fine dining, but the place is always packed. Not many restaurants around can beat the spectacular scenery. The dock is right on the water and overlooks Shelter Island, a quiet residential town a short ferry ride away. Sailboats and small yachts slip by or dock right here, some with local license plates, others from as far away as Florida.

"Girls, I've got the perfect opener for us," Hallie says. "I figured we could start out talking about the spring fling. At least that sounds exciting, right?" Hallie fingers her green V-neck sweater that brings out her eyes. It's her favorite shirt and she's wearing it with a denim skirt, tights, and her brown knee-high boots that we covet.

We all nod. "What do you think, guys?" I ask the crew, but their faces are blank. Fourth wall. Fourth wall. I have to remember that. They're not going to answer us.

"Perfect!" Addison says enthusiastically. "Let's try it on for size." She turns to the crew, who jumps into action, yells out a few commands, and then someone says "Rolling," faster than I can even catch my breath.

"Can you guys believe the spring fling is next month?" Hallie asks, trying to sound natural even though I know her voice is an octave higher than it should be.

"Um, yeah, that's pretty close," Keiran seconds, her eyes moving toward the cameras and back again. I notice she's shredding the napkin in front of her.

"Has anyone started thinking about dates?" Brooke asks, a mischievous smile on her face. "It's never too early to start." She turns to me. "I know Charlie has her eye on someone."

My face burns—and it's not that hot out. Thanks, Brooke! "Maybe," I say cryptically. "Don't you?"

"I always keep my options open." Brooke winks.

"What are you thinking of wearing?" Hallie asks. "It's never too early to think of a dress."

"Oooh! I saw something in *Seventeen* that was sweet," Keiran gushes and then she's off and running describing it. This somehow turns into a conversation about the lack of great places to shop out here on NOFO. And then before I know it, I'm weighing in on where to find cute clothes, and Brooke is boasting about her amazing sales collection, and Addison is calling cut.

"Girls, that was amazing!" Addison says and sounds like she means it. "You guys totally forgot the camera was there."

"We did, didn't we?" I say to the others excitedly, my confidence growing. "That was fun."

"And surprisingly easy," Brooke admits.

"A total rush," Hallie agrees.

"Take a breather, get a drink, and we'll start up again in a few minutes," Addison says as she walks away to take yet another call.

"Brooke, I loved that line you gave about Tanger being the new Target—everyone who is anyone goes there." Tanger is the outlet mall where we shop.

Brooke grins. "That was good, wasn't it? And Kiki, you were so cute describing that dress."

"Do you think we were trying too hard?" Hallie asks with a frown. "I had to work it to be that witty."

"Nah," I dismiss her. "It's good for us to be funny on camera. They'll like us more, won't they? It's not like we were lying." I did notice our conversation was hipper than normal, but who cares? It was still us. I'm sure it will tone down the more comfortable we get.

The four of us are so busy rehashing our lines, we barely hear Keiran's phone ringing, "It's my mom," she says. "Hello? What?" She freaks out, making me jump. "Now? I can't. I'm *working*. Remember, *working?* But, Mom? Mom? FINE." She runs her fingers through her hair and looks at us worriedly. "I have to go. My mom needs me to watch my brother while she runs to a parent-teacher conference."

"Kiki, you can't go now!" Brooke complains. "We're in the middle of taping."

"I have no choice," Keiran says, coming down off her high.

She throws tip money down on the table and grabs her bag. "I'm sorry," she says, looking at Addison.

"It's okay," Addison tells her and motions to some of the guys. "We'll send a small crew with you on your babysitting gig and the rest of us will hang here. Keiran, tell your mom we're coming and we just need a few minutes to set up, okay?"

"Really? You don't mind?" Keiran asks, her shoulders relaxing.

"Of course not," Addison says. "We knew your babysitting skills were very much in demand. We love shooting this sort of stuff."

"You guys are awesome," says a camera guy named Hank. "The way the sun hits Charlie's hair is perfect."

"Perfect," seconds Phil. "She looks like an angel."

"Me? An angel?" I joke. "That's a new one."

"The rest of you look great too," Addison adds and I hear her phone ring. Again. Her face darkens. "I have to take this. Excuse me."

I lean back in my chair as Keiran gets whisked home with a small camera crew of three people. "This is pretty cool," I say to the others. "I thought it might be a little weird taping our conversations, but I don't mind it."

"Me either. But I hope we all get to shoot some individual scenes, don't you?" Brooke asks.

"I'm sure we will," says Hallie and nudges me.

"Hal! Hal! Someone here for you," a voice crackles over the intercom. We turn toward the Crab Shack window and see a cute guy wearing shorts (in April no less) and a hoodie, with curly blond hair, waving at Hallie.

"Whoa, who is he?" I have to ask.

Hallie's whole face flushes. "Patrick Waters. He goes to Greenport. He works here at the restaurant and—guys, do I look okay?"

"You look great," Brooke tells her. "I dressed you so I should know. Go talk to him. Why do you look so nervous? You never have trouble talking to guys, Hallie."

"This one is different," Hallie says shyly.

Addison appears again. "Oooh...who's that?" she asks Hallie.

"Hallie's crush," Brooke teases.

"Do you think he'd appear on camera?" Addison asks. "If so we just need to ask him to sign a release."

"Let me run and ask him," says Hallie. Hallie talks animatedly for a few minutes and then we watch as Phil hurries over with a camera while Patrick signs the form. Hallie backs up and they tape her walking over as if it's for the first time.

Brooke sighs. "She's getting good airtime." I hit her. "I know, we're all going to get it. I just wish mine was now. I really like being in front of the camera."

"You?" I tease. "Never." She swats me back.

"All this talking is making me thirsty," Brooke says, holding up her empty Coke.

"Me too," I realize. "I'll get us refills," I grab our cups and head to the counter. Hallie's mom is always telling me to just walk into the kitchen, but I feel funny doing that when there are paying customers around. Instead, I wait in line, making sure to stay out of the way of the cameras taping Hallie. I feel a tap on my shoulder and turn around quickly, almost knocking the cups of ice into the person's chest.

"Whoa. I wanted a cool drink, but not extra ice." It's Zac, and we're standing so close, with the cups between our chests, that I can smell his minty mouthwash. His curly hair is damp and he's wearing a plain navy long-sleeved shirt and khakis. But it's his eyes, those awesome blue eyes that seem to pick up every speck of light in this place and reflect my image back at me.

"Hey." I try to sound calm and natural even though I'm anything but.

"Hey yourself," he says. "I have a confession to make: I thought I might find you here."

"Really?" He came here looking for me?

Zac nods. "I didn't see you at the office at lunch, and someone mentioned you were heading here after school, so I decided to track you down."

He tracked me down? Wow. "Here I am." I try to smile. "Everything okay? They didn't kill my piece on the band's trip to Disney World, did they?"

"Nope, nothing like that," Zac says. "I just wanted to make sure we were still on for Friday night. I was hoping you weren't avoiding me."

"I wasn't avoiding you," I say quickly. God no. Never. It killed me not to go to the office today. "I had to get some homework done early since I'm..." I realize I've never told Zac about the show.

Zac looks over to where Hallie is talking to Patrick. "Is there a reason why a camera crew is following Hallie?"

"Um…" Okay, this is awkward. How do I explain this in less than five minutes? "You see…"

"Charlie?" Addison has now joined our little twosome. Her clipboard is in hand and she's smiling. "Who is your friend?"

"I'm Zac," he says, extending his hand and shaking Addison's.

"Addison," she says. "I'm Charlie's show producer."

"Show producer?" Zac says with a cock of his head and a curious grin. "As in theater?"

"As in TV," Addison corrects. "For *The Cliffs,* Charlie's new TV show."

"Charlie is getting her own TV show?" Zac looks really confused now.

"Um…yeah," I admit, feeling awkward.

Addison looks at me apologetically, but I smile. "Addison, could you give us two minutes so I can explain?"

Addison nods. "Sure, and make sure you explain this too." She hands me a release. She walks away, dialing her phone again.

I stand there holding the release in my hand. "So."

"So," Zac repeats. "Let me guess, you're secretly Hannah Montana and you've never told me?"

"Not exactly," I tell him sheepishly. "Remember how we were talking last week about paying for college? Well, the short story is that I was approached to do my own reality show on the Fire and Ice Network. If I do this for even one season, it will probably pay off all my college and then some."

"What kind of reality show?" Zac looks interested. We've moved off the line now and I'm still holding the empty cups, which are freezing my hands thanks to all the ice.

"One about me and Keiran, Brooke, and Hallie," I say, knowing how silly it sounds out loud. "This executive from the network was watching me at work and she approached me about the show. Today is our first day of taping." I glance over at the table where Brooke is talking to Hallie and Patrick. Addison motions for me to hurry up.

"Do you they follow you all the time?" Zac wants to know.

"No, they have to get our permission to tape things before-hand, which is why I'm holding this release," I explain, feeling embarrassed. "If I talk to you on camera, you have to sign this saying you're okay with being on the show."

"I think I'll leave the spotlight to you today," Zac says, and winks. "I want to hear more about your new career tomorrow though. See you at the office? Without the cameras, of course."

"Of course! I'll see you there," I tell him.

When I walk back over to the girls, Addison is eagerly waiting. "Charlie, he's adorable! Did he sign a release?" She watches Zac closely and I see him grab a brown bag from the pickup window and take it to go. He gives me a little wave and I wave back. "Where is he going?" Addison asks worriedly.

"He didn't want to be on camera today," I tell Addison.

"Oh, okay," Addison says, looking dejected. "He's just so cute. He'd look gorgeous on celluloid."

I giggle. "Back off, Addison, he's *my* crush." She laughs.

"Did you tell him Patrick signed a waver?" Hallie asks me. I shake my head.

"Maybe he'll change his mind," Addison suggests. "The more, the merrier! We want to feature you four and your larger circle. Patrick is a cute addition, and Brooke said she has some prospects that sound good. Zac would be perfect too. We want this show to cover your whole lives, not just pieces, so we're interested in seeing everyone who's a part of it if we can."

"Sure," I promise. I like how into showing the real us Addison seems to be.

"Okay then, let's get back to work." Addison puts her headset back on and I feel a rush of excitement. "Hallie? Make sure you talk about Patrick now that he's gone," Addison instructs us. "And Brooke, tell that story about the girl in gym class. I loved that. And Charlie?" She smiles. "You just be Charlie. Got it?"

"I think so," I tell her.

Addison grins. "Good. And we're rolling!"

Welcome to Poppy.

A poppy is a beautiful blooming red flower
(like the one on the spine of this book). It is also
the name of the home of your favorite books.

Poppy takes the real world and makes it
a little funnier, a little more fabulous.

Poppy novels are wild, witty, and inspiring.
They were written just for you.

So sit back, get comfy, and pick a Poppy.

poppy

www.pickapoppy.com

THE A-LIST
HOLLYWOOD ROYALTY

gossip girl

THE CLIQUE

ALPHAS

SECRETS OF MY
HOLLYWOOD LIFE

the it
girl

POSEUR